AT THE HEART OF THE UNIVERSE

Also by Samuel Shem

NOVELS
The House of God
Fine
Mount Misery
The Spirit of the Place

PLAYS
Room for One Woman
Napoleon's Dinner
Bill W. and Dr. Bob (with Janet Surrey)

NONFICTION
(with Janet Surrey)
We Have To Talk: Healing Dialogues Between Women and Men
*Making Connections: Building Gender Dialogue and
Community in Secondary Schools*

NOVELLA/NONFICTION
(with Janet Surrey)
The Buddha's Wife: The Path of Awakening Together

AT THE HEART OF THE UNIVERSE

A Novel

SAMUEL SHEM

SEVEN STORIES PRESS
New York • Oakland

With thanks to Tianjia Dong, for his wisdom and calligraphy, and to Ross Terrill

Seven Stories Press
140 Watts Street
New York, NY 10013
sevenstories.com

"Green Jade Plum Trees in Spring" by Kenneth Rexroth, from *One Hundred Poems from the Chinese*, © 1971 by Kenneth Rexroth. Reprinted by permission of New Directions Publishing Corp.

"'A Dream of Night' by Mei Yao Ch'en" by Kenneth Rexroth, from the original by Ch'en Mei Yao, from *One Hundred Poems from the Chinese*, © 1971 by Kenneth Rexroth. Reprinted by permission of New Directions Publishing Corp.

"To a Traveler " by Kenneth Rexroth, from the original by Su Tung P'o, from *One Hundred Poems from the Chinese*, © 1971 by Kenneth Rexroth. Reprinted by permission of New Directions Publishing Corp.

"Written on the Wall at Chang's Hermitage" by Kenneth Rexroth, from the original by Tu Fu, from *One Hundred Poems from the Chinese*, © 1971 by Kenneth Rexroth. Reprinted by permission of New Directions Publishing Corp.

"South Wind" by Kenneth Rexroth, translated from Chinese, from *One Hundred Poems from the Chinese*, © 1971 by Kenneth Rexroth. Reprinted by permission of New Directions Publishing Corp.

Library of Congress Cataloging-in-Publication Data

Names: Shem, Samuel, author.
Title: At the heart of the universe : a novel / Samuel Shem.
Description: Seven Stories Press first edition. | New York : Seven Stories Press, [2016]
Identifiers: LCCN 2016008702 (print) | LCCN 2016015648 (ebook) | ISBN 9781609806415 (hardcover : acid-free paper) | ISBN 9781609806422 (ebook)
Subjects: LCSH: Mothers and daughters--Fiction. | Americans--China--Fiction. | Adopted children--Fiction. | China--Social life and customs--20th century--Fiction. | Domestic fiction. | BISAC: FICTION / Cultural Heritage. | FICTION / Sagas.
Classification: LCC PS3569.H39374 A95 2016 (print) | LCC PS3569.H39374 (ebook) | DDC 813/.54--dc23
LC record available at https://lccn.loc.gov/2016008702

Printed in the United States of America

9 8 7 6 5 4 3 2 1

For K.C. and her children, and for Janet
And to my dear friend John Updike

It is Spring in the mountains.
I come alone seeking you.
The sound of chopping wood
Echos among the silent peaks.
The streams are still icy.
There is snow on the trail.
At sunset I reach your grove
In the stony mountain pass.

You want nothing, although at night
You can see the aura of gold
And silver ore all around you.
You have learned to be gentle
Like the mountain deer you have tamed.

The way back forgotten, hidden away,
I become like you,
An empty boat, floating, adrift.

—Tu Fu (713–770),
"Written on the Wall at Chang's Hermitage"

PART ONE

For a woman to be without talents
Is synonymous with virtue.
—Anonymous, Song Dynasty

1

Sitting on the train, the baby at her breast, the young woman thinks, *They say there's a machine in Changsha City that will tell you if it's a boy or a girl. If I had had one of those machines I would not be doing this now. If I'd made this trip before, I wouldn't have to be making it now. I didn't have to do it. Jiwei said he would do it for me. Jiwei's father said he would do it for me. I said no. I am the only one to do this, I said.*

Thinking, *But can I? Maybe there is a way of saving her?*

Xiao Lu sits on the hard bench of the train. It is an early morning in late July, already deathly hot, and the train is crowded and stifling. A sign says that the bench seats four, but six are squeezed in. She wears a plain dark-blue cotton dress, without sleeves, and is, as usual in her daily life, barefoot. Her feet rest on the wooden floor, on either side of her pink plastic sandals. No one seems to take any notice of her. She has always been terribly shy, an observer more than an actor. Not one to dress up, or use makeup.

Because of the stain of "landlord" on her family, it was hard for them to find her a husband. Her parents had to look farther away, to farmers living on one of the mountains several hours from their village. She married late—at twenty-two—and in the end her dowry had to be increased by a dozen fat ducks. Her mother would have been happy if she had never married, and stayed at home, especially after what had happened to her two older girls. Her age and shyness did not bother the man chosen to be her husband, Jiwei. He said it didn't matter.

He has a kind streak, she thinks, *although less so, now.*

11

She is slender—skinny even, after her month-long ordeal, for she has had no appetite, none at all—with the slight bulge of her belly from the pregnancy. Her arms are strong, hands calloused. Her dark hair, if you saw it in bright sunlight, would have the slightest glint of russet. Her face has a certain modest beauty, although that too has been marred by the recent strain. Her eyes are worried, exhausted, and sad, and her mouth is set so that it won't tremble. It is a face of innocence curtailed and bitterness rising, held back by the pure power of obligation if not of will. All this by age twenty-eight.

She has never been on a train before, never seen a train before. Under other circumstances it would be exciting. But it is just a train—no, now, to her, it feels like a death train.

○ ○ ○

The journey started at four in the morning. Unable to sleep, she walked with the baby in her arms around the courtyard, up and down the path, even out on the ancient raised soft-dirt paths hemming the rice paddies. It was deep summer, but the mosquitoes didn't seem as harsh as usual. She protected the baby with a piece of old netting. There was no wind, and the stream was silent. "When the wind dies, the moon is clearly seen." That ancient text was the first calligraphy she had ever drawn as a schoolgirl. On still moonlit nights, it played in her mind. *My teacher said I had talent. Some talent. A farmer's wife. Living with his parents. On the farm. Maybe this will be better for her. For her, some other life.*

Last night by the light of the full moon she wrote slowly, in a neat, patient hand, the characters of the message she would put into her baby's swaddling clothes the next day. Just before four in the morning she awakened Jiwei. She wondered how he could sleep that night, but he did, and he grumbled when he awoke—despite it being almost his usual time to start out to the fields—until he remembered what he had to do. Silently he got the old bicycle and wheeled it out of the courtyard onto the narrow dirt path.

"Are you sure?" he asked.

"Of doing it?"

"No, of *you* doing it, not me?"

"Yes, I'm sure." All her life, secretly, she had been sure. Except the last month, plunged into the torment of what to do, now that it had turned out to be a girl. She had a sudden thought that maybe she had said she would do it because then she could change her mind, disappear with her baby, go somewhere else, start again. But no. Xia, her older daughter, was almost two now. She could never do that to Xia. And there had already been one sister who had disappeared. Her own sister, First Sister, the oldest of the three of them, had gone off one day when she was fourteen to a meeting of the Red Guards downriver in the valley, in the town of Tienja, and had never come back. When she had not returned by nightfall, Father, Mother, Second Sister, and she had all gone to Tienja to try to find her. They tried everything, and all they found out was that she had gone into the schoolhouse where the meeting was held, and no one had seen her leave. No one saw her ever again. She was fourteen, then, in 1972.

Now it is 1991. July 25. First Sister would be—what?—thirty-three? *She is thirty-three. She is not dead, she can't be dead. I never tell anyone she's dead. I say she's disappeared. My mother and father and Second Sister might as well have disappeared. It is no different. I never see them anymore.*

An hour before sunrise, Xiao Lu, holding the baby, got on the back of the bicycle, and Jiwei started off. The road down the mountain from the farmhouse was bumpy, and bumpier as they pedaled over the cobblestones of the village, but she was used to riding this way and balanced out the bumps easily, and the baby slept. *The second is easier*, all the women had told her, and this turned out to be true. An easy birth. A wonderful, beautiful baby, unblemished. *Today, one month old. Fresh as spring.* She remembered the calligraphy she practiced as a girl: "When spring comes, the plants, unseen, come to life." *Her name. Chun. Spring.*

The bicycle went easily downhill through the persimmon trees for which the village was known, and soon they were pedaling alongside the river. The sights were familiar, but seemed new in their portending. They rode along the river through high-standing sugarcane and ancient lychee trees drooping down over the water. A water buffalo lowed at their passing. Fish flipped, and fell. Sugary ripples in the moonlight.

Within an hour they were in Chindu town. The sun was bringing to life the smell of sewage, spreading a pestilential heat through the silent streets. She had been to Chindu twice, but never farther. She had rarely been outside the village, and never outside the district. On the far edge of Chindu was the bus station. She had never seen a bus, never ridden on any motorized vehicle other than the village's rattling old tractor. Other bus passengers were throwing their luggage up onto the racks on top. She had none. She turned to say goodbye to her husband and risked a look into his eyes. They were as she'd never before seen them, both shamed and terrified. As if it had just sunk in. He was biting his lower lip hard. His face was deathly white.

"Say goodbye to her," she said. He hesitated. She uncovered the baby's face.

"Goodbye, little one," he said. "I'm sorry."

She clenched down on something inside and turned away and walked to the bus.

"I'll meet you here tonight."

Ever so slightly she nodded, not sure anymore of anything, especially not of the distant uncertainty of "tonight." She got on the bus. Jiwei ped- aled alongside the noisy, dust-spewing bus for a while, waving weakly, then fell behind. The baby had not made a sound. Two hours later the bus let her off at the train in Tienja.

The Tienja station was crowded and confusing. Huge piles of coal glis- tened black. Coal dust stung her eyes, her throat. By the time she got onto the train there were no seats. Even the standing room was limited. She made no eye contact, but after a while a man tapped her on the shoulder and, gesturing to the baby, offered her his seat on a hard bench. Crammed in, she couldn't see out the windows except when someone got up to go to the toilet. They said the trip was four hours. The odd thing about the train was that it was so smooth, like a boat on the river of her childhood, but for the rhythmic *tick-de-tack tick-de-tack*, which, when the baby slept, brought sleep to her as well. The other odd thing was that for the first time in her life she was in a crowd where she knew no one, and no one knew her. This made her think back to her mother and father, and, once again, to her sisters. *How much can people stand?*

Because of a few fields and a shack they had owned, they had been called "landlords," and, although her father had not been sent away, he had been shamed. After First Sister disappeared into the schoolhouse in Tienja, nothing was the same. Father went around like a hungry ghost, smoking huge wads of tobacco rolled in inky newspaper, muttering to himself, doing so poorly at the farm that her mother and the girls had had to pitch in. Mother was sustained by her kitchen altar, her little box of gods, her small hidden Buddhas and her bowings and her silent prayers to her ancestors and Kwan Yin and the Earth God and the Sun God, and the Water God and the Rice God and sometimes the new moon itself—and, when there was money enough for it, her incense. When First Sister disappeared, Second Sister began looking around for a man, with a sensual ferocity no one had ever seen in her before. She found a discarded bicycle and with a friend fixed it up enough to ride downriver all the way to Tienja, and she wound up marrying the son of the policeman who had helped them look for First Sister. The policeman's son had taken over a tiny store selling women's clothes. The store became her life, and they saw her at home only for the first few holidays.

○ ○ ○

Now, every time she looks into her baby's eyes, she starts to weep. If she looks, but tries not to respond to her, the baby gets frantic. The one thing the baby can't stand is a stiff face looking back at her. So she looks, and responds, and weeps—gradually the tears ease. She tries to forget the past month, or what she is about to do. Tries hard.

Cannot.

The more she tries to forget, the more the memories float up and through her mind, and she gives in to them. She recalls the joy she felt at finding out she was pregnant again, with her second child, but at the same moment she felt a jolt of dread—*what if it was another girl?* She tried to talk about it with her husband, but he could not. The official policy was one child per family. They already had a girl, Xia, age two. If it was another girl, to keep it would be a disaster for the family—the cost of the penalty, the shame of still not having a son.

Girls are shame; boys are pride. Girls leave to marry, boys stay to work, carry on the blood and the land, bring status and maybe a better future, bring a wife to care for the grandparents in their old age. A second girl would only bring twice the shame.

"If this one had been a boy," said her mother-in-law, smiling, "We'd be glad to pay the penalty. A boy would be worth it. He'd pay for himself, many times over."

The tension of carrying the baby during the pregnancy was almost unbearable, not knowing which it would be. She said that if it was a girl she did not want to see it because if she saw it she couldn't give it away.

The birth was easy. They took the baby away, so she knew. She heard the baby cry, and asked to see it.

"No," her husband said.

"Bring her. I need her. She needs me."

Life. Saving a life, her life. Beautiful, more than my first.

And then the hell started. Her husband said he would take her away right then. His mother said it was better that way. His father, she thought, could have done the unthinkable, from the old days, drowned her or let her die somewhere farther up the mountain, and maybe that was why she insisted to see her, to be with her, thinking, *I'll fight to keep her, as long as I can.*

It was a month. A long time and a short time. She saw in her husband's father's eyes the not-thereness of the baby. In his mother's eyes, as if little wheels were clicking along inside, *How can I get rid of this one without fuss.* The touch of her poor baby's lips on her nipple, fists on her breast, made her vow to keep her with her always. They tried to force her not to, even keeping her first daughter away, making Xia view the tiny baby as a thing, like the sow or the little barnyard duckling who, confused and having lost its mother, followed the chickens around thinking it was a chick. Jiwei's mother tried to talk with her, tried to tell her what shame she would bring on the family and on herself, what hardship, for girls grow up and leave, and they needed a strong boy, they were barely surviving, they needed help.

Jiwei started out confused, but as the days and weeks went on, any of the fire she had seen in him, buffeted by the constant pounding of his mother and father, died out under a smothering obedience. Even inside her, there was a sense of losing face in the family for having a girl. They sent her to a fortune-teller, a rancorous, skeletal old woman, who, hearing everything, said the next child was certain to be a boy. A boy that would bring her status, a boy she could keep with her forever so she would never have to part with him as she would the girls—this brought a little flicker of agreement with them. But still she would not let the baby lie in someone else's arms, arms that wanted to get rid of her as if she were a piglet, or a crazy duck.

They worked on Xia, they "reeducated" Xia so that her natural jealousy of being replaced came out in a look on her face never seen before, a look of contempt, and in the way that she avoided her and the baby. The last straw was when her little girl refused to sing with her anymore, and sang only with her grandmother.

It took a month for their assault to work. Someone said that a woman in the village had done it once, two years ago, and knew how. They brought the woman, not the mother—she had not done it herself, for everyone said that was too hard—but the mother-in-law, who had done it for her. They brought the mother-in-law to tell them and forced her to listen. Round-trip it would cost a lot—for the bus and the train and the bus in Changsha and tea, it would really cost a lot, maybe nine yuan—a month's earnings. They handed the money to her wrapped in a knotted kerchief, and told her to count it. She had to put the baby down to do so.

○ ○ ○

Now, Changsha City is overwhelming. The train station is huge but filled with people running and shouting and jostling and not looking into each other's eyes but looking to the place they are going next. The faces are lighter skinned, tanned but not burnished like country faces. She stands in the midst of the chaos, searching for the bus they told her to take, the bus up the Nan Da Lu. The baby is screaming, and she rocks it and comforts it with a finger and then, again, a breast. Mixed in with the crowd are men in uniforms of various types, soldiers in olive-green Mao suits and beaked caps with stars, and also local police in blue. She goes outside and finds the buses. Dozens of them are lined up with their motors running, others are pulling in or pulling out. She knows heat from the farm, from working all day in the fields, but she has never felt heat like this, a dirty heat, for the air is thick with acrid smoke, engine exhaust, and oil fumes. The honking is incessant. She starts to cough. The baby starts to scream again. She walks from bus to bus and cannot find any that says "Nan Da Lu." She thinks to ask, but is ashamed, and starts to go up to a woman sweeping the street but stops because she thinks, *Maybe I won't do it. Maybe I'll go back home. No, I can't do that. Maybe I'll keep going, use my last yuan to get back on the train and go out past the other side of the city, find another village, another farm, another life.* This thought lasts only a few seconds before all the impossibilities arise and crowd in. In her despair the only thing that prompts her to go up to the woman is the fact that she is saving her little baby, and that there is hope for life to go on if she has a son.

"Where is the bus to Nan Da Lu?" she asks.

The woman stops sweeping, and stares unkindly at her. She spits in the street. "The bus runs only up and down Nan Da Lu. You have to take a bus to get to that bus."

"Which bus?" she says, suddenly afraid. No one told her about two buses. It will cost double. Does she have enough money for two buses, back and forth?

"The Shaoshan Lu bus, going south. Walk down Wuyi Lu three blocks. Over there. Wait for Shaoshan bus. Get off at the Nan Da Lu."

She thanks her, and starts to walk. There are hundreds of bicycles fighting the trucks and buses. The bicycles are carrying not just extra people, as in the roads around the village, but everything imaginable— animals and pots and pans and boxes and even huge oil drums strapped across, and some have trailers or small truck beds attached and are carrying things stacked twice as high as the cyclist. Soldiers and police are everywhere, in uniforms and caps with red stars. Many of the people are in worn Mao clothes, light blue or dark blue. The street is as wide as the river at home. The noise is like no other she has ever heard, like being in a small field with a hundred tractors, each with a differently pitched horn. She can hardly hear or breathe. Her chest feels clogged. She passes a sign: "ONE CHILD FAMILY IS HAPPIER AND BETTER."

Coughing and spitting, she keeps on, finds the Shaoshan bus, pays, gets on. It is packed, and she has to stand. Suddenly she feels lost, and fights her way to the front, to the conductor—a woman with an astonishing scar across her forehead.

"Can you tell me when we get to the Nan Da Lu?" she shouts over the racket.

The conductor nods.

She stands nearby, waiting.

Maybe one of my mother's gods will keep me from finding where to go to leave her, and I can go home with her. Maybe the Wrong Bus God, yes.

She fingers the piece of jade around her neck, a gift from her mother when she left home to marry. "It's my oldest Buddha," her mother said, "and is so worn, and so small, that you can wear it in safety—no one but us would ever know it is a Buddha."

"But I don't bow to the Buddha as you do. That god is yours."

"Wear it, dear one, and you will know that I am with you."

Now she fingers the smooth jade, its slight soft contour and worn lines of carving bringing up not so much the shape of any Enlightened One, but the sense of her mother, with her now. She did not even tell her mother of the pregnancy, afraid of what might happen, and when it did, she did not get in touch with her. She had the idea of taking Chun and going back to her mother, to live with her and her crazed father—but she knew that they would never allow her to take Xia. She wasn't ready to give up her husband and child, no. Now she thinks, *How could I brave the shame? How could my own mother have sent me, her beloved, away from her—to this?*

"Nan Da Lu!" the conductor announces. "Let her out, you barbarians," she shouts to the people standing in the way. "Let the country girl out."

"How did you know that?" she asks, turning before she goes down the steps.

The conductor smiles, and shakes her head kindly. "I was one too. Why did you come to big city?"

"Why did you?"

"To get my scar!" She laughs, crazily. "Good luck."

"Thank you. How far is the police station?"

The woman glances at the baby. Her eyes widen, and then narrow with suspicion, or understanding. People shout for the bus to get going. "I don't know," she says. "Try the market. Two blocks up, you'll see it."

"Try the market?"

"Try the market. They have excellent celery. Like at home. *Safe* to eat too." More shouts from the crowd. "All right, you animals! We'll move your cage someplace else. Get out now, dearie. And listen: be careful." She nods her head for emphasis and, glancing around, whispers, "Be careful."

Try the market? Excellent celery? Like home? Safe? She takes this as a sign.

○ ○ ○

The Nan Da Lu is not as broad as the other roads, the traffic lighter, although the flow of bicycles is undiminished. She focuses on finding the market. The baby is sleeping, comforted by the familiar rocking of her strides. Sure enough, in two blocks there it is, an alley street going off perpendicular to the road, back toward a park, a narrow alley of stalls much like the Thursday market in the village. She wanders along with the crowd, hiding her baby under her dress. She passes down and back the whole length of the alley, glancing at the stalls selling clothes on racks, all bright colors hanging limp in the scorching noon sun, and woks sizzling vegetables and butchers with ducks and chickens and pigeons in cages and a wooden board drenched with blood and a hose and a mangy dog hanging around hoping, eternally hoping, and bicycle repairers and, yes, midway down, the long wooden trays piled with all kinds of vegetables.

This is it. No. I can't. This is why they told me not to do it myself, why the woman in the village sent her mother-in-law to do it. Saying goodbye at home is like not really saying goodbye. I can't do it, no.

She turns and starts to walk out of the alley, but—unused to her plastic sandals—stumbles on a stone and almost falls. Pain shoots up her leg, hot and sharp, but she dares not attract attention and keeps walking on. Out on the main street, she sits down on the curb. She thinks, *If you do it, you have to be sure. But the conductor said, "Be careful." There are soldiers and police around. Can't ask here. Walk farther away and ask.* She walks back down the road, finds two young girls in bright dresses—perhaps going home for lunch from school?—and asks them.

"Is the Nan Da Lu police station nearby?"

"Yes. Just down there in the other direction. Can we see your baby?"

"Yes." She unwraps her. The baby blinks in the sun.

"Ohhh! Beautiful! Boy or girl?"

She can barely say it. "Girl."

"How old?"

"One . . ." She puts her hand over her face and turns and rushes off, away.

But not far. There is no time to go far and still make it back to the station for the last train home. Her mind fills again with fantasies of ways out, and in each she sees her mother-in-law's face, and in it her husband's face, and her other daughter's face, and the facts and the fantasies go around and around until she thinks she will scream or run out into the traffic on the road with the baby in her arms. The heat and the fact that she has not eaten or drunk anything for hours make her feel dizzy, so that people and things seem part of a dream from which she will soon awaken.

And then something else takes over and it is as if some other hand is leading her back to the alley of the market. Before she gets there the baby starts to fuss again, and saying to herself, *This is for the last time*, she sits in a doorway and takes out her breast and uses her two fingers to help her beautiful one take her nipple in her lips and suck, suck lustily, sending a warm chill through her, and on one hand she doesn't want to look into those eyes set like smooth dark jade in that face but she can't not look, and she forces a smile and the forcing brings a real smile, the smile, at best, of possibility for this little lost one. She takes the carefully calligraphed note and ties it firmly into the swaddling clothes and smells her one last time, that smell like no other, baby-soft and fragrant, like spring's own hair, and puts her lips to the soft skin of her face her little nose her rosebud lips, and then she seems to float over the sidewalk over the dirt of the alley of the market crowded at noon and hiding the baby in a fold of her dress she goes straight to the vegetable stand trying to blend in and yes the celery is piled high and the stalks healthy and easily parted and, yes, *safe*, and she places the tiny bundle in the little nest she makes for her and without looking back rushes off, away, resolving not to watch what happens but then at a safe distance from behind the pile of iron and tires and pumps of the bicycle-repair stall, she watches.

It takes no time at all. Vegetable sellers know their vegetables. She watches a short, stout woman wearing a blue bandanna go to rearrange the celery and suddenly look down, recoil, look again, and realize, and pick up the baby and shout:

"Whose baby? Whose baby?" People turn to look. "Whose baby?"

Mine! To keep this from escaping she puts a fist to her mouth, jams it hard, smashing her lips against her teeth.

"Whose baby?" the woman shouts. People stare, look around for the mother.

Mine! Fist to her mouth, she turns away.

"Whose baby whose baby?" echoes and echoes.

Turns back, blood on her hand now, on her fist.

"*Whose baby whose baby whose babywhosebabywhosebaby . . .*"

Turns away, huddles up inside, crouches over as if the fist is coming down on her head, her back, her belly, runs away.

2

The air-conditioned minibus turns up the narrow alley, swerves to avoid an oncoming motorcycle piled high with live chickens and ducks, and heads toward a skinny ash-gray dog lying in a puddle of shade cast by six brick-layers perched on a scaffold of bamboo, working hard to build just a little bit more of modern China. At the imminent death of the dog the three Western passengers scream, perhaps thinking of their own family dog, Cinnamon, left behind in Columbia, New York. The bus driver hits the horn. They barrel by, listening for the *kuh-chunk!* of the dog's death, but hear none. The bus bounces on over the rutted dirt of the alley. Clutching their seats, the family of three turns back and sees, through the dust, the dog, sitting against a wall of the alley, yawning. The two Chinese—the driver and the tour guide—burst out laughing. The bus rocks on toward what looks like a dead end where the alley walls converge but at the last moment it goes left through an open gate into a small courtyard enclosed on three sides by one-story cement buildings with black-tile roofs, and stops.

"Nan Da Lu Police Station," says Rhett Wong, the guide. "Everybody out."

Rising quickly from her seat in the front of the bus, Clio checks on her daughter and her husband and moves with an athlete's ease down the steps and out onto the dusty ground of the courtyard, thinking, *Finally, here. Finally we're facing it, finally we'll find out whatever facts there are. Something else might happen here, of which we three—and she—are a part.*

She looks around at the series of one-story buildings edging the bare dirt square. The overhangs of each roof are supported by wooden columns to offer shade—giving the place the feel of an outpost in the Wild West. Here and there a policeman stands or squats, a cigarette in hand or mouth, staring at her, not moving. She finds herself focusing on the open gate, two stuccoed concrete pillars at the end of the elbows of the embracing walls. *This is where she would have come. In the dark, just before dawn, crouching here, the baby in her arms. Looking at the bare bulb over the doorway, there. Waiting. Fearing, hoping. Desperate, both ways. Here, to there. Mine, to yours. She did it. Did she stay and watch, or did she just keep running? Right here, in that gateway. Broken.*

Suddenly she feels the seriousness of this endeavor, returning to the place where her beloved girl was abandoned, and perhaps even the place with some record of it. *Is this a wise thing to do? We could have just kept on exploring China, stayed with the tour. We didn't have to come here, risk this.* Her anxiety rises, but then, feeling the searing, heavy heat of a June afternoon in south China, her fear flips over into excitement, for it reminds her of the most adventurous time in her life—the years after college when she broke from the Family Hale and wandered the Caribbean. Sailing along, one day much the same as the next except for whether the wind was blowing or not blowing, or how long the day's rain would last. Showing up here and there, sometimes in the most elegant harbors, sometimes, like now, in dusty, hot places where everyone stood around or squatted and smoked, staring at her and not moving, and where she was the only white woman, and where at first she was scared and worried and after a while found herself on the other edge of scared and worried, the edge of portent.

Thinking, *In the days before Katie, before caution. Well then, girl, seize those days again! Be brave for your daughter. View it as an adventure.*

She wears an upscale version of the same kind of clothes she wore back then—a tan safari shirt with multiple pockets each latched by Velcro, matching shorts, and navy-blue New Balance tennis shoes. Tall and full-bodied, she keeps herself in shape, working out with a trainer at Schooner's Spa at the mall, jogging with her daughter, playing tennis regularly with her friends and golf rarely with her husband. She stands there with a certain solidity, planted but ready to move. At home she seems always on the go between child, husband, job, lessons, and errands, racing around in what she and her circle of mothers call "the daily scavenger hunt of Life As Supermom." She's fifty-one, older than the other moms—she married late, at thirty-eight. Deep down she still feels twenty-seven. Under the conical straw peasant's hat she bought a week ago in the Terra Cotta Warrior Gift Shop in Xi'an, her sun-bleached blond hair is in a ponytail. Above her straight nose, her light-blue eyes scan the shapes and colors around her—now suddenly an architect's eyes, an art dealer's eyes—searching for pieces she might buy for her gallery.

Nothing. This is post-Mao modern, or post-modern Mao: concrete, and spiritless. Artless. She tilts the straw hat back on her head and feels the flat sudden burn of the sun on her cheeks and chin and—a focus of her allure—on her plump lips, and thinks, *Sunscreen.* Sunscreen for fair-skinned Pep, peeling away, and, just to be on the safe side, for Katie. Katie's amber skin never seems to burn, just to burnish, but still. With melanoma on the rise, with studies showing that it takes just one or two real bad sunburns in childhood to start it brewing, you can't be too cautious. From her backpack she takes out her tube of Coppertone 45, maximum strength.

Watching Katie step down from the bus and bounce out into the light— her yellow hat with a chicken logo pulled down over her sunglasses so that she seems older, even glamorous—Clio feels a lump rise in her throat, a sudden sorrow that brings tears to her eyes. *She's so innocent, so expectant and vulnerable. She still sees the best in everything. Totally unable to tell a lie. A fierce, sure spirit. Still a pure soul. What will she make of all this? God help her.* You *help her.*

○ ○ ○

Katie Chun Hale-Macy, tall for ten, and slender, steps down slowly out of the air-conditioning onto the dusty ground, pulling down the beak of her yellow baseball cap with the chicken logo and "CHINA CULTURE CAMP 2001." She feels the wet heat slap her like a big, sweaty hand. She tries to see, but everything's blurry. "My sunglasses are like all fogged up?"

Clio smiles. Lately Katie's every sentence ends in an upward inflection, making it sound like a question. It bothers Pep, but Clio has assured him that all of Katie's fourth-grade girlfriends talk that way.

"Yeah," Pep says now, squinting into the harsh glare from under his floppy hat. "It's like breathing wet fire. Must be a hundred, and a hundred percent humidity. Hot as hell." He stretches up to his full six-four height, his arms high, his fingers waving in the turgid air, his khaki, multi-pocketed safari shirt riding up over his belly. His height, for him, has always been defining. Reassuring. He uses it, keeps his body tuned up. He jogs and bicycles with Clio and Katie and golfs with his buddies and considers himself fairly fit and trim. His size 12 Nikes feel solid on the packed dirt. He lowers his arms again and takes a long breath out, thinking, *This could be hard, really hard. God knows what we'll find out.* Looking around more carefully, his bright-green eyes narrow. He feels the risk, the possibility that all that he and Clio have created to make this family, to make it theirs, this American family that's doing pretty damn well in the world, all of this could be changed forever by this encounter with the police, or tomorrow at the orphanage. This ain't gonna be easy. A lot is at stake. He purses his thin lips. All at once he feels apprehensive, if not scared. *Don't let them see. Be careful. Take care of them.*

He shifts his weight to a more solid stance, feet apart, crosses his arms on his chest, and tilts his head, flashing a Paul Newman cocky smile. "Where's the lush green?" he says, feigning a great yearning and puzzlement. "Where's the green? I want the lush green—"

"Here he goes again, Mom—"

"—And all I get is dusty brown, all I get is dusty brown!"

"Pep!"

"Daddy, don't—"

"Okay, okay." Squinting, he looks around. "It is beautiful, in its own way, yeah. I love this light, this dusty haze—where's my camera?" He rubs the sweat up off his brow and back over his lank light-red hair and, to his chagrin, dislodges a piece of the scab that has finally—finally!—started to form on the bald top of his head. Three days before, at lunch at a scummy restaurant in Chengdu, he bashed it against the low ceiling of what he considered the filthiest pit toilet in all of China.

"Shit," he says, staring at the blood on his hand, "I'm bleeding again."

He is too tall for China, and something of a claustrophobe—which has made the trip difficult. Three things you don't want to be in China, he's realized, are tall, claustrophobic, and invested in keeping clean—phobic to dirt. *At fifty-six, you're too old for China too.* He worries that the scrape on his head from the pit toilet ceiling is brewing up rare, exotic germs that might sicken him, and he feels his sudden sweat as a fever. Thinking, *Band-Aid*, as well as *Camera*, he unzips the Citibank fanny pack that contains credit cards, passports, and airplane tickets, as well as sterile wipes and mini-packs of Kleenexes and a Swiss Army knife and a blue laser flashlight. And various pills including antibiotics and Pepto-Bismol for diarrhea and the sleeping pill Ambien to fight the week of wretched jet-lagged nights and the hot, noisy rooms and the overnight train ride from Beijing to Pingyao, wherever the hell *that* unheard-of city of six million was! And the pack of sterile needles and syringes in case any of them are in a car crash and need blood. All the things that Rosemary Ahern, the organizer of the trip, told them to bring.

The latest in a long line of Macys in Whale City Insurance, his business is risk. The first Macys were Nantucket whalers who settled Columbia, New

York, a Hudson River town, in 1775—they are mentioned in *Moby Dick*. That's what he tells new accounts, "We go back to *Moby Dick*"—thinking, *Big shit*. His work is out on that dire leading edge with morticians, oncologists, hospice workers—making a living out of disease, disaster, and death. Lately his job has been a burden—more so for his inability to think of anything without thinking of the risk to Katie and Clio. *As if I'm constantly underwriting our lives.* He finds a sterile wipe in his fanny pack and blots his bleeding scalp.

"Good," Clio says. "Are we ready?" Katie has moved close to Pep, and is leaning up against him, one hand in his. "Are you all right, Katie?"

3

When Clio told Pep that China Culture Camp 2001 was a guided tour with twelve adopted Chinese girls of Katie's age and their twenty-two American parents, a three-week tour focused on making the trip fun for the kids by visiting zoos and schools and playgrounds and Burger Kings and Pizza Huts, Pep thought it over and said, "I don't *think* so, honey. You know I don't do groups all that well. Doesn't sound like much fun, no."

Clio was surprised. But the refusal reverberated with other no's that had crept into the marriage over the years—it had started with the shock, humiliation, and profound sorrow that they'd gone through when they'd failed to produce a baby of their own—what they now refer to as "a bio," a "biological" as opposed to an adopted baby. The creep of no's had only gotten worse as they tried to move on to adoption. At their advanced age there had been another series of hurdles—what he christened "The Adoption Olympics." When Katie arrived, the sorrow lifted—it was no match for their joy—but as the years went on they realized that the sorrow was not gone entirely.

When Clio brought up the idea of the trip a second time, he said, "I need a *vacation*, a cheap vacation—how 'bout the reliable Adirondacks?"

"It has to be China."

"Why? Maybe if Katie were interested in China, okay. But she doesn't seem to be in the slightest." It was true. Over the years Katie had mostly resisted Clio's repeated efforts to keep her Chinese heritage alive in the backwater town of Columbia. Despite her talent and passion for drawing and painting, Katie rarely drew or painted anything that seemed inspired by the Chinese art that Clio had shown her. Despite their finding a tutor from the Chinese restaurant, Katie hadn't shown much interest in learning Chinese—"I want to learn Spanish, like everybody else in my class."

"But the trip isn't only for Katie's sake," Clio went on, "it's for all of ours. The books I've read, the people I've talked to—they all say it's a terrific thing, to go back as a family. Age ten is about right. The timing's perfect. We'll leave the tour early and go back to her orphanage in Changsha—we can be there on her birthday. Returning ten years later, imagine? And we can visit the police station too."

"What police station too?"

"Where she was abandoned. We can visit both. To see if they have any more information. We've got to try, Pep. To find out anything we can about her birth mother. Agreed?"

He hesitated, trying to assess the risk. "Mostly, yes."

"We probably won't find out anything. No one ever has. But we have to try. We need to be able to say to her—maybe now, maybe when she's older—that we did everything we could. We followed up. Completely. For *her* sake, Pep. Okay?"

"Not if she doesn't want to." More and more lately, he felt that Clio was being too lenient with Katie, making him be the firm one, which put him in the position of the bad guy.

"You think I'd make her do it if she didn't want to?" Clio said, surprised.

"There's a first time for everything, Clee."

Clio stared at him, hurt by the accusation. "Thanks a lot," she said. "Y'know I can take your compliments, Pep, but when you turn on the charm, I go all weak in the knees."

○ ○ ○

For a while, Clio gave up the idea. But then one night a few months later when they went in to put Katie to bed they were surprised to find that she had arranged her treasures from China in a kind of altar. Her banner with the character for "Chun" hung over her bed. Upon her big bright-red Chinese box, under a bamboo umbrella, and in front of a fan filled with the magical mountains of Guilin, several of her Beanie Babies were gathered with a small red Chinese flag, a framed embroidery of a panda, and a propped-up Katie drawing of the Disney video *Mulan*—and in her writing "*China's Bravest Girl*."Also, Pep's green-bronze replica of a Tang Dynasty horse frozen at full gallop with flowing mane, Clio's statue of Kwan Yin, and "Shirty"—Katie's most prized possession, the soft purple-and-white-striped cotton shirt that was her security blanket. Clio took Pep's hand, squeezed it, smiled, and led him to Katie's canopied bed. She was just closing her book—*Your Dog's Mind*—and curling up to sleep. They sat together on the edge of the bed. Each kissed her goodnight, said, "I love you," one after the other, and she murmured, "Love you too" to each in turn, and suddenly was asleep.

The next morning, when they asked Katie if she'd like to go on a trip to China, she was thrilled, and more thrilled when they told her they'd be in China on her tenth birthday. "Cool! I'll turn ten in China!"

"Not just China, love," Clio said, delighted at her enthusiasm. "Changsha. Where you're from."

"*Way* cool! Thanks, Mom, thanks, Dad. It'll be like the best birthday present *ever*. When do we leave?"

That night, with Clio out at a business meeting, Pep curled up with Katie to put her to sleep, as he had done when she was a baby, before she had—as he saw it—turned so totally to Clio. The whole first year he had been the one to put her to bed, and the love he felt for his tiny, beautiful *Asian* daughter astonished him. That night once again he hugged his nine-year-old gently close, feeling again her little smooth shoulder against his chest, her hair a black silk wave flowing across his face. "Hey, Dad," she said, "remember Lion Army, Lion Army?" Once when she was small and he was cuddling her this way, she'd called out, "Lion Army, Lion Army," and he asked, what was this army? and she lifted up her head and put his arm under it and said, "No, I mean lie on arm-ey, lie on arm-ey!" and they'd laughed and laughed. Now she put her head on his arm and he read her another chapter of *The Wind in the Willows*. As he read, feeling that smooth cheek against his, he flushed, and his voice cracked.

"What's wrong with your voice, Dad?"

"Nothing." *Why can't I tell her?*

He finished, and started to rub her back—another ritual.

"Dad?" she said, after a while.

"Yes, foozle?"

"I hate school."

"What? I thought you liked school. This whole year with Miss Witters, studying the Greeks?"

"I do, but I don't like, you know, *school*? Can I stay home tomorrow?"

"Nope. It's your job, like mine and Mom's. You have to go." Katie groaned. "Why don't you like school?"

Katie paused. "Never mind."

"C'mon, c'mon, tell your dad."

"Like no one wants to be my friend anymore—Tara hangs out with Kissy now in recess, they don't want me with them. I feel like I'm *outsidered*!" Tears came to her eyes. She felt his strong arms around her, caught the earthy scent of his skin and his nightly beer, heard him ask why, and blurted out, "I think it's because I'm different?"

"Different how?"

"When they look at me it's like I can *feel* them saying, 'She's different.' Like they look at the outside of me and see I'm Chinese and there aren't any other Chinese in my class—in the whole school!—and they don't like me from the outside and they don't *see* that inside I'm the same as them, and I just want to be friends? I hate Spook Rock—they're all stuck up and into being popular." She wasn't crying now, and turned over to look at him. "Can I go to public school the rest of the year?"

Pep had never seen such a sad look on her face. She was, as always, laser-like in her intensity, and he'd seen her in tears before, but this was something else—a deep hurt, a sorrow. "I'm really sorry you feel bad, hon, but how would that help?"

"'Cause there are Chinese kids there, some of 'em are my age, like the kids whose mom and dad own the Chinese restaurant we go to? I want to change schools. Please?"

Pep was shocked. He'd known that lately, most mornings, she hadn't wanted to go to school, but he'd never realized why.

"Mom and I'll talk about it tomorrow. We'll try to work something out. I'm really sorry you're having such a hard time, Kate-zer. It's *sad*."

"Really, really sad, yeah."

"We'll try to help. We'll take it *gentle-gentle*, like always, okay?"

"Okay, but don't say *anything* to any kids or teachers or other parents, okay?"

"Of course not, hon." She laid her head down on his arm again, and he said what he had always said to her in the old days, "Coazy-coazy! It's so coazy-coazy!" and he rubbed her back and felt her calm down. Her confiding in him, and the feeling of being so close to her, like they once had been, brought a sudden bolt of despair. *How has it happened? How have I lost this? Somehow or other, with my wife and my daughter, I've become outsidered too, and I've got no idea how to get back in.* Close to tears, feeling her calm breathing, he realized the depth and intensity of his love for her—and for Clio. It made him realize how lonely he had become. *Katie and Clio have their own world together now. I've gotten pushed out—and they don't even know I feel it.* He sighed. Figuring she was asleep, he eased his arm out from under her and got up.

"Check on me, Dad, will you?"

"Sure, hon."

"And keep checking on me."

"I will. Have a beautiful sleep. Love you."

"Love you too."

He got up, tucked her in, and left. Maybe this was why she'd had such trouble going to sleep lately. Ever since her last sleepover, at Kissy's, when she'd called in the middle of the night and they'd had to go all the way out to Copake Falls to get her and bring her home. She said, then, that she had been the last one awake, left alone in the dark, unable to fall asleep. Alone. Left. Scared. Ever since, they'd had the night ritual of going back into her bedroom every few minutes so she knew they were there, until she was asleep. *Maybe it is from her being abandoned, left alone in the dark, at only a month old. Clio's right. In Changsha, we have to find out what we can.*

○ ○ ○

The next day Katie came home from school with a gift for Clio, a Chinese-style drawing she had done—a bunch of purple grapes on a branch—and a poem:

We both have hearts.
Your in mine and mine in yours.
Even if your far away I'll
Always carry you in my heart.

Later that night Pep and Clio talked over what Katie had said. Clio talked with Katie alone as well. Talking seemed to help, but they couldn't send her to public school, no. Spook Rock Country Day was elitist, yes, but Columbia Public was like a war zone.

A week later, when Clio was driving her after school, Katie, from the backseat, said, "Mom, I've been thinking of like when we're in China?"

"Yes, dear?"

"I bet my birth mom will recognize me, and I think I'll want to stay a while?"

Clio was startled. The Volvo jumped toward a ditch, then swerved back. Ever since the adoption, the image of Katie's birth mom had never been far from Clio's mind. The woman was always a presence, always *there*. Almost every day Clio would be surprised to find herself thinking of her—no, not thinking, more that she was just *there*. Not as a vision, never as a particular image, just a *sense*—like from time to time she still sensed her own dead mother *there* with her. The *sense* was of a slender, pretty but worn woman of thirty-something in a peasant's shirt and pants, poor beyond belief but proud, even elegant, both shy and strangely sure. And soulful. Like Katie—whose sureness, Clio had come to realize, was a reaction to her own shyness, her own deep soulfulness. Only rarely would Katie mention her birth mom. On Katie's birthday they'd light a twenty-one-year candle to her birth mother and say a prayer, to remember that wherever in China she might be, she too was remembering Katie that day. The first time Katie mentioned her she was about four. They were in the car, and suddenly from the backseat came, "Mommy, I came from another mommy's tummy, right?" Clio was stunned, but ready. "Yes, darling, in China before we met you, you grew in another mommy's tummy and they weren't able to take care of you because they didn't have enough food and money, so we went and got you and brought you home." From the backseat, total silence. Clio held her breath. Finally she said, "Do you understand?"

"Yeah," Katie said, "can I have french fries for dinner?" Pep broke out laughing, as did Clio—and Katie too, even though she didn't know why. She screeched with laughter, like a happy bird.

And so now when Katie brought up finding her birth mother on their trip back to China, Clio said, "What a great thought, hon. But it's a big country—over a billion people—we probably won't even meet her."

"Yeah, but if we do she'll recognize me."

"Yes, maybe she would."

"She *will*. And if we have a like *chance* to meet her, you'll make it happen?"

"Of course."

"As hard as you can?"

Clio loved this in Katie, her focus, her optimism, her being so quietly *tenacious*. Right from the first time they saw her, at four months. "Yes."

"Promise?"

"Promise."

"We'll meet her and stay for a while! Thanks, Mom."

Clio's heart was beating fast, pulsing in her temples. Not so much at the "meeting her" part, but at the "stay for a while." It wrenched her, a hand reaching in, twisting.

"China's the biggest country in the world, right?" Katie asked.

"Yes, but India is catching up fast, and—"

"China will win. Trust me."

"Okay. Call me if I need you." Clio said, using their funny goodnight line.

○ ○ ○

As they drove on to Mary's Farm, Katie was strangely silent. They pulled into the rutted dirt road leading up to the barn. The woman who ran the place was a kind of earth mother, a divorced fifty-something who had inherited a plot of farmland and kept herself going by boarding horses and giving riding lessons to the rich New Yorkers who had moved upriver a hundred miles into Kinderhook County. But lately business had been bad. A brand-new, sparkly clean upscale riding venture called Ascot Equestrian was siphoning away her clientele. All of Katie's private school friends went to Ascot now, but Katie insisted on sticking with Mary. The "Farm" was a ramshackle place with run-down old barns and leaky fences and haphazard cages and coops. Mary had horses and goats that shared the stable, and chickens and miniature ponies that could pull a cart and rabbits and a pig and a snake and any other stray animal that wandered in. Katie loved riding, but also loved just hanging out with Mary, doing chores and talking with her. At Mary's, Katie was in animal heaven. She'd always loved animals, especially babies, and wanted to work in a shelter some day. Twice a week here she could spend as much time as she wanted with whatever animals she wanted.

Mary, muddy and smiling, waved to them from up the lane.

Katie waved back, opened the door, and said, "Bye, Mom."

"Bye, dear." Clio leaned toward her, into the backseat. "See you soon."

Katie hesitated, and then shut the door again. "Mom, I'm feeling a little sad."

"Why's that?"

"Well, I'm thinking over and over about my birth mom leaving me and never seeing me again. And it's really sad to think when I had to say goodbye to her." Tears came to her eyes. Clio reached for her, hugged her across the seat, feeling the little shoulders shake. After a few moments Katie sat back, and wiped away the tears with the back of her hand. Clio handed her a tissue. She blew her nose. Again she was quiet, sitting there still, head down. Finally she said, "But *every* mom has to leave her daughter sometime and never see her again. *All* moms and dads have to say goodbye to their kids, and their kids to them?"

"I know, dear. But that's a long, long time away, and when that time comes, Daddy and I are going to make sure that you're ready."

"You can't promise that."

"No, we can't. But we'll try our best. And life has a way of making sure you're ready. It may sound weird, but it's true."

Katie considered this. "'Kay." She opened the door again.

"Hi there," Mary said to them both, her eyes telling Clio that she knew something was up. Her broad face and even her hair were coated with dirt.

"How'd you get so muddy?" Katie asked.

"That horse Velcro! He's such a brat! Pushed me into a big mudhole!" She laughed, heartily. "A brat, right, Katie?"

"A real brat, yeah!"

"C'mon, I need some help."

"You got it!" Katie cried happily. "Bye, Mom."

"Don't get too dirty, hon."

"Oh Mom!" She rolled her eyes and ran off.

As Mary went to her house to wash up, Katie walked toward the barn, head down. She kicked resentfully at the yellow, red, and purple leaves in her path. Magically, as if in answer, a whirlwind of leaves spiraled up and around her, riding an unseen breeze. She watched them fly away, free as birds. *Like they're little sads, flying away.* She smiled. At the barn, she pulled hard on the weight-balanced door and suddenly she was inside. *Smell of hay and moldy stuff and pine needles and dirt and horse poop and goat poop and Velcro and leather and earth like when you turn it up for the plants in spring. I love the smell of earth and pine.*

"Cheep cheep! Cheepcheep! Cheep!"

She looked up. A barn swallow nest on a crossbeam. *Two tiny beaks, three, four! Wide open like pink clamshells waiting for food—babies! I love it here. It feels like home.*

4

Now Katie stands in the hot sun of the courtyard of the police station, leaning up against Pep. Her mother is staring at her, expecting an answer to her question. *Am I all right? Not really.* Katie can see the worry in her mother's eyes, and senses a tension in her father's body. *They are really nervous!* For the first time she senses what a big deal it is for them to come back here, and for her too. *I think I want to find out about what happened to me, but maybe not.* She glances around at all the policemen staring at them, *like they're wondering what I'm doing with these two people who aren't Chinese, like they think they kidnapped me or something? No way I'm going in there and sit in front of a bunch of policemen who are going to talk about it to them and me.*

"Mom, I'm hot," she says, adjusting her baseball hat. "Please can I go wait in the bus?"

"You don't want to meet the policeman, dear?" Clio asks.

"Yeah sort of but I don't, you know, really *want* to? Like in front of everybody?"

"Are you sure, sweetie?"

"Yeah. Can I just wait in the bus and be cool? I mean like *cold*-cool, not, you know, *cool*-cool?"

"Sure, Kate-zer," Pep says, squeezing her shoulder. "It's okay."

"Just stay in the bus," Clio says, "till we get back."

"I will." Katie knocks on the door. The driver, cigarette hanging from a corner of his smile, opens the door. Katie gets in and he closes the door behind her.

○ ○ ○

Pep takes out his camera.

"No way!" Rhett cries out, and grabs the camera, concealing it quickly under his shirt. "Are you crazy?"

"No photos?" Pep asks. "Why not?"

"Because these are the *po-leece*!" He says it in perfect imitation of Eddie Murphy. "Going to a police station is the last thing—the very last thing— any Chinese wants to do. You never go there voluntarily. And if you're forced to go there, you do *not* take pictures of them. *They* take pictures of *you*. Jesus!" He lights a cigarette, his hand shaking ominously. Unlike most Chinese they've met, Rhett speaks an astonishing brand of English, one you'd hear on the street at home, laced with Afro-American slang. How did he learn it? "From watching American movies," he said. "A *lot* of American movies." What were his favorites? "*Dumb and Dumber*, and *Gladiator*, and *any* Eddie Murphy film. America is great, just great!" Had he ever been there? "No, but if I could, dudes—and little dude Katie—I'm like *there*, tomorrow?"

Of all the Chinese they've met, Rhett Wong is the only one whom Pep feels has a touch of not exactly cool but of a *reach* for cool. He is thirty-two, chubby, dressed all in black and gray with aviator sunglasses that never leave his face and a cell phone always in his hand, a cigarette that pops into his fingers at will, and pointy leather shoes that give him, with his bulk above, the appearance of a small dancing bear. "Rhett"? He told them that, at a certain age, an educated Chinese takes a Western name. When it came time for him, his elder brother, at college studying English, was reading *Gone With The Wind*.

"A *camera*?" he goes on. "You wanna take a *picture*? Let's just hope they didn't see it!" His tone implies real danger. Yesterday, at the Changsha airport, when they mentioned the police station, he balked. It was all they could do to convince him, and he said he would require additional "combat pay."

"You think, with the camera, I'd be in danger?"

"Not just you, man, *me*."

"What would happen to you?"

"You don't wanna go there." He puffs, considers. "At best—at the very *best*—I'm selling beans off a blanket in the street." He stubs out his butt on the tire of the minibus. "If we're unlucky, they may already have seen your camera on *their* cameras. Here." He sidles up to Pep like a thief selling a stolen Rolex and slips the camera into his hand. "Sneak it back in the bus."

"But if they're watching, won't they want to *see* me putting it back in the bus?"

Rhett stares at him as if he is an idiot. "Pep. Sneak it back in the bus."

Pep knocks on the door, and puts the camera on the front seat of the bus.

"Okay, guys," Rhett says. "One for all and all for one! *We're goin' in!*"

Pep looks at Clio and rolls his eyes. She's glad to connect with him, and rolls her eyes too, and smiles reassuringly. "Ready?" Clio asks.

"Sure." Pep has little desire to talk to a Chinese policeman, but he has to be there, not only for marital solidarity but so that, if Clio starts talking about Tibet or Human Rights or the Enslavement of Women or the One-Child-Per-Family Policy, he can step in and avert an international incident.

○ ○ ○

They walk across the courtyard and in under the overhanging roof to a kind of veranda, a shelter from the dusty heat. Turning left they go through a low doorway and into a small concrete-walled room, another smaller room to their left with a table and three chairs—maybe an interrogation room. Rhett walks to a door in the first room and knocks. He motions Pep and Clio into the interrogation room. The walls are bare but for a poster of the men, ships, and planes of the Chinese army, navy, and air force, in formation beneath a large red star. Through a rectangular hole in one wall they glimpse several men lying on mats on the floor, smoking. Some of the men are only partially in uniform, their '30s-style undershirts an affront to the image of authority. Pep and Clio sit at the table and wait, listening to Rhett talk to the lounging policemen for what seems a long time.

Finally in comes a policeman, followed by Rhett. The policeman has a striking head—large, square, framed by a brush cut of black hair. His dark eyes show his suspicion and, because of the reddened sclera, his fatigue or dissipation. As if, Pep muses, he's been up all night tormenting a suspect and drinking it off the rest of the day in the back room with his buddies. His cheeks are lightly pocked, giving him a tough look, but this doesn't fit with his lips, which are small and curled and impish. You can see, in the man, the boy, and the boy is not the bully of the class but the astute observer of the bully. Not the gunslinger, but the sidekick. The top two buttons of his uniform shirt are open, revealing a hairless chest. Rhett introduces him— neither Clio nor Pep catches his name but from three weeks in China they are used to never catching names and don't ask again—and his handshake, like that of most Chinese, is limp. Rhett says he will translate. The chief and Rhett look to Pep for his questions. Pep looks to Clio.

Clio, on the spot, fingers the smooth jade Kwan Yin on the red thread around her neck that she bought ten years ago at the temple on Mount Yuelu here in Changsha. Jade to dispel ghosts, red thread for luck, Kwan Yin the Chinese bodhisattva of compassion. This helps. As does looking at the kindest part of the chief, his lips, and then looking into his Chinese face as a whole, for this suddenly brings back a warm rush of familiarity—she sees in it the beloved Chinese-ness of her daughter's face. Ever since Katie was a baby, whenever Clio sees an Asian face, she feels this rush of connection, of affection. After the first three months of staring into her baby's eyes, one day she went out to shop at the mall and was shocked to realize that it was the *Caucasian* babies who looked strange—noses too big, faces too custard white, eyes too round, all dull expressions and huge heads on rubbery necks. *Assume that he is, at heart, kind. A father of a daughter.*

"Thank you for taking the time to see us. We adopted our daughter from Changsha ten years ago—she's sitting out there in the bus, the nice air-conditioned bus?" She stops, hoping that this mention of air-conditioning might amuse the chief. Rhett conveys her words. The chief is not amused. "Her documents say that she was brought to Nan Du Lu Police Station. We wanted to find out if there are any records."

To Clio, Rhett's Chinese seems even stranger than usual, filled with clangs and bangs—someone from Beijing told them that the Changsha dialect sounds like a bunch of knives and forks and spoons being jangled around in a cloth bag. Clio is sweating hard. When Rhett finishes, the chief gives a slight smile. When he speaks, his voice reveals vocal chords weathered by many years of barely cured tobacco, an unpaved roadway along which his words jounce and swerve crazily. The chief says that this is a new police station and there are no records from the old police station.

Clio's face falls. The chief is still smiling, but the smile is now more malicious than welcoming. He is in charge and there is no question he can't counter. Clearly this interview, for him, has a low degree of difficulty. "I understand," she says, "that there are no records of our daughter Katie, but can I ask you about the general policy of the police station in dealing with abandoned babies, with foundlings?"

The chief nods. Answering Clio's series of questions and follow-up questions, he seems frank, clear, and matter-of-fact, even bored at telling her the obvious, things of little interest to him. The police get a call from someone who finds a baby where it has been left, almost always in a public place—a railway station bench, a bus station, a busy street corner or park at dawn where the people are gathering to start their tai chi, a busy market, under an overpass where merchants sell things, the front step of a department store. There is even a hole—a kind of ledge in a wall at the entrance to the Martyr's Park—that is known to be a place where babies can be safely put. The baby is always left where it will be found right away. Whoever finds it knows to call the police. The police go and pick up the baby, bring it back to the police station, make a record of it, take the baby to the orphanage. Each police station has been assigned an orphanage. His is Changsha Social Welfare Center Number One. Katie's orphanage.

"Is there ever anything left with the baby when it is found?"

Sometimes, the chief says, there is a note pinned to the baby's swaddling clothes, which has the date of birth and the name. Is there ever anything more? Never, says the chief. *Never?* Clio asks. The chief, with a certain smugness, says maybe once or twice there is a message. What does the message say? The chief shrugs. Can you remember what any of the messages were? Another shrug.

"Are you saying that you don't read them or you just don't care?"

"Easy does it, Clio," Pep says, finding himself suddenly drenched in sweat. The chief turns and looks at him, amused at seeing the first fracture of the marital whole. "You don't have to translate that, Rhett—"

"Go ahead, Rhett."

Rhett glances at Pep, and Pep senses that he also doesn't want to offend the chief. Smiling, Rhett translates. But before the chief can answer, another policeman walks in. He too is hefty, but not quite as hefty, imposing, but not quite as imposing, and without acknowledging the existence of anyone but the chief he hands two small plastic envelopes to him. The chief opens them—two brass medals suspended from red ribbons. The chief admires the medals, and tucks them into his shirt pocket. The other policeman leaves. As if his receiving these two medals has somehow erased whatever latest pointless question Rhett has asked, the chief sits back and says nothing.

"What do you do with the notes, the messages?" Clio asks.

Rhett translates. The chief smiles and makes the gesture of lighting a match and holding it to a piece of paper, watching as it turns to ashes.

Tears come to Clio's eyes. *Oh God don't, don't cry here now!* She wipes them away with her hand but they keep coming. All at once on a wave of sorrow she is back in Columbia a dozen years ago, waking up one night beside her husband and feeling crampy in her stomach, no, lower down in her womb! Three months pregnant. After all the anxiety of trying to conceive, all the humiliation of charting her fertile period and calling Pep up wherever he was to come and have sex (not "make love") right away on demand, and then finally, after six months of failure, getting pregnant and letting herself go, imagining their baby, their child, and feeling suffused with joy—feeling like the Mona Lisa! That one night, waking up beside her husband, not wanting to disturb him, and going to the bathroom and something terrible starting to happen and the cramp becoming a tearing and a loss and she knew it before she looked but she had to. There, in the toilet—the *toilet!*—a bright red blossoming out from a stringy central bud. Dissolving. Her cry awoke Pep, brought him running—she tried to flush it before he arrived but he saw it too. She never got pregnant again. Years of trying, and never again.

Dazed by her sudden anguish, she feels Pep's arm around her shoulders, and she takes the tissue he offers. She focuses on her breath. Gradually calms down. The chief stares at her, a stare she sees as containing all the detached slyness of a skilled interrogator who now knows his victim's vulnerability. But then all at once she thinks she sees in his eyes his sense of her despair, even a flicker of kindness. At least a lack of cruelty. Which is something. She feels herself soften, and to her surprise she smiles at him. When she goes on her voice is calm.

"Who are the mothers?"

The chief seems surprised. "They are either from the country and married, or from the city and single."

"Do the mothers ever leave the babies right here at the police station?"

The chief seems indignant at this, and with a hint of passion says something that Rhett translates as "They can't. It's *illegal.*"

"But does it happen?"

"Don't push him," Rhett warns.

"Clio—"

"Please ask."

Rhett asks. The chief stares at Clio, then at Pep, and says nothing.

"Have you ever had a mother come here looking for her baby?"

The chief, hearing this, seems amazed, and laughs. He speaks with inordinate slowness, looking at Clio and then at Pep, rather than at Rhett. "No. It's illegal. It's *all* illegal. You don't understand. These women have a problem. They want to solve their problem. They solve their problem and it is over with, and they go on with their lives. It is a relief. To find them is what *you* want, not what *they* want. They don't want to be found. They don't think about it, they don't care about it. It's over."

"They don't care what happens to their babies?"

"They don't care."

"But . . . on their birthdays . . . these are their little girls—"

"Look," the chief says, getting up. "They are in a terrible time in their lives. They are in pain. Some of them kill themselves. They have a problem. We solve their problem. Don't be *selfish.*" He smiles, and says, "Thank you for coming to talk."

They thank the chief for taking the time and walk out of the tiny rooms onto the veranda, blinded by the sun and heat and dust.

5

Clio steps out of the shade of the veranda into the searing heat and walks quickly through what seems like solid yellow dust toward the minibus, searching for Katie. "Where's Katie? I don't see her!" Her heart sinks, her ankles go all watery.

On tip-toe she looks in. Katie is lying down, curled up on the seat, asleep.

Clio looks up at the damp dusty sky and sends up a prayer of thanks to God, or to the gods. As she brings her eyes back down she sees a puzzling sight. There in a far corner of the courtyard is what looks like a pile of dirty rags, but it's moving. She walks over, Rhett and Pep following.

As she gets closer she sees that the rags are human beings. One is a small old Chinese woman with a deeply lined and weather-beaten face, dressed in tattered clothes. She squats on her heels in the dust, staring straight ahead as if she's blind, one hand out, palm up, begging. The palm is the same color as the rest of her skin, a dirty dark tan. It moves back and forth like a broken-down metronome, pleading. Before her, and tied to her other wrist by a bit of worn twine, is a skinny child, a toddler, still a little wobbly on his feet. The boy walks unsteadily back and forth to the limit of the twine. His face and hands and bare feet are filthy, the same yellow-tan dirt color as the old woman's. He totters toward Clio and holds out a hand to her—even the palm is filthy. The fingers are thin as pencils, the arm hardly as thick as a broomstick. The old woman, alerted by the sharp tug on the twine, smiles—her teeth are stained almost black by a lifetime of betel chew—and starts talking to them.

Wanting to remove himself from this scene, Pep looks away.

As he stares at the entrance to the courtyard, he sees a woman walk in from around the corner and come toward them. She is tall and slender—"willowy" is the word that comes to mind—and young, maybe in her thirties. Unlike many of the women they've seen in Changsha, she wears a white silk dress slit up the side and covered with pink lotus blossoms, the silk flowing down to just above her ankles, revealing tan feet in blood-red sandals. A matching red parasol protects her from the heat. As she gets closer, his breath catches in his chest—she is beautiful. Beautiful and sensual. A long oval face with high cheekbones and large, dark eyes and shoulder-length black hair—which, in the bright sun, glints with an almost imaginary touch of red—like Katie's. Thin and graceful like Katie, too. And unlike most of the Chinese women he's seen, she looks straight into his eyes and holds his gaze. Her smile seems to him, somehow, not casual, but deep, even *elegant*—also unusual, here in rural China. He smiles back. She turns and walks across the yard and goes up onto the veranda and into an office of the police station. He can still see her standing in line, waiting her turn.

"Pep," Clio whispers to him, clutching his arm, "did you see that woman?"

"Beautiful—incredibly beautiful."

"No, no—I mean she looks just like Katie."

"Yeah, I thought that too—"

"*Just* like! Of all the thousands of Chinese faces we've seen, she's the only one who looks just like Katie."

"Yes, she does, but—"

"The same face, eyes, hair—the same build?"

They stare at her, standing in line in the doorway.

"What's up, doc?" says Rhett, badly mimicking a Bugs Bunny accent. He too is staring at the woman in the doorway. Clearly he has overheard their conversation.

Clio feels a tug on her sleeve, and reflexively pulls away.

The beggar woman is standing up, pulling at her insistently, roughly. Rhett speaks harshly to her, but she doesn't let go. He tries to pry her fingers off Clio's sleeve. It takes him a while to do so, and meanwhile the twine has come loose from her wrist and the little boy is wandering across the courtyard, straight into the traffic of bicycles and motorbikes and cars.

"Rhett! Pep!" Clio cries out, afraid for the child. "Hold her—I'll get him."

She rushes off toward the boy, who is disappearing down into another doorway in the rabbit warren of the police station.

Rhett takes hold of the woman, but she struggles free. Pep, repelled by the smell and dirt, helps Rhett walk the woman back to the wall. Wailing, gesturing toward them for money and then to where the boy has disappeared, she squats down again. Pep looks over to Clio, who has the boy by the hand. The child is resisting her grip, but feebly.

Pep turns away again, and sees the woman in the white silk dress and red sandals come back out of the doorway. She glances at him once more and smiles, then puts up her red parasol against the sun and turns and walks away, disappearing again around the concrete gateway into the alley.

He thinks to tell Clio, but she is in the far corner of the courtyard, trying to get the boy to move. About fifteen Chinese men and women have gathered around them and are talking loudly. Rhett and Pep leave the old woman and help Clio bring the boy back. Rhett shoos away the Chinese, and ties the twine around the old woman's wrist.

"Pep, let's give her something."

"Fine," he says, taking out a five-yuan bill—nothing for them, a lot for the beggar. Clio puts it in the boy's hand. The boy immediately gives it to the old woman, who smiles her black smile and bows her head up and down in thanks, and reaches out to try to grasp Clio's hand. Clio smiles and nods at her, but backs away.

They walk to the bus. Clio looks in. Katie is still asleep on the seat. "Thank God Katie didn't see that!"

"No fooling," Pep says, taking out his packet of sterile Handi Wipes. "But you did good. Want one?"

She wipes her hands, looking toward the alcove where they saw the woman with Katie's face.

"She left," Pep says.

"What?"

"I saw her walk out."

"And you didn't *tell* me? I wanted to, you know, well, talk to her."

"Why?"

"Because she . . ." She stops herself. "Hurry, come on, get in the bus." She pushes Pep and Rhett inside. "Rhett, tell the driver to try to find her. Go back down that road. Shit! Hurry up!"

Rhett blinks, and stares at her for a long moment, as if calculating something mysterious or, Pep thinks, profitable. "Sure. No problem. Let's go. Saddle up!"

With what seems to Clio like excruciating slowness, the driver backs up, out, and into the narrow alley they came in on. The woman is gone.

"Go to the end," Clio says, "try the other roads. Pep, you look out that side, I'll do this—Rhett, please—faster?"

"Okay, okay." He leans over the driver's shoulder and whips him on with a few harsh exhortations. The bus jumps, reaches the end of the alley, turns onto a larger road. Nothing. They drive up and down, staring into every doorway and alley. Nothing.

The bus bangs through the fractious traffic. They drive here and there, up and down the nearby streets where she might have walked. No luck.

"Who are you looking for?" Katie asks, sleepily.

Back at the hotel there is a new banner in the lobby:

WELCOME TO SEE YOU AGAIN

They hire Rhett for some sightseeing the next afternoon.

Up in their room, Katie grabs her bathing suit and bolts for the pool. They try to keep up, calling out to her to wait in the lobby. Her long legs seem to glide down the grand marble staircase. She has always been athletic, like Clio. When they go for runs together Katie seems to float, as if she's imitating one of her beloved animals, a fawn, or a foal.

Soon they are sitting beside the pool, watching her play in the water.

"Clio, listen," Pep says. He feels the chilly fizz of his first Tsingtao since lunch flow down into his body. "It's impossible."

"Yes," she says. "Yes, of course. Impossible."

6

That evening they decide on nostalgia—a birthday bash for Katie at the Jiangjiang Hotel, where they stayed when they came to Changsha to adopt her. Rhett has gone for the day, but the Grand Sun concierge arranges for a taxi to take them, wait, and bring them back—writing the instructions in Chinese on a hotel card. As they drive across Changsha in a taxi, they recognize almost nothing of the city. In a decade it has grown from three million to six. It used to be a quaint jumble of small streets and two-lane roads lined with one-story shacks where people sold their wares; now the roads have been widened, the small buildings destroyed. Blunt new skyscrapers are everywhere.

Chinese Culture Camp has taken them through one dirty, noisy, polluted city of five million after another, seeking out tourist sites among the ratcheted construction and rising nondescript buildings. Changsha—like many of the other cities—could almost be Anywhere, USA, say, Atlanta. The China that they fell in love with ten years before has mostly vanished. Changsha traffic is fierce; driving, perilous. Before, there were few cars and a million bikes; now it seems the reverse. The roads are jammed. There used to be only a few traffic lights, now there are many—mostly ignored. Instead of Mao hanging from the taxi's rearview mirror for good luck, it's Michael Jordan. Their taxi driver acts like a kid with a new toy. The ride is heart-stopping. Pep and Clio white-knuckle their seats. After a few close calls, even Katie curls down in the backseat covering her eyes. Whenever Clio sees a young woman in a long white dress she scans her face, looking for *her*.

The Jiangjiang Hotel has survived. Pep gets out of the cab and reenacts with Katie what he said to her the first time, bringing her back from the orphanage:

"Katie Chun, this is your *hotel!*"

Ten years ago, it was the best hotel in Changsha. Now it is shabby. In the lobby are several elegantly dressed "ladies of the night"—Clio can't help but scan *their* faces too. In one of the private function rooms, there is karaoke—a man in a cheap suit up in front of his fellow workers, mike in hand, singing along with a woman in a bikini on TV. But the shabbiness makes it seem quaint, campy, even funky. Pep has difficulty explaining to the manager that they need his help in finding the room on the ninth floor where they lived during their first week with their baby. Like most Chinese who know English, he speaks a stiff, formal, textbook style. Even in five-star hotels, the translations of signs are literal, and often comical. Yesterday when they checked into the Grand Sun they laughed out loud at the sign over the courtesy phone in the lobby: "TOURISTS COMPLAINING PHONE." Two days ago, south of Chengdu, at the colossal Grand Buddha of Leshan, the brochure started out okay—"At 71 meters he is the biggest ancient stone carved figure of Buddha in the world"—but then floated out into a religious/historical morass—"He was originated and built for reducing flood and serving for mass by monk Hai Tong rabbi in Tang dynasty."

Finally the manager understands, and accompanies them to floor nine.

The wide, red-carpeted, dim hallway still has the same smell—pungent, earthy, mushroomy—with a hint of antiseptic. Four girls in scarlet uniforms are still there to attend to the wishes of the ninth-floor guests, though the rack of Communist propaganda is gone. Pep and Clio remember that the room is on the right side near the end of the hallway, facing the street where, every morning, a street cleaner truck playing a calliope tune awoke them, but they aren't sure which room it is. They choose 921.

It is much smaller than they recall, like returning to your hometown as a grown-up. Someone is occupying the room, but they aren't there. A mahjong game lies orphaned on a low table. But it is much the same as it was—two single beds, a tiny refrigerator, large chrome thermoses of boiled water. They go into the small bathroom.

"We gave you your first bath here," Clio says, "right there in the sink. It was the first time you made a sound—you wailed! In the orphanage, you never made a single sound."

"Why not?"

"We don't know—you were all bundled up, and peaceful. It's a mystery."

Katie wonders at that, that she didn't make a sound. *Why not? Was I scared? Weird not to know why.* She looks at her mom, who is inspecting the bathroom as if it has some secret passage in it. *A mystery? Like when Tara and Kissy were asking each other, "What time were you born?" And they each said what time they were born and then they asked me and I said the truth, "I don't know," and they gave me a weird look and I had to say something else so I said, "I'm a child of mystery," and I felt outsidered.*

"You were so stuffed up," Pep is saying, "you couldn't sleep. So we all got naked and turned on the hot water and stayed in here till the steam cleared you out."

"I fit in that sink? It's weird not to remember—I mean except what you told me."

"We tried everything to get you to sleep," Clio says, "and nothing worked, and finally we looked over—we didn't have a crib, they just gave us a baby carriage, one of those massive old-fashioned ones with big wheels?—and we saw, up over the side, you had one hand held up straight in the air, and you were asleep."

"Like I was saluting or something?"

"Or maybe surrendering," Pep says.

"Yeah, I remember—I mean you told me. Maybe I was trying to get out of the baby carriage and sleep with you guys? You told me there were two babies in every crib in the orphanage, so maybe I was scared being alone?"

"Think so?" Clio asks.

"I'm *really* hungry. Can we like eat?"

Pep and Clio look at each other and smile. To her, and now to them too, it's just a room. Worse, someone else's room. They leave easily, not wanting any more of the other room, the magical room, to disappear. The restaurant they remembered is still there, but the cuisine has gone downhill. Picking at the chicken with vegetables, Katie happens upon a head—complete with beak. In disgust she pronounces the food the worst on the trip—a lot worse than the food back home in Columbia at Chinese Restaurant or even at the new one, Shalom Hunan.

○ ○ ○

Outside on the street, they are accosted by several beggars. One, a shriveled old man with a cane, blocks their way and pecks at Katie with his free hand, screeching at her as if she understands. Two weeks of beggars in the new China have put Pep on edge—you never saw a beggar in China ten years ago, it was safer than America. He puts one arm around Katie, the other around Clio, and starts for the cab, parked up the street.

The old man suddenly sidesteps, blocking their way. Another beggar approaches. Pep starts to get anxious. Thinking quickly, he points to a spot behind the old man, and as the man turns to look, Pep leads Katie and Clio quickly to safety.

They get into the cab, and rocket on off, away.

Katie is embarrassed. *Did he have to trick him like that?*

Clio and Katie clutch each other as the cab careens along in crazy lane changes and close calls.

Across the street from the slick and sparkly thirty-story Grand Sun Hotel, there is a new banner:

HELP TURN CHANGSHA INTO CLEAN MODERN CIVILIZED CITY.

7

An hour later, they are lying in their terrific beds. The air-conditioning hums softly. Katie is in bed with Clio, Pep in the next bed by himself—the usual arrangement on the trip. Katie finishes a chapter of *Harry Potter and the Goblet of Fire*. Pep turns out the lights. Clio rubs Katie's back and waits to see if she'll start to talk. In the dark at the end of the day, Katie often gets chatty. But not tonight.

Clio has been disappointed by how little time she's had alone with Katie. Katie's friend Heather Ho McGinnity from New York City came along on the first part of the trip, and the two of them were inseparable. Sitting together on the bus, running around the tourist sites, sitting together at restaurants and every night watching TV in the hotel—it's been a glorious two-week playdate. For the whole past year, Clio has felt Katie spiraling out, less and less interested in spending time with her, preferring to be with her friends—or Mary. Sleepovers are all the rage. Spook Rock Country Day School is a hidden world, a kind of British-Visigothic fortress from which parents are mostly forbidden—except from the first-rate Development Office. The teachers are fuzzy but not warm. At home Katie has killer homework, and then dives into her computer, or the TV—*and we let her*.

The tight, close "I can tell you anything" bond that they shared for years has frayed. They used to talk about everything—*everything*! Katie would open up completely, and with the most heart-wrenching innocence, as if it were natural not to have any separation between them. Clio had never had conversations like that with anyone before. And now, is it ending? *What if she and I can never talk that way again?*

Clio had hoped that the trip would break the pattern, that it would be a chance for her to spend time with Katie—it's been anything but. Even when Clio's been alone with Pep, her mind has been on her daughter—she knows he senses her divided attention. She hopes that these few days alone with Katie and Pep in Changsha will be a real chance for all of them.

"I'm sorry, Katie," she says now. "It wasn't the greatest birthday in the world. We'll do better tomorrow. After the orphanage, you get to do anything you want."

"Okay, Mom. Thanks." She pauses. "You know, coming here to China, I thought it would be like a quest, like the Greeks this year in school, like

Ulysses on his adventures, or in our class play when Orpheus goes like looking for Eurydice down in Hades? Where the hero goes on a journey and discovers things? I mean discovers what's *really* happening, not what he *thinks* is happening or *wants* to happen or whatever? So I've been trying to act like that, trying to kinda journey-like and discover what's *really* happening, I mean as much as I can?"

"Good, honey. Daddy and I feel that way about this trip too."

"Thanks. But the bad news is, is that . . . well, coming here to China and seeing everything like the people and how different they look and how poor they are and all?"

"Yes, honey?"

"Mom, I can't *believe* I came from here, from China. Like I'm Chinese, but I'm really more Chinese *American*? Like I'm Chinese, but not Chinese? People look at us and they're wondering why these two Americans are with this Chinese girl? At the police station, it was like the policemen were thinking you kidnapped me or something! It's all pretty weird. So all the time I feel weird here, people coming up to me talking to me and expecting me to speak Chinese? Before I got here I thought Chinese was like in the back of my brain and it would just come out when I'm here but it hasn't?"

"It's hard, honey," Clio says. "But I know exactly what you mean. We're all feeling that, aren't we, Dad? Strange, and trying to put it all together to make sense?"

"We sure are," Pep says.

"We're glad that you're really trying to understand it."

"You are?"

"Yes. We're all on the same quest, together."

"Right," Pep says, "and we're learning a lot, and we'll go home a lot better for it. Just like Orpheus and Eurydice."

"Da-ad—Orpheus *lost* Eurydice! *She rotted forever in Hell!*"

"Oh. Sorry."

Katie is silent for a few moments. "I'm . . . I don't know, I'm trying to think like if I'd grown up in China I'd be *different*—shorter and smaller and browner?"

"Really?"

"Un hunh."

"You think you'd be a lot different?"

"Yeah, this isn't like home."

"That's why we came," Clio says. "To try to understand all this, together."

"Cool. G'night."

"Goodnight, hon. Love you."

"Love you too."

"G'night, Kate-zer," Pep says. "Love you."

Silence. Finally, Katie says, "Dad?"

"Yeah?"

"You shouldn't treat beggars so rough-like?"

"You mean like outside the hotel?"

"Yeah and like the waiters too?"

"Waiters *too*? What waiters?"

"All the waiters if you don't get what you want right away like if they don't know what a Sprite is, you yell at them?"

"You think?"

"Most definitely. Mom and me don't like it."

Hearing the "Mom and me," Pep feels a rush of shame, and then irritation. For the past several years, he's felt the two of them bond together, at odds with him. They're mother/daughter, of course, but still. Sometimes he feels his position in the family has fallen to a niche somewhere below Cinnamon the dog and above Dave the lovebird. Lying in bed now, he feels cast out, alone. Like the loneliness he increasingly feels at home when the two of them are out at a horse show or gymnastics or art or music or shopping or Mary's Farm and he's left rattling around the big, empty house throwing the ball to Cinnamon or playing his trombone—with only the dog listening.

Clio has her circle of friends, mostly moms. Then there is Carter, her best friend from Wellesley, and her partner Sue, who lived in her building in New York and who moved up to Columbia and started Oblique Antique, where Clio sometimes works. It was while Clio was visiting Carter that she and Pep first met. Last year Clio invited him to join her and Carter in taking meditation lessons from Tulku, the cash-poor Tibetan janitor at Katie's school. He tried, but at his age neither his body nor his mind could bend that way. Clio thinks he doesn't like Carter—not true. It's more complicated than that. He's amazed at how easily women can connect— even on this trip the fourteen women—hetero, gay, single, whatever—all of them got along like quote sisters. And what does he have? Golf pals and poker buddies and Rotarians, a lot of 'em Columbians he's known since kindergarten, and if they ask, "How are you?", well, you could be dying of cancer but you say, "Fine," or "Pretty good," and that's that. Meanwhile Clio makes her daily rounds of "cancer calls" to her stricken friends. She seems to think he's uneasy with lesbians and even homophobic. She doesn't know that deep down it isn't resentment at all, but envy. His envy of their closeness, and his having no way of getting there. The closeness he and she had before the infertility crap, before Katie.

Suddenly chilled, he shivers. He knows that if he could just admit to his loneliness, Clio might respond, but he can't seem to. *Why the hell not?*

He feels terrible, almost like crying. What is it that Clio said last month, about Katie being so "authentic" all the time?—"She's got a genius for the real. It's like living with a Zen master, twenty-four hours a day." Once, after Katie painted a red horse galloping on the original oil painting of Pep's great-great-grandfather, Gifford Macy—he had been cleaning it, had left it lying on his desk—he said through clenched teeth: "Please, Katie, don't do that again." She looked at him and said, "You said that without love in your voice." Startled, with difficulty he swallowed his pride and said, "Okay. You're right. I did." She paused and said, "You said *that* without love in your voice too!"

The girl has a light beam for anything cruel or phony—she'll call you on it with such innocence, you melt. And she even had it the first time they saw her, when she was brought out into the bright October sunlight and handed to them and he opened like a flower, felt a blast of love from his toes to his head and he started to say, "What a little muffin," but the "muffin" part got lost in the choking tears of joy, the love he had never felt before, and when he looked into her eyes they held his gaze, dark eyes so electric!—and he fell in love with the peacefulness of the three of them, the birth of this finally family he'd yearned for, sitting together in the concrete courtyard with old iron play gyms and bamboo seats that kept the toddlers imprisoned, and the bright flash of a rainbow of baby clothes hanging on a line, flapping in the wind of south China in the glorious fall, and all of it blurred like a rushed photo because he was weeping.

Now he counts to ten to calm himself.

"Okay, Kate-zer. With the beautiful nice beggars and the waiters? I'll try."

"You'll do it, Daddy, I know you will. Love you too." As she slips down the steep slope of sleep Katie remembers a girl she saw outside the Beijing Zoo. *She had a hurted arm in a sling she looked real sad and hungry. That could have been me, if . . . if something else happened to me. Why was it me who was given up? Why me?*

Clio feels Katie relax, turn over, and go out like a light. She doesn't feel sleepy. Her mind is going over and over what Katie has just said. Chinese but not Chinese. Chinese *American*? It's true. Watching her walk down the street here, you know she's not Chinese—she doesn't walk stiffly like they do, or gesture like they do, or cover her mouth when she laughs. What a relief, to have her see the *real* China. Katie's back, in sleep, molds against her front—like she herself used to mold against Pep, warm, *there*.

○ ○ ○

With Katie breathing deeply, Clio senses the sexual in the air. Even though they've had a lot of time alone on the trip, nothing has happened—they've both been strangely reluctant. When they first met, their attraction was immediate and intense.

Clio had been invited up from the city by her friend Carter for a charity event at Olana, the home of the great painter Frederick Church. Perched high on a hill just south of Columbia, it faced a glorious panorama overlooking the Hudson River with its glittering silver bracelet of the Rip Van Winkle Bridge, and the granite Catskills. It was Victorian Day and Pep was working as a volunteer guide. A tall, red-haired, boyish man dressed in formal Victorian leisurewear: dark suit, white shirt and cravat, purple cape. He was standing in front of a ten-foot-tall Persian window, all done in amber—her favorite stone since a trip to Morocco with her family— with a hand-cut black stencil latticework of arches within arches like the Alhambra. She liked him at once, for the gentleness in his face.

She asked: "Is the window positioned there for the seasons?"

"Yes," he said enthusiastically, as if happy to be asked a good question, "Church was often depressed—a lot of family tragedy—and he craved the light, for relief. The window is perfectly set to catch the most light, the whole year round. I admire that about him. He was a great artist, but marvelously practical."

"And the amber?"

"He loved amber, the way it shines against the dark. My favorite painting is all amber—*The Entrance to Persepolis*—would you like to see it?" He led her to it: a view through the dark scalloped cliffs to the ruins. It took her breath away—a foreboding that gave way to the soft light on limestone, the Greek temple facade.

Pep went on, "I see it as his coming out of his depression over the death of his little son, finding a glimmer of light."

"Wonderful. I've always wanted to go there."

"To the light?"

She wondered if he was joking, but no. "Yes. But first, Persepolis."

"Well then," he said, gallantly crooking his arm for her to take. "Shall we? I'll change."

It was so good-natured, he was so *with* her right then, she actually blushed.

They began. A new beginning for them both. She thirty-seven, he forty-three. To any new adventure, they said, "Yes!" Later, he told her that she had tipped him out of his middle-aged leaning into aloneness—into the dead history and expectations of his Mayflower family: his father Phillip Noble Macy, a rock of insurance and curiously *disinterested* in him, and his Boston-bred mother Faith Cabot Macy, fragile and cautious, cowed and fearful and early dead. Yes, she had tipped him out of all this shit into something new and exciting and sexy and fun and of great meaning—a leaning *into* life. Those were his words, "of great meaning, a leaning *into* life." It *was* an adventure, one of meaning, which she too was ready for after wandering the tropics and then bucking the slithery and glib New York art scene. And the essence of their adventure was not the two of them alone, but their shared vision of a child with them.

The electricity of the romance led to a startling passion—they were a great match in making love. She loved his horizontal height on the bed, his strength, and his attentiveness to her. And his playfulness—as he put it, one long sensual afternoon, "There's nothing for endurance like a man who sells insurance." Why have they had so much trouble getting back to lovemaking? When they do, it's still great. But they don't get there easily. She wonders, why not? Part of it is Katie, to be sure, always around—for years sleeping in their bed—and if not there in person, there all the time in her awareness. He resents it, but all her friends say that it's normal. The real crusher was the infertility—having to do what their doctor in Columbia, Orville Rose, called "work sex"—doing it at certain times no matter what, poor Pep feeling like a bull with a ring in his nose having to "get it up," hoping that it would take and then each month—month after month of failure—the sorrow and rage when she got her period. And then the miscarriage. At one point Pep himself–despite his squeamishness—was giving her tightly scheduled hormone shots—running upstairs at a party, pulling up her dress and pulling down her panties and jabbing her in the butt.

But still, every month, bleeding. No explanation, no diagnosis, just that they were maybe too old. The trauma of having to see other women cradling their babies—she'd cross the street rather than meet one of them. One failure after another. And then, both of them depressed as hell, a profound and mostly unspoken sorrow eating away at the marriage, trying to try to drag themselves out of their exhausted desolation and get it up to *adopt*? More failures—they soon found out that they were either too old to adopt, or they hadn't been married long enough, so that when they *had* been married long enough they would be too old—every avenue they tried leading to a dead end.

They were ready to give up, to say no, until a trip to visit old friends in Vermont. The friends with a perfect house, a perfect garden, perfect jobs—and no children. And after that weekend, on the drive home she and he agreed that it all really was perfect, and absolutely sterile. That was his word, "sterile." She said to him, "I can't give up." He asked, why not? She said, "Because I just keep seeing that little face!" What little face? "I don't know, just a little face that needs us and that we need too. Just that little face."

Two weeks later, the agency called and told them that China had opened up for adoption, and they could be among the first group to go. No age requirement, no marriage requirement. If they hurried with their documents, they could have a baby girl in eight weeks. After being so close to saying no, now they said, "Yes!"

"Peppie?" she says to him now, in a whisper so as not to wake Katie.

"Yes?"

"I've missed you."

"And I you."

"It's my fault."

"Nope. It takes two, you know."

She disengages carefully from Katie, and slips in beside him. Clio knows that he won't push her. She feels the familiar big body, and as she settles into the crook of his neck, she breathes in the comforting scent of his hair, his aftershave. They caress each other, she his chest, he her breasts.

Soon she hears him breathing deeply, asleep. Katie mumbles something from a dream. At once, Clio is attuned to her daughter's needs. She finds herself thinking once again that she's made a mistake in sending Katie to Spook Rock, an almost all-white school. She's the only Asian, one of only two kids of color, the other an African American boy named Nigel, who is driven to school every day in a limo. Year after year of school photos of white children but for those two faces. How much of Katie's growing isolation is from being Chinese? How much from being adopted?

Clio needs to be close to her, and slips out of Pep's bed into Katie's. She puts her arms around her again. Her mind is too awake for her body. She finds herself thinking of their first trip to the orphanage, ten years ago. From the moment she first saw her, when the Chinese woman in the long white coat came out of the one-story redbrick building into the slanting autumn sunlight of the concrete playground with two babies in her arms and called out, first, "Ying!" for the one who, just then, became Faith Ying Schenckberg, and then, "Chwin! Chwin-Chwin!" for Chun, Katie Chun Hale-Macy, she knew they'd done the right thing. The sight of her baby stunned her, enfolded all her senses into one sense, of awe. There she was—her black hair tinted red in the sun and sticking straight up on top of her head, her round face and plump cheeks and fair skin and lips a pink of roses. Beautiful big eyes like teardrops on their sides and pupils dark as history. Dark irises too, with a catch of blue—but maybe it was only the reflection of the dazzling late-October sky. She was swaddled tightly in a tattered purple sweater, and wrapped up and tied with plain twine. She had just awakened and looked at them sleepily but steadily, as if strangely *sure*. From the start her eyes were so alive! As if, Clio said to Pep, she had been so tightly swaddled for so long—three months in the orphanage—that her arms couldn't move and her fingers couldn't touch, and she had learned to touch everything with her eyes. Her hair grew out from two dark whorls, a "double crown," which her caretaker said was a sign of great wisdom. The hair on the back of her head was rubbed off, showing bare scalp—Clio realized with a sense of horror she had been kept lying on her back, unmoving, for hours at a time. Her heart went out to her. She fell in love instantly. Pep was weeping. *In that one moment we went from two to three. Tomorrow we go back there again.*

Her mind floats this way and that over the incredible images of the day and settles on the vision of the woman at the police station in the white silk dress and blood-red sandals and umbrella and with the face of Katie at thirty. Again she watches her walk in, stare at her and Pep, disappear into a doorway and then into Changsha and seemingly off the face of the earth, this impossible possibility come on this tenth birthday, less an actual woman than an aura or a divine presence or even a sinister one, a break-away spirit a rising and falling on a jasmine sea sure it's impossible but happens . . .

8

The next morning Katie decides to wear her best dress to the orphanage. It is bright red, with white flowers on sinewy vines. It fits her frame closely, making her look older, less a girl than a stunning young woman. She and Clio take care with her long hair—no ponytail today, but straight down on her shoulders, pulled back by a purple headband. Like Clio's.

The four bellboys in red with pillbox hats escort them out the great brass revolving door. A sudden heavy rain has started to fall. They turn around and go back to find hotel umbrellas, one of which shelters all three of them. Huddled together under the umbrella they tiptoe through the yellowish mud and screaming machinery widening the road, wading alongside a dozen barefoot men in tattered undershirts, who are digging more trench with pickaxes and shovels. Suddenly there it is, in the middle of a block of low shops being destroyed, the exact same red pagoda-like gatehouse. Clio looks up and sees, once again, the roof gods on the upcurved beams, the last in line "the man riding the chicken," who, she knows from her study of Chinese art and architecture, is prevented from bedeviling the inhabitants of the building below because a man can't fly down there on a chicken. A sign, in Chinese and English:

CHANGSHA SOCIAL WELFARE CENTER NUMBER ONE
FAMILY PLANNING IS EVERYBODY'S BUSINESS

The entrance is the same as they recall but for a uniformed guard who carefully checks identification, and a shiny new chest-high steel gate, which completely blocks the entrance. The guard swings the massive gate open.

Inside, everything has changed. To the right, the spot where the one-story redbrick building with the courtyard/playground once stood, the spot where they were handed Katie, is a pile of rubble and bricks. To the left, where the low recreation room was located, is a four-story building, the administrative offices. Nearby, where the room for the newborns and the schools for the older, special needs children used to be, is an eight-story concrete building looking like a new apartment house. Shocked at how the place has grown, they go into the administration building for their meeting with the new director.

Mr. Ma is about thirty-five, a chunky, handsome man with eyes that seem alert, humorless, and firm. He wears a robin's-egg-blue short-sleeved shirt and khaki pants. But for his face, Pep thinks, he could be a Columbian neighbor in high-summer garb—say, a golfer. He sits at the head of a boardroom-type table on a marble floor, with eight cushy leather high-backed chairs on rollers; standing up in a corner of the room is a ferocious air conditioner. Damp from the rain, they are soon chilled. The place gives a feel of being well funded. *Probably*, Pep thinks, *by grateful Westerners like us.*

Pep explains who they are and why they've come. Mr. Ma shows little reaction—it's hard to tell how good his English is. Pep speaks slowly and gestures every question, like charades. Has Mr. Ma gotten the photos they sent showing Katie in the arms of her nurses when they adopted her? No. Where are they? He doesn't know. He gets a lot of letters and photos, it is hard to keep track of them all. Pep asks to see whatever documents the orphanage has on Katie.

Mr. Ma asks for her full name, and then sends an assistant out to find them.

Clio takes out the little album that Katie and she have prepared, to show to the orphanage workers, and hands Mr. Ma a photo of Katie in the arms of her caretaker, a rail-thin woman with a squirrelly face and a prominent gold front tooth.

Mr. Ma sends another assistant out with the photo.

Maybe money will talk. Pep tells Mr. Ma that they have brought a donation to the orphanage on behalf of their group of eight families. Mr. Ma nods. Pep zips open his fanny pack and finds the envelope containing the thousand-dollar check. As Pep opens the envelope there is a ripping sound. Two weeks of humidity have sealed the flap onto the check. A piece of the flap sticks to the check, obscuring his name and address. Mr. Ma inspects the check meticulously and shakes his head no. No bank will cash a damaged check. Katie slumps into a high-backed chair and twirls around in it.

"This is not going well," Clio says softly to Pep.

"It's a disaster. I can't believe he didn't blink at the thousand bucks."

An assistant comes back with the documents for "Chun" and sets the folder down.

"These are your records from the orphanage, dear," Clio says.

"Can I see?" Katie asks. Clio looks to Pep and, getting his okay, nods.

A tense moment. They bend over the documents. But they are merely copies of the official adoption documents they already have: Chun was brought to the Nan Da Lu police station at one month of age and, later that same day, brought to the orphanage.

Clio goes on to ask Mr. Ma about Katie—whether there are any other records, any notes found in her swaddling clothes, any *anything*? Mr. Ma says no.

"Chwin? Chwin-Chwin!" Someone is calling to them from a group of women standing in the doorway.

Pep and Clio turn. It is the woman with the wizened face and the gold front tooth—the woman in the photo who was Katie's nursemaid from one to four months old. Ten years ago she carried Katie out of the little redbrick building, called out her name—*Chwin!*—and handed their baby to them.

"Oh my, she *remembers* her!" Clio cries and, taking Katie's hand, goes to her.

Clio greets her excitedly. Katie holds back. The woman kneels to her level and looks her in the eye, and hugs her.

The woman points to herself and says, "Name, Hongyen." Smiling, she goes on, "Hongyen *Ayi. Ayi* mean 'Auntie.' Chwin Auntie."

"Kate-zer, this is the woman who took care of you when you were a tiny baby!"

Katie, still being hugged, feels strange. Released, she finds herself looking up into the woman's eyes, sticking out her hand and saying, "Nee how, nee how, Ayi."

Hongyen bursts into tears and puts her hand over her face. Pep and Clio are tearful as well, amazed that Katie has spoken Chinese.

Mr. Ma has called in another man, who is examining the check. They may be able to steam off the piece of gummed envelope flap. Mr. Ma presents a gift to Katie, a china plate with a fish on it. Katie thanks him and, looking into *his* eyes, shakes his hand. She sits down with Hongyen Ayi at the end of the table and begins demonstrating her red Squeeze Breeze. It's a plastic water bottle with a small rubber fan on top, battery operated. At the push of the button the fan sprays a fine cooling mist in your face. Katie has Squeeze-Breezed her way through the searing heat of south China. Hongyen feels the mist on her face and laughs hard.

Mr. Ma indicates to the Macys that the meeting is over and they can now tour the orphanage with the caretakers. They leave his office and walk to the nine-story building and wait at the elevator. The walls are rough concrete. As they wait, the elevator empties out several old people in wheelchairs—it is an old age home as well.

○ ○ ○

Suddenly they are in a room filled with infants, ages about one to three, most of them in motion, tooling around in those cruiser seats on wheels that years ago were banned in America as unsafe. Some children are sitting in chairs—not the handcrafted bamboo ones Pep and Clio recall from the old courtyard, but plastic. An abundance of caretakers follows them around, the tails of their long white coats making them seem like mother geese tending their goslings. Crude, colorful murals grace the wall. The activity is lively and noisy. *Fluttery*, Clio thinks, *bright-fangled birds on a lost Caribbean island.*

They know that there are only girls here.

Clio is moving toward the babies. A little girl, one eye clouded over completely, toddles up to Katie, silent but curious about Katie's red Squeeze Breeze. Katie looks embarrassed, but the toddler persists, following her as she retreats behind Pep's legs. She is dressed in lime green and carries a small purple plastic rake. Pep takes Katie into another room, where younger children lie, one to a crib. One child has an IV tube taped to her scalp. Katie, curious, asks what it is, and Pep tells her that the girl must be sick and is getting special medicine. Katie stares down at her. The one-eyed girl comes close again, and they move on.

Meanwhile Clio has been handed a baby, and is cooing to her delightedly, walking around absently among the kids and caretakers.

"Dad," Katie says, "that little girl with the one eye is bothering me."

"Okay. Let's try to get away from her."

"Mom said maybe I should give her my Squeeze Breeze?"

"Nice idea."

"Come with me, Dad."

Katie leads Pep to the girl and gives her the Squeeze Breeze, showing her how to use it. Suddenly Pep flips into his risk-assessment mode, personal injury division, and wonders about giving a toy with a motorized fan to a child with only one eye. Lawsuit, trial, headline in *International Herald Trib*—"Insurance Agent Should've Known Better, Ten Million for Lost Last Eye." He thinks to take the Squeeze Breeze back, but the girl is gone. *Wait. The thing is American-made, to code; a soft rubber fan. Safe.* Katie and Pep rejoin Clio in the large room reserved for the newborn babies.

There is good light and warmth and a flock of white-coated nurses. The cribs are the same old ones Pep and Clio recall, the dark-green-painted wood, handmade, that Katie and the others lay in on their backs in the cute little brick house, Katie Chun sharing a crib with Faith Ying. Seeing these old green slats and the same red quilts with the white impatiens, Clio senses, finally, the red thread of meaning unspool back ten years and catch—pulling tight against the past. There are, as before, two newborns to a crib. One is only ten days old, lying asleep on a bamboo mat, in a Western-style onesie that keeps her warm. Clio stares at her, and at Katie, wondering what she is making of it all. *Does she see herself in this tiny baby?*

"Look, hon," Clio says, "the quilts are the same colors as your dress. And they're the same quilts you had on you when you were that old."

"I remember, from the pictures you took." She contemplates them quietly. "Can I look at the other babies?"

"Sure, sweetie. But don't go far." Katie walks off to another crib, and stands there once again, staring down intently.

"She's taking it all in," Clio says. "She's got that look. Everything."

"Yeah. It's big." Pep sighs. "The conditions are so much better now."

"Yes. They're not swaddled up and tied up with twine—their fingers can touch. But I don't much like this high-rise building. I doubt they get outside much. I liked the other better. Our little brick house and playground?"

"Yeah. It was special."

"Remember the newborns?" He nods.

Back then, she and Pep had wandered away from the group at the red-brick ward and had come upon a dimly lit room. There, in two long rows of cribs in a narrow high-ceilinged space filled with a gritty, sooty attempt at warmth from a coal stove at one end, were newborn baby girls, maybe twenty of them, covered up by the red quilts with the white impatiens, a continuous long line of quilts, door to far wall. Some were completely buried under the quilts; some had faces showing. Above each baby, tacked to the plaster wall, was a plastic pouch in which was placed—in which, she realized, *could be placed and then replaced*—a piece of paper and a few Chinese characters: name and date of birth. The oldest was barely two months. Despite the stove, it was chill, and deathly still, the silence punctuated only by a cough or a sneeze from one of the covered-up bodies, up or down the line. Occasionally there was a whimper. One baby, and only one, was crying weakly. Clio uncovered the tiny face, flushed and frail. She put her finger on the forehead, across a blue thread of vein. The skin felt hot. There was no attendant in sight. She looked at Pep, and saw such a sense of desolation in his face that tears came to her eyes. They left, and went out again into the autumn light.

"Incredibly sad!" Clio said.

"Yeah. I guess only the healthiest make it out of here to the brick building." His voice was hoarse. "The survivors. The ones that survive the first month."

"Selected for special care, to be adopted."

"The odds against them—it breaks your heart, Clee, doesn't it?"

"Into little pieces."

○ ○ ○

Now Pep is following Katie into a sunroom. He worries that she is getting overwhelmed, and he wants to get her out of there as soon as possible, but Clio isn't ready to leave—he watches her walking around with a baby in her arms and a big smile on her face. *She wants another. Me too. I'd love to go back to life with a baby. But we're way too old. But if it were easy, if we could just walk out with one now? Sure.*

The sunroom is empty but for a single girl of about three with a bandage on her head that makes her look like a Maoist urban guerrilla. She stands quietly, unmoving, hands stiffly at her sides, her big dark eyes staring at them.

"Dad, I want to talk to you?"

"Yeah? Come sit, and tell me." Pep is glad to be the one she wants to talk to now—he feels *valued*. He offers her his lap, and she curls up into it, playing with the hem of her dress. He readies himself for a heart-to-heart, happy to listen. "Okay, hon, what's up?"

"I've been thinking . . . when I grow up, I think I want to adopt a Chinese baby, because I know how to do it. *Anybody* can have a *bio*, but not everybody knows how to be a parent to an adopted baby, especially if she's Chinese. What do you think?"

Pep hides a smile, amused at how she's picked up their lingo. "You certainly do know all about it. But why wouldn't you want your own bio?"

"Because anybody can have a bio. It's easy, I mean, except for you and Mom."

"That's right. We tried hard, but it didn't work."

"Why not?"

"We never found out. The doctors never found a reason."

"Well I'm glad, 'cause that's the only way you could get me."

"Me too, honey." He hugs her. "Me too."

Finally Clio appears, ready to leave. They try to find Hongyen Ayi to say goodbye, but she is gone.

9

It is still raining hard. As they wait for the guard to open the gate, they see Hongyen Ayi rushing toward them, shielding her head with a pink plastic coat. Pep raises his umbrella and urges her in.

The four of them huddle under the Grand Sun umbrella. In a frank language of her eyes and face and hands, Hongyen conveys that she is touched by them coming back, and that she has something for them. She looks around to make sure no one can see her. Quickly, as if scratching her neck, she reaches into her bra and brings out a small envelope and slips it into Clio's hand. She smiles, bows to each of them, hugs Katie, and splashes through the muddy puddles back to the orphanage.

The forbidding gate opens, and closes hard behind them. Under the umbrella they walk through the mud alongside the ditch to the hotel. Pep stops, and pops some shots of the bare-chested workmen in the ditch and the striped plastic sheets that serve as the walls of their makeshift huts, floating out in the rainy wind like spinnakers.

Clio waits, her arm around her daughter, trying not to agonize about what could be in the envelope. She finds herself staring up at the sleek hotel. What irony! These dirt-poor orphans, given up for nothing, wind up at the most expensive houses and schools in the richest country in the world, studying the Greek gods and goddesses in fourth grade at Spook Rock Country Day. Finishing up the year—*just two weeks ago!?*—by putting on a musical called *Orpheus and Eurydice*—Katie so shy that she'd only take a "barking part," as one head of the three-headed dog, Cerberus, guarding the gates of Hell. What a world. Where does she fit in?

The four bellboys escort them into the soaring lobby with a marble floor and the kind of immense flower arrangement on a marble stand that you see in the great hotels of the world. Pep wonders, again, where all the money is coming from.

○ ○ ○

While Katie swims, Clio and Pep, sitting at the bar overlooking the pool, open the envelope. Two pieces of paper. One, on orphanage stationery, from Hongyen Ayi:

> Dear Macy. I find this in baby Chun's swaddling clothes ten years ago and I ask friend to make translation and keep secret. I give it now because of good *ch'i* today when we meet. Good fortune to you Macy and most to beautiful Chun.

The second note is in Chinese, with the English translation:

在我們農村，重男輕女的思想
很嚴重，这不是我一個人能推翻得了
的。但我相信在这茫茫世界中一定會
有好心的叔叔、婶婶能搭救我的女儿
春春，她生日是六月二十五日。我願意来生
做牛做馬報答这大恩大德。

生母

In our country-side the thought which man is more important than woman is very popular. I myself don't have the strength to say something against it and overthrow it. But I believe on this big world there must be some kind, good-hearted uncles or aunties who can rescue my little daughter Chun, born June 25. I would do anything for him or her on my next life if I have another life.

Her mother

They read it over and over. They stare at each other, at first unable to say a word.

"*Her* hand," Clio says. "But I'm not sure we should show it to Katie now—with all she's got to take in already?"

"Right. We'll do it next week, when we're home." He fingers the document, examines it as he would an insurance contract, as if looking for a catch: the thin, fragile paper, the squid-ink-black strokes of a calligraphy brush, the "Chun," the "rescue," the "her mother"—all in a clumsy, concrete-sounding translation. But there can be no catch. *It just is.* How will their daughter react to this, the first real evidence of a mother who loved her passionately but who didn't "have the strength to say something against it and overthrow it," the "it" being that her girl is worthless, compared to a boy? How will Katie stand it? How will she feel? There's no way to know.

He thinks for a moment of hiding it from her, maybe until she's eighteen or twenty-one. But no.

"Yes," Clio is saying, "maybe when we're all curled up together in our bed, safe and sound." But her feelings are raging—she can almost *see* the young woman writing this the night before she will give up her baby, tormented but trying to hold the faith that "on this big world"—why "big"? Does she feel hers is small?—"there must be some kind, good-hearted uncles or aunties"—*people like us.* People who she "would do anything for . . . on my next life if I have another life." As if this life of hers, with this act, is over—and she's not counting on any other. It's so sad! And yet, when Katie sees this, it will be with her forever. It will make whatever image Katie has of her more real, maybe even make Pep and her less so—no, not less real, but *different*—"uncle and auntie," not mother and father? Clio's spirit starts to sink—but suddenly revives, fiercely. *Feel for her, yes, feel everything for her, yes! But protect Katie! Katie is ours!*

"Very safe and sound," Pep says, taking her hand. "A low-risk moment, yes."

Clio folds the letter carefully, puts it back in the envelope, and hands it to him. "Keep it safe, Peppie, it's a treasure."

○ ○ ○

At lunch in the hotel. Katie seems subdued, picking at her rice.

"So what did you think of the orphanage, dear?" Clio asks.

"It was all right, but I don't know, seeing all the girls maybe bothered me?" Her tone is dead serious.

"How did it bother you?"

"Well, you and Dad told me Chinese families can only have one child, right?" Clio nods. "And they want boys, and keep the boys? And give the girls away?"

"That's right." Clio says. *Or worse.* She glances at Pep.

"So like they think girls aren't special. But girls *are* special! I mean don't they realize that girls are *goddesses*?"

"*Of course* girls are goddesses," Pep says, "we feel that way for sure."

Katie pushes her rice here and there on her plate, her face somber.

"How did they get there? I mean, how did the mothers get them there?"

"They leave them here in the city, somewhere where they'll be found right away, and whoever finds them takes them to the police station, and then they come to the orphanage, and the birth mom goes back to her family in the country."

"Who's in her family?"

"Well, maybe she already had a baby girl, and then tried for a boy, and when it turned out to be a girl they decided they couldn't keep her."

"So I have a big sister somewhere!" Katie's eyes are wide with surprise.

"Maybe," Pep says. "That's why we went to the orphanage and the police station. To see if we could find out anything."

"Did you?"

"No, sweetheart," Clio says. "We didn't."

Katie nods, but says nothing. They hold their breath. Katie's lip turns down, and she tries bravely to stop it, breathing hard for the longest time. They don't dare move.

"Mom?"

"Yes, dear?"

"I wish I knew who my birth mom was." Her eyes pool with tears.

"We wish that too, Daddy and me."

"Yes, honey, we all do."

Katie just sits there, still as a statue, staring nowhere, tears easing down her face.

"It's sad, so sad." Clio says. She realizes that for the first time in her life Katie has *gotten* it, the fact of her abandonment, the fact that *they are it*, for her.

Katie just sits there silently, tears lying on her cheeks like pale scars.

"Here, love, come here." Clio helps her climb over the chair and into her lap. The little body shakes with sobs. Clio hugs her.

Pep scrapes back his chair, goes over to them, and puts his arms around them both.

10

"Even if a Changsha-ese doesn't have enough money for lunch," Rhett is saying, "he'll find a way to have a big dinner." He puffs his cigarette, laughs. "We're Hunan Cool, man, we're entrepreneurs."

It is afternoon, and they are on the way to Yuelu Mountain, just over the Xiangjiang River from Changsha. When Rhett arrived at the hotel, he announced that he had found the perfect thing for Katie to see, an aviary. She asked, what's an aviary?

"Birds, baby, birds! *Free-flying* birds—they eat out of your hand, and do tricks! They've even got lovebirds, like your little Dave." Katie is delighted.

The minibus is clean, cool, and provisioned with bottled water. From the bridge across the Xiangjiang, Katie spots boatmen fishing with cormorants. Rhett knows about cormorants. "They're the only diving bird without oil sacs, which is why they sit with their wings stretched out—to dry them in the sun. The fishermen tie a rope around their necks to keep them from swallowing the fish, and mostly take them out at night. They put oil lamps on the bows of their boats, 'cause cormorants are afraid of the dark."

"Cool. When my dog Cinnamon was a puppy—he was afraid of the dark too."

"My pets *love* the dark," Rhett says. "All twenty of 'em."

"What kind of pets?" Katie asks.

"Crickets. Fighting crickets, each in its own little bitty cage."

"You're like kidding me, right?"

"No way, little José! I'll bring my best fighter—Goliath—tomorrow."

On the footbridge that runs across the river to the north, there is a horse pulling a heavily laden wagon, and then another, and another—a horse caravan. Katie's eyes are glued to the bus window. The traffic jam is fierce. She gets a good look. Rhett points out, in mid-river, Juzi (Orange) Island. "Mao was born near here, and as a teacher he often met with students on the tip of that island, and composed the poem 'Changsha—To the Tune of Quin—'" His cell phone rings. With a slick movement he flips it open, barks, waits, shouts a torrent of what seems extremely harsh Chinese, flips it closed.

They drive through a pleached arbor of plane trees on the campus of

Hunan University—Rhett's alma mater—past a forty-foot-tall statue of Mao in alabaster, and then past the Yuelu Academy of Classical Learning, founded in 976 during the Song Dynasty. Rhett recites the slogan on the stone tablet entombed there, "'Loyalty, Filial Piety, Honesty, and Chastity'—in that order—haha!"

"So, Little Britches," Rhett says to Katie now—she recognizes the term from Disney's *Jungle Book*—"what music you dig?" Katie, shy, shrugs. "Rock? Country? Reggae?"

"Mom loves Bob Marley."

"Get *out*!" Clio laughs, and nods. "Momma, you are *bad*! How 'bout you, Katie?"

She hesitates a moment, then risks it. "Britney."

"Britney?! No way! I *love* Britney!" He sings the first few bars of "Oops! . . . I Did It Again" in a brassy Britney falsetto. "C'mon, c'mon, I *need* you with me, girl!" Katie joins in, at first softly, then louder, as the bus climbs the winding road up Mount Yuelu.

At the summit they get out for the view. It's as if they've entered a blast furnace. Rhett takes Katie off for an ice cream. Clio and Pep climb the pagoda, and at the top they wade through a wind-scattered deck of playing cards to the railing. To the east, shrouded in urban smog, they see the glittering skyscrapers of Changsha, surrounded by a gleam of sprawl, threaded by superhighways. To the west is a range of green mountains piled up as if by a big hand pushing earth, the far western peaks blending with haze and obscuring the horizon. Ribbons of rivers feeding the distant Yangtze curl through dark-green valleys that rise to terraced rice paddies, sparkling like shards of glass in the afternoon sun. There are rare shrouded clumps of small towns and villages.

As Clio stands there, the aura of the woman in the police station seems to coalesce—a concrete image of the dream woman she has lived with for ten years.

"Out there, honey," Pep says, pointing toward the river valleys, "is probably where she came from."

Clio is startled. She strokes his back. He smiles, and takes her hand—in the special way he always does, one finger interlaced between two of hers, the rest clasped. *Sensual, yes, like before.* Their eyes hold. His innocent, curious look reminds her of the moment they met.

Now, a gust of wind from the distant mountains catches the playing cards. They float and flicker like chanced-upon butterflies, down from the pavilion, away.

○ ○ ○

"Stop! Rhett, please tell him to stop!" Clio is up out of her seat. Rhett gets off the phone, shouts something at the driver. The minibus stops.

"Hey, this isn't the aviary," Katie says. "What's going on?"

"It's on the way, hon, it's the Lushan Temple. We came here the day we met you—just after. I just want a quick look in. It'll only take a second."

They climb up the steep path to the entrance to the temple, pay their next-to-nothing admittance, and walk in.

"Pep, look! Look, it's magnificent! Just as it was, unchanged!"

He's already shooting pictures. "Beautiful." He looks around. "And for the first time in China, we're alone! It's deserted! It's breezy and shady and roomy . . . and *quiet*!"

Clio floats through the first courtyard to a large building. Her eyes are drawn up to the graceful oblique way that the temple columns and beams handle the stress of the arches. Song and Yuan constructions. The cantilever arms—or *angs*—ride freely, balancing the bracketing system, a play of forces like the arches at Chartres. She looks down to the great open space within. There, fifty feet tall, are the three golden Buddhas, each on a golden lotus blossom, each holding its hands in a different position.

This time around she feels more awed. Through her meditation lessons, she understands something of the person who gave birth to this sacred and beautiful place—and this time she isn't focused on the four-month-old baby she's just held in her arms for the first time and then had to leave for another day in the orphanage, but on the ten-year-old who is achingly real and right here with her and loved in a known way. She is tempted to kneel on the carpeted bench and light a stick of celebratory incense, but no. *Not yet.* Feeling guilty for taking time from her daughter, she moves quickly away, along through the silent courtyards and past the barred-up classrooms and through an arched moon gate framing a garden. She stops, staring at the garden. Mountains are symbolized by water-pocked rock; water is symbolized by a current of gleaming pebbles cracked off a mountain and worn smooth by thousands of years of river.

She is amazed at the layers of beauty, both in the lushly flowered terraces and pavilions and gold-leafed statues and carvings and pools with carp reflecting the red-tile upsweeping lines of the pavilions, and in the metaphor—the enduring of this spirit, two thousand years later, in the midst of China's prestressed concrete. She looks back.

Katie and Rhett are together, he with his hand waving in front of her, conducting her in a song, perhaps Britney; Pep is clicking away.

She hurries ahead—recalling, hoping *she* is still there—up to a final level, into the largest temple and a final gold Buddha of immense proportions. She walks around to the left, past piles of yellowing documents and abandoned prayer ribbons, into the shadow behind the big Buddha where thin light comes in through a slim door, and *yes*!

Just as she remembers. Kwan Yin, the Chinese goddess of compassion, a bodhisattva: one who, on the verge of nirvana, turns back to help others along. The goddess of a thousand hands. Hands to reach back to all people to help them with their suffering. A twenty-foot-tall statue in shiny black wood, a smiling face filled with love, a small Buddha sitting on her head, another Buddha sitting in her raised right hand, and surrounding her a circle of arms and hands each with a small Buddha, hundreds of them, and a final outer circle of arms and hands, the Buddhas so small as to be almost unrecognizable, little buds. Clio recalls how, ten years ago, she happened to wander back here while the others lingered at the big golden Buddha, and found herself, alone, looking into these wise kind eyes. She stood there and suddenly and without thinking asked this goddess for help in mothering, in being a mother to whoever this little baby was, is, would be: "Please, goddess, help me to be a good mother. Amen."

Now again she is alone. Her hurry to get here has given her privacy from her husband and child. She stares up at Kwan Yin. A new sensation arises—of being lifted up, of gratitude. *Kwan Yin. She who hears all the cries of the world—and is still smiling!*

For the first time in her life she goes down on her knees to an image of a divinity. She places her hands palm to palm under her chin and touches her forehead to the wood, and says out loud:

"Thank you, goddess. Please help me to be an instrument of your compassion and your—"

"Mom, what are you *doing*?"

Clio lifts her head off the wood and turns.

Katie, standing there beside Pep.

Rhett too.

Pep is raising his Olympus.

"Don't! Pep, don't!" He lowers it. Clio rises and turns to Katie. "I was offering a prayer to Kwan Yin. You remember, the goddess of compassion."

"Yeah. What did you pray?"

"I asked for her help in being . . . kind to other people, being compassionate. And I thanked her for helping me, these ten years, to be a mother to you. Right from that first moment, at home in the kitchen ten years ago, when we got the phone call from the adoption agency, telling us that you were ours."

"Now *that*," Pep says, "was an *amazing*!"

"I *kinda* remember," Katie says, puzzled. "Some thingee with a card?"

"Yes," Clio says. "We were scheduled to be in the first group of eight couples to go to China to adopt, but we were too late with our documents, so instead of us, some friends went first. We decided to buy them a card to congratulate them when they came home. We found a card from the *I Ching*, an ancient Chinese book of fortune telling. It was Hexagram Three, 'New Beginnings,' with a Chinese character on it. And below it was a poem. I memorized it:

> *Times of birth and growth start unseen, below the surface.*
> *Everything is dark and still unformed, yet teeming with*
>   *motion.*
> *Difficulties and chaos loom.*
> *Despite this struggle, energy and resources are collected,*
> *and form begins to take shape.*
> *The young plant takes root, rises above the ground, and is*
>   *brought to light.*

"But we liked it so much," she goes on, "the 'New Beginnings,' that we kept it for ourselves—and got them another card. We even made a big poster of it, and kept it by our bed."

"So I would be your like new beginning?"

"Yes, dear," Clio says, "our young plant, brought to light."

"And then," Pep says, "a few weeks later, we're in the kitchen and the phone rings, and I pick it up. It's the lady from the adoption agency. She says she has good news. I say, 'Hold on while I put you on speaker.' She says that the orphanage has a baby for us, and that the only two things she knows about our baby are her date of birth—June 25, 1991—and her name. And her name is . . . *Chun*! The same name on the card! It means 'Spring' or 'New Beginnings.'"

Katie's mouth is open in amazement. "Wow."

"Yeah!" Pep says. "Out of all the thousands and thousands of Chinese characters, 'Chun' was the one we picked out. And it turned out to be *you*."

"And then what happened?"

"Dad and I started to cry, and I fell down on the floor."

"You really fell down?"

"On the floor, yes. I fell down and I was so happy I cried. It was a miracle."

"We knew then . . ." Pep says, choking up, so he has to catch his breath. "We knew that you were the baby meant for us."

"And that you were meant for me too, right?"

Clio nods.

Pep throws big arms around the two of them, and squeezes.

Katie, released, laughs and says, "It *is* an amazing, yeah! Hey, I've got an idea—let's light a stick of incense to it, to the Chun, and to the goddess too?"

They do. Clio says, "Thank you, goddess, for your loving-kindness and your wisdom, for this wonderful girl and wonderful dad and wonderful trip back to you."

Another hug, and they walk down to the van.

With a final glance back at the temple, Clio says, "Ironic, isn't it, Pep—the only permanence left in China now is from the people who specialize in impermanence?"

11

Katie's in heaven at the courtyard of the aviary or, as the sign says:

THE SQUARE OF COMMUNICATION BETWEEN HUMANS AND BIRDS

She's on her fourth cup of birdseed—and the birds, sensing in the profligate American an easy touch, are clustering around her. They have been an hour in the aviary, a ravine enclosed by netting strung from tall pylons, a habitat for thousands of birds. There are parrots who say "Nee how" (Hello) and "Sigh-chen" (Goodbye), and one that as you leave says "Eee-ho-yeh" (See you soon), peacocks that flaunt glorious erections of thousand-eyed featherings, and red-headed cranes wearing wheat-colored crests that, Rhett points out, look like those on the helmets of the combatants in *Gladiator*. In the Square of Communication an attendant throws grain up into the sky and it is snatched in midair by what must be fifty snowy egrets, swooping and fighting for the food, and then strutting like old-time parsons. The ducks and geese squatting forlornly in a dried-up pond are a downer, but nearby a Chinese guy, dressed like a cowboy, is riding an irritated ostrich around a barren enclosure. Along an avenue of caged lovebirds, the peach-faced ones remind them of their lovebird, Dave.

It is furnace-hot. Katie is fed a constant diet of ice creams and sodas to keep her hydrated in the sizzling, breezeless wet heat of the ravine—but she is in kid heaven, communing with her "second-favorite animal"—her first being, of course, the horse.

Pep walks desultorily along with Rhett. The heat and glare has Pep thinking he is seeing things, as, when a monstrous feather duster alongside a little path seems to be staring at him with snake eyes, full of reproach, it takes him a good second to place it as an emu. Strolling along, Rhett waxes philosophical, talking about his humble beginnings on a farm a few hundred kilometers down the road. His parents were teachers sent out of Changsha to the country during the Cultural Revolution. The whole family, including grandparents, lived in one big room. They heated hot water for washing and bathing over a coal stove.

"What about toilets?" Pep asks.

"You don't wanna go there." Rhett followed his brother Ashley into

Hunan University, and then took the job as a guide in a tourist agency. "But I gotta get to the States, to Hollywood." Pep asks why. "It'd be like Eddie Murphy in *Beverly Hills Cop*, going from Detroit to L.A." Dreamily he recites, "Nina Ricci, Rolls Royce. Grauman's Chinese Theatre. L.A.'s the cutting edge, the center of the world! China's heading there fast—as I'm sure you've noticed—but not fast enough."

"It's totally changed. Beijing looks like Dallas now. Almost a capitalist country."

"No joke. An authoritarian, militaristic central government controlled by the multinational corporations—a tiny number of filthy rich guys lording it over an immense number of poor bastards—just like *America*!" He laughs. "You say 'Communist Party' now, everybody yawns. People are getting *so* rich—a guy in Shanghai built a house the exact replica of the White House. Another, the Hearst Mansion. And listen up, Pep!" He pauses. "There ain't no more *government* insurance—no 'Iron Rice Bowl' anymore. So everybody has to buy *private* insurance. The market's five hundred million—*easy*! *Somebody's* gonna capture that space—why not you and me? Move fast, and we're first in. Billions!" He sighs, as if wistful about perfect love and lots of money. "I'm wired in, Mr. Pep, here in Hunan. I can get in through the back door—we call it *homer*—bribes? Pep, with your brains and my good looks, all we need is *money*!"

He laughs hard, holding his belly with his hands, screwing up his eyes against the smoke from the cigarette. His phone rings, and he flicks it open, attacks it with a rattling chain of words, closes it. "Y'know how *much* money's coming into China now?" Pep avers he does not. "Well, neither does anybody else, but it's big. It's like the Wild West here. *Yu shu ju jin*! 'Watch out, world, here we come!'"

○   ○   ○

The high point for Katie is the bird show. She and Clio and Pep and Rhett sit on bleachers watching three girls, in bright-pink dresses and sashes, make cockatoos do tricks. One girl at a microphone keeps up a patter in Chinese. The volume is high and the sounds of what Pep calls the "cymbal-ic" language jar his Western ears. Two other girls put the troupe of cockatoos through their paces—one bird is able to count, another rides a tiny bicycle, a third picks a fake orange from a tree and carries it back to the stage. At one point when Rhett, in response to a question to the audience, holds up a ten-yuan bill, the bird flies over and snatches it. Katie screeches with delight and asks Pep for a note so she can try. Pep digs, and hands her another note.

Rhett's phone rings again, but this time he doesn't talk much, just takes out a pad and pen and writes something down. Katie raises the ten-yuan note for the bird.

Rhett hangs up and turns to Clio. "Have *I* got something for *you.*"

"What?" Clio asks. "What?"

"I found her."

"Who?"

"The woman in the police station."

Clio's whole body jerks, like a current has passed through her. "Oh my."

"Wait, wait," Pep says. "Nobody *asked* you to find her."

"I know. I did it on spec. And I found her."

"Are you sure it's her?" Clio asks, surprised at how shaky her voice sounds.

"Positive."

"How in the world?" Pep asks.

"Like I said. I'm plugged in. *Homer*, remember? 'Back door'—a bribe."

"Impossible," Pep says.

"In China we have a saying: 'Everything's difficult, nothing's impossible.'"

The bird ignores Katie and takes the money from another kid. "Found who, Mom?" She is staring at Clio intently.

"Nothing, dear, just some woman—"

"Liar liar pants on fire. Who is it?"

Clio glances at Pep, who is shaking his head no. His fear snaps her awake—there's no way she'll hide this from Katie. "When we were at the police station—while you were asleep in the bus—a woman came along who, well . . . she looked a lot like you—very beautiful, dressed really nicely, and she smiled at us, and, well—"

"She looked like *me*?" Clio nods. "Exactly?"

"No—she was a lot older, thirty-something."

"Oh." Katie turns away, and starts waving the ten-yuan note again as the next bird sails out toward the audience. But then her hand comes down. She stares at Clio. "*I get it*! You could tell she looked like me when she was my age. Let's go see her!"

Clio feels her heart thumping hard, and her head starts to feel fuzzy, her legs weak, everything misty and drenched in sweat. Before she can speak, Pep does.

"Sorry, honey," he says, "we can't."

"Why not?"

"There's no reason to. Just because she looks like you is no—"

"But maybe she's my birth mom trying to find me."

Pep and Clio say nothing. Katie looks from one to the other.

"Look, Katie," Pep says. "There are a *billion* people in China, so the chance that on *that* day she'd be in *that* place, the same place as us, is just about zero."

"*Duh*, Dad—on my *birthday*? When I'm ten? Where *else* would she be, if she's looking for me?"

"Honey," he goes on, "she didn't even stop to talk with us."

"She didn't *see* me—I was sleeping in the bus, right?" Katie stares at him, and then at Clio. *They don't get it. Tell them for real.* "Mom, Dad, I *want* to go see her."

Pep has never heard this tone in her voice before—dead serious, clear—undeniably *mature*. Rhett sits there nodding, a slight smile on his face.

"Why *can't* we?"

"You'll just be disappointed, Kate-zer, and—"

"No, I won't. I know it's her." She looks down at her feet, and then goes on, again dead serious. "I told you. I said I wish I knew my birth mom. Now I can."

"It's a risk," Pep says.

"Why?"

"Well," Clio says, "suppose it turns out to be somebody else?"

"But then we *tried*, right? We were brave. You guys are always *telling* me to be more brave, right? Right, Dad? Right, Mom?"

Clio nods. Pep too. Clio turns to Rhett. "Who is she, and where is she?"

"Her name is Li Ming Tao. Lives in a city to the west, Tienja. I was there once. All I remember is coal—coal mines, whole town smells of coal. 'Tienja' means 'Heaven.'" He rolls his eyes. "Like in a movie. Name and address is all I got."

"How long a ride in the van?" Pep asks.

"Can't get there by van, the roads are crap. By train it's four, maybe five, hours."

"Five hours?" Pep says. "Forget it. We don't have the time. We have to be back here tomorrow night, for our flight out on Thursday, at noon."

"Is there a train tonight?" Clio asks.

"Lemme check." Rhett dials, talks, waits, talks. "The last train today leaves in two hours. We get in about ten or eleven tonight, stay over, do our thing tomorrow, and catch the last train back tomorrow night. You still leave Thursday noon."

"Ten hours on a train," Pep says, "for a few hours there?"

"Unless you cancel the flight, stay longer? A wild weekend in rural Hunan?"

He thinks of the compounded risk of it all, and the insane cost of changing their flights back—and he also has a rising suspicion that Rhett wants them to stay longer just to push his insurance scheme, or something else.

"We *do* have to be back on time," Clio says. "My family always gets together on the Fourth, at the compound on the ocean in Annisquam. We never miss it. Shouldn't." She thinks this over. "But if we catch tonight's train, at least we'd have tomorrow."

"Yeah, if we leave right now," Rhett says. "But for this, I need *hazardous* duty pay—heavy *homer*." Pep asks how much. "A coupla C-notes. So?"

Clio glances at Pep, then at Katie. "Well, why not?" she says. "We can't leave China till Thursday anyway, and we have no firm plans. No harm in trying, being brave. It's way out in the country—maybe it's even scenic, right, Rhett?"

Rhett bursts out laughing. "Oh it's *scenic*, oh yes, it's *real* scenic, Clio gurl, oh yeah!" He keeps on chuckling to himself, his hand over his mouth.

"Yes!" Katie cries, raising her fist in triumph.

"Wait!" Pep says, wondering why he's always the one to try to bring some reason into things like this. "Rhett. Is this trip risky?"

"No more risky than staying here."

"You'll be with us every step of the way?"

"Like white on rice, Mr. Pep, like white on rice!"

"Come on, Dad, be brave! It's an adventure! Mom says yes, right?" Clio nods.

"Why am I always the bad guy? Why am I always the guy who says no?"

"Good question, Daddy!" He looks at her like he's just swallowed a toad. "Heeee! Hee heeee!"

Pep laughs too. "Okay," he says, "let's go."

"Yes!" Katie shouts again. "Onward ho!" She jumps up and bounces down the bleachers toward the stage, disrupting the communication between the humans and the birds.

12

In the twenty minutes since Rhett disappeared up the mouth of Mad Dog Lane, a crowd of Chinese has gathered closer and closer around them and the van. People point to Katie and smile, and laugh, and talk to her as if she understands. They point at Pep and Clio, puzzled at why they are with Katie. Pep indicates, through wide-eyed mimicry, that he can't understand it either, and that her birth to them was some kind of miracle.

Many go up to Katie and try to touch her. She seeks refuge between Pep's knees as he sits on a concrete bench overlooking the grayish-yellow Yu Yu River far below. She pulls down her beaked yellow China Culture Camp cap to the level of her reflecting sunglasses and opens *Harry Potter*. Pep feels good, protecting her. In the hellish wet heat, in the mist of the coal dust that has plagued them since they stepped off the train last night, these people seem like specters from an inferno, dusted a devilish black.

"This is like a scene from Dante," he says to Clio, "The Second Ring of Hell."

Her artist's eye tries to find form in this loud, explicit confusion. "All gray and rough—it's great in a way, though, isn't it?"

"It's a matter of taste." He resents her interrupting his resentment at what he sees as a surreal living hymn to poverty, chaos, dirt, stench, and disease. He feels more and more claustrophobic with the crowd so close, and is fighting an impulse to stand up to his full height and scream, "Get out of my face!" But no, he sits there silently in what clearly is the bad part of Tienja, itself a kind of West Virginia of south China. He clenches Katie harder between his knees, between what now seem, given the diminutive Chinese, his *immense* bony white knees—and scowls.

Clio paces back and forth a few yards up the cobble-and-dirt lane, toward the sharp turn around which Rhett disappeared, and down to the narrow paved street and low stone wall overlooking the muddy river and forlorn, sooty town. She stares at the black-tile-roofed shacks piled on top of one another, boxes balanced so precariously on the steep hillside that it seems a slight tremor could send them sliding down into the river. She nods and smiles at the crowd, all the while counting her lucky stars that she isn't forced to live in this filthy place, breathe this black air—and feels guilty for it. Her heart is racing in her chest. High, on edge, she is super alert to what they could all find out in the next few moments. If Rhett comes back with nothing, it'll be a huge disappointment for Katie. *And for me? Disappointment and relief, both.*

Katie, at least, seems to be tuning things out, and is happily into her *Harry Potter.* Perched on her knapsack between Pep's legs, knees akimbo, she's calmest of them all, into a world of transparently good guys and bad guys.

○ ○ ○

The train trip, fractured by breakages, took five-plus hours. They were late getting to the Changsha station. Rhett had to squeeze them into a "hard-bench" car, so packed with travelers that they'd had to stand, everyone smelling of sweat, garlic-breathed shouting, and pushing. When Pep pushed back, they laughed. It took Rhett an hour to shove his way through to first class, bribe somebody, get back, and drag them out. Pep's bowels reacted badly and he had several phantasmagorical episodes in the train toilets—a hole in the floor with the rails blasting past underneath. In Tienja, the heat seemed turned up a notch further. An acrid, smoky scent hit them at once, a scent that coalesced to the ground in three-story-high piles of black coal surrounding the station, aglitter in the harsh klieg lights that reminded Pep of World War II films, and Clio of scenes from the more moribund passages of Dickens. All three of them started coughing spasmodically.

Once they'd checked into FIRST SNAIL UNDER HEAVEN HOTEL, Pep led them into their tiny, low-ceilinged room and shouted, "Well, here we are, family, in the beautiful nice First Ring of Hell! Enjoy!"

"Yeah," said Katie, wrinkling up her nose in disgust, sneezing out two plumes that seemed, in the harsh light of a ripped-shade lamp, quite gray. "And no Cerberus."

Punchy from the horrendous trip, Pep demonstrated how he could not stand upright, thanks to the "nice low ceilings." He snaked his index finger along the dresser-top and showed them the whorls covered in inky black. "Great for taking fingerprints, in case of a beautiful murder here tonight? No toilet in the room—good—much more sanitary that way. And what's this under the pillow?" He lifted a well-worn thin pillow, peeked under it, then reached. "*Snails*! And look—room service! 'Snail Pizza, Taco Snails, Peanut Butter and Snail Jelly sandwich'—*ow*!"

Katie was whacking him with a pillow, Clio joining in. Coal dust flew up, the motes glistening in the harsh light like slivers of diamonds. They sneezed crazily and realized that if they disturbed anything in the room they'd aerosolize the anthracite. They moved in the room as if it were mined, afraid of setting off the hellish black.

The beds sagged like hammocks, the sheets felt used and unlaundered, and the thin pillows were the consistency of dough. It was steaming hot, but when they opened the window a stream of mosquitoes came in, and they spent the next hour swatting, sweating. They slept in their clothes that night with the sheets pulled over their heads. Katie went out like a light. Pep and Clio each took a dose of Ambien.

The next morning, groggy and itchy in the hazy daylight, they faced into Tienja Town—now less ominous, more ugly. For the first time during their visit in China, they saw no other Westerners, and as they walked the desolate twisting streets, crowds of dully clothed people stared and pointed. They followed Rhett up a sinuous alley to the address he had been given. The store—MING TAO'S DRESS—was tiny, maybe ten feet across. Two floor-to-ceiling windows displayed dresses and hats and shoes trying to look stylish, and rip-offs of Western skirts and slacks.

As agreed, Rhett went in alone first. Clio had suggested this, to cushion Katie from any shock, and to abort the mission if necessary. Pep was suspicious, thinking that without them present, Rhett might try to pull something funny, but then realized that Clio and he wouldn't know what was going on anyway—they didn't understand the language, and the Chinese body language didn't mean anything familiar. A hearty laugh could mean stark tragedy; a grin, rage.

With a thumbs-up, Rhett went in.

Clio felt the breath go out of her body. *This is it.*

In no time he came back out.

"Not here," he said, "at home. Let's go. And try not to stick out, Pep, okay? Turns out that this place is a 'restricted zone.' Let's hop! *Hop!*"

"A what?" Pep asked, as he actually hopped. "What the hell's a 'restricted zone'?"

"No Westerners allowed. Recent change. There's a big prison just outside town. C'mon, let's rock and roll! Try to be cool, 'kay?"

"Oh, sure," Pep said, "we'll just blend right in."

Rhett chuckled. They ducked into the van and rode along a yellow-mud river working hard to float coal barges and fishing boats, and past endless railway cars and trucks loading coal. They soon found themselves going uphill on smaller and smaller streets until they came to Mad Dog Lane, too narrow for the van to pass. They got out to walk.

"It's one of those houses, up there. By the base of those two palms." They all stared up into the distance at the lines of low shacks and the slender, gray-ringed palm trunks, the serrated green leaves at the top hanging down together like two punk-rock sisters on a bad-hair day. "Wait here." He looked at the group of Chinese already gathering around them, and shook his head. "Blend, big fella, blend."

○ ○ ○

Pep is first to spot Rhett reappear around a bend in Mad Dog. The crowd now is large and, from its sheer mass, pushing in on them. For the first time in China he feels real danger. Several of the young men seem to be eyeing his watch and camera and fanny pack, like wolves might eye a stray puppy. Pep is standing with his arm around Clio and his knees tight around Katie's shoulders. Rhett is walking fast down to them.

"I got good news and bad news," Rhett says, slipping through the crowd as if coated with graphite. "The good news—she *is* Li Ming Tao, the woman in the police station. She *did* come because she thought you might be there." He pauses.

For Clio the scene around her fades out, her total focus is on Rhett's lips and on what the next words will be. *Oh God. Everything hinges on this.*

"The bad news—she's not your mother, Katie. She's your mother's older sister."

"But . . . but then where is her sister?" Clio asks, but no one hears her, and she realizes she is whispering. She clears her throat. "But where *is* her sister?"

"She knows where she is, she saw her within the last year." The three Macys stare at each other. "She lives two or three days away. Doesn't have a phone."

They start to throw questions at Rhett. He motions them to stop. "Ask her yourself." He looks at his watch. "She needs ten more minutes to get ready."

They wait silently. Clio and Pep look at each other, see the fear in each other's eyes, and look away.

Katie senses that something weird is going on with them. Even with the crowd pressing in all around, it's really quiet. *Too* quiet.

"Okay," Rhett says finally, "let's go." He turns and heads up the narrow lane.

They follow close behind. The crowd spreads out in their wake. The lane is part cobblestone, mostly dirt. As they climb they are immersed in the aromas they have come to identify with the poor of China—waste, smoke, food, sweat, garbage, dirt, burnt coal—and unfathomed others. Water runs down the gutters on either side. Each house is much like another, yet each is in small ways different, immediately identifiable. Clothes hang overhead, woks and pots are being washed. Old women and children sit in groups, pointing and smiling at them as they pass. The climb gets tricky, the cobbles slippery with suspect liquid, the path slanting to one side. They turn a corner and there before them are the two soaring palms, trunks thick as elephant legs, curving up into the murky air—curving, Clio thinks, in great catenary arcs like the Gehry Museum in Bilbao—with dark green leaves stroking each other in the summer morning sun.

Rhett stops before a wooden door. The crowd falls silent. He calls, a woman's voice answers. Rhett opens the door and leads them in, first Clio, then Katie, then, bending his head to slip under the low lintel without scraping his tender scab, Pep.

○ ○ ○

Clio is startled to actually *see* the woman once again. She wears the same long white silk dress and blood-red sandals. Her black hair flows gracefully down over her shoulders, her oval face—yes, Katie's face, older—is subtly made-up, and her smooth, tanned skin glows. She is sitting before one of two windows, the one catching the sun. The red parasol hangs from a nail on the wall. The kitchen table is covered with a white tablecloth, upon which are plates and cups and glasses. A pot of water for tea is on the electric stove, a coal stove sits forlornly in a corner, and a single bulb in a small pink shade hangs down. The walls are plastered, and the paint is old and dusted with soot. On one wall is a calendar with a faded photo of the strange finger-like mountains and deep gorges of Guilin; on another is a framed photo of a Western woman with platinum-blond hair in a low-cut silver sheath, maybe Madonna several incarnations ago. The ceiling is low. The woman's beauty and clothing—and the delicate jasmine, rose, and vanilla of a musky perfume—speak to Clio not so much of a life trapped in a drab room but of a life trapped in a life, of an enticement, of a possible sorrow, or of a possible nostalgia that blossoms from the sorrow itself.

Clio stares at this woman, the first blood relative of her baby—seeing even more of Katie in her now—and feels a sob rise in her throat, but quickly clicks back into control. Her arm is around Katie's shoulder, protectively.

Pep, despite another hard shock of claustrophobia that makes him duck his head as if he's in a tight tunnel, is stunned again at the woman's beauty. He watches her rise as they enter, and smooth her silk dress down along her waist, accentuating the lines and lace of her bra. Willowy. Sensual. And yes, she does look like an older Katie, remarkably so.

Katie glances up at the woman, their eyes meet. Katie shies away. *Nah, she doesn't look that much like me really. And she's really my birth mom's sister, my aunt?*

Rhett introduces them all, pointing to each in turn as if identifying dishes at a banquet table: "Ming Tao, Clio, Pep, and Katie. Katie—this is your aunt, Tao Ayi."

Clio watches as Ming Tao stares at Katie for a long moment, nodding her head and smiling. As she speaks, her voice is surprisingly coarse—a cigarette voice.

"She says Katie is very beautiful."

"And so is *she*," Pep says, with a broad smile. Rhett gives him a look, and translates. Ming Tao laughs, pats her hair, extends her hand. Each of them shakes it. Tao says something to Rhett.

"She says please sit down and she will make you some silver needle tea."

They sit around the table, on four unrelated wooden chairs.

"Silver needle tea," Clio says. "That sounds so fascinating. What is it?"

Ming Tao speaks for a while, to Clio's ears all clangs and bangs, and gestures gracefully out the window toward the palms—are they to think that the tea comes from palm fronds? Tao puts a hand on each hip and, smiling, waits for Rhett to translate.

"She says it is a very special tea that comes from Junshan Island. It is one of the greatest teas in all of China. It will amaze you because when you put it in your cup it stands up on its end like silver needles, and emits a fragrant odor."

"Tell her we will be very happy to share her silver needle tea," Clio says.

"Can I have a Sprite?" Katie asks.

Rhett translates. Ming Tao seems embarrassed, and says that she does not have soda, just water. Bottled water? No, from the tap. She offers to go out and buy some.

"No, no, it's okay," Pep says quickly. "Tell her we don't have time."

Rhett tells her, and she nods. She prepares and pours the tea. Sure enough, the leaves are all silvery, and in the cups, they do stand up on end. Clio watches Pep put his nose almost into the needles to catch the fragrance. By his glance she knows that he hasn't smelled anything, but he nods and smiles at Ming Tao as if he has.

"You don't smell anything?" Ming Tao asks, through Rhett.

On his face is a startled look—Clio knows he realizes that Ming Tao has read him correctly. "Nope," he says, "I can't."

"I smell it," Clio says, "and it's delicate, very wonderful. Very fragrant, yes, yes. Thank you so much. Shay shay. Want a taste, Katie?"

"Mom, you *know* I don't like tea." *Why's she embarrassing me, in front of her?*

More smiles, then silence.

Pep looks around. A tiny room. A door leads to another, what has to be a bedroom. A narrow stairway up. Cement walls, gray and unpainted. Two small windows, one partly blocked by the palms. Little color, no plants.

He finds himself staring at a spot above the stove where there is a wooden panel to which spidery wires come, join up with each other in little boxes, and then go out again. The wires travel on the wall making right-angle turns here and there, walking to the stove and snaking up across the ceiling to the hanging wire of the light bulb, the wires tacked to the bare wall and ceiling by small steel brackets. No covering for the wires, the wooden panel, the little boxes. No insurance coverage possible. A risk.

From a large nail on another wall, a black plastic hanger hangs. On the crosspiece, two plastic clothespins, in pink. The higher up he looks, the sootier it grows. It is overwhelmingly ugly, dead ugly. As he looks back at her he is startled—she has seen, in his eyes, his sensing the ugliness and maybe even the potential danger of living here. She holds his glance for a second, and he realizes that she feels the same. She shifts in her chair and runs her hand through her luxurious hair, sending fresh fingers of alluring perfume into the air, and smiles at him—a smile he takes to mean "Yeah, it's a dump. I deserve better, maybe even deserve what you've got, and I'll do what it takes to get out."

"I saw you at the police station," Ming Tao says suddenly, through Rhett.

"Yes, we saw you too," Clio answers.

"But I did not see her," she says, pointing to Katie.

"She was lying down in the bus."

Ming Tao laughs heartily. She takes out a pack of Chinese cigarettes and offers them around. Rhett smiles, and proudly produces a pack of his own, clearly a luxury brand. Tao nods appreciatively and takes one. Rhett flicks his Tang-Dynasty-warrior lighter. They puff contentedly. To Pep, the smoke is as harsh as Ming Tao's voice. He starts to worry about his and his family's breathing. He looks around the tiny hot kitchen for a source of circulating air, and finds none. The room grows dim.

"And if you don't mind us asking," Clio says, "why were you there?"

13

Ming Tao tells the story rapidly and in a voice that seems to Pep way too loud for the room. He worries that the crowd outside is hearing it all, and wishes they had some privacy. Rhett translates rapidly. "I am Second Sister, Big Sister to your mother."

Katie looks up quickly, then back down. She keeps her face stiff, not showing anything, but she feels her belly go funny.

"Okay," Pep says, in a tone of let's-get-down-to-it, "what about her mother."

Clio locks eyes with him. To her he seems incredibly blunt about this, a delicate matter, and his imbecilic use of the term "mother" instead of "birth mother" feels to her like a betrayal. Should she ask Rhett to clarify the terms?

"She is Third Sister. Her name is Xiao Lu."

Clio feels a chill. Her name. Finally. Once again she feels like she's about to break down. As she tries to get herself under control Pep barges in.

"Is she alive?" he asks.

"Yes."

"When is the last time you saw her?"

"I saw her, let's see, about one year ago."

"And, Tao Ayi," Clio says quietly, shyly, bringing a smile to Ming Tao's lips, "your sister, um . . . Xiao Lu, she is quite well?"

Ming Tao hesitates.

Clio and Pep glance at each other.

"Yes." She smiles. "And no."

More smiles, but when she goes on she seems more tentative, or even irritated, or perhaps contemptuous—all of which Clio finds strange. But perhaps she simply is misreading the woman, for Ming Tao is smiling all the while. "Two years ago, on the eighth anniversary of the day she left baby Chwin in Changsha, my sister took the train back there, back to Changsha." She pauses, takes out another cigarette. Rhett lights it for her, flicking his Tang-warrior lighter with a certain flair.

Clio reacts strongly to this, the first time she's heard Ming Tao call Katie by her Chinese name. She has heard it from Hongyen Ayi at the orphanage, but still is struck to hear it here, as if it is confirmation that Katie truly is someone else, that everything Clio has only partly admitted she is now forced to face, to admit with a terrifying certainty. To her she is Katie, not Chun, and certainly not this "Chun" that sounds like "Chwin." But the stiff way that even Rhett pronounces "Katie" and the easy lilting pronunciation of "Chwin" drive the point home with the sudden pain of a splinter.

"Xiao Lu waited all day outside Social Welfare Center Number One. She hoped to find out something, anything, about what happened to her baby—if she was still there, if she was still in Changsha, or in some other part of China. She saw nothing, spoke to no one. Third Sister is very shy. Not like me!" She laughs hard at this. "But on that day she saw a group of Western people with Chinese babies going into the Grand Sun Hotel. She went up to the Chinese doorman outside the hotel and asked who they were. He said they were Norwegian people, who had just taken eight babies from the orphanage the day before. She asked more about this. The guard told her that all the babies are adopted by Western people, some from Europe, most from America. This upsets my sister very much. She thinks—America! That is so far away! My baby is *gone!*" Ming Tao strikes a dramatic pose of exaggerated grief, and waits for Rhett to translate. "So then she takes the train back—she is so upset she doesn't even stop and see me here in Tienja—and she goes back home, to her home on the mountain. But then the next year—one year ago now—on the same day, the anniversary of when she left her baby, she gets on the train here again, to go there. But she can't do it. She gets on the train and *she can't breathe!* She feels she will die if she doesn't get off the train! She is used to breathing *clean* air—she lives in mountains for the last *three years!* The mountain air is very good, and the air here is terrible, and . . ." She takes a deep drag, blows out two dragon plumes of significant smoke, and laughs hard at the terribleness of this air.

"And what?" Pep asks, pressing harder, as if ferreting out a lie on an insurance application, trying to uncover "a disease or mental defect."

"Oh I don't know."

"Okay, trouble with the bad air here." He tries to clear his throat of the jagged black needles of cigarette smoke. "So a year ago she gets off the train?"

"And visits me here, right here in this room." She gestures around the room. Pep, Clio, and Katie look around, as if something of her is still there. "And she tells me this story, and she is sad that she will never go back to

Changsha again, never find her baby, and she is very broken-down by this, crying and crying, and she leaves, and that is the last time I see her. But anyway, for my business, my dress shop, I go to Changsha maybe every other month—to see the new clothes from Hong Kong—and from Milan and America too!—I love Milan and America very much!—Donna Karan DKNY! I love Changsha City—such a lively city and the shops are so bright and full of things to buy—like the Apollo Commercial City on Shaoshan Lu—did you go there?"

"No, we missed it," Clio says. "But what happened to her?"

"So big and clean and magic! And at night, Changsha City comes alive! Like it must be Times Square, or Broadway, or SoHo—Donna Karan lives in SoHo, no?"

"We don't know where Donna lives," Pep says. "Rhett, help!"

"And so," Ming Tao goes on, "after my talk with Third Sister, and her being *broken-down so badly* by abandoning Chwin, the next time when I go to Changsha on business, I take the bus to Social Welfare Center, to find out more. The big gate is closed. There is a guard. He will not talk to me. I talk to the doorman at the Grand Sun, and we talk a lot about Americans he sees there with their babies, and he tells me one thing very important—Americans go nuts with their child's birthday. Sometimes he sees Americans have a birthday party in the hotel, for their other kids? They take over the whole restaurant! Back in America they hire clowns, animals, magicians, even a circus! Spend a *lot* of money! So I think, hmm, Tao, if they come back here with Chun, maybe they come back on her birthday—*what an opportunity!*" She laughs, stubs out her cigarette, and stands before them, an actress on a stage. "I know Chwin's birthday, so I plan my next dress shop trip for that day. Last Monday, on her birthday, I watch from a store across from Welfare Center. But I don't see anyone! Third Sister said other mothers told her to leave Chwin near a police station, because when she is found she will be taken right to the police station, then to the orphanage. She found the Nan Da Lu station, and left Chwin in the nearest market, down an alley, in the vegetable stand. Hidden in a pile of celery. They find her right away. Xiao Lu visited that market again, the time she went back."

Celery! In a pile of celery? Clio looks down at Katie, who seems caught up in thought. She brings her chair closer, so their legs touch, and puts her arm around her.

Katie tries to picture herself as a baby in a pile of celery. Suddenly she feels a clenching up inside, like her insides have turned into a big fist, twisting.

"So I think maybe Chwin on her birthday will visit the police station. I leave a friend to keep watching the closed gate of the Welfare Center and I walk the one block over to the police station. I see you, but I do not see a Chinese girl with you. It is dangerous for someone like me to be there all the way from Tienja, so I go in and pretend to have business, give them my name and address, and get out fast." With a satisfied smile, the performance done, she sits back down.

"Incredible," Clio says. "Like magic, Katie, isn't it?"

"I *told* you, didn't I?"

"Okay. Now." Pep is trying to bring the thing back down to earth, to the facts they need. "When we asked about her health, why'd you say 'yes and no'—is she sick?"

"She's very good."

"Is there something more, something wrong with her, physical or mental?"

"Pep, please—"

"It's important. Ask her, Rhett."

When Rhett translates, a shadow flickers across her face, but she brightens again. "No, she needs clean air, that's all. *Very* shy, and lives alone on the mountain, and she is not interested in fashion, but she is good. Smart. Artistic. Our father, *he* is crazy."

"*Crazy?*" Pep blurts out, imagining a dozen genetic risk factors.

"Broken by the Red Guards. They left him his house and a few fields, but he . . . After our mother died he stops. He sits and talks to himself. And sees things that aren't there and talks to them, talks to his past. He wraps up tobacco leaves in newspaper, big rolls, and smokes them." She laughs, takes a newspaper, and, with comic drama, demonstrates, making a funny face at Katie, who smiles awkwardly. "But he is happy! His mind is focused on the time before Cultural Revolution, the Great Leap Forward! The Years of Starvation when I and Third Sister were born. In the Great Leap Forward we had nothing to eat! We ate nuts and berries!" She laughs, earthily, as if, Pep thinks, she's enjoying her insane father's predicament and the irony of Mao's dictate that all Chinese have to leap forward by starving to death. Is her blunt laughter of derision? Horror? The mere folly of it all? Who knows.

"And your mother died of . . . ?" Pep asks, actuarial to his core.

"Exploding heart."

"Heart attack—good to know. At what age?" She thinks about sixty. *Make a mental note: get Katie screened for cholesterol/lipids.*

"Are you okay hearing all this, dear?" Clio asks Katie.

"He went crazy? Like *why*?"

"Because the Chinese government treated him very badly."

"Was my birth mom tortured too?"

"No, she was only a child. No one would've hurt a child."

Ming Tao asks, "But why didn't I *see* you go in the Welfare Center on her birthday?"

"We were supposed to go there on her birthday," Pep says, "but there was a mistake—our meeting was cancelled. We went the next day." *Was it only yesterday?*

She laughs at this mix-up.

"But it's quite a thing for you to do," Clio says, "go all the way, alone, to Changsha, spend a whole day or two trying to find us, and then the long ride back."

"Yes," Ming Tao says, "it is *very* hard for me to do."

"And why did you go on this . . . this mission for her?"

"I feel bad for her, her life is not good. Both my sisters' lives are not good, both First Sister and Third Sister. I feel bad I did not take care of Third Sister. I was Second Sister, *her* big sister, we swam in our river together, swam and swam!—and then I didn't take care of her. Now I have a debt. So I pay her—whenever I go to Changsha, I look for her baby—and now I pay her by finding Chwin and bringing her to her."

"Yeah, well," Pep says, with a look to Clio, "we'll have to think about that."

"But you, Ming Tao, you did this because you felt guilty?"

Rhett translates this. Ming Tao does not understand. They go back and forth, with little luck. Finally Rhett says, "Guilt is not what she is saying. She feels 'bad' and 'owes her sister a debt,' which she has now partly paid, but there's more to pay, by bringing you together with her and by being a good ayi to Katie. She said again how she has discovered pleasure in her life but her sister has not. That's the best I can do."

Clio is startled to realize that she has forgotten Katie's birth mom's name. "God, Pep, these Chinese names—what was she called, Katie's birth mom?"

"I'm drawing a blank."

"Shi-ow Lu, Mom," Katie says, and then emphasizes it. "*Shi-ow Lu.*"

"Shi-ow Lu. Thanks. Oh—and Tao—you mentioned First Sister? Where is she?"

Rhett translates, but Tao does not answer. Her face turns somber.

Katie notices, feels how the flow of talk has been cut like with scissors, wonders about this First Sister.

Finally, with a sigh, and a thin smile, Ming Tao asks, "Will you have more tea?"

"No, no," Pep says, abruptly. "Bottom line: Where is Xiao Lu right now?"

"She lives alone on a mountain, far away. No phone."

"Can you give us her address?" Pep asks.

She hesitates. "I am the only one who knows how to find her. You cannot find her without me. I can take you but . . . I am so busy here, with my shop, my family . . ."

From Rhett's tone, and his look, Pep gets it. This is a woman on the make. She sees, in them, a way out of this filthy hot room. He is on guard.

"Yes, yes," Clio says, wanting to shift the tone away from Pep's rude interrogation. "Yes, Tao Ayi, we were at your dress shop—a lovely, elegant shop, and you must get a *great* deal of pleasure from it, shay shay." After she says these last words she realizes they mean "thank you" and wonders why she used them.

"How far is it to visit Third Sister?" Pep asks.

"A nine-hour journey, first by train, then by bus. And then you take a brand-new cable car up the mountain—but you still have to climb two hundred more steps to the Elephant Temple, and then hike up through the woods to her little house. I have never been there, but I think it will take, to go and come back, three days."

"Can't do it," Pep says, relief in his voice, "We have to leave Tienja tonight, on an eight o'clock train back to Changsha, and then back to America." He turns to Clio, praying that she will not think it's a good idea to go.

Clio looks at Katie, who shrugs and says nothing. To Clio, this sudden possibility of meeting the birth mom is fraught. She feels she *should* do it, but now that it's real, it feels too sudden, too risky. Maybe someday, when they've thought it all out, prepared themselves—someday when Katie's more mature, and really *prepared* for it, okay. But to go nine hours up into the mountains, into the unknown, after what she's heard about her here? "No," she says, "there's really no time, is there?"

"Right," Pep says. "We'll spend the day, find out all about Katie's birth mom, and write her a message that someone can get to her, and then plan, next time, to visit with her."

Clio looks at him, and again at Katie. "Honey, do you want to stay here three more days to go visit your birth mom?"

"Oh God, Clio, come on—"

"Katie?"

14

She glances up at her mother. All of them are staring at her. The room feels tight and hot, hard to breathe in. She feels confused, and flustered. So far this meeting with her birth aunt isn't fun. *It's meeting the wrong one. Don't they know that?*

"Yeah, I do," she says, answering her mother.

"You sure?"

"I *told* you I wanted to, remember? I still do."

Clio and Pep exchange looks. "Let's just talk a little more about it, dear, before we decide for good?" Pep groans and shakes his head. "Rhett?" Clio goes on. "Could you ask her to tell us more about Xiao Lu—how old she is, if she has other children, what happened to her husband?"

"I have only seen her twice in twelve years," Ming Tao says. "Once, a few years ago at our mother's funeral, and once last year. At our mother's funeral I said to her, 'I have discovered the pleasures in life!'" She laughs so hard at this, tears come to her eyes. "She married a farmer near a town called Chindu. She lived there with him and his parents, and had a daughter named Xia. But she left them all, went to a mountain, three years ago. She takes a big risk, to leave them. *Big* risk!"

"Katie," Pep says, "You have a sister! Her name is Xia."

"Awesome! How old?"

Rhett asks. Tao says, "Xia is a few years older than Chwin."

"And do I have a brother too?" Katie asks. After Rhett translates, Tao shakes her head no.

"But why?" Clio asks sharply. "Why would she *ever* leave her *first* child?" She sees Katie staring at her, her eyes showing her surprise.

"Mom, she musta *had* to. She wouldn't of done it except she had to. Like she had to put me in the celery, but she made sure I was safe, right?"

"Right." As always, Clio thinks, Katie sees the glass as half-full, finds the good. No depressed Hale genes for her. "She knew you'd be found right away—it was the *best* place to put you, really."

"I don't know why she left Xia," Ming Tao says. "She left, and never went back."

"So," Pep says, "Katie's sister and birth father still live on the farm?"

"Yes. But you stay here today with me, we get my two children—your cousins—they are a little older than you, and you play with them and we have a banquet, and we take you to your train back to Changsha at eight. We go to their school. Tomorrow is the last day of school, and I will take them out today to play with you all day."

"What kind of farm does my birth dad have?"

"Rice, like everybody else. I've never been there."

"Do they have animals? Horses and birds?"

"Yes, there are many animals—water buffalo, and birds, and pigs and chickens and ducks, but no horses. There aren't many horses around here."

"Okay, so, Mom, if we can't go meet my birth mom today, can we go *there*?"

"You'd rather do that," Clio asks, "than stay here and meet your cousins?"

"Yeah. It'd be a lot funner to find my sister and my birth dad and his farm."

All this talk of "birth dad" is having a strange effect on Pep. For ten years he's listened to Clio and her friends talk only about birth *mom*. Now, suddenly, *he's* here? The *other* guy? The guy who can bang out child after child, while he has to sit in the fertility doctor's bathroom whacking off to see if there are enough sperm for maybe one of their own? Images of the other guy crowd in, and he tries to push them, and him, back out.

"What's the matter, hon?" Clio is leaning over, whispering to him.

"I don't know. All of a sudden I've got to deal with a birth *dad*? *Another* dad? *Her* dad? I mean, her *dad*? *I'm* her dad, aren't I?"

"Join the crowd."

He stares at her. "You mean this is what *you've* been going through?"

"Every day, for ten years, un hunh."

"Shit. I don't know if I can do it, face the guy yet. I've got to get ready for it."

"I know. But if we can, we've *got* to have her meet her sister. Agreed?"

Pep stares at Katie. How could he deny her her sister? "Agreed, sure . . . But," he whispers to Clio—but barely able to keep it to a whisper now, "but the thing is, is that the sister, well . . . the sister comes with a *dad*!"

"It's the price you pay." She can hardly suppress a chuckle.

"Okay," Pep says to Rhett. "Ask her how long it'll take to get to this farm."

"Oh, it is far away, very far," Ming Tao says, "a very long, hot journey. Many hours by bus, then bicycle, then on foot."

Pep is sure she is lying. While looking her in the eye, he speaks to Rhett in a slow, firm tone, with a certain toughness he has learned from decades of closing insurance deals with tight-fisted Columbians. "We want to go meet Katie's birth father and sister and grandparents. If there's time, we'll meet her cousins and uncle too. And tell her that even though it is too long and too hot a journey, we have a van, a beautiful nice air-conditioned van stocked with cold bottled water, which is waiting for us down at the end of the street, and maybe we can all—her too—go there today, and still get back to meet our beautiful train at eight? Do you get what I'm saying here, Rhett?"

"Pep!" Clio says. "There's no need to speak to her that way."

"Yeah, Daddy, I told you not to! And don't say 'beautiful'!"

Pep starts to burn, but hides it. "Okay." He whispers to Clio, "She's ripping us off. She's lying. I don't know what to believe now—it may not even *be* her sister and birth dad for all we know—I mean she's obviously on the make—but there's no risk to spending the afternoon in the bus, stopping off at this farm, and then we're gone."

"Pep, please?" Clio has seen—in the universal woman-to-woman wordless language—that Ming Tao is picking all this up.

"Fine." He smiles at Ming Tao. "I'll try to be more polite, Katie. Rhett? Deal."

"Got it, big guy." As he translates, Pep plays a little game of eye tag with Ming Tao. She listens carefully, hearing the nuance. He sees that she gets it.

"A beautiful *van!*" she exclaims, acting like an innocent who has been severely mistaken and takes correction gratefully. "If so, you can get there and back in time for your train."

"Can we call ahead?" Clio asks. "On the farm, do they have a phone?"

"No. But first we go visit my children's school—"

"No," Pep says. "We go *right* now." In her eyes he sees a certain calculation, like a client trying to find the catch in the policy. He has to give her something. "Tell her that after we come back we will make a generous gift to her and her family."

Rhett translates. Ming Tao smiles, and nods, and starts to clear the teacups.

"Do you have any photos of Xiao Lu and her family?" Clio asks. Tao says no. "Of your mother and father and—who did you say?—was it *First Sister?*"

"In those days we were too poor to have a camera." She seems to sense Clio's disappointment, and moves to stand behind Pep and Katie. She puts a hand on Katie's head, and on Pep's shoulder.

Katie doesn't like to be touched by anyone other than Clio and Pep. She wishes she could get away.

Through Pep's thin Hawaiian shirt, Tao's hand feels *warm*. His skin tingles. He has an impulse to touch that hand. Her voice now is light, nuanced, almost lilting.

Rhett translates. "She says that she means what she says from her heart—in Chinese the saying is 'down to earth.' Meeting you and her beautiful niece is one of the greatest things in her life. After you leave China tonight she wants to be great friends with you and a great ayi to Katie and you *must* come back very soon. And next time you will all go together to visit her dear Third Sister up in the mountains. And one day she will visit you in America." He smiles. "And me too. We're a package."

Despite her sensual touch, Pep discounts this—her "down to earth" reminds him of someone saying "to be honest with you," which only means they have some reason not to be honest and might well be lying—but he feels that he's gotten things moving in a direction that will work. He'll need to stay on his toes in dealing with these two.

Clio fingers her Kwan Yin. She sees Ming Tao as a messenger to them, much as the Goddess of Compassion is a messenger to all. A woman who has kept her beauty and savvy and created a business in the new, cutthroat

China. "Tell her," Clio says, in a hushed tone, as if the moment is both sanctified and profaned by the stark truth of their inequality, "that we'll try to meet her children and that she's welcome to come to America to see us. And that we'll come back, soon as we can."

"I will leave a note for my husband and children," Ming Tao says. The stick figures dance across the page, like characters onstage. She places it carefully on the table, a teacup on a corner to secure it.

Rhett hustles them out. The crowd has built. Rhett is the prow of their ship, they follow in his wake. The Chinese shout to Ming Tao. The heat clutches at them, letting go when a high shack brings a rhomboid of shade—but then knifing in again when they walk back out into the sun.

As they get closer to the van they are forced to go more slowly. The crowd is packed from the center of Mad Dog Lane all the way to the walls of the shacks, and not only is it streaming down from above but it has been drawn up from below by the snazzy Toyota van. They can see the uniformed driver holed up inside, smoking and reading the paper, ignoring the crowd and its pleas to be let in. The engine growls.

They stand there for a moment, stopped by the crush of people. Ming Tao suddenly cries out, and points to Katie.

"Look! She has the same red sheen to her hair as me." Rhett translates. She bends down to Katie's height. Sure enough, the red glows in the bright sun. Two russet auras of the blood.

Pep can't help but stare down the cleft of Ming Tao's silk dress, to the deeper, softer cleft of her breasts, coddled in a lacy pink bra. Tao looks up, sees him looking, and smiles. *Ah, to be twenty years younger and a cool Chinese! Like Rhett!*

"And," Clio says, having to shout to be heard over the din of the crowd, "does Xiao Lu have the same reddish glow to her hair?"

"Not like me. Third Sister is the smart, shy, artistic sister, not the beautiful, fun-loving sister. Beautiful, lively, fun sister is me!"

Clio realizes that Pep is right—this woman is on the make, and suspect. The sudden weight of trusting her to be the source of all truth about Katie's birth mother and father, sister, and grandparents comes crashing down. How can they trust her? They can't, but they've got no one else. No DNA here, no. At least not this time around. And when would they ever come back?

With Rhett leading, they rush to the van. The door opens, and Katie,

Clio, and Ming Tao step in. Pep, a bit panicked by the mass of people crowding around him, bounds up the steps of the bus and feels a blow come down on his head, and staggers on the top step as if he's going to tumble back down. He sees stars, hears screams—"Pep!", "Daddy!"—and starts to topple, but an iron hand from above seizes his wrist, and two hands from below smack into his butt and give a great push and he is up the three steps into the van and on his knees, then up on his feet and being lifted by those iron hands to a seat. His hat is thrown into his lap. He wipes the sweat from his face and to his horror finds it a greasy red—fresh blood.

"Shit!" he cries. "Not again!"

"Daddy, you forgot to duck!"

"Feels like I was hit with a sledgehammer. How bad is it?"

"Very bad, Dad. It's gross."

"Let me see, darling." Clio takes a sterile wipe from the packet.

As she tends to Pep, Rhett barks orders to the driver to get going.

The driver, without regard for the mass of humans encircling his van like bees around their primping queen, backs up, moves forward, up, forward, and they are soon bouncing down out of the mouth of Mad Dog Lane toward the river laden with coal barges and dotted with fishermen's boats, long thin gondola-like vessels whose necks mimic the necks of the coal-black cormorants sitting in their bows, dark birds sitting as impassively as dream warriors resting up for the next battle in an ancient blood feud which, in the grand scheme of things, of course, means nothing, nothing at all.

PART TWO

In broad daylight I dream
I am with her.
At night I dream
She is still at my side.
—Mei Yao Ch'en, "A Dream at Night"
Song Dynasty, 10th–12th century

15

Forget it, they told her, when she got home late that night, forget it.

The trip back had been like a ghost trip, she like a ghost of herself, a ghostly red thread stretching tighter and tighter away from her baby for four hours until, when she got off the train again in Tienja, got off the train in the succulent dark and walked to the bus station, it snapped. But not a clean snap, no. *I am not free*, she thought, *no. I have made a terrible mistake, for all of us—Jiwei and Xia and me and Chun—and also for this life itself because I have added to the missing, to First Sister and to my own mother and father; I have added to the suffering.*

From the moment her husband saw her again when she got off the bus at Chindu, she saw in his eyes that he knew—despite everything—that they had done the wrong thing. And she knew he would never admit it.

"How did it go?" he asked.

"I put her in a pile of celery. She was found at once."

"Good."

He didn't ask her how she was. He touched her arm, but the touch seemed far away. They walked back to the bicycle. She felt like she wasn't all there, that she should be carrying something else, someone else, in a bundle in her arms.

Forget it, Xiao Lu, they told her, have another. Try for a boy.

Xiao Lu told them, "Maybe I can forget it, but I can't forget her. I see her in my mind all the time."

They—first her mother-in-law, then her father-in-law (a kindly man, as poor farmers go), and then her husband—didn't seem to know what to say to this, and so they said nothing. They went on with their lives and assumed that after a while she would go on with her life too.

○ ○ ○

Which she tried her hardest to do. It wasn't that hard a life, not compared to how she had grown up—her family were so poor at one point that they owned only one pair of decent pants, and had to choose who would wear them. She had been born in 1962, the Year of Starvation. First, lack of rain had made the crops fail. Then the Chairman's policies made it worse. Years of famine followed, when they had gone out to search for berries and mushrooms and nuts in the hill forests, and then roots and, at the end, even the sorghum grasses that animals ate.

Now on the farm the normal rains and sun brought plenty of food, and the thick clusters of persimmon trees brought shade and the rich fruit that she never tired of eating. But the fact of the abandonment of her baby was always there, like the memory of that drought, those bitter roots that burned your lips, your tongue, your throat. Another life was inside her, a hellish other life spreading out in pain from that act of abandonment, like a defective clock, ticking.

She immersed herself in little Xia, and in working the rice paddies and wheat fields and fava bean fields, and in cooking and cleaning and sewing, but it was always as if she were doing it left-handed, or at a slight distance. In the distance was not just her baby but her baby's unknown life and for-tune—where she had been taken and who she was with now. There was never a question of whether or not she would survive. Chun was a sturdy baby, much more sturdy than Xia had been, and she had seen her rescued from the celery, and knew which police station and which orphanage she would be taken to. Xia had always been frail—maybe from the hepatitis she had shortly before getting pregnant—and had caught every cold, and sometimes in the dusty seasons would have frightening attacks of wheezing. She grew up small and delicate. Xiao Lu worried more about Xia's well-being than about Chun's.

Forget about it, they all said.

I can't forget about it, she answered.

Your problem, they said, is that you can't forget about it.

She tried to act as if she had forgotten about it.

And it worked, for a while. Her acting as if the pain were gone was helped by the hellish work of the second rice harvest that summer. Once the rice had ripened, it had to be harvested quickly. Every hand was needed, and although Xiao Lu could have stayed in the compound with Xia, she left her with her mother-in-law and went up the foothills with everyone else to the rice paddies. The work was backbreaking. It started before dawn, at the sound of the village boss's gong, went through the whole white-hot day, and ended after dark. A thousand years ago the paddies had been carved up onto Black Dome Mountain in dragon-backed plates, flooded and drained by an ancient system of bamboo pipes. The curving dams of mud served as footpaths, and constantly needed repair. Despite the height of the mountain, the heat seemed to reflect off the water of the paddies rather than be tempered by the altitude. The hard work with the sickles on the rice stalks was made all that much harder by having to constantly climb up or down, the only level place being the paddy itself.

Xiao Lu was unused to this work. She had grown up many hours away in a less mountainous spot, where the river was more central than the hills, and where the crops were soy and wheat and lychee and sugarcane and fish. Because of Xia and the pregnancy with Chun, she hadn't worked in the fields in several years. Now she found it exhausting. She was not used to going out in the cool predawn and, when she stepped into the mucky water to start cutting, feeling all kinds of animals slithering and nipping at her feet—eels and worms and water rats and the odd startled frog and all kinds of voracious insects. The knee-high rice stalks cut her uncalloused hands, and raised welts on her arms and face. Her back, unused to constant bending, ached so that shooting pains went down her left leg and her toes tingled constantly. Her legs cramped and trembled. The Hunan summer sun was relentless. The time until the lunch break seemed a white-hot eternity.

It was harsh, hard, painful work, but as each day went on her pain began to feel more welcome to her. Not only did it, for little spaces of time, obscure the memory of actually having placed her dear baby in the pile of celery, but it also felt like just retribution for what she had done. Her huge conical straw hat hid her face from the others, and hid their world from her. Nights were easier. Exhausted, Jiwei fell asleep instantly, snoring—she didn't have to rebuff his unwelcome sexual advances. Even though she was filthy with sweat and itchy from bug bites the size of small acorns, with Xia close beside her she too would collapse into sleep, into the enigma of her dreams.

The work never stopped. After the second rice harvest, the fields had to be prepared again, to try for a third. There was plowing and seeding and fertilizing to do. Many paddies were too precariously placed on the mountain for water buffalo, and had to be hoed and seeded by hand. The night waste had to be hauled uphill from the village for fertilizer, in two five-gallon plastic cans balanced on a bamboo yoke across her shoulders. Again, the stench was a perverse comfort, one of guilt and retribution.

Through that second rice harvest and immediate first plantings of the new seedlings for the third crop, through the fava bean harvest and the picking and drying of the persimmons, and then into the autumn and the planting of the winter wheat, all through this, the ancient rhythm of the farm, Xiao Lu maintained a sense of calm, and gave the appearance that she had forgotten. To everyone except her husband—and perhaps her daughter Xia—she seemed almost back to normal.

o o o

But that year the winter was early, and harsh. The family house had been built partway up the mountain, for protection, and despite its carefully chosen spot in the lee of a hill, if the wind shifted to come out of the east, the weather was fierce. That winter would turn out to be one of the worst. It started with incessant rain and then came windy sleet and hail and even snow—almost unheard-of at that latitude and altitude. Luckily for the family, it was the quiet season for tending the crops, and much of their time was spent sitting around the coal fire. They were lucky in another way—there was a coal mine not far from them, on the west side of the mountain, and they were friends with a man who hauled coal to the nearby village. Every year he would drive his horse and old wooden cart with car tires up to the farm and unload the cheapest grade, glistening rough black rocks of coal, which would last all winter. To Xiao Lu it was always a frightening sight—the horse, the cart, and the man were black, covered in coal dust. Rather than a farmer's straw hat, the coal man wore a floppy train-engineer's cap, and his coal-streaked face showed white only in his eyes and, when he ate, his teeth. Everyone else seemed to like him, and he often spent the evening drinking rice wine with Jiwei and his father. They got drunk, told stupid stories, and laughed too loud. She alone was fearful of him. When Jiwei asked her why, she couldn't tell him. Maybe because he limped. She had always been afraid of cripples.

The bad weather was the beginning of her undoing. All of them were forced to stay inside, keeping warm with the coal fire in the big main room, the fire throwing its light onto the large Mao poster, which, to her, seemed a threat. As she sat there staring into those intended-to-be-seen-as-benevolent eyes, she started to count off, as if in one of her mother's prayers to the Buddha or her other kitchen gods, the ways that each great grief in her life had come from the Chairman's orders: famine, "landlordism," lost sister, crazed father, and now, lost baby. As the family chattered, she clicked each of these over in her mind like pieces of a game played with bones on an alabaster stone. While she could hide her grief—it had turned, with time, from a sharp knife slash to a dull ache—she could not hide her distraction. The farm family, unlike her own but like most of the families she had come to know in her life in western Hunan, could not abide frank feeling, but were acutely sensitive to anyone's distraction, figuring it meant a hidden plan that could not be good for them.

She became the focus of their attention, by it not being directed at her.

"She's gotten even more quiet, Jiwei," her mother-in-law said.

"She's always quiet."

"But not like this. She sits there, but she's not there."

"She's all right, Mom."

"No, she is not. Watch her carefully. Get her pregnant again soon."

But her husband knew what no one else knew. She did not want to get pregnant again.

○ ○ ○

When he had first approached her sexually, a few days after she had come back from Changsha, she had refused him, saying that she was too upset to start in again so soon. At first he had been understanding, and she appreciated it enough that she in fact was the one who initiated their lovemaking. She did not tell him that she had been to the village doctor for pills. Several months went by, with no pregnancy. She had gotten pregnant easily—within two months—the first two times.

"She got birth control," Jiwei's mother said to him after three months.

"How do you know?"

"I asked my friend to ask her friend to ask the doctor's wife."

"Did you get birth control?" Jiwei asked her that night.

"Yes."

"You don't want a son?" he asked, astonished.

"I do. A son would make me very happy, very proud. But I can't know if it will be a son or another daughter, and I can't stand giving away another daughter."

"What can we do?"

"Wait. Maybe I will change my mind."

She tried very hard. But whenever she envisioned being pregnant, her mind filled with the memory of the increasing horror she had felt when she was pregnant with Chun. At the start of that pregnancy, to give the baby up if it wasn't a boy had just been an idea, something in the air, an expectation, not talked about. But as the pregnancy went on, especially when the baby started to kick, she began to live with the portent of it being a girl. It was a strange new feeling, of being of two minds. Up until that time in her life, she had usually seen things as simple, based on pragmatic solutions to problems of food, clothing, shelter, shame. Even injustice of the kind that had rained down on her family had been clear—it came from the Chairman, and they were unlucky enough to have owned a little land and a house that they had rented to others. And if it had led to the Red Guard putting a dunce cap on her father's head and hanging a sign that said "Landlord!" around his neck and during the New Year celebrations with firecrackers popping like pistols parading him down the main street of their village in front of everyone and then loading him onto a fisherman's boat and rowing him up and down the river, the fisherman's cormorant sitting like a sentry in the bow of the sleek narrow boat—well, it was understandable, they were just following the Chairman's orders. And if, as soon as the Chairman died, there were new orders, and if millions of lives had been lost because of the old orders that were now wrong orders, and tens of millions more lives, connected by fine threads to the dead, had been ruined—First Sister's among them—well, how to understand that?

"Karma," her mother had said to this question. "We have bad karma."

It was not satisfying to her, but she had nothing else to satisfy her, so it would have to do.

This was virgin territory for her, to yearn for the baby and fear the baby, to carry a vision of nursing a sweet-smelling little baby and then have the vision darken when she saw it was a girl. By the end of the pregnancy with Chun she was hardly eating, and feeling half-crazed. The trip to Changsha made her feel more so.

"I can't go through that again!" she said to her husband.

"You have no choice," he said tensely. "To live here we need a boy."

"I can't bear giving up another girl, I would die—I can't do it."

"We can't afford another daughter! Where can we get money for the penalty? They can take our land, destroy our house! It costs *too much*—unless it's a boy!"

"I will die!"

He looked at her, incomprehension in his eyes, and walked away.

○ ○ ○

Not so his mother. When she heard that Xiao Lu did not want to get pregnant again, she was furious. One day as soon as the men had gone off to weed the winter wheat she cornered Xiao Lu and said the thing that she knew would hurt her the most—thinking that the thing that hurts the most brings the most result.

"You gave away your daughter so that we could have a son, and now you won't have a son? Are you crazy?"

Xiao Lu said nothing.

"If you don't even try for a son it makes your giving away your daughter worse!" In her worn and tightly wrinkled old face, her eyes narrowed, and her mouth settled into a grimace that almost looked like a smile. And then, to Xiao Lu's horror, she did smile, and said, "You gave away your child—your own flesh and blood—for *nothing*?"

Xiao Lu was stunned by the cruelty of this accusation. The tension in the air was solid, like a clod of earth.

Her mother-in-law burst out laughing. When she calmed down, she said, "You say your mother was Buddhist. Go to the temple in Ja, it's not far—take two lengths of red cloth and a bundle of incense. There is a famous Kwan Yin there, the goddess who brings sons. Give her the cloth, light the incense, pray to her. She will give us a son."

"I will do that." Trying to make the best of it, Xiao Lu asked, "But if it's still a girl, will you let me keep it?"

"Yes." She laughed so hard and so long that tears rolled down her cheeks.

Xiao Lu looked into her mother-in-law's eyes, eyes yellowish where white should have been, eyes lying in the face like dead oysters. "Forgive me, Mother, but I don't believe you."

That winter there came a truce, but an uneasy one, as if Jiwei's mother was giving her a chance to get pregnant. The only hint that she was furious and contemptuous was her laughter. Of course it was usual in the family to laugh at any hint of trouble, or of strong feeling behind it, and as they sat in front of the coal stove mending clothes or playing cards, or games with Xia, from time to time it was clear that Jiwei's mother was laughing at her, at her misfortune. If she did a bad job on a stitch, or distractedly fell behind in shelling fava beans or attending to Xia—even if she, flustered, made a stupid move at cards—his mother would make a digging comment and laugh, and the others would join in. Xiao Lu, embarrassed, would be even more awkward with the next stitches, or shellings, or card, and more laughter would come. At first, Jiwei resisted this, but after a while he too joined in. Much to her horror, so did Xia.

○ ○ ○

Spring came early. The fields needed to be prepared for the first rice. Every hand was needed. Again she left little Xia with her mother-in-law, and went with the men into the fields. It was so cold that soon she couldn't feel her bare feet as they sank at each step into the mud. The hoe seemed theoretical, bouncing off the hard earth with every other blow. The wind was from the east, and carried a thick stinging mist. She had to squint to see, and had to plant her feet wide apart to steady herself. But the pain helped her to forget, and to go on.

After a few days of this she noticed a change in Xia. Nothing tangible, but it seemed that the little girl was less attached to her, looking less often first for her, and to her. She was now almost four, though, so Xiao Lu figured it must just be a step in her growing up, and a healthy step at that. But then she noticed that the person Xia went to, first, was her mother-in-law.

She realized what was happening. They had used Xia before, as the reason to give away Chun, and that had worked. Now they figured that they would use Xia again. If they could turn Xia against her, if she had the feeling that if she didn't get pregnant again and produce a son she would lose Xia too, they would do it.

"You're turning Xia against me," she said to Jiwei.

"Talk to my mother."

"You're turning my daughter against me," she said to his mother, who, from the stove, stared up at her with a mixture of contempt and cruel curiosity.

"Did you get yourself sterilized without telling us?"

"No! I want a son too!"

"Are you pregnant?"

"No."

"If you don't get pregnant, you cannot stay."

"And Xia?"

"Will stay with us."

"You cannot do that to me, and to her."

"We can."

"You would not."

She smiled, and then, without covering her almost toothless mouth with her hand, she laughed, and her laughter made her laugh even harder, so that her face in the dim light had the icy eyes of a cruel ghost. She seemed oblivious to Xiao Lu staring at her in revulsion. Finally, holding her little belly, she said, "It is up to you. It is your choice. Give us a son."

○ ○ ○

Nothing changed, and everything did. Little by little, day by day, as the seasons rolled into one another, despite all of Xiao Lu's efforts, Xia was being pulled away from her, pulled toward Jiwei and his mother and father. In all of the compound and farmland, Xiao Lu had found one spot of comfort, one actual spot, on the ground. Up the path out of sight of the house was an ancient guava tree. It had not borne fruit in anyone's memory, and some of its branches were dead, snapped off at the ends by storms. Yet Xiao Lu had been struck from the first by the tremendous life force in it. In two places where horizontal branches had been snapped off, new branches had grown straight up toward the light. It spoke to her of a living thing that, broken off bluntly in two places, had channeled the blocked flow of chi out toward the phantom limb to flow up in healthy, straight, flowering new trunks. She had heard how, on the swampy south coast, banyan trees—called "walking trees"—would, when blocked in one direction, send down suckers from the branches and trunk to root in the mud and surround it, protecting it and extending it in another direction.

But the guava tree seemed even more to speak to her own life. When she first had married and come to live at Jiwei's compound, feeling that there was no privacy in the house—they had a tiny room in the loft, with a makeshift door—she and Jiwei had found this place. They could mold their backs to the trunk, and nestle on the big fallen guava leaves, and look out and down to the curl of the river through the paddies in the valley below, and watch the sun set over the far mountains. It was their special place—a place where two young strangers had fallen into liking each other, a like that soon blossomed, through touch, into love. They played there like children, chasing each other around the weathered trunk, ducking under the branches, screeching and laughing. When Xia came, it was the special place for the three of them. The little girl loved playing around the trunk of the tree—hide-and-seek, and running here and there to the edge of the path, and onto the dikes of the nearby paddy. The guava tree seemed, to both Jiwei and her, to respond to their joy and laughter. Blossoms threaded out along limbs that seemed totally dead and, tenacious, persisted, a few bearing fruit. To them, a magical place.

It was to this tree that Xiao Lu retreated during these months and years—the one place of comfort in the world that she had left. Jiwei sometimes would come there with her, but the vision of a son and her reluctance would never leave them alone, and he soon stopped. Xia came less and less.

One day Xia bit into a piece of bread and squealed in pain and reached into her mouth.

"I lost my first tooth! Look!"

In her hand was an upper tooth. "Good for you, Xia!" Xiao Lu said. "Does it hurt?"

"Yes!"

"Here." Xiao Lu took her on her lap and pressed an edge of her shirt to the gap, to stop the bleeding. Xia quieted. "Now we have to go outside and, since it was an upper tooth, throw it up on the roof for good luck."

"What happens if it's a lower tooth?"

"We bury it in the ground. You hold it, and I'll just wash my shirt and then I'll throw it for you." She went to the bucket to wash the blood off, and when her back was turned, Jiwei's mother took Xia outside. Xiao Lu rushed out after them, and got there in time to see her mother-in-law throw the tooth up onto the roof. Xia screeched with delight, clapped her hands, and screeched some more.

"Why did you do that?" Xiao Lu screamed, furious. "I am her mother. I am to do it!"

Xia stared at her, stunned by this side of her mother that she had never, ever, seen before, this fierceness and anger. Her eyes got big.

Jiwei's mother just smiled.

"You witch!" Xiao Lu screamed. "Stay away! Stop it! I won't allow it!"

Xia stared.

Jiwei's mother mimicked her to Xia and laughed, and Xia broke out of her surprise and fear and laughed too. They both stood there laughing, until Xiao Lu snatched up Xia in her arms and, carrying her on her hip, started walking up the path to the guava tree.

"No, no, let me down!" Xia cried, struggling against her.

Xiao Lu held on until they got to the ancient guava tree, and then, still holding her, sat down in her usual place, her back against the rough old trunk.

"Why are you laughing at your mother?" she asked.

"I don't know! I want to go back to Grandma."

"What is Grandma telling you about me?"

"That you don't want to give me a brother."

"But I do, I really do."

"Why don't you then?"

"I can't, not yet."

Xia seemed to calm down, and with a puzzled look in her eyes, she said, "They say you are sick. Are you sick?"

"Who says?"

"Grandma."

"Anybody else?"

"I want to go back."

"Tell me if anybody else?"

"I want to go back."

She knew then for sure that Jiwei had been converted to his mother's cause. "No, Xia dear," she said, taking her hand, "I am not sick. Not sick at all."

"Then why do you act sick?"

"How?"

"I don't know!" She tried to pull her hand away. Xiao Lu held tight. "Let me go!"

Xiao Lu forced her daughter to look at her, and saw, in her eyes, not her anger with her, no, but a distance from her, and a wish not to be there with her right then, right there. She let her go.

Freed, Xia started to run down the path to the house. Xiao Lu thought to call out to her, but held back. As if hearing her hesitation, Xia stopped, and turned around. Her spindly legs were slightly bowed, her arms sticks, her little chest sunken. *Maybe her body is telling her the truth.*

"Momma?"

"Yes, Xia?"

"Will you come back?"

Xiao Lu smiled, thinking, *It is still possible, yes.* She got up, patted the trunk of the tree once for comfort, and walked to her. "Yes."

The next day she was awakened by distant sounds she'd never heard before, *thunck thunck thunck.* She left Xia asleep, and went outside. The sounds were coming from up the path. She realized it before she saw it. It was the sound of an ax, of axes. The men were chopping down her tree.

○ ○ ○

Year after year Xiao Lu struggled, made the best of it, and yet year after year she saw ever more clearly the trap that would destroy her: to risk being pregnant again. The ridicule and laughter spread from the family compound to the village down the hill. It wasn't just that she hadn't produced a son—many of the families had only a daughter—but that she would not *decide* what to do. The word was that she had not said no to trying for a son, but that she would not say yes either. People said she was stubborn, or maybe crazy—wasn't there a rumor that her father had gone crazy?—or that she was *emotional*, and not reasonable. But not yet so emotional as to be locked up with the insane ones, in the hospital in Tienja. And the worst that was said about her? "She is putting *herself* first."

At times she seemed on the verge of making the choice to try once again. For all his dull obedience to his mother, Jiwei tried to respect her. They went through a stretch of time when Xia was about six when she was on the verge of deciding to try again. But it was just around that time that she got word that her dear mother had died, suddenly, of a burst heart.

She traveled alone down the mountain, across the several valleys to the river, and then, by a narrow fisherman's boat, upriver to her parents' house in the village on the shore. The journey took nine hours. She had not been back there since she'd left to marry Jiwei. She had wanted to bring Xia, but they would not allow it, thinking that if she took her child, she might never come back. At the funeral she was stunned to see just how crazy her father was—crazy but not willing to leave the land, insisting he could still farm it, although it hadn't been properly taken care of for years. The village boss felt sorry for him and said he would let him stay.

The only other people at the funeral were Second Sister and her husband, daughter, and son. After First Sister had disappeared, Second Sister had begun fighting terribly with their mother, and had soon left the family and married the policeman's son, and moved all the way to Tienja. Like Xiao Lu, she hadn't seen anyone in the family for many years, and the two sisters hadn't seen each other since Xiao Lu's wedding. Now, to Xiao Lu, she was almost unrecognizable—her face made-up like a movie star, her manner sophisticated—they had nothing in common anymore. Her children were dressed like royalty, little emperor and empress. "I have discovered the pleasures in life," she said. "No, I have heard nothing about First Sister, not a word." No one had.

The funeral was horrible. There had been no money for proper transport of the body to the monks who did the cremation, several hours away. They loaded the corpse into a wheelbarrow and took turns helping to wheel it up the harrowing hilly path to the run-down temple. At each bridge, as was the old custom, Xiao Lu said a prayer to the gods and sent a leaf of paper money into the stream below. Thinking, *It is what my mother would have done at my funeral, or if the body of First Sister had ever been found. If she is dead.*

The only thing she took back with her when she returned home was her mother's little box of gods.

○ ○ ○

Back in the family Xiao Lu limped on for about another year, until finally one day she found that she had been replaced. The rumor was that Jiwei had been seen talking to another young woman, in the shack that served as a bar down in the village. He began to drink rice wine after work, and sometimes it put him to sleep, and sometimes it awoke in him cruelties toward her and, to her amazement and fear, toward Xia. Xia took refuge—from both of them, Xiao Lu realized, for she herself had become a picture of gloom, now that her mother was dead—took refuge in her grandparents' bed. His mother had won.

What to do? She thought of killing herself. Some women who had given away their babies did. It was easy. You drink fertilizer, get drunk, lie down, and you are dead. But she could not do that, because of Xia and Chun, at least not yet. She thought of doing the unheard-of, the thing that no one she knew had ever done—leave. Thinking, over and over, *I can't stay, but I have nowhere else to go.*

Before dawn one spring day she tiptoed into the grandparents' room. Xia was almost nine, and slept on a cot at the foot of their bed. Xiao Lu put a note—of the most careful calligraphy, like the note she'd put in Chun's swaddling clothes—into a fold of Xia's sleeping gown.

"I love you and will always love you and know that you love me. For now, dear one, it is best for you and Daddy that I go away. When I find a place to live, I will send word, so you can come to me for a visit or to stay. Or I will come to you. If I do not come back in body, I will always be with you in spirit. Love, Mother."

She left without saying goodbye to anyone else. The only things she took with her were her mother's jade Buddha and little box of gods, her work clothes, some soap and a toothbrush and her rice bowl and chopsticks, combs for her hair, and the pink plastic sandals she had worn on the trip to Changsha City.

Where would she go? In the western distance, across the valley, was a mountain range. The tallest of the mountains was Emei Shan—Hundred Mile Mountain. When she and Jiwei had rested with their backs against the old guava tree, the two of them alone and then with their daughter, when they had been happy and hopeful, they had always been drawn to the ragged outline of Emei Shan. Some said it was a sacred mountain, but some were always saying that about mountains they could see but not reach. Not that she was looking for sacred, but she had heard that there were protected temples there, and a wild expanse of land protected from farming and people.

She had heard that sometimes people could find a place to live on that immense wild mountain, live alone among the trees and streams and rocks and caves and friendly animals—mountain deer, monkeys. This was her craving. To embrace her shyness, to be alone. Life with people was too hard. She was defective with people, always had been—except with her mother—and couldn't be with them anymore.

Starting out in that crisp spring morning, she felt at every step a shock of pain, but it was also a shock of surprise, and a shock of relief at her new sense of—what? yes, freedom!—for her pain had less to do with any of the family she was leaving—even Xia, right then—and had more to do with that robust little girl she had abandoned in Changsha, now almost seven years ago.

16

We're going back to the place where she was born. Clio, sitting next to Pep in the van, realizes this suddenly, about an hour into their horrendous journey. The trip has been unreal—no seat belts, terrible roads, the driver seeming intent on killing them all. She keeps picturing the fragile little head of her daughter hitting the steel side of the van. Pep has a bandage on his head, secured under his chin, which makes him look like a man with a toothache in one of those old Dürer engravings you see in your dentist's office.

How could she not have realized this before? Of *course* she would have been born there, probably in the farmhouse. Clio feels excited, hopeful. To actually meet Katie's blood family, her grandparents, father, big sister Xia—she's sky-high, super alert, sharp. She imagines them as simple, kind people, close to the earth and wise to the seasons, the sky, the rainfall, and the sun—of course the sun. She can almost see their faces, stretched with amazement as the three of them walk in. *A sister! And they can tell us all about her birth mother, all the reasons why she left.* A hard bounce jolts her. Carter and Sue and Tulku and her other friends in the Columbian meditation class would call this a sacred journey, to be treated with care and concern. Like the placement of the keystone at the apex of an arch—in itself, ordinary, but in the moment of placement, of extraordinary import.

Thinking, *What is sacred? To find what you have never lost.*

She checks on Katie. Despite the jolting, she's curled up asleep two seats behind. Shirty is clutched in her fist against her cheek, her mouth is open a little so that a sliver of drool stains her soft cheek and her braces emit silvery flashes when the bright sun sweeps across them, like a powerful little lighthouse, like Annisquam Light. During the first part of the ride they played the game of "counting animals," and counted thirty-four water buffalo before she fell asleep.

Ming Tao. Clio simply can't believe that she's sitting next to Katie's aunt. She never expected to have the opportunity to encounter any blood relative. The time is so short. Rhett says they'll be in Chindu in about fifteen minutes.

○ ○ ○

All during the bone-jolting ride in the van from Tienja, she has talked and listened to Ming Tao. Clio and Pep have been sitting across the narrow aisle from her, and Rhett, leaning in between them from the seat behind to interpret, chain-smoking Chinese cigarettes, seemed really *into* the conversation, so that she felt she was speaking directly to her. For a while Katie listened to what her aunt was telling them about the family. She too was in great spirits, really attentive to what was being said, at one point looking at Pep and Clio wide-eyed, saying, "I can't believe I'm going to see my sister, my big sister." Clio made sure to ask her more about her birth mother, Xiao Lu. It seemed a strange name, but Rhett said it is common, means "Winding Path." *Entrancing,* Clio thought, *the spiritual names given to many Chinese.*

As she spoke, Clio took notes, all the while watching how Katie was reacting. She said that Xiao Lu was a shy, studious girl of firm opinions—even, under the surface, a rebellious streak. She loved swimming in the river that passed by their house, and playing in the paddies and fields. As Third Sister, she was their own mother's "baby," closest to her of all three sisters. Like Katie, though shy, she always seemed sure of herself. Her main passion and talent were much like Katie's—she loved animals, and was a gifted artist; her great talent was calligraphy. She had won a prize in school, and studied with a master who lived as a hermit an hour's bicycle ride from them, upriver toward the Yangtze.

Hearing this, Katie said, "That's an 'amazing'! So I'm a lot like her?"

"In those two ways," Ming Tao answered, "yes."

"When she was ten," Pep asked, "did she look like Katie?"

"A little. She too has a double crown of hair. But Katie is more beautiful—Katie looks like me." She laughed gaily and, glancing at Rhett, threw her long hair back over one shoulder and readjusted the scooped neckline of her long silk dress.

At this, Katie looked uncomfortable. Her lips, Clio noticed, were set in a familiar, firm, protective way that signified embarrassment. She yawned. "Mom, I'm taking a nap."

"Fine, dear. Do you want Shirty?"

"Yeah." Clio is the caretaker of Shirty, and dug into her knapsack. "Be careful taking him out." She felt nervous about Shirty being so torn and tattered, so worn that he couldn't even be re-sewn. "This trip isn't too easy for him."

Clio and Pep smiled at each other. Shirty stood for Katie.

"We're all so pumped up," he said, "it makes it a little scary, eh?"

"Yeah." She took Shirty two seats back and lay down.

○ ○ ○

Now, with Katie asleep, Clio and Pep feel freer. Since the mention of "birth father," Pep has been obsessed with images of the guy. He sees him sometimes as a burly, rough, tough peasant, honest and plain but totally unaware of the bigger world, and other times as a slim, graceful young man barely old enough to be his own biological son—after all, he's probably between twenty-eight and thirty-five—trying to educate himself as best he can in this rural backwater, keeping up by reading and traveling long distances to see movies and maybe even having a pen pal. These are the two extremes of his vision. And the vision of each of them and all the fleeting visions in between are colored by the fact that this guy produced a baby, and he didn't. *Like sometimes in the locker room, naked, feeling like I've got a big scarlet letter on my chest: F for Failed.*

Pep is amazed at how quickly his images of the birth dad bring up his vulnerability, his sense of failure that he thought Katie's arrival had obliterated, or at least blunted. But the more he tries to push it down, the more it pops up. He needs to get a grip on it, and now, with Ming Tao, seizes his chance.

"So," he says, his voice pitched a little higher—something he knows Clio notices, "what is Xiao Lu's husband like?"

"Very handsome," she says, "I like him very much."

"What does he look like?"

"He is as tall as me, and has beautiful eyes—like mine!" She laughs at this.

"But, um, what color hair—and is he thin or, you know, bulky, muscular?"

"Black hair, and no, he is not fat, he is thin."

"Good." Pep is relieved that the guy is not a hunk. "What kind of person is he?"

Rhett and she go back and forth on this. Clearly Rhett is trying to individualize, and she is having difficulty. "All she can say," Rhett says, "is that he is a 'normal' person who is a hard worker. Nothing else comes to mind. She only saw him once, at her sister's wedding in the village." Ming Tao speaks insistently to Rhett. "She asks why you don't want to know his name."

Pep is startled that he hasn't asked his name. "Okay, what is it?"

"William Tu."

"William?" Pep is surprised. "*William*? What's his Chinese name?"

"Wei. His name is Tu Jiwei, but he wants to be called William."

"Not Bill?" Pep asks. "Not Billy?"

"No. Always William. At the wedding he was always Jiwei William."

Pep turns this over in his mind. The formal "William," not the familiar "Bill"? Does this show a social yearning, a striving to better himself, to leave the farm for college?

"Tao Ayi," Clio is asking, "did you ever meet Xiao Lu's daughter Xia?"

"No. After a Chinese girl goes off to live with her husband, the family does not see her much. I was not so close to Third Sister because soon after First Sister left, I left and went to Tienja and got married. My husband's father was assistant chief of police. We have not been lucky in making money. A prison guard does not make much. The shop is not doing well because the big stores come to Tienja now. The owners are in Hong Kong. I make little money. Our children—my husband will bring them to see you later at the train—they need better food, medicine. The boy is wild! Gets into trouble in school. He has attention deficit. He takes Ritalin. Very expensive drug from America. I am sad about all this."

"Yes," Clio says, "boys in America are wild too. Tell us more about Xiao Lu?"

"What is there to tell? She was shy, and always, I don't know, *different*."

"In what way?"

"Not fitting in, not social, not like me or First Sister. She didn't like to use makeup, or wear nice clothes. More interested in books and calligraphy than boys. She didn't want to get married, but we needed all the girls to get married. I like nice clothes, I have many silk dresses like this. Here, feel it." She takes Clio's hand and runs it over the diaphanous fabric. It feels light, airy, almost magical. "Do you like it? I can give you one like it, or I can give you this one."

"Yes, fine. I'd like that. But tell me about First Sister?"

She sighs, puffs, considers. "She is four years older than me. Beautiful, and very smart." She taps her forehead. "A *thinker*. I loved her very much. She got interested in politics, trying to help Father with what was done to him by Red Guard, trying to convince the cadres he is no 'capitalist roader.' She was in school in Tienja. One night when she was fourteen she went to a meeting of the Red Guards at Tienja Schoolhouse Number Two. She disappeared. We never heard from her again."

"*Never*?"

"No. We tried. Father was going crazy. Mother was crying all the time, lying in her bed. I had to take over the family. I was the mother of the family, I did all the work, I took care of Third Sister, of everything. I made sure that the family was okay. All the time I was writing to the son of the police chief who I met when I went to Tienja to find First Sister. He came to our village. He wanted to marry me. I did not want to go, leave our family, but I knew I could get money and send it home. Maybe because his father was assistant police chief, I can clear my father's name—and find First Sister. I was clever. If anyone knew where First Sister disappeared to, it would be the police. I had a secret motive for my life. I tried and tried for years, but did not succeed. I am the hero of the family. Like in a movie." She lights up, and goes on excitedly, "Like the woman in *The Road Home*, do you know it?" They did not. "She is very steady in her love for the schoolteacher who comes to her village, and waits for him to return, and spends her life happy, and then when he dies, far away from the village in the winter, she insists that the men of the village follow the old custom and carry him on their shoulders, home. In a snowstorm! A real woman! Like me. I stayed and tried to help. I helped you find Xiao Lu, didn't I? And now *I* am the one who needs help."

"Do you think First Sister is alive?" Pep asks.

She looks down into her lap. "No, I don't think so. But I never stop thinking of her. I am always searching. Whenever I go to Changsha City, I look at every face to see if it is *her*." She pauses. Rhett and Clio wait. "I am the one of our family who is left. Father is insane; Mother dead; First Sister gone, Third Sister some kind of fresh-air-needing hermit on a mountain? She is crazy too I think."

"*Crazy?*" Pep says. The word comes out like a shot.

"Wait, wait," Rhett says. "I don't think that's what she means. Chill." He goes back and forth with her, trying to clarify. Clio and Pep feel a clutch of real fear—what if Katie's biological mother is mentally ill? Often when Clio or Pep asks Katie a question she just spaces out and doesn't answer—and both of them have been worried that their daughter's addiction to anything on a video screen is a willful withdrawal from human contact. Especially now, when she's started to talk about feeling "outsidered" socially at Spook Rock. As if dealing with people is just too hard, or even just being with people is. Animals, Katie said once to them, are easier. She often seems to prefer solitude, with her animals or her drawings.

"Okay," Rhett says, finally. "Not 'crazy'-insane—the *father* is crazy-insane."

"Wonderful," Pep says, sarcastically. "Great, just great."

"She means 'selfish.' Giving up her family, going off by herself. *Selfish.* In China, being selfish is *worse* than crazy. You stick out from the group at your peril."

"Ah yes," Clio says, relieved. "In America it's the opposite."

Ming Tao is talking rapidly, and seems indignant. Rhett tries to catch up, though she keeps on talking as if they now can understand. "She's saying *she* didn't put herself first and run away, she *stayed*—'I stayed and took care of everybody, and what do I get? I and my family, *we* need help now.' She feels she's gotten a bad deal in life."

Clio begins to catch on to what Pep said before, that her idealized family reunion is descending to the level of a mercenary exchange. Rhett confirms that this is the direction things are headed.

"Bottom line, guys, is what do you want to know, and what'll you pay?"

"I want to know," Clio says, with distaste, "*specifically* how to get in touch with Xiao Lu. How to get a message to her, in Chinese, for certain. Specifically and for certain I want her address." Clio again opens her little notebook—a Shreve, Crump & Lowe silver case with lined light purple pages—and her Whale City Insurance pen. "She can write the address in Chinese here. You can write out the English."

"Cool." He hands Ming Tao the notepad, conveys Clio's message in slow, firm tones. She hefts the notebook admiringly, opens and closes the cover, looks at her reflection in the high-polished silver. She takes a finger and smooths out a trailing edge of eyeliner, turns her head this way and that, pleased—and writes nothing.

"She's not writing," Pep says.

"I noticed." Rhett asks her something. She smiles and nods and, looking Clio in the eye, talks a long time to Rhett.

"She says that even if she writes it down, she's not sure you can ever find it yourself, without her. She lives where there are no streets—she lives like a hermit in the woods—and you don't know what she looks like. She will go with you."

"But we're not *going* there this trip," Clio says, "and we can't come back for, well, I figured not until spring, at best. We can write a note—we'll do it on the ride back, after we clarify what's what in the birth father's family here—maybe there will even be a message we can send to her from her husband and daughter and in-laws—but *we need the information!*"

Rhett tells her this, echoing Clio's passion. Ming smiles broadly, and replies.

"Okay," Rhett says. "Make her an offer."

"We'll discuss it," Pep says.

Ming Tao nods her head. She reaches out to shake hands, as if now that money is to be exchanged they can be great friends. To Clio her hand feels rough, coarser than you'd think, her grasp stronger, like a workingman's. For all her silky dresses and makeup she seems to have no empathy for Clio as a woman and a mother wanting to connect, nor to know what this one day might mean to her and Pep and Katie.

○ ○ ○

With a final desperate lurch the van heaves itself up into a small square in the center of the town of Chindu, shudders, and wheezes to a stop. The driver and Rhett hop out to ask for directions. Clio awakens Katie. Rhett and the driver get back on, and Rhett says that they can't go much farther in the van. They'll drive a few blocks to the other edge of town, to the road to the village.

"The family farm is not far from the village."

"The farm!" Katie says, with excitement. "Dad, this really *is* an 'amazing'!"

A few minutes later the van reaches the limit of its ambition—it is too wide for the narrow lane ahead. "Ohh-kay!" Rhett says. "All ashore that's goin' ashore!" He makes a special show of escorting Katie out.

Stiff-limbed and sore all over, they step into the sunlight. The heat is the usual hellish wet fuzz. They are at what looks like a dead end but for a narrow cart path shimmering a bright red-dirt aura up into the metallic glare as it rides along the bank of a narrow river and then curves away through what look like high stalks of sugarcane, out of sight.

Katie looks up the road with such excitement and hope that it's as if she could travel the distance to the farm in an instant.

"How many people here are excited?" Pep asks, with a big smile. "Raise hands?"

Katie's hand shoots up, as does Clio's, and then Rhett's. Pep's stays down.

"Daddy, aren't you excited too?"

He starts to jump this way and that, crazily. "Excited?" he says. "Look at me, I'm jumping out of my skin!"

"Daddy, don't!" Katie says, embarrassed, as a small crowd gathers around them.

Rhett starts to talk to them, and one man shouts back. They go back and forth like jazz musicians on a riff of dueling drums and muscular trombones. "This is as far as the van can go. We can rent motorbikes, or bicycles. By motorbike it's about fifteen minutes, and by bike it may be half an hour."

"Motorbikes!" Katie cries out.

"Is it a difficult ride?" Clio asks.

Rhett asks someone in the crowd. "No. It's level, along the river. Then it's a little uphill for ten minutes. We have to go to a village called Ja Ja—and there we have to ask for direc—"

"Listen," Clio says, "everything is taking longer than we planned. It's already eleven thirty—to make the train back we've got to leave here again by . . ." She checks her Movado. "To be on the safe side, by about five thirty. With travel to and from the farm, we'll have at best a couple of hours there. Bicycles will do."

"Deal." Rhett turns back to the man who can arrange this.

"And don't forget the helmets," Clio calls out. Rhett stares at her. "Helmets. Plastic helmets. We don't ride without helmets. Katie can't ride without a helmet."

"Mom!" Katie whispers to her harshly, embarrassed. "Stop!"

Rhett asks about helmets. The man bursts out laughing, repeats the Chinese word for "helmets," and everybody else gathered around laughs too, presenting risk-ridden mouths that Pep sees as a "Before" in a commercial for reconstructive dentistry.

"He says he has no helmets."

"Shit!" Clio says. "Why is everything in this country so difficult?"

"Welcome to China!" Rhett gestures to the three of them and says, "Where everything is difficult, and . . ."

Pep and Katie join in. "—And nothing is impossible!"

"Okay, okay—no helmets—but *total* caution. Let's go!"

○ ○ ○

"Look, Peppy," Clio shouts back over her shoulder, "finally you've got your 'lush green, lush green'!"

Pep smiles. For the first time in China they're all having fun—as if the landscape is living up to their high hopes. The bicycle ride along the river *is* lush green lush green, mostly past rice paddies and fava bean fields and wheat, with some sorghum and soy. Water buffalo abound. The greenish-brown noodle of water curls this way and that with hardly a ripple but for the rare fish flipping. Rhett points out ancient lychee trees bending down over the slow-flowing water like courtesans bowing before a stream of passing empresses. Great stands of rare ming aurelias and the more common mimosas—trees that look like they came to life out of classic Chinese scroll paintings—and all kinds of flowers in bloom, from red and purple wildflowers and fragrant jasmine, through great gatherings in backwaters of lotus pads sprouting sturdy tubes of stems that explode in big creamy flowers with streaks of pink like in Renoir's lily gardens, to wild clematis of deep purple and banks of bougainvillea, a rush of red and pink flowers piling on top of one another like kids playing capture the flag.

And then around a curve suddenly they see before them a small mountain. Lush green, yes, with sinewy plates of rice paddies glistening all over it like the scales of a snake or, as Rhett points out, like the scales of a dragon, for they are called in Chinese "dragon-backed mountains." At the bottom of it they can make out the reflections of tin roofs—the tiny village of Ja Ja—"Nothing Village." The village seems to float, suspended, in the lap of the little mountain, cradled in a hazy cloud of light green dotted finely with bright orange. Clio asks what the orange dots are.

"Persimmons," he says. "Hunan persimmons are dynamite!"

"What's a persimmon?" Katie asks.

"The world's greatest fruit. You'll see."

Pedaling easily up a slight incline, they are among the persimmon trees. They ride down a shaded lane, the ripe orange fruit hanging down all around them. Rhett stops, picks a few, and hands them around. Pep and Katie look at their fruits casually. Clio stares at hers carefully, a signature of the closest village to her daughter's birthplace. The fruit is as big as a man's fist, shaped like a tomato. Four perfectly interwoven leaves spiral out from the stem to lie flat over the dome of the fruit. The color is deceptive. Orange, but a subtle orange, as if underlaid with earthy brown, tanned like Chinese skin.

"We can't eat 'em," Pep says. "Nothing unpeeled or raw. Not with the skins."

"*Pep—my man*! You *can't* eat the skins—they're bitter. You skin 'em!" He takes out a jackknife, opens the blade.

Ming Tao asks him what they said. He tells her. "When I was a girl," she says, "in the Years of Starvation, we ate the skins of *everything*, to survive. We even ate acorns, and sorghum—which made all of us very constipated."

"Rhett!" Pep cries, having suffered through booming diarrhea for days. "Can she get me some of those?"

Laughing, Rhett peels one of the fruits, sections it, hands it around, licks the juice, and starts on another. Ming Tao is slurping hers, in heaven. Clio takes a taste. Her eyes widen. "My God!" Katie licks a tiny wedge, shrugs, and hands it back. Pep now inspects his piece assiduously for any trace of skin, and bites. "Golly that's good. Gimmee another!"

They sit in the shade, popping pieces of persimmon into their mouths, the sticky juice making runlets down their chins. It is quiet but for the sound of a solitary bird—a sound Clio hears as that velvety one, of nostalgia.

"You know, Katie," Clio says, "we're going back to the place you were born."

"We are?" Clio nods. "You mean the hospital?"

"No, there aren't any hospitals out here. The farmhouse where they live."

"I always thought I was born in a hospital, like everybody else."

"Well, hon, it was like everybody else *here*," Clio says.

○ ○ ○

Ja Ja is hardly more than ten low houses around an open patch of dirt. Now, in early afternoon, the village seems deserted. In the open patch sits a pool table, balls unracked, cues abandoned like pick-up sticks. One building looks like a store. They follow Rhett in.

One counter, one dormant coal stove, a table and several chairs. A shaft of light squeezes itself through a lone and clouded window. The scent is of garlic, tobacco, and ash. An old man is asleep in a chair, in his lax hand an unlit clay pipe. In the golden, shadowy light his face seems all lines, a leathery persimmon. Rhett awakens him and says something. The man answers but Rhett can't understand him, and tries again. Again, nothing.

"It's either him or the local dialect," Rhett says. He tries again. The old man goes to a freezer and produces ice creams on sticks. They lick hungrily, the ice cream washing down the sticky persimmon. Rhett asks where the farmhouse is. Another long back and forth ensues. At one point the old man makes a face like he's just swallowed a bad piece of water buffalo and spits on the earth floor and sneers. Rhett asks him a few more questions. The spitting and sneering continues. Rhett leads them out into the sunlight.

"That was quite something," Clio says. "What was he saying?"

"The farm is just up there. They're not his favorite people." Rhett glances up at the sky. "Looks like we might get a shower. We better hurry."

17

The red-dirt road to the farmhouse turns immediately up. They get off their bikes and walk them along. The air is still: a dark line of clouds hovers over a range of high mountain peaks far to the west. They go slowly, owing to the brutal heat. The persimmon trees close in, scratching them. Clio, glad to contain her wild hopes by doing something physical, is in the lead, and holds the branches to keep them from whipping back at the others.

Finally, after a long uphill serpentine, they come to a clearing.

A single fig tree marks a fork in the road. The path to the right dips into a valley of early rice. A series of paddies climbs the hills on either side. Some fields are green, others are flooded with no sign of plantings and reflect, in slivers, the high, flat sun. Far down in the valley Pep spots a single white-yellow dot poking up out of the green rice grass—the yellow is a conical straw hat, and the white a shirt: a lone person bent over nearly at a right angle.

"Man or woman?" Pep asks.

"Can't tell," Rhett says. "Pulling weeds. The house is the other way, up there to the left. Let's go."

A turn in the path, and then a climb up at a harsh angle, through flooded paddies and dikes and narrow mud footpaths between them, some paddies a muddy brown and with no sign of rice-life, some furry with early sprout-lings, others flush with knee-high grass. No sign of houses or people.

"I could see sitting here all day long with a fishing pole," Pep says, with a wistful sigh, "just fishing. Nobody else around. Throw in your line. Sit. Fish."

"How can you think of fishing at a time like this?" Clio says.

"It's the only way I can stay calm," he says, "and it's not working worth a damn."

A few more minutes of uphill pedaling and they turn the corner onto level ground, and see the farmhouse. Set back from a dirt courtyard, it is a concrete-walled one-and-a-half-story structure huddled under a red-tile roof. To the right is a half-dug-out foundation and an attempt at an enclosure for small animals—chicken wire strung between steel rods sitting akimbo in the holes of cinder blocks. Pep notes that the attempt has been weak, and abandoned, with clear gaps exposed. Chickens are pecking in the hard dirt of the courtyard and in the wilted, dusty undergrowth.

Katie stares at it, surprised at how run-down it is. She thought it would be like in pictures of China, or movies, or even some of the farms she's seen in their travels, with a neat stone fence, and walls and a roof that look really solid and can withstand a hurricane, and lots of trees and flowers. She looks at Clio, and sees the surprise and disappointment on her face. *And Mom thinks* Mary's *Farm is a falling-down wreck? She doesn't look too happy about this. What's that she always is saying, "A hard dose of reality"? And I was born in there? But the people are what count—my grandparents and birth dad and sister are what really matter—like Mary really matters. Where are they?*

As if to affirm her optimism, among the chickens a bantam hen is strutting around, followed closely by a fuzzy yellow duckling. "Look, guys, a baby. A baby duck following a chicken!"

Pep stares, assessing the property for clues to its inhabitants. Against the front wall of the house are farm implements of some ancient sort, long wooden handles leading to what looks like a scythe and some kind of wooden-pegged rake. The windows on either side of the doorway are open to the air, but barred. On one side of the door are several twig brooms in various stages of deterioration, like women in skirts once fashionable, now tattered. A ruined woven basket lies on the ground, like a partly submerged boat. Junk—botttles, plastic bags, cans, rotting greens—are scattered around some broken brown bricks. On the other side of the door is a tall iron container with a hinged mouth used for transport, maybe of coal? Shocks of straw lie on top of it, as if tossed by a recalcitrant cow, or a bloated water buffalo. The tall, wide wooden door, in several crudely fitted sliding sections, is open. Over the doorway is a tile mosaic with many pieces missing—a dragon? A phoenix? *This is a house of people who are not quite making it through the basics of the day.*

"Well, here we are," he says in a somber tone, putting his arm around Katie, feeling her trembling.

"Stay close," Clio says, clutching Katie's hand hard.

"Okay," Rhett says. "Let's see who's here. Ming Tao and I'll go in first."

They walk to the door and disappear into the dark. Pep and Clio try to see inside. On the wall facing the doorway is a large framed portrait of Chairman Mao. The walls are barren, with black streaks. Dark wooden furniture is scattered about.

Suddenly they hear shouting, screaming, a high-pitched voice filled with venom, which, once started, seems to go on without interruption. Then they hear Rhett's voice, also shouting, trying to interrupt without success, and then another high-pitched voice, maybe Ming Tao's, shouting, and the screaming and shouting goes on and on. Abruptly it stops. A few more high-pitched screams. Rhett and Ming Tao hurry out of the doorway into the hazy day. They blink in the glare and, looking back a few times, walk toward the Macys, shaking their heads and talking.

"Okay," Rhett says, "let's get out of here."

"But . . . but is this the right place?" Clio asks.

"Un hunh. Too right. C'mon." He picks up his fallen bicycle.

"No! What's going on? We are not moving until you explain. Who were you talking to?"

"The grandmother. Katie's father's mother. The grandfather's in there too, but he didn't say anything. I don't think he can hear." He starts to wheel his bicycle.

"And?"

"Look. She wants no part of this. She doesn't want to see you, she doesn't want to talk to you, she wants you to go away."

"But why?"

"I couldn't tell why. Lotta hatred there, that's all I picked up. The minute she found out who we were, she started screaming."

"And where's the father, and the sister?"

"She says they're not here. Won't tell me where they are."

"Do you believe her?"

"Who knows. But there's no way—"

"You've got to help us," Pep says. "Come with us back in there."

"You do *not* want to do that," Rhett says, shaking his head.

"All right," Clio says, "I'm going in there."

"Let's go," Pep says. "Katie, you wait with Rhett and Ming Tao."

"I'm going too," Katie says. "It's my . . ." She stops and stares.

A woman is coming out, wheeling a wheelbarrow in which lies a man. Both are old, tiny, skinny. With each step the old woman takes, the old man's head lolls side to side. She stops in the sunlight, puts a thin hand to her brow, and stares at them. For a long moment there is silence. The old woman wears faded blue Mao pajamas, the old man the combat-green version. The woman is emaciated, lips mere wrinkles in a desiccated face that seems to Clio, in its darkness, charred. In that dry carved oval, the eyes are rheumy.

Clio finds herself stepping forward, hands clasped in front of her, and bowing slightly. "*Ni hao ni hao*," she says, taking another step.

The old woman's eyes glance past her. Clio stops, looks back at Katie. Pep has stepped up behind Katie, has a big hand clasped over her chest, holding her tight to him. The old woman screams—Clio sees Katie jump. Clio turns back to her and sees that she has snatched up one of the twig brooms and is shaking it with pathetic weak movements. Her mouth is her real weapon, wide open and toothless. Clio tries again to make contact. Out of that gummy hole comes a series of shrieks and rages, all of it saying in the universal human language of hatred, "Get out of here. Now!"

They pick up their bicycles. They pedal off, down, away.

At the fig tree where the path forks, Rhett stops. They all get off their bikes.

"That was terrible!" Clio says. Katie looks ashen, in shock. Clio reaches over to her, her own hand shaking before it touches Katie's cheek. "Honey, are you okay?"

"What's *wrong* with her?" Katie says. "We didn't do anything to *her*. Jeez!" Thinking, *She's like a bad witch in* Harry. *And why did we find her anyway? My birth mom wouldn't be mean.* She's *the one we should find. Her and my sister.*

"We certainly didn't," Pep says. "Rhett? What happened?"

"What can I tell you?" He smiles. "She's crazy about you."

"I have never, ever—" Clio starts to say, and then points. "Look, down there." In the valley, the figure in white with the yellow straw hat is walking through the rice fields toward them. "Come on."

They pedal downhill a short way and then stop, laying down their bicycles at the opening of a footpath on top of the dike—across from the figure approaching them between several flooded paddies. They walk single file toward the person. The path curves this way and that with an ancient elegance and logic, but the curves lengthen the distance to the figure in the field. The air suddenly feels cooler, denser. They slip and slide on the narrow, mucky path. As they get closer to the figure approaching them through the waist-high grass, they see it is a woman.

Rhett shouts to her. She sees them, stops, squints. Rhett shouts again.

After a hesitating movement toward them, the woman turns and walks back quickly into the field, heading for the far dike, curving along down the valley. Rhett and the others try to move faster, but come to the end of the path, at the edge of the flooded rice field, and have to stop.

The woman gives one backward glance and moves resolutely, faster than seemed possible, away through the muck and high grass. She's soon a tiny straw spot—then nothing.

"Shit!" Clio says. "I'm sure she'd know something. Why are they all so afraid?"

Ming Tao says something, illustrating her thought by pointing her index finger at her temple and making a twirling motion—the universal sign of "crazy."

"She says," Rhett offers, "that all of them are crazy here."

"And what do you think, I mean from trying to talk with them?"

He puffs, thinks. "Nah. It's just China—the *old* China. You see a stranger, you figure nothing good can come of it for you. You get out, or get them out, fast."

"We've come this far," Pep says, "we've got to do everything we can to try to find the . . . well, the father, William, and the sister? Can you ask again in the village?"

"Fine," Rhett says, dejectedly. "I'll try someone else."

In the square of the village, Rhett wanders off in search of information. He soon returns. "I asked around. They don't live here anymore, but maybe—*maybe*—live on another farm, maybe an hour away."

"Another farm?" Clio asks. "Did he remarry?"

"If they know, they ain't tellin'. That's all I got." He lights another cigarette, puffs. "There's an old Chinese saying, 'The bird sings, but the snake is silent.' They don't want to get involved. Now. If you want to make your train, we've got to go."

18

As her bicycle spins noisily back along the river, Clio replays it over and over: the grandmother's face, the father, who has taken the daughter and moved away, the fact that no one wants to talk about any of them. Then the immediate past lets go, and something more urgent hooks her: We are on the path *she* took, the baby in her arms, this same ride from the farmhouse down through the village and along this river, and then from Chindu by bus to Tienja, and then the long train ride to Changsha. *This journey brought her baby from there—that grandmother, that farm, that poverty of dirt—to me.*

Clio has always thought that the birth mom's misfortune was her own good fortune. But from time to time she's wondered whether or not it truly was good fortune for Katie. Now it's clear—health-wise and opportunity-wise, yes, no question. But love-wise? Sometimes lately Clio's doubted that she's good enough. Katie's birth mother gave her up unwillingly—maybe *she* could have loved her better? A fertile woman, and young. Strong enough to live alone on a mountain, make a new life for herself. But what kind of "new life" is it when you abandon your child, both children? The shapes of path and river float by. She feels a clear moment of peace. *Yes. Xiao Lu's misfortune is Katie's good fortune too.*

○ ○ ○

In the van, Katie sits looking out a window, Clio and Pep beside her. They could almost *see* the collision between her expectation and the reality—their experience as well. But soon a second shockwave seems to go through Katie, and she crumples down into Clio's lap. Her desolation shakes them. Clio strokes her hair.

Finally she sighs deeply, turns pensive, and sits up again.

"Do you want to try to talk about it, honey?" Clio asks.

"No, I want to think about other things, better things, that's all."

Ming Tao and Rhett are sitting together, smoking, drinking cold beer straight from sweaty bottles. Both are smiling. They seem to be talking more intimately. Clio senses a mutual attraction; Pep sees a mutual endeavor.

"Rhett?" Pep calls out. Rhett comes over and sits down across the aisle, Ming Tao sitting in the seat behind him. "We've decided that we *do* want to leave a note with Ming Tao," Pep says, "for Xiao Lu. And we will negotiate a fee, for all her trouble. For the fee you will promise to deliver the note, and give us her address, okay?" Ming Tao smiles and says yes.

"But I have one more question?" Clio says. Tao nods. "She tried, herself, to find us in Changsha, and then asked you to try. Why does she want to meet us?"

"I asked her that," Ming Tao says, smiling in a way Clio reads as self-congratulatory. "'Why open this up again, it is over. Why?' And she said . . ." She stops, closes her eyes. When she opens her eyes again, for the first time since they met her she is unsmiling. Clio senses that her lips are set against the danger of being flamboyant. "She said, 'When I gave up my baby I thought it would be over, but giving her up made sure it would never be over. I did not solve a problem, I created more problem. But I learned one thing." Tao pauses. "And then she tells me a saying she heard somewhere, tells it in a serious voice: 'The opposite of mindful is forgetting.'"

Clio is surprised at this, at the wisdom in this "mindful"—mindfulness is part of the Eightfold Path—surprised at the wisdom of the whole phrase. She catches herself. *Why shouldn't she be wise?*

"What does that mean?" Pep asks.

"I don't know," says Tao. "And then Xiao Lu said to me, 'If they ever come back, the most important thing in my life is that they know I want to see my baby and meet them.'"

Clio glances at Katie, concerned about where this is going, and yet needing to go on with it. Katie is turned away, seeming to be preoccupied. In a whisper so that Katie can't hear, Clio asks, "Do you think that she wants her back?"

Ming Tao thinks for a long time, and whispers, "I don't know."

"But what do you *think*?" Pep asks.

"Maybe she does. Her heart is broken. She is broken-down. But I don't know."

Clio is digging in her fanny pack for a Kleenex before she knows she's weeping.

Katie is looking at her. "You okay, Mom?"

Clio nods through her tears and takes Katie's hand, unable to reassure her. Pep has his arm around her, and she glances at Ming Tao. She is staring at her, with a softening in her eyes—*finally she has gotten what this is all about.* The harder Clio cries, the less noise she makes. Pep hugs her firmly, his bulk reassuring. He hands her another Kleenex. "I'm sorry . . . so . . ." She wipes her nose and eyes, and sits quite still, the wet tissue in the palm of her hand like a crumpled lotus offered, and rejected.

"Okay," Ming Tao says, opening her red plastic pocketbook and taking out an envelope, handing it to Rhett. "I give this to you now."

Clio stares at the characters, written by the same woman who wrote the note in the swaddling clothes ten years before. Rhett writes out the English translation.

"'Bai Li Shan'—Hundred Mile Mountain—also called Emei Shan. One of China's four sacred mountains, the highest—you see it for a hundred miles." He goes on reading, "Then she says, 'Go to Elephant Temple—ask for me.'"

Clio feels her stomach churn, the air go out of her. A temple? A sacred mountain? Is *that* why she left? Or did something happen, back there, to force her out? She gave up everything to do that? She, the *other*, is one strong woman. One strong *young* woman. *Daring, as I was, once.*

"And then," Rhett is reading, "go to . . ." He hesitates, looking for the English words, "Dusk-Enjoying Pavilion, where the path forks, and go to the left." Rhett smiles. "Everyone's heard of Emei Shan. It's a famous tourist zone now, right, Ming Tao?" They talk together for a few minutes. "Yes, she says it is a big tourist zone. She heard they have a brand-new cable car that takes you up the mountain to the temples. Many Western tourists go there. They have English translators and she thinks even one Pizza Hut, and they take Visa. They want to make it like Disneyland, Enchanted Kingdom and rides and games and fun. And skiing."

"And that's where my birth mom lives?" Katie asks.

"That's right," she says. "Third Sister." She reaches out and strokes Katie's hair, trailing a long finger down her cheek. The red nail polish gleams against Katie's skin. Clio is amazed—for the first time she seems really *interested* in Katie. Ming Tao says something with clear affection and enticement.

Rhett translates. "She told me there are many animals there, where she lives. It is famous for two kinds of animals: tame mountain deer—the mountain deer have no fear of humans, and they come up to you and you can feed them—and, on that mountain, the biggest Joking-Monkey Zone in all of China!"

"What's a 'joking-monkey zone'?" Katie asks.

"The monkeys play with tourists—come down and let you feed them, and sometimes they take your hat, or throw fruits down for you—it's great fun!"

"Monkeys in their natural habitat! Mom, can we go there?"

"It's far away, sweetheart, three whole days, there and back. We have to catch our flight tomorrow, we can't. Maybe next time—"

"But we have to, since we're already here."

"We can't," Pep says, "we can't stay here just for some monkeys."

"It's not for them—it's to find my birth mom. Please?"

"Yeah, it'd be great to do that, Kate-zer, but our plane leaves tomorrow—we've got Mommy's family reunion in Annisquam, and then summer camp, and—"

"I hate that reunion, it's cheesy!" Katie says, with unusual anger. "Everyone asks me the stupidest questions—'How's school?' Good. 'You got so tall!' Duhh. Yap yappety yap. I can't even swim there—the water freezes your noogies! And stupid Aunt Thalia won't call me 'Katie'—she always calls me '*Kate*'! And you two hate it too, right? I mean that's what you always say when the time comes to visit them."

"Katie, they're family," Clio says.

"My birth mom's family too! And it's our only chance to find her."

"We'll write a note to her," Clio says, "you, me, and Daddy will write a note to your birth mom telling her we'll schedule a trip back after Christmas, and—"

"But it's so far to here, we'll never come back!"

"We'll write her a nice beautiful letter, Kate-zer, get everybody ready to meet—"

"Cheater! You said you'd *never* say 'beautiful' again, *ever*!"

"Goddamnit Katie—"

"A swear! You used a swear on *me*?"

"We have a schedule, darling, and—"

"Mahh-ahhm—I want to go there, say yes, okay?"

Clio looks to Pep, who shakes his head no, but says nothing. "Sorry, dear—"

"Yeah, but what's more important?" She stares at them, desperate and angry, and then folds her arms over her chest and turns and marches back to the last seat of the van, pulling the beak of her cap over her face. Clio glances at Pep, and then goes to Katie. He follows.

"You're upset about what happened at the farm, aren't you?"

"Yeah, I am, and not seeing my sister either."

"And after all that, you'd still want to see your birth mom?"

"Yeah. Don't you?"

"Yes, but—"

"I don't want to talk now." She turns away, slouching against the back of the seat. Clio, shut out, feels terrible. She sees in Pep's eyes her own question: *Is it possible to stay?* He says, "Let's talk. C'mon." Going handhold to handhold on the seatbacks of the lurching van they move to seats halfway between Katie and Rhett and Ming Tao.

"Listen," he whispers, "there's one other factor here. I'm getting suspicious of these people. All these years in the insurance industry have made me a pretty good judge of when people are lying, right?" She nods. "Bottom line, I'm not sure I believe any of this. *Any* of it—that she's her aunt, or that those were her nasty grandparents or that the lost sister and birth dad live nearby, the Elephant Temple and funny monkeys—it's smells like a setup. A con. Whether it is or not, there's no way of knowing the truth. Everything we know comes through Rhett. 'On spec,' okay? We have no idea what he's translating to us."

Clio is startled. It's like entering a whole new universe, alien to her, of deception. "Sure it's possible," she says. "But *why*? Why would they do that?"

"They're desperate to get out. They'll do *anything*. You saw Ming Tao's shop, her house—the jazzy new China is passing her by. Passing both of 'em by. You heard Rhett—he wants a visa, out."

"You don't think she's Katie's aunt?"

"Maybe, maybe not. Maybe she's just some woman who happened by the police station just then. We saw Katie in her and wanted to believe it. Rhett overheard us. Don't forget—Rhett had a half hour with her in her house before he came back to get us. She's staring at the bare wires feeding that electric box on the wall, thinking about the lights in the big city. She wants a way out of her life; he shows up with a big smile and says, 'Have *I* got something for *you!*'" He shakes his head in wonderment.

"True, we can't be sure," Clio says. "And, I don't know—I feel bad saying it, but after seeing the viciousness in those grandparents, and hearing about the crazy father and how Xiao Lu is so fragile, so broken-down—I just don't know if we should risk it. Even if we were sure they were telling the truth."

"*Especially* if we were."

She considers this. "Yes. I mean, if she's been obsessed all these years with finding her baby, well . . . maybe it's all about . . . well, trying to get her back?"

"Could be," he says, nodding soberly. "If so, big risk."

She sighs. "Okay. We'll write a letter to her. If she writes back when we're home, we'll assess things, and maybe implement them, maybe not. But for now, we're done." She looks back at Katie. "Poor little girl. I feel so *bad* for her! Having to see that old crone screaming at her, as if she were a . . . I don't know, something she threw into the trash that somehow came back?"

"It was a nightmare."

"But even after all that, she still wants to go."

"Unless," Pep says, "it is really the deer and the monkeys."

Clio sits quietly, and then raises her eyes to his. "You think she'll be okay?"

"I do. As long as we are, she will be, yes."

Katie sits in the back of the van, still mad. *Write a letter that's all? She promised! Like last year in our school play Orpheus rescuing his bride Eurydice from the Underworld he promised Hades not to look back at her until they were safe again in the Realm of the Living—but then just when he saw the dim light ahead he turned around to make sure she was there and that was it. He lost her forever.*

○ ○ ○

On the outskirts of Tienja they get caught in bumper-to-bumper, wheel-to-wheel traffic—a rush-hour movement of fierce commerce, born of different sizes and shapes of the dark mountains of coal—and of the overflow from the Dragon Boat Festival down below, on the river. Trucks, buses, taxis, cars, motorcycles, bicycles with trailers, floods of pedestrians—all inch along in the fierce glare, honking angrily at the rubbish-lined, unblinking streets. Pep watches his watch obsessively, praying they'll make their train. Suddenly his skin starts to itch, bad. *Could it be hives?* He's never *had* hives, but his golf buddy, Toby Updike, editor of *The Columbia Crier, started* with hives—which soon *exploded into psoriasis! Bad news, if this is that!*

The train has left.

Pep starts to get angry, but Rhett checks and tells him that there is another train, which leaves for Changsha City at five in the morning. It arrives at nine thirty. They can still make their noon flight out. Rhett arranges a hotel. Pep gives some of his remaining cash to Ming Tao, and they all say goodbye.

With great relief, by ten they are in their room at the Dripping Water Cave Hotel. They've feared the worst, but are pleasantly surprised. Hot water, flush toilet, no dripping, and no snails. The room is air-conditioned and has a reasonable bed for Clio and Pep, and a tiny bed in the entryway near the door for Katie. Rhett is in the next room. He will wake them at four a.m. for the five o'clock train. To be on the safe side, Clio sets their own two alarms.

Katie, in her pajamas, sits on their bed. Clio is doing the nightly combing of the hair. Katie hasn't said a dozen words since their argument in the van.

"What's wrong, hon?"

"I told you I want to stay and find my birth mom. Why can't we?"

"Mommy and I have thought carefully about it," Pep says, "we've really tried to see if there was a way that we could safely do it, but we can't, we just can't."

"On the plane tomorrow we'll start planning everything out to come back. Your birth mom will still be there after Christmas."

"How do you know? She could be *dead* then. It might be now or never."

"Please, dear," Clio says, "don't think like that—"

"But you *promised*. I said, 'Do you promise if we have a chance to find my birth mom you'll try your hardest to do it?' and you said, 'Yes, I promise.' Remember?"

"Yes, I do, sweetheart, but—"

"And you're gonna *break your promise*?"

"Not break, just delay it until the next—"

"You promised on *this* trip, now!" Katie jumps up off their bed and walks to her own bed near the door and lies down. Clio is mortified.

"You *promised*?" Pep whispers. She nods.

"I never imagined that there was the slightest chance . . ."

"Jesus." He groans and shakes his head in incredulity.

Clio stares at Katie, her back turned away, her face to the wall. She gets up and walks over to Katie's bed. She's still facing the wall. "Want me to rub your back?"

"No."

Clio feels this like a punch in the gut. "Please, let me . . ."

Silence, then, "Nope. G'night."

"Goodnight, dear. Love you." She waits for Katie to say, "Love you too." Nothing.

Back in bed, in the dark, Clio can't fall asleep. She hears Pep groaning and grumbling, awake. "You can't sleep either?"

"Nope. Incredible headache. Aspirin won't touch it."

"Is it safe to do an Ambien? We can't afford to sleep through the alarms."

"With three alarm clocks among three consenting adults? Sure. We'll just do a five. It'll wear off by four." He takes one. Clio abstains.

○ ○ ○

When the alarms go off at four, Clio struggles up out of sleep, calls to Pep, turns on the light, and moves toward the bathroom. Katie isn't in her bed. She goes into the bathroom. No Katie.

"Katie?"

No answer.

"Katie!"

Someone is knocking on the door. Clio opens it. Rhett.

"Is Katie with you?"

"No, why?"

Her legs turn to water. She finds herself sitting on the floor, in shock.

19

A hundred things go through her mind and one thing only. She's on her feet and at Pep, shaking him. "Get up! C'mon, get up! Pep!" He's sleeping on his side as if dead—groggy from the Ambien. She shouts in his ear. "Wake up!" A feeble groan. "Damnit!" She rolls him over on his back and grabs his nose and twists it hard, until he winces and wakes up. "Katie's gone! Come on!"

Pep is trying to push off the covers of the sleeping pill but he can't seem to claw his way back out to her. Pain shoots through his nose and then from cheek to skull, and ricochets back like a metal echo. "Okay, don't panic—"

"Katie's gone! I woke up and she wasn't in her bed. Gone! We've got to find her! Get your clothes on and come on!"

He snaps to, reaching for his clothes. "Any ideas?"

"None! Hurry!" She is pulling a shirt on over her pajama top and slipping on her shorts. "Let's go."

She leads Pep and Rhett out into the gloomy hallway. No Katie. She takes a deep breath. The elevator takes an age. She waits, and waits, and suddenly finds herself pounding on the closed elevator door and screaming, "Come on down, damnit, come on down!" She feels totally clear. Clear and fierce, ferocious.

"Any idea where she went?" Rhett said.

"None. She'd never go anywhere by herself, not at this hour. Lobby. Come on."

She stares around the lobby. Empty. Her focus falls on a clerk, asleep behind the reception desk. Every detail leaps out—skinny, with lank black hair and a thin moustache, a bow tie hanging from one point of his collar. Rhett awakens him. Clio and Pep look around every nook and cranny, into the tiny restaurant and kitchen and the bathroom. No Katie. Back to the desk clerk. Barely awake, he is spasmodically grasping at his bow tie, trying to attach it to the other point of his collar.

"He hasn't seen her," Rhett says.

"He *has* to have seen her," Clio says. "You saw her. Someone kidnapped her. Where is she?" The clerk's thick-lidded eyes bulge in fear. "Rhett. Get him to talk."

Rhett shouts at the young man. More fear in his eyes. He's seen nothing of Katie.

"Maybe," Rhett says, "she just went out on one of her adventures."

"At three in the morning in China she does not go adventuring. I *knew* we should've just waited at the station!"

"Let's look out on the street," Pep says. "Maybe somebody saw her."

To Clio the full moon seems ominous. The street is coated in a tin light. Sooty night moisture seems to lather the empty streets and shops with dangerous stuff. They stare around, up and down, and see no sign of life. For the first time in China, no people.

"Pep, what time is it? I forgot my watch—"

"Four ten. Let's look around the block—" He starts off.

"Wait," Rhett says. "Let's think this through. Like a detective would."

"Rhett, do *not* start that movie shit now," Clio says. "Stay focused."

"We think it through while we look," Pep says. "Anybody we meet, we ask if they've seen her. Move it!"

Clio is already ahead, calling out at the top of her voice, "Katie? Kay-tee!"

They follow, calling out. Everything is shut down, boarded up as if under attack. Finally they find a human, standing guard over several piles of coal. Rhett asks him if he's seen Katie. He has not. They keep going. To Clio the lack of any readable signs and the cruel metallic light of the moon coating the dingy, run-down buildings make her feel even more terrified of where their daughter is, and what she could possibly have gotten herself into. *Please God.* A woman sweeping the street. No, she's seen nothing. For a moment they stop, stand there forlornly. Clio shivers with a sense of doom, teeters—and fights it off.

"Okay," Rhett says. "Let's go back, try to figure this out. I want to check out everything in the room—the bed, the floor, the door and lock, and make some calls—train station, bus station—"

"Police," Clio says.

Rhett sighs. "Not sure about that—this is a restricted zone, and—"

"Rhett, listen carefully," Pep says, firmly. "We call the police. Now."

With a shrug, Rhett leads them back to the hotel, and calls the police. Next he calls the driver of the van, telling him to come at once, and then the train and bus stations. They go back up to the room. Clio can barely stand to look at Katie's bed. Rhett inspects it carefully. It still has the indentation of her body. In a rumple of the covers he finds a tattered rag. "What's this?"

"Shirty!" Clio says, bursting into tears. "Her security blanket."

"Okay. Anything unusual here?" Clio shakes her head. Pep too. "Okay.

No sign of a struggle. Good. The lock on the door is not broken or forced. Did you lock it before you went to bed?"

"Absolutely," Pep says. "Always."

"Good—so no one broke in. So that means one of two things: either she let someone in who she knew, or she went out of her own free will."

"I can't see her doing either," Clio says. "Not without asking us first. Why aren't the police here yet? You really called them?"

"Whoa," Rhett says, holding his hands up in defense. "I called them, okay?" Clio doesn't say it's okay, but Rhett goes on, "What about clothes, shoes?"

Clio looks around. "Her running shoes are gone."

"Good. That argues against anything forceful."

"But her cap is here," Pep says, seeing the yellow cap with the chicken.

"That could mean anything. Did either of you hear anything in the night?" They say no. "Do you remember the last time you saw her, and exactly where?"

"I woke up at about twelve thirty," Clio says, "and checked on her, and she was sleeping quietly, and I went back to bed. Once she's asleep, she's out—she never wakes up. Someone or something must have woken her up."

"So she's been gone, at *most*, four hours?"

As this sinks in, this amazingly long amount of time that her daughter has been gone, Clio sits down heavily on the edge of their bed. Suddenly she jumps up again.

"Rhett," she says, "where is she."

Rhett's face goes tight, as if slapped. "What?"

"I said where *is* she." Clio moves toward him and tries to grab his shirt, but he slips behind a dresser. She traps him, is about to grab him again, but Pep's hands are on her, stopping her.

"Let go!" She shoves Pep away, grabs Rhett's shirt with two hands, and shouts, "Where is she? She'd let *you* in, wouldn't she? You better tell me right now, or you're finished!" He doesn't answer. "Only two people knew where we were—you, and Ming Tao. She'd never let her in without waking us—that leaves you."

"I did not take your daughter. No way."

She stares into his eyes, trying to fathom, and sees only dark. "For all we know, you've been lying to us all along—you might have cooked up this whole scheme—Ming Tao, the farm, her birth mom, everything. We need to know the truth here. All of it. Right now."

Rhett is staring at Clio, his mouth open in a little *o* of disbelief. Soberly, he says, "Truth is, I tried to help you." He looks at Pep. "Sure, I want you to help me. I told you that from the start. But I've told you the truth. I don't know about this Ming Tao gal, she could be lying—but I don't think so. That's 'movie shit.' As you said."

"Is *she* the birth mother?" Clio asks.

"*Her*?" Rhett looks shocked. He thinks it over. "No. Never. No way."

"Okay," Pep says, believing him. "Clio, we just have to plan on what we do while we wait for the police."

They send the van driver cruising around, his cell phone at the ready in case he spots Katie. Pep will stay in the room with the door open to keep an eye on the hallway, and Rhett with his cell will stay in the lobby and keep grilling the staff and guests for information. Clio wants to go out on the streets to search. Rhett starts to make a sign for her to carry, with Katie's photo and the message that she is missing and that there is a one-hundred-dollar reward for her return. Left with the vision of her child lost out in the chaos of this city in the middle of China, Clio collapses on the bed, shaking. Disbelief turns to horror. From time to time she convulses in sobs. Pep sits on the bed beside her, feeling her shoulders shake the way their daughter's do on the rare times now when she cries.

20

Beepbeep . . . beepbeep . . . beepbeep—

Lying on her cot, hearing the alarm on her Baby-G wristwatch, Katie clicks it off and thinks, *It sounds so loud I hope they didn't hear it—it would ruin everything.* She presses the tiny button for the pale-blue light. 3:00 a.m.

Thinking, *But can I really do this? Maybe it's the only way ever to find her.*

She listens for any sound that means they heard it too, but hears only her own breathing. She holds her breath and listens. Nothing. Just her father snoring. She lies there for a moment, trying to shake off her dream. This one was about a tame deer on a path through the woods on a mountain, and a weird dream because the deer had a Chinese face. Thinking, *Now, be as quiet as a deer.*

She slips on her shorts and socks and shirt but not her Nikes, which she holds in her hands. She tiptoes on deer feet to the door. Only one lock. *They'll be mad but I'm mad too. It is the only way, no question. Be gentle-gentle with the lock—click! Uh-oh.* She holds her breath again and doesn't move, listening. It's like her mother has eyes in the back of her head and sees whatever she's doing, especially if it's bad. Nothing. Just her dad snoring.

She hopes the door doesn't squeak like it would in a cartoon and wake up Wile E. Coyote after the Road Runner's gone. It doesn't. She squeezes around it and out, closing it softly. Done. She runs. She decides not to take the elevator because when it opens in the lobby someone might hear it. She goes down the stairs. Yuck. Yucky smell, worse each floor down. She puts on her Nikes, runs down all the way, then gently opens the door. Wrong floor, the basement—it's *really* yucky. She goes back up one flight. She's worried that there's a doorman or clerk there who might see her and stop her. She should have worn a disguise, even a boy disguise, like Mulan did. It's too late now. She peeks out. No doorman. The lobby is dim. A clerk has his head down on his arms on the desk; he's asleep. Quickly she dashes across the lobby and the door closes and she's out! It's 3:04 a.m. by her Baby-G.

Nobody is on the street. No cars or trucks or bicycles. It's quiet except for the humming of the street lights like the rays are fighting their way through the foggy night. Now she will just wait from 3:04 to 5:00 and go back in. The train will be gone and they'll have to stay. That's the plan. She hurries down the street a block and ducks into an alley where she sits down on a big wooden crate to wait. *You go girl! That's what Mary always says to me when I hesitate like with Velcro. "You can't hesitate with a horse," she says, and then when I don't hesitate and that brat does what I want she always gives me a thumbs-up and says, "You go girl!" And I tingle all over at how I did go girl and did good.*

As she waits, she goes back over what has happened. She feels that she tried everything to get them to understand how much she wants to stay to find her birth mom. She tried everything and they hardly even listened. Do they think that she didn't *hear* them ask Tao if her birth mom wants her back? *How can I tell them that it doesn't matter if she wants me back? There's no way I'd go back to her—I've already got a mother and father, I don't need any others. But a sister's a different story.*

Katie finds herself staring out at a little shop across the alleyway, a shop whose sign she can't read but whose window display has all kinds of metal parts and some tools that look already used, rescued from trash. All over China she's seen Chinese people combing through trash barrels and junk piles, hunting for anything of value. She is amazed at how everything in China is used, how anything that is thrown away is recycled.

Thinking, *Like I was.*

The thought surprises her. It's weird at first, but then something else happens. Something else seems to surround it like darkness surrounds day with a shadowy sadness and it pulls her down so that she feels like she's fallen into a black pit in the middle of her stomach and she wants to cry but another brand-new thought stops the falling and stops the something else.

It's not only that I want to find my birth mom. I need to find my birth mom. That's what they don't understand. When I see them again, when they've missed the train and the plane, I'll tell them that. I never understood that before and now I do and once you understand something like that you never forget it ever how can you?

"I'll tell them that," she whispers to the shop, to the metal parts and orphaned tools, as quiet sitting there in their shop window as she is sitting there on her crate in the alley in the coal-y dark night. She looks at her watch—3:16. She can't imagine waiting one hour and forty-four more minutes just sitting there in the alley, and besides, she has to pee. In China kids can pee on the street, in alleys, in corners. That's an idea, she even carries some tissues in her left-hand pants pocket—like her dad always does. *Good idea, Dad.* She goes deeper into the little alley. If she just makes sure not to let her shorts touch the—God what's *that*? An animal or a plant—maybe a brown furry vegetable—is hiding by the wall a few inches from her feet. She tries to hurry, but it's hard to hurry your pee. She hasn't touched anything but her hands feel gross anyway. *Now* what.

There's a rustling nearby. She jumps, scared. A dog.

She doesn't touch it. They told her that just about every animal in China has rabies—but she doesn't have to touch it to be friends with it. It's more scared of her than she is of it—she can see that. It looks like a dingo dog in Africa or is it Australia, big, wide, pointy ears and a narrow black snout, and mostly yellow but you can see her hungry ribs. Her nipples are really big and black and her breasts are full of milk so that means she's got *babies*! "Hey, little dingo dog!" Her tail's wagging. Anything she can give her to eat? There's that dumpling Mom put in her pocket just in case. She takes it out and offers it. "Here, dingo dog, here you go." The dog slinks back, so she tosses it. The dingo edges closer, sniffs, grabs the dumpling, and gobbles it up, then turns to go.

"Hey, wait! Wait for me!" The dog waits. Katie follows her. The dog keeps on, turning her head away and then back like she wants to show Katie her babies. "Okay, let's go!" *That's what we say to Cinnamon Our Fluffy Pup I call him Dad calls him Our Pampered Pooch or Our Yuppie Puppy when we take him for a walk.*

○ ○ ○

She is lost. She looks around, and the small street she is on looks exactly like every other small street she has been on. There are street signs and other signs, but all of them are in Chinese, and she wishes she tried to learn the language when she had the chance. She feels bad that her parents tried so hard, and she didn't see the sense in it. She wanted to take Spanish because her friends at Spook did. *Big* mistake. She lost her friends and didn't learn Chinese or even Spanish that well either. Now she feels bad at how worried they'll feel when they wake up for the trip back and find her gone. She should've written a note but she was too mad. They'll go bananas.

The night seems even darker; the air is really wet and even thicker and smells a lot like coal dust. She thought she could remember which way she came, but now she can't. Dingo dog is looking back at her, still trying to get her to follow. Maybe if she did, she'd lead her back, because dogs have an instinct to find their way home. But maybe that wasn't her home and she was just out hunting for food, and her babies are where her real home is. She knows she shouldn't follow her any farther. This is no joke. It's 3:44.

Her mother has told her that if you're lost the most important thing is not to panic. She takes a deep breath and looks around. She decides to find her own way. Little streets have to lead to bigger streets. If she can get to a big street where there are lots of people or a park or a bus station or train station or even a police station, someone might speak English and take her back to the hotel. The Dripping Cave Hotel.

She wishes she could say it in Chinese, but all she can say is "hello" and "goodbye" and "thank you" and the word for "American," which she thinks now is "A-mo-ran" or "Meg-oh-ran." So she figures if she walks far enough she'll come to a big street and maybe somebody will speak English and she will say, "I am lost please take me to the Dripping Cave Hotel?" The Chinese people are kind. If they understand her they will help her. Safer than in America, her father always says. She feels better now that she has a plan. But it's so dark and misty and there haven't been any people around, none! and her plan doesn't seem that good a plan really, and she is getting more and more scared. She walks on. She tries to keep her spirits up by whistling, but the sound is so lonesome in the dark, tight streets, disappearing into the bitter-tasting coal mist like light into a long, curvy tunnel, that she stops, and just walks.

○ ○ ○

She walks for almost another half hour and has not found a main street or a person. She finds herself in a maze of tiny alleys lined by darkened shops and low, dead buildings, and once in a while, behind a high fence with barbed wire on top, a huge pile of coal glistening under a humming streetlamp. The only things she recognizes are signs for Coca-Cola. It's after four, which means that her parents are up. Up and panicking, wondering where she is. She thinks they'll probably figure it out, but still. And even if they knew why, they wouldn't be able to find her.

Nobody who knows me can find me!

Exhausted, hungry, and thirsty, she sits down on the edge of a stone, next to where water is dripping out of a metal pipe sprouting out of a stone wall. It's drinking water probably—but she knows not to drink it, it's drinking water only for Chinese. Suddenly she feels scared, and then *real* scared. She is alone and unknown in the middle of nowhere and she can't even take a drink and can't tell anybody anything and she starts to panic—it hits her belly and then goes up into her head so everything goes fuzzy and she feels totally alone, abandoned but not out in a wilderness with nothing in sight but under something, in and under something cool and damp and all ridgy and leafy, closing in, rubbing against her, weighing down and over her so she can't breathe and no one's there no one hears her cries no one! She starts to cry, just lets go and wails. *Please God help me please let them find me please I'm sorry I'll never do this again just get me back to them safe and sound!* Her body shakes, everything blurs, she screams, "Momma! Momma! *Momma!*"

Stops. Hears her voice echo off the stone walls. Silence. Nobody answers. She has stopped sobbing, but keeps on shivering inside. She sits, waits, not knowing what she's waiting for, except to be saved.

After a while, the far end of the narrow street brightens, and then glows. Dawn is a relief. The first angel rays of sun thread their way through the opening of the street, making the coal dust sparkle, and hit the tops of the buildings, changing the stone all around her to a weird-like rosy color. She checks her watch—5:21. They missed their train. She sits and sits.

○ ○ ○

Pa-clop pa-clop pa-clop pa-clop . . .

A horse coming up the small street toward her, totally black. He is pulling a wooden cart with car tires and a man is sitting on the cart. The man has a round straw hat like a big nipple on a bottle. It's pulled down so he can see into the blinding low rays of the sun. Half his face is hidden but what she can see of it is all black too. He wears a black long-sleeved shirt and she can't tell what he's sitting on in the cart but it's black too. Like in *Orpheus and Eurydice* where the Underworld People were all in black including her and the two others playing Cerberus the three-headed dog guarding the Gates of Hell. *Maybe this is help. Maybe I'm going to be saved!*

Pa-clop! Pa-clop! PA-CLOP!

She loves the sound of horseshoes on stone. It's coming right along toward her. She wishes she had a carrot or a peppermint like she gives Velcro at Mary's Farm. She wishes she had something to give him, to make friends and be saved by the man on the cart. The horse starts to turn a corner, away. She runs.

"Hey! Nee how nee how! Neeeeee HOWWWW!"

The horse's ears turn but the man keeps on going like he doesn't hear her. She runs, gets closer and closer, and goes around in front, stopping the horse so the man can't miss her.

"Nee how!" she says as loud as she can. It echoes off the stone walls of the street.

The man is looking. He nods, says, "Nee how." His voice is wobbly and loud.

"I'm lost!"

He nods and says something in Chinese.

"Help me!"

Another nod, and a smile. He's pushing his big straw nipple hat up on the back of his head and the line above where it was is all white, where the sun never shines. She wonders why his face and hands are all black and then realizes that it's because the cart is piled high with huge lumps of coal. The coal lumps glisten wet in the slant of dawn. That's why the man and horse and cart and everything are totally black—the coal dust coats everything. He sells coal. Maybe if she goes with him he can take her to where there are other people. What else can she say to him?

"Pizza Hut?" He seems hard of hearing. "*Pizza Hut!*" He smiles, and says nothing. He doesn't know Pizza Hut but why would he, he's just a coal guy. "*Burger King!?*" Nothing. Doesn't like burgers. "*Dripping Water Cave Hotel!?*" Another smile, but this time maybe he seems to understand. "Meg-oh-ran!" *Point to yourself.* "*Meg-oh-ran!*"

He definitely nods and smiles and motions for her to come up and sit beside him. She hesitates. Never take a ride from a stranger never *ever* take a ride from a stranger.

But she's totally lost and there's nobody else and maybe he can at least take her to the main street where people who speak English are. She tries one more time.

"MEG-OH-RAN?" He blinks his eyes—the lids are white!—and nods, and gets down from the pile of coal he's sitting on, and gestures for her to get up and in. As if he'll help her. Does that mean he knows she's American? "MEG-OH-RAN!"

"Ming-wan," he says. She hesitates to go with him. But there's nobody else. She goes to the horse and pats it. It is thin and tired looking and the harness is old and worn and a big heavy yoke and just old leather and rope tied here and there. Not a happy horse, no. What's he doing now?

The coal man is walking over to the side of the street—and he's limping.

Like in our Delores's Book of Greek Myths *it said, "He walked like a flickering flame." Who was it oh yeah Hephaestus the god of fires and black-*

smiths when Zeus threw him off Mount Olympus he fell for a whole day that's how high it was and crashed and forever after "he walked like a flickering flame."

Now he's sorting through a trash pile and he's picking up something, looking carefully at it. He's coming back and holding out one of the things to her—rotten vegetables. He feeds them to his horse. Again, more insistently, he gestures for her to get up on the wagon.

She looks into his eyes and sees two little nuggets of coal gleaming back at her. Terrified, she backs away. He limps toward her. She starts to run. She runs to the next twist of the narrow street, and looks back. He is standing, watching her. She runs on and on until she's out of breath, stops and looks back again. No sign of him. Her chest feels like it's on fire. She starts coughing and sneezing and, when she tries to get her breath, making a wheezing sound. She takes out a tissue and blows her nose—on the white tissue there are two circles of black soot! Gradually she calms down, breathes more easily.

She looks around, and finds that she is standing at the entrance to what seems like a park. The sun is now bright, melting the killer mist of this scary night. She sighs with relief.

A man carrying a bird in a cage, a red macaw, passes her and goes into the park. She takes a few steps after, and is amazed at the expanse opening up before her, and the numbers of Chinese people already in the park at dawn, doing exercises and martial arts with swords and ballroom dancing and meditations and playing soccer and badminton and basketball. Someone there must know English. She follows the man with the bird into the park.

He goes to the Men-With-Birds-In-Cages section. In a little grove are about twenty men and all different kinds of birds, their cages swinging from low branches of trees. The men smoke and talk, and they look happy. Anyone who loves birds can't be all bad. Maybe one of them will speak enough English.

"Nee how, nee how," she says to the bird guys, and they say the same back and start talking to her in Chinese. She makes gestures with her hands that she doesn't understand, and points to herself and says, "Meg-oh-ran, megoran, do you speak English?"

"Megoran!" they say, and laugh, and start to show her their birds.

21

Pep sits alone in the hotel room. The Chinese police have come and gone, taking Rhett with them. Clio is out walking the streets with the sign Rhett made, while he waits in the room for any news. The police questioned Rhett harshly. They spoke no English and didn't allow Rhett to say anything to Pep and Clio. They examined the room, the bed, the bathroom, the door lock— but seemed to find nothing. Then they sat Rhett down and grilled him. It was obvious they were not happy that Rhett had brought three Americans to this restricted zone. Suddenly they got up, and without a word hauled Rhett away. Before the police arrived, Rhett warned Pep and Clio that if they took him away, he would not be able to come back. He would need some money to bribe them to let him go—to just warn him and put him on a train back to Changsha. Pep gave him as much cash as he could.

He can't stand it. He has to do something. For some strange reason, he finds himself staring into the bathroom mirror, shaving. He soaps his cheeks, his chin, his neck, and when the first scent of the almond oil lather hits him he stops, stunned as if he's been hit by a plank, remembering how Katie loves to snuggle with him when he wakes her up in the morning and the scent of almond oil is fresh, how she says, "It's my favorite scent in the world and not just because it's almond but because it's *you*, my daddy!" He watches his face crumple and distort into tears and he drops the brush in the sink and holds on for dear life. *For dear life, yes.*

○ ○ ○

Clio has wandered the streets around the hotel for hours. She carries the sign written in Chinese. It shows a photo of Katie, and her name and "THE DRIPPING WATER CAVE HOTEL" and the phone number and their names and "Big Reward $100." The Chinese sometimes stop and stare and smile and go on. She searches their faces as if for clues or complicity and finds nothing.

Over and over like a dirge comes the thought, *China has taken her back.*

"Oww!" she cries out as a man jostles her hard, almost knocking her down. Reflexively she lashes out, slamming her arm awkwardly into his neck as he passes. He stops cold—it's a hard hit, even for China—and stares at her with puzzlement, a thin, rough man dressed in a cheap short-sleeved shirt and smoking a cigarette. She stares back, hoping he'll do something else. He laughs and laughs. Soon a crowd stops and stares, pointing at this crazy Westerner. She pushes her way through the crowd and hurries down an alley off the main street.

Just walk.

She learned walking meditation from reading Thich Nhat Hanh. With each step, count your breaths: three breaths in, four breaths out. Breathing in, think, *Calm*, breathing out, *Smile*. Place each foot with the awareness that the whole earth is underneath. Walking on lotus pads, greeting the earth rising up to meet you.

Breathing in, calm. Breathing out, smile. Can't.

She holds the sign in front of her so everyone can see it, and after a while she finds herself walking not to a Buddhist mantra but to the Episcopal *The Lord be with you. And also with you. Lift up your hearts. We lift them up to the Lord. Let us give thanks to the Lord our God. It is right to give our thanks and praise. It is truly right, and good and joyful, to give you thanks, all-holy God, source of life and fountain of mercy. Give her back to me, and I'll do anything . . .*

The crowd flows past. Most glance at her photo with its message; many of them smile. Trucks and buses and bicycles and motorbikes shred the air, stir the hellish heat, the dust, the dirt, the coal-throated evil. She is lost. *China has taken her back.*

○ ○ ○

She has no idea how long she has been walking. She turns a corner and sees "DRIPPING WATER CAVE HOTEL." There is a finality to the sign, an accusation of incredible negligence, of the most profound failure of any mother, the failure to take care of your child. As if the sign will mark the place where she lost her daughter. She stands for a long time that is no time, tears in her eyes. She watches dully as one of the frantic, crippled buses puts on its brakes and shrieks to a stop at the end of the block. Oily black fumes blast out from a tailpipe. Out of the bus stream the Chinese, and one of them, a tall, thin young man in a white shirt and tie, stops after he gets out and turns around and reaches back into the bus for something and that something is—

"Katie!"

Clio starts to run, elbowing people out of her way and, when that doesn't work, jumping off the curb into the street and screaming at the top of her voice her daughter's name over and over, but Katie doesn't hear her and isn't looking and there's not only the man in the tie but a young woman in a flamingo-pink dress and Clio keeps running and shouting, "KatieKa-tieKatieKatie!" and finally Katie hears and sees and she's shouting too and running in a frantic yet graceful way toward her she's alive she's alive in her arms heart-searing joy.

○ ○ ○

Hugging her with all her might, feeling that little thin body rock-solid against her own, Clio sobs and sobs and tries to stop and cannot, and can't even speak for the longest time. Katie is crying her heart out and bur-rowing into Clio's breast. Finally, when the rough, fierce tears of joy have softened to a glow of relief, Clio looks her up and down and asks, in a shaky voice, "Are you all right?"

"Yeah."

"You're filthy—are you sure you're okay?"

"Yes."

"What happened?"

"I got lost. I went out of the hotel and I was just waiting and I followed a dog—big mistake!—and I got *so* lost? But these kids"—she points to the two young Chinese—"they found me. They speak English and are really nice. I told them 'Dripping Cave Hotel' and they said, 'You mean Dripping *Water* Cave Hotel?' And I said yeah, and they took me back here on the bus—on two buses actually."

Clio turns to the boy and girl. "Introduce me, dear."

"Mom, this is Leston, and this is Happy."

"Good morning, Mrs. Macy," Leston says, taking her hand.

"Good morning, Leston." His handshake is watery.

"Good morning, Mrs. Macy," says Happy, also taking Clio's hand.

"Good morning. Thank you so much for finding our daughter and bringing her back to us. We were so worried, you can't imagine!"

"It was very scared, yes?" Happy asks. "He is lost?"

Clio nods. "You just left the hotel on your own?"

"Yeah."

"But why?"

Katie hesitates. "I . . . I'll tell you and Dad together, okay? Where is he?"

"In the hotel, waiting—come on, let's go." She turns to Leston and Happy, thinking they deserve a reward but not having any money to give them. "Please, will you come into the hotel and meet my husband?"

"Thank you. We have to go back to learning for school. It is a far a way. Two buses under a far distance. We are welcome to thank you."

"Come meet Pep. Come into the hotel—you're late already, come."

They smile, and follow. Clio stops to look again, deeply, at Katie, and then, her arm around her, walks on. Leston and Happy go on ahead.

They enter the Dripping Water Cave Hotel. The desk clerk sees them and smiles. The elevator takes a long time.

They knock on the door. Pep opens it at once. "Katie!" She buries herself into his chest, and he starts to cry. His sobs come out in weird coughs. The three of them are in a tight hug together, crying.

Finally Katie pulls away and looks up at his face. "Dad, you sound like Cinnamon throwing up."

They laugh through their tears. "But he's a cute pup, isn't he?" Pep says.

"You *always* say that, Dad!"

Pep feels like he has been brought back from the dead. He breathes out a long, trembling sigh, the tension riding on it out, away, gone. *Thank God.*

Katie again nestles into him, into the fresh scents of almond oil soap and beer, the familiar scents of her dad. When Katie pulls away there's an imprint of her two cheeks in black soot on Pep's white shirt.

"I want to give Leston and Happy a reward," Clio says.

"Absolutely! Let me get my wallet!" He comes back and takes out as many yuan as he can find and offers the money to them.

"Oh no," Leston says, "we cannot give money to you. No."

"Sure you can. This is what we do in America when someone does a good deed."

"No," says Happy, "we do not give money. It is good deed, it is very triumph yes?"

"Well, let us give you something anyway, to remember us by."

They ransack the room for gifts, wanting to give them *everything*!— and find a deck of playing cards featuring Goofy, Mickey, and Donald, a Rotary International pin, two photos of Katie and Cinnamon, Pep's copy of Ben Hogan's *Power Golf* and Clio's copy of Thich Nhat Hanh's *Being Peace* and—to Pep and Clio's surprise—Katie's *Harry Potter and the Goblet of Fire.* They hold out these presents for the two Samaritans to choose from. Each takes a photo. Leston takes the Disney playing cards, the golf book, and the Rotary International pin. Happy spots the *Harry Potter,* and screeches. *Being Peace* is remaindered. They exchange contact information, say goodbye.

The Macys sit together on one of the beds, their arms around each other.

"Are you sure you are okay, darling?" Clio asks.

"Yeah, I am."

"Nothing, um, happened to hurt you?"

"Nope. I'm okay. Just a little dirty." She yawns, and the yawn is contagious. Pep yawns too, then Clio. They laugh through their yawns.

"But what happened?" Pep says.

"I set my Baby-G for three and ran away, and I was gonna come back at five, but I got lost, really, really lost! It was dark, and lonely, and I was in all these wind-ey streets like a maze and then I got *so* scared I like panicked?" She feels like she'll cry and tries not to by keeping on talking but then out it all comes, crying and talking all at once. "I missed you *so* much!" They hold her tight, and finally she stops. Pep gives them all Kleenex from his left pocket. All blow their noses. "I'm sorry, really, really sorry."

"But why . . ." Clio starts to say, and then gets it, and see that Pep gets it too.

"Oh my God," Pep says.

"You didn't figure it out?" Katie asks, surprised.

"You did this so we'd miss our train?" Clio says.

"So that then we'd have to stay, and then you'd agree to go find my birth mom—I had to do *something*!" They're staring at her like they've seen a ghost. "But then I got so lost, like for hours! You musta gone crazy not knowing."

"We *were* going crazy," Pep says. "We were afraid of the worst."

"Yeah, me too. I was mad because you didn't do what I wanted, and I did a dumb thing."

They sit quietly with each other. Over and over again Katie looks at each of them in turn, and they at her, as if drinking in all the life in each other's eyes.

"But you know," Katie goes on, "something happened, I mean inside me." She fidgets between them, and then gets up and walks to the cot, picks up Shirty, and stands facing them, running the soft cloth through her palm with the fingers of a hand. "When I was just really lonely, before I got really scared? And I like imagined if I ever got back here what I'd say to you?"

"Go ahead," Pep says.

Katie hesitates. The old feeling of not wanting to be the center of attention comes up, of not wanting anyone—not even them—to stare at her. *Stop it, don't be scared, you have to say this you want to say it just say it.* She can't. She turns away, and holding Shirty she walks up and down the room with him until finally she can say what she promised herself she'd tell them if she ever saw them again. The words come out as if they were already spoken before she even thought of what they were, so that they sound fresh to her, and alive. "What I found out is that it *is* really scary out there and dangerous—*really*. And that you protect me from it all the time." She glances at Pep. "From the risk?"

"Exactly," Pep says. "You got it."

"But that you don't do it just to . . . um . . . to keep me back, like from growing?"

"Never. It's to keep you safe."

"Even maybe *too* safe?"

Pep smiles. "Maybe. We're wrong sometimes too, you know."

"I know. So I decided something." She takes a deep breath. "If you don't want to risk going to find my birth mom, that's okay with me. It's okay if you decide that. Because I want to thank you for taking like really good care of me?" She glances at each of them. Her mom has her hands clasped together over her heart, and is nodding slowly. Her dad is wide-eyed, his mouth open. "But there's one thing I never knew that you have to know."

Pep is amazed. *She's never been like this with us before. Astonishing.* He glances at Clio, sees his amazement mirrored in her eyes. He squeezes her hand. She squeezes back.

"Well, I always said that I wanted to find my birth mom, and that's true but it's not all. I don't just *want* to find her, I *need* to find her. And maybe *you* need to find her too. All of us, together?"

Clio has the urge to hold out her arms for Katie to come to her, but something stops her. Her daughter has changed. Not a child standing there, but—is it possible at ten?—a young woman. Tears come to her eyes again, tears of pride, tears of loss. *The loss of that four-month-old baby who*

I could almost hold in my hand. The loss of the wide-open child who shared everything with us. All the losses that nourish this luminous moment.

"Katie!" Pep says, "You grew up!"

"Not totally, Dad, but yeah, I think a lot."

PART THREE

Spring comes early to the gardens
Of the South, with dancing flowers
. . . . .
The willow leaves are long,
And really are curved like a girl's eyebrows.
—Ou Yang Hsiu, "Green Jade Plum Trees in Spring"
Song Dynasty, 10th–12th century

22

Sleep comes fitfully to her now. It is her hellish time of year. Her first thought upon awakening? *Five days ago was Chun's tenth birthday and in less than a month it will be the tenth anniversary of taking her to Changsha and abandoning her.*

Dawn is a relief. Her favorite time of day. The first sunlight hits the tops of the high white spruce and transforms to a russet glow. Clearing the eastern peaks, the dawn pours down through the tree trunks on a million splinters of hazy light. The forest is still, crisp, the air metallic, like the taste of a cold metal coin. The silence is that mysterious one of mountains— immense, dead, alive, expectant. A time for her to sit in silence, to listen to the dawn awakening the birds awakening the day.

She sits, following the movement of her breath, and when that fails, following the movement of her mind. *Busy mind. Always, busy mind.* She gets up, goes out, washes in the icy brook and hauls water for tea, and feeds goodnight cookies to the gentle, expectant deer, the dawn being their bedtime. Now it is time for calligraphy.

She unrolls a fresh sheet of rice paper on the long, smooth board she has fashioned and shellacked to a deep maroon, and then places the four black stream-polished stones that hold the paper in place. Often she awakens with an image of the day's four characters. The first strokes—not always now, but often—are each day's variant on the character for Chun, "Spring." This practice began three years ago in the long, lonely days and nights when she first found the abandoned hut on this, the shy side of the mountain. She started with drawings on scraps of paper. Not having practiced calligraphy since she left her mother and father to get married, at first she was hesitant and reluctant, unsure. It was a burden merely to get through one day, and then another. Like putting one foot ahead of another on a narrow log spanning a ravine. To do more was out of the question—such was the sorrow in her heart at abandoning not one daughter, but two. Xia she would see again; poor little Chun was gone. She thought often of killing herself, of going up to the highest peak of the mountain, Sacrifice Rock, and, like so many other souls crippled by abandonment, throwing herself off to her death. One winter day, when the streams were still icy and there was snow on the trail, she found herself standing there on the edge of that precipice for a long time. *To abandon your beloved is to abandon yourself.*

But something else happened. Rather than jump, she walked. At first she walked the trails on the mountain, and then she just walked, scratched and cut by the bushes and grasses and low-lying limbs and bruised by the slippery rocks and frozen at night and drenched during the day, as if saying to the world, "If by my wandering I die, it is my karma"—in fact saying, "I hope I come across one of those poisonous brown snakes that kill you before you know it." For a while stepping heavily, hoping to chance upon one and quickly die.

But she didn't die, and after a while, lost, weak from hunger and fatigue, her clothes in tatters and her face masked with scratches and dirt, she happened to circle close enough to a temple to be found by an old nun who was gathering kindling. In the nun's eyes she could see surprise at finding this wild . . . wild *thing*—human, but barely. Seeing in the nun's eyes a horror and disgust, despite her vow to avoid humans she fell down and cried out like a baby. She recalled her cheek lying against a smooth stone, and then something wet—blood? water?—and then she felt thin old arms around her head, pulling her head up from the rivulet of the stream she had fallen down into and placing her cheek on the rough grass of the bank and a word came into her mind, which began the salvage of her soul: *celery.*

The nun helped her back to the Elephant Temple where, with the two other nuns who lived there, she nursed her back to health. Three nuns only, for, ever since Mao, the Elephant Temple had been preserved as a tourist site, with only the three nuns and twenty monks, to keep things going, for show. The care of these kind women, after so many years of uncaring in her husband's family, touched her heart, and the *something else* began to happen.

Perhaps her silence appealed to them. They saw the worn jade Buddha around her neck, and took it as a sign. They invited her into their Buddhist practices: sitting in silence and following the movement of the breath and the mind, and walking meditation, and chanting. The *something else* arising from these Buddhist practices reminding her of those of her mother, whose chants were done so softly in the middle of the night in the kitchen so as not to be heard—but they were heard by her as her two sisters slept. One day, in gratitude, she showed the nuns her mother's little box of gods.

Like a muscle unused, her heart strengthened. Eating only vegetables cleansed her. Her job was hauling water. When the nuns tried to talk with her, their voices seemed to pierce her sealed vessel of sadness. She resented it, and remained silent. They wondered if she could make sounds. When they found out that she indeed could—they heard her talking to one of the tame monkeys, and to the trees—they saw it as a sign of her suffering that she did not.

One day, wandering far upstream on the wild mountain, she came to an abandoned small hut in the woods near a stream. Set against the mountain, it was one room, of rough planks and logs, with a wood bed and table. Although neglected for many years it was well made, solid as the rock it touched. It must have been there for countless years, for the beams were darkened and mossy from the rain and mist of the secluded site. Beside it in the cliff face was an abandoned cave. It was said to have been the cave of a hermit, a holy man. She claimed the hut and cave for her own, and told the nuns. It was so far into the woods, so far above the last sacred outlying structure of the home temple—the Dusk-Enjoying Pavilion—that the path to it had been overgrown by ferns and saplings and low brush, and could no longer be seen from any of the other cleared paths.

A refuge.

For almost three years she walked to and fro once each day, to her new task at the monastery. This new job, a job she asked them to give her—one of the rare times she spoke out loud, and the only time she asked for anything—was to sweep the stone path and the two hundred steps that started at the mouth of the trail coming up the mountain from below, and ended at the top of the steps, at the grand gate of the Elephant Temple. To keep the ancient bamboo grove lining the path clean and neat, and free of tourist litter. All visitors came up by this path. She grew to know every inch—every tree, leaf, stone, every ribbon of velvet moss. When the visitors passed by and left tracks on the path, she swept the path clear once again.

If you saw her walking to and from her hut each day you would think she was at best peculiar and at worst deluded, for she walked in a slow meditation, placing each foot with awareness, and each day taking different routes so as not to trample a more obvious path through the hungry jumble of the underbrush to her hut. She wanted no one to wander toward her unwanted. *I am a failure at being with human beings. I can't be with them anymore.*

Her loneliness began to turn to solitude, her despair to surrender. It didn't turn, no, but it *began* to turn. She realized this one day, in the way she broke the silence with the deer, for there was a slight lilt in her greeting, a slight acceptance of her plight: *I'm just a being too, in a new beginning.* She said it out loud to the deer, "I'm just a being too, in a new beginning."

All the deers' ears flicked up like flags. The big doe's eyes showed fear. It turned, ready to spring away. For a long moment it stood still, half there and half gone, its deer-spirit twisted between the past and the possible. And then it came back for the dawn's goodnight cookie, and as it took it from her hand she whispered as soothingly as possible, "I'm just a being too, in a new beginning."

New Beginning. The words startled her, for they were also the words for "Spring," and in that moment two urges surfaced with a clarity that was frightening in its nostalgia: the urge to do calligraphy, and the urge to try to find her lost child.

On the eighth anniversary of the day she had traveled to Changsha and left her baby in a pile of celery, she again took the train from Tienja to Changsha. She was determined to find out anything she could about what had happened to her baby. There she learned that the worst had happened— she had probably been adopted by white people from Europe or America, as far away on this big earth as her child could be. All hope was lost.

Despite this, the next year, driven by the same relentless need to relive her catastrophe, she tried to go again, but had an attack—finding herself breathless and panicked on the train. She got off, returned to Tienja, unburdened herself to Second Sister, knowing that it was finally over. Desolate, she went back to her mountain refuge.

Calligraphy was the only way she had found to bring her lost daughter back to her. At first the stories she told, over and over again in the five characters stepping down the paper, always began with "Chun." The first drawings were unadventurous. She merely tried to write the character for "Spring" with ease. Over and over she did what school children are taught to do, make the nine strokes in perfect order and style. And at first, rather than trying to create a story with the remaining four characters, she merely wrote "Chun" again and again. Each time she drew it, she recalled how her elementary school teacher had described it to the class:

First, the three strokes for the character for "three": 三

Next, the two strokes for the character for "person": 夫

Next, the four strokes for the character for "sun": 春

"Three people sitting in the sun," the teacher would say, "this means 'Spring'!"

Oh, how she and her young schoolmates in that one-room schoolhouse by the river had laughed at that, delighted by the way that a character tells a story from the real world. They couldn't wait to draw it!

The nuns of the Elephant Temple had taught her about mantras, magic chanted formulas that had the power to change things. They tried to teach her Buddhist mantras, but she did not respond—she had no need to chant words that seemed far from her heart and soul. *But this, this is my mantra, yes!*

As she made the character for "Chun" she would repeat to herself, "Three persons sitting in the sun—Spring, a new beginning . . . Three persons sitting in the sun—Spring, a new beginning . . ."

At first it was a small comfort. And then it became a great comfort.

After many months of just drawing "Chun," she began to fill in the other four characters in vertical order down the long run of paper.

At first she drew the aphorism that she had practiced as a girl—a girl of Chun's age—the calligraphy that had won her a prize:

Spring 春

Returns 歸

Flower 花

No

Fade

Her teacher said there were many ways to interpret this: "Spring comes and in the dark the plant comes to life," or "Whatever is alive will always bloom," or simply "Stillness and Aliveness, in profound harmony."

It was astonishing to her, the complexity and profundity behind these simple ink marks on a piece of rice paper. A skeleton for such imaginings! Best of all for her despair, it was totally absorbing, both in itself and as a vessel to her lost child, an artery to another heart that had once been her own and would never be other. Calligraphy became her world.

As the months passed, as memory turned to imagination, her strokes grew into a complex and willful attempt at simplicity, but not simplicity itself. It was infuriating to her, to see the mess she was always making. She tried new brushes, she tried better paper—mulberry paper in fact, a single sheet, brought all the way up the mountain by one of the porters, costing two weeks' pay. The harder she tried, the worse it got. She asked a monk who did calligraphy about that, and was told that *will* cannot work in calligraphy, rather that calligraphy *is*, and makes the essence of the person move, and in the movement in relationship, the character, like an unbidden ghost, *appears*. This was difficult for her. She thought back to the few childhood lessons taken from the strange old master in his hut on the river. He always smelled of jasmine water and seemed attached at the lips to his clay pipe and never seemed to eat. He grew more and more thin and his characters grew more and more full until one day his wife found him dead at his art, the long sheet of rice paper filled with a single stroke of the fattest brush in his collection, a single long, fat black character that was no character, no character at all, but any and all characters that anyone who wished could find in it. A stroke to begin from, contain in, break out of, to something else. She has thought about this stroke for the rest of her life, this message before dying.

"The character reflects the soul, the soul the character," her teacher said.

It has taken her three decades to start to understand that, and over a year of practice alone on this mountain with each journey of five characters down a rice paper sheet beginning with the character for "Chun." Each "Chun," she understands now, when viewed from a distance is a stark black measure of her soul, and when viewed so close up that each bristle of the brush appears is a measure of the struggle still raging within it. The views from the closest place in paper and brush are beyond herself, and the views from the farthest place across the little hut and even out the door into the air of the mountain are beyond herself—and all are views of herself, too. As in an ancient painting, where the artist is so dwarfed by the mountains and rivers that his figure is hard to find—until suddenly you see it, floating in thin air between the peaks. *The mineral ink of a pliant soul.*

Now she chants out loud:

"All of it is my soul, all of it is my not-soul.

"All of it is me, all of it is not-me.

"All of me is made of non-me elements, all of soul of non-soul elements.

"All of it is in Chun."

She smiles, thinking, *All of it is in Spring.*

It was only when she first understood this about her soul and her art that she made the first journey to find her lost daughter. Two years ago now, and she only found out that she had been taken away to the ends of the earth. Five days ago now it was her birthday. Last Monday, and it is now Saturday. She was ten.

She sighs, feels herself sinking once again, and gathers all that she has endured over these ten years to right herself.

This morning she has finished the day's "Chun," and has already looked deeply into it from near and far. But on this particular day her mind is still funneling around and around in a whirlpool like that below the waterfall upstream. *She is gone.*

Her heart strikes sorrow. Tears come rolling down.

But whatever has been learned comes blossoming up to meet the tears. Whatever has kept her going keeps her going now. She hangs the day's "Chun" up to dry—as if for the first time now seeing what has been written:

It is a simple "Chun." Simple strokes that are like the ancient carving on an oracle bone or a tortoise shell she once saw in a photograph. A seedling struggling for the light, strokes that have reversed the complexity of centuries, which evolved the nine-stroke character for "Spring" out of this elegant three. A simple "Chun" she has gotten back to, back to that single shoot struggling in darkness to find the light and grow toward the sun and blossom and give back seeds. Whatever she has learned and seen now in this day's simple character, she realizes that she has come to understand not only sorrow but love, not only depth but lightness, and so she is surprised to find herself saying out loud—to the lush pines and magnolias, to the stream and the fallen log spanning it, to the deer she has tamed who are curling into their beds nearby and to her playmates the erratic monkeys in the forests up the mountain—yes, breaking her silence, saying out loud:

"So? So, fancy lady, put on your plastic orange jacket and take your broom and go to work."

A blue jay appears, the sharp face reminding her of her old calligraphy teacher. He chatters at her. She chatters back at him in blue jay, and walks out of the clearing.

The low, tilted morning sunlight casts the black shadows of the pine tree trunks across the bed of ferns. In one moment the shadows seem to her like a ladder laid down toward the most heavenly heart of nature, and in the next moment they seem like lines on her dead mother's sallow, waxy brow, and in another moment like a mere calligraphy of the number three, counted over and over again in her path.

23

The beaten-up bus sways around the hairpin turns of the steep, narrow road and stumbles up onto a small field, a shallow bowl partway up Emei Shan, the towering Hundred Mile Mountain. Hardly hesitating, the bus then swerves around sharply so that it is pointing back to where it came from. The driver gestures for them to get out. Pep peers out the window and can't believe that after traveling for two days this is the right destination. He sees no cable car, no signs in English, nothing. Definitely not a tourist-friendly zone. It's the wrong place. He tries to argue, but the driver is adamant.

They get out. With a cough of oily exhaust and a spray of dust the bus is gone.

Emei Shan rises all around, up into the clouds. At one end of the field is a two-story concrete building with a single opening as large as a garage door, and several windows with iron bars. Dimly seen inside are white tiles, an open fire, and two men in white caps. Outside, a third man stands under a large, stained pink umbrella that shades an iron table. His hands are on his hips and he is staring at them hungrily. A red fire hydrant rises up nearby, tilted, as if suffering. They look around more carefully up into the surrounding mountains for the entrance to the cable cars. Seeing none, in sign language they try to get information from the men in the building. No, there is no cable car, definitely not. There is a trail, the entrance of which is at the far end of the field.

"This does not feel good," Pep says. "Rhett and Ming Tao were lying to us."

"Maybe," Clio says. "But they never said they were sure there was a cable car."

"But they *were* sure that it was a popular tourist zone, like Disney. This ain't Disney." They look at each other—the unspoken goes back and forth between them: *If they lied about this, maybe they've lied about everything and then what the hell are we doing here?*

"There's the sign for the trail, guys," Katie says. "Let's go."

Clio's guidebook says that the path up to the Elephant Temple is winding, steep, and rises almost two thousand feet. At first the incline is gradual. The path, though ancient, is well marked, with stone steps chiseled into the mountain. Starting out at well over four thousand feet, they hike only an hour over an increasingly steep path before they have to stop. They sit, panting like puppies chasing their breath, unable to quite catch it. Pep wonders, at what altitude do you have to worry about altitude sickness?

A long line of Chinese men starts coming down the mountain toward them. They wear thin-soled rope sandals, either long pants with the legs rolled up or shorts, and polo shirts or singlets. They seem emaciated, without an ounce of extra fat. Wiry. Their calf and thigh muscles bulge, strung to bone with tendons that look like guy-wires. Most are smoking.

Each has a four-foot-tall wooden carrying harness on his back from which dangles a half-gallon plastic water bottle and a sweat rag. The harnesses are empty. Clearly they have carried their loads of supplies several thousand feet up the trail to the temple, and now they are coming back down.

Seeing Westerners is an obvious rarity for them. They seem cheerful and curious, and ask Katie questions. Through sign language Clio conveys that they are going up the mountain to the Elephant Temple, and tries to ask how far it is. Several of the men indicate that it is far, and a hard climb. They offer to carry each of them up, for a price. Clio is astonished—these little men carry them up? How? On their backs. A startling idea, which Katie pronounces "Gross!" They decline, and go on.

After another hour or so on the trail, Pep and Katie, in the lead, find themselves at a clearing on the banks of a stream. A shelf of rock reaches out into a natural eddy of the water, a deep pool. Rocks pop up all around, a seating arrangement. Pines, larch, immense rhododendrons in red, purple, pink, and white, and a gathering of giant azalea shelter the glade. The afternoon sun seems caught between hot and easing. Hanging from a tree are a few tin ladles. The grotto is of an altitude to discourage serious insects. The only litter is cigarette butts. Pep cracks the seal on a fresh bottle of water and hands it to Katie. It isn't cold, but it is safe, and both of them sigh contentedly. Clio arrives and sits next to Katie on the natural stone seat. Pep goes upstream a little to wash his face.

Katie sits there picking at her fingers—a bad habit Clio has tried to stop, using umpteen strategies gleaned from the good doctor Orville Rose and a book called *How To Stop Your Child Picking*, with no effect. She vows not to say anything now. Katie keeps on picking. She can't stand it. "Please, sweetie, don't pick, okay?"

"I'm thinking about your birthday before we left home. How old were you?"

They had celebrated in Columbia with dinner at Gourmet Restaurant, a brand-new place between the hospital and the cemetery. "I was fifty-one."

"So when I'm twenty you'll be sixty-one and when I'm thirty you'll be seventy-one and when I'm forty you'll be eighty-one! And fifty, ninety-one!"

"That's right, but—but I'm—"

"I mean if I get married when I'm thirty-five you'll be . . . what?"

"Seventy-six," Clio says, she too feeling appalled. What a sad, awful image.

Katie does some counting on her fingers. "And if I adopt a baby you could be like eighty?" Clio nods. "Why did you wait so long to adopt me?"

"We told you—we didn't meet each other until we were older, and then we tried for a while to have a biological baby, and as soon as we could after that we—"

"You're not going to die, Mom, I mean before some of this, are you?"

"Are you worried about that, dear?"

"Yeah, you're old and Daddy's older even than you and I'm thinking you might die, you *both* might die, and then you'd never get to see me married or become a mother?" She glances up at Clio, and looks away again, picking. And then, after a sad, harsh sigh, she says, "You're older than *any* of my friends' parents or any in China Culture Camp, and if you die soon, who's gonna take care of me?"

In Katie's eyes Clio sees a terrible vulnerability—it always makes her think of Katie's abandonment. Yet in that same vulnerability is a steely focus that Katie's always had, calling her and Pep to be *real*. Abandoned, yes, but also found. "It's scary, it really is, and not just for you but for us. But Daddy and I are in good health—you don't have to worry—"

"I *am* worried, Mom." She falls silent and looks past Clio, as if to something else.

Clio recalls the only other time she has ever seen Katie this way. She must have been about three. Pep and she had just finished singing and reading to her; had put her into her crib. "Goodnight, dear, love you." Usually Katie would have said, "Love you too," and gone right to sleep. But that night she just lay there and looked up at them, and asked, "Does *everybody* die?" Startled, they looked at each other. Clio thought to lie, but she could see that Katie had already seen her hesitation and knew her answer. "Yes, dear, you live a long time, a long, long time hopefully, and then you die." "Am *I* going to die?" Again she hesitated. Pep started to say, "You're really young, honey, and"—but Clio put her arm on his and stopped him because in Katie's eyes she saw the realization, the first glimpse of her own mortality. As she watched, her baby's eyes got glassy. She saw that Katie *knew*. Clio reached down and picked her up but Katie didn't make a sound. The tears stopped. When they put her back down, she was calm. Her eyes were dry, but now she was looking past them, elsewhere.

Clio and Pep talked to her, sang to her, rocked her, and tried to get her to play, but she wouldn't. It was as if part of her had gone missing. Clio held her, and Katie stayed that way for a long time in her arms, quiet, not crying, but with a—what?—yes, a first distance between daughter and mother, as if saying, *How could you do this to me, bring me into your world when I have to leave it, when I have to leave you! How? Why?* She stayed that way, quiet and still and somber, almost sorrowful, and distant, until she fell asleep. It broke Clio's heart—Pep's too, he said.

"Yes," Clio says now, "I know how worried you are. It's the scariest thing in the world, to think of someone dying. We'll try to live a long time for you, dear, but if we die, we've arranged for you to be taken care of till you can take care of yourself."

"Who'll take care of me?"

"My sisters. Aunt Thalia and Aunt Faith."

"I don't want *them*—Aunt Thalia doesn't even call me my right name— she calls me 'Kate'—she's *retarded*! Aunt Faith's older than you! I want Carter and Sue."

"Do you really?"

"Yeah. They're really cool and they live close by and they let me stay up real late and sleep late and they have two *real* dogs—like Cinnamon—not *goldens*. Can I?"

"Sounds good to me, hon. I'm sure that Dad will agree, and we'll tell them when we get back. But why are you thinking about all this now?"

"'Cause of your birthday."

"And maybe because we might meet your birth mom soon?"

"Maybe, yeah."

○ ○ ○

It is the last slip of afternoon by the time they emerge from the tunnel of thick, tall trees onto an open terrace. The terrace is under construction, stone being chiseled from the mountain. Tripods of bamboo poles hold pulleys and ropes for lifting. In a pit of muddy earth below, a dozen barefoot men in an assortment of faded shirts and long pants are digging. They haul dirt up to the terrace in woven wicker baskets with open tongues, two baskets per carrying pole across their shoulders, dump it, and then walk back down into the pit, their empty baskets dangling, tongue-side down, as if in supplication. From a different direction two men, a carrying pole sagging between them, are struggling valiantly to move a coffin-sized chunk of red stone across the terrace to its place in the scheme of things.

When they see the Macys, they stop and stare and, laughing loudly, call out to Katie. The Macys—even Katie—wave back at them and offer up Nee hows. Clio's guidebook says that a paved path leads along to a final two-hundred-step stairway up to the Elephant Temple. Sure enough, they spot a path of square concrete stones snaking around between tree trunks, leading away on level ground.

"This is it," Clio says. She looks up the narrow path. It tunnels through a grove of old bamboo. The trunks are thick and dark green. Her eyes are led up the lattice of stalks to the feathery tops, soaring high above, caressing the breeze. "Isn't this divine?"

"Wonderful!" Pep says, starting on ahead. "Lush green lush green . . ."

Clio walks behind Pep, with her arm around Katie's shoulders. A great old eucalyptus rises at the edge of the path, leaning over it. Clio ducks to pass under it, holding on to the trunk to stay on the path. Katie, talking to her, walks upright under it. The trunk is worn to silk from many decades of human hands holding on.

A young Chinese woman wearing a bright orange plastic vest is sweeping the path. When she sees them coming, she stops. Pep passes her. As Clio draws near she notices the woman staring intently, first at Katie, then at her. Clio nods, and says, "Nee how." The woman says nothing. She looks again at Katie. The expression on her face is peculiar—Clio reads it as embarrassment, or even fear. They pass by.

24

There is a commotion at the mouth of the path. She turns to look.

The construction workers are laughing and chattering.

Soon a large white man comes up the path. He puts his hand on the trunk of the great leaning eucalyptus and, with care not to hit his head, ducks under and goes on. Behind him is a white woman, wearing shorts that go down to just above her knees, and a tan shirt with many pockets all over it. With her is a girl.

A Chinese girl. A Chinese girl who could be ten.

As she watches, her heart starts to strike hard in her chest. Her eyes are riveted to the Chinese girl. She holds the woman's hand. Her step is light, like a deer, easy and fluid. She and the woman are talking, and seem more caught up in each other than in the world around them. Xiao Lu understands then that the white woman is the girl's mother. The little girl is trying to get her mother to understand something, or agree to something, and waves her arms and nods her head. The girl, focused on the woman, doesn't notice the leaning eucalyptus and barely passes under it; the woman, at the last moment, ducks.

Could it be? Could Second Sister have found them?

She watches them approach. The stones of the path are narrow. There is only room for two people side by side. Over and over when people come up the path she steps off it, onto the packed dirt of the bamboo grove. Steps off it because they are tourists and she is a worker. Most people are Chinese. It is rare to have white people come here. The cable car will bring more white people.

They come closer. She is straining to see her more clearly, to find, in this girl, the baby she placed in the pile of celery ten years before. She is slender, graceful. She wears blue shorts and a bright-pink shirt and carries a yellow beaked cap with a chicken on it. Her long hair is tied back. And her face? Oval more than square, her lips could be *her* lips, her eyes *her* eyes—and look!—she smiles. Is it *her* smile?

Could be, yes. They are here now. They have come to this particular place at this particular time. Of all places this place; of all times this time. Has to be!

They are upon her, the mother and girl. She steps aside but watches them. The girl doesn't look at her. The mother glances at her and smiles and says something that maybe is "Ni hao" but sounds strange. She nods and says nothing and turns her eyes again to the girl, who is staring ahead and talking a foreign language.

They pass by. She sees the double crown, two whorls from which her hair flows.

Say something! Talk to them. Run up to them. Even if they are not them, the price of saying nothing is too high. It is better to be wrong. Shout out her name!

It is the moment she has waited for, ever since she turned away from that woman at the vegetable stand who was screaming, "Whose baby whose baby?" It is the moment she has waited for to undo the regret, the fierce, relentless guilt, the shame. It is finally, for someone whose heart had stopped fully beating ten years ago and who has lived for something in the future—for this very moment—it is finally that moment.

And in that moment something inside of her says no.

Do I want to do this? What will happen if I do this? I have a life now. I have a life that I can live. I have reached a level of peace. Why disturb that? Who am I to do this? Who am I to disturb these people, this child? It is all for me, me! I, I. Selfish woman! Selfish!

They are walking down the path. Their lives are whole. Let them go. Let *her* go.

But if she *is* her, she has come here to have her life disturbed. Not her, but them, they have come here not to disturb their lives, but to find their missing lives.

"Chwin?"

They keep walking. *Louder.*

"Chwin?"

If she turns, it is her. If not, not.

"Chwin-Chwin?"

The little girl turns. The mother turns. The father turns.

They stare at her. They stand absolutely still and stare at her.

As if in a dream she is floating lightly upon water, weighing nothing and lifted up onto the stones of the path and moving toward her baby.

The mother and father and child stand there as if they too are in the gossamer paralysis of a dream. She keeps walking toward them, and then something stops her. She puts her two hands flat on her belly, and stands there that way. She looks first at the child, and then at the woman. The woman's eyes get big and her hands fly to her face, cover her mouth. Not a sound comes out. She finds herself down on her knees, feels the harsh grit of the concrete stone on her skin as a caress. Down on her knees, looking into the eyes of her beloved lost one, she says, softly now, "Chun."

The girl looks terrified. The man pulls her closer to him, and the woman moves quickly to her and puts an arm around her shoulders. She wants to reach out her hands, her arms, to her child, she wants more than anything to hold her in her arms as she has imagined doing for all these years, but suddenly she feels a roaring in her ears that spins her around so that she feels she is falling, and she cannot hold out her arms, she cannot reach out. Shame fills her eyes with tears, shame for what she has done not only to this little girl but to these kind people, and she lowers her head and weeps. She has not wept like this since the day she left her, gave her up. The world around her dissolves. Nothing exists but shame.

They are speaking to her, the woman is speaking to her. She raises her head.

"Xiao Lu?"

Their eyes meet. She nods. The child is standing between the man and the woman, protected by both. On her knees, Xiao Lu is at eye level with the girl. Her eyes show fear.

"Chun, don't be afraid."

The man, standing next to the child, wipes his eyes, and then whispers something to her. The girl shakes her head no.

He gestures to her to get up. She does. They are all very tall. Even Chun is tall, almost as tall as she.

The man is holding out his hand.

She takes it. It is very large, fat and fleshy. His eyes are wet with tears. The woman holds out her hand. It too is large, but not fat, the skin buttery soft. For a moment the woman's eyes are wide open and bright, but then they veil, wet. Her face is calm, but she bites her lip.

She looks down at the girl, and she holds out her own hand.

The girl reaches out.

She takes her child's hand.

In the touch is the world.

25

In moments of overwhelm, Katie mostly reaches for her dad. He is almost always bigger than anyone else, and always solid—she can count on his being *there*. Now, as she takes this woman's hand she feels a tingle go through her like when you hit your funny bone but going up and down her whole body. She trembles. For a second things blur. She nestles her head into Pep's side and reaches her other arm around his thigh. He curls his big hand down around her shoulder to her back, and holds her tight. It helps. The tingling leaves her, and her eyes clear.

The Chinese woman's hand feels the same size as her own, but the skin is roughened, and her nails look worn. *And she's so small! Just a little taller than me! But her face isn't a kid's face. It's a lot older. Her tan cheeks and forehead have tiny squint lines like sun rays around her eyes, like she's outdoors a lot. As she's so thin—like she doesn't eat enough. Her hair is totally black, and cut short like a boy's—she's pretty, in a way, but she looks like she's been through the wringer, as Mom would say. Her eyes are like mine, and her lips too I think, kind of plump in her worried face. She seems shy, like me when I meet someone new. She's really crying—a lot!*

Katie feels her mother's arm press more tightly around her shoulder and looks up at her. Clio's eyes are pooling with tears, her lips trembling. And all of a sudden Katie is startled to feel her father's body shake, like a rock slipping suddenly out of place in a pile—a shudder—and she looks up at him and *he's* crying! He *never* cries.

Clio is feeling like everything is happening in slow motion. *This is it. No doubt now. This is she. And she's so young! The age our daughter should be. Katie by rights should be our grand daughter.* Xiao Lu has gone down on her knees in a crude but absolutely right gesture identifying Katie as the baby who came from her "tummy," and is weeping. Clio's own tears flow easily, in relief. Thinking, *This is, because that is. We are, because she is. Finally, now, a chance to understand.*

Pep is taking a closer look at her. She's poor, she sweeps up trash for a living. Despite her poverty she's fastidious. A good sign. Though her clothes are plain, they're clean. A collared shirt with fine blue stripes, sleeves rolled up above her wrists—strong wrists and hands—and brown sweatpants that loop around the soles of her feet, white socks. Well-worn clunky shoes with thin black rubber soles. The shoes are a strange color, a lime-green, matching the duct tape around her twig broom where the wad of reddish twigs meets the rough-hewn wooden handle. The once-bright-orange plastic vest that identifies menial workers all over the world. Her hair, cut short as a boy's, is almost stylish. He searches her face for his daughter's—*her* daughter's too! It stuns him, this *actuality. She is the daughter of both of us, all three of us. Not to mention William, good old fertile farmer Bill!* The Chinese woman's face is long and slender with lips and eyes like Katie's. Exquisite eyes, really, and full of feeling.

Pep feels Katie, who he is holding tight against him, tremble as she holds the hand of her birth mother. Seeing that touch, sensing all that is in that touch, cracks the enamel of his denial. A gritty warmth rises in his throat and rages into his sinuses. Katie looks up, having felt him shudder. She's puzzled, a little scared. He hugs her harder, whispers that it's okay. It's more than okay—he feels glad that Katie sees him crying. The myth in the family is that he never cries—and it's true he mostly breaks down when he's alone. In an instant he realizes that he doesn't want to always be the one with the dry eyes, the one unaffected, the he-man holding things together. *That too, sure—but not only that. Not always outside-tough.* He looks again down at Xiao Lu, still kneeling there but now with her reddened eyes raised to them, and he looks at Katie. Incredible, to actually find her.

Clio and Pep reach down to Xiao Lu, offer their hands to her, palms up. She puts her hands in theirs, and rises.

The four of them stand there awkwardly, wiping away tears, blowing noses on Pep's tissues. The Macys try out some basic English words, and realize that Xiao Lu understands nothing. They've got to find a translator, but they realize they don't even have a way of telling her where they are from.

"Anybody know the word for 'English'?" Clio asks.

"I'll try 'American,'" Katie says. Pointing to the three of them she says, "Megoran."

Xiao Lu has no idea what this is, except maybe their family name. She nods and smiles and points to herself, and says, "Li Xiao Lu."

Pep shakes his head, and points to each of them, and says, "Macy. Macy. Macy." Then, as if talking to an idiot, he says slowly, loudly, pointing to each, "Pep Macy. Clio Macy. Katie Macy—Katie Chun Macy."

Xiao Lu repeats this, "Pep Macy, Crio Macy, Katie Chun Macy." She feels good about getting this right, and she smiles.

"Good, good," Pep says. "Now." He points to each of the Macys, to all of the Macys as a group, and says, "Megoran." Xiao Lu wrinkles her brow.

"Try charades," Clio says.

"*You're* the whiz at charades, you do it."

Clio makes the gesture of pointing to herself, Pep and Katie, and then with one hand moving back and forth between them and Xiao Lu, and the other hand at her mouth she moves her thumb and fingers like a duck quacking.

Xiao Lu thinks that for some strange reason she is interested in ducks, and mirrors her gesture.

Clio smiles and shakes her head no, and then takes both hands and moves them out from her mouth in a gesture of speaking and says, slowly, "Meg-oh-ran?"

Now Xiao Lu is puzzled. She is getting that the duck is sending out a message called "Megoran." She shakes her head no, and says, "*Bu* megoran."

"We're sunk," Pep says.

"Hey, Dad, why don't we show her our passports? The visa is in Chinese right?"

"*Good* thinking." Pep takes out Katie's passport, shows Xiao Lu the great seal of the United States. Xiao Lu admires the photo of Katie, laughing. Then Pep shows her the visa stamp, written in both Chinese and English. As he does so, he is startled to see that their visas have expired that very day. *We are now illegal in China.* In the past, this would have floored him; now he is surprised at his reaction: *Big shit.*

Xiao Lu stares at Katie's visa, reading the Chinese—dates of entry and exit, days for each stay, and then a number that sends a shock through her, the date of her birth. It brings it all back, the birth, the month of horror, the trip to Changsha. She starts to feel ashamed, looking down past the little blue booklet to the ground. But then she understands where they come from, and says, "Mei guo ren!" They nod and laugh. Now she understands. They want to find someone who speaks Mei guo ren. *They want to talk with me—and how good it would be to talk with her, with them!* Suddenly she realizes that this is the reason for her silence ever since she came to the mountain, her isolation from people and her silence when she is with people. *If I could not talk with my lost child, I had nothing to talk about with anyone.*

Maybe one of the monks or nuns knows Mei guo ren. She gestures for them to go with her, along the path up to the temple, to see if someone up there can translate for them. They seem to understand, and wait for her to lead. She cannot lead, she has to sweep up after them all. Through gesture she makes them understand. They start to go, glancing back all the time as she sweeps up their trail. She smiles at them. She senses that they don't understand that this is not so much a job as a practice. That she is clearing the old path of human intrusion so that it can be a new beginning for the goddesses and gods. Usually she concentrates so wholly on her job that for a time she forgets her past, and can't imagine her future. This is new. For the first time she cannot concentrate. It is not easy to sweep or even walk, for her legs have gone wobbly, hardly in touch with the stone. Her mind is busy with questions and hopes, and her heart is full of memories and fears.

They climb the two hundred wide stone steps leading up to the Elephant Temple. The steps are steep, and ratchet out of sight—a hard climb. Above the horizon of the top step, only the peaks of the encircling mountain can be seen, and then the sky, full with the first russet of dusk. But if you could ask each of them about the steepness of the steps, the portent of the dark, even the beauty of that russet or the other scenery, each might say, "What effort, what portent, what scenery?" Each of them feels light, the climb not a matter of effort and portent but of challenge and seeking, like when you are hungry in a city and searching for a place to eat, you don't notice the passing crowds, the buses, the parks. From time to time one or another of them will stop, stare, and then smile and bow—a way of saying, *It's a miracle, this, our having found each other at last!*

They arrive at a great ancient moon gate, a capricious pink set in a fading orange-pastel wall. An aged monk, in robes that once might have been saffron but now have gone brown, stops them. One yuan each. Pep digs into his fanny pack.

Xiao Lu comes forward. "This is my daughter I was forced to give away ten years ago. Now she has found me again. These kind people have raised her. Please show them every courtesy. Thank you, Venerable Father." She sees, in the old monk's eyes, his surprise—not only that she has broken her habitual silence, or that she has left her sweeping early, but that she is a mother. Wordlessly, he motions them through.

She leads them through the first square of two small temples that store the centuries of wooden Buddhas and bodhisattvas, then up the steps of the second square of empty, neglected classrooms, and into the vast open courtyard of the Elephant Temple, its domed roof supported by four soaring, gleaming tree trunks. The front and back are open to the air, and in the center stands the white elephant atop which is the lotus with the golden Buddha. She stops and raises her eyes to the sky. Her ritual devotions are now, for the first time, freed from her burden of sorrow, freed for what she has longed for: to be *new*. Whenever she enters this place she stares up at the mountain and feels it shadowing the temple like the underbelly of a black dragon, the trees and bushes and flowers all around like its shed scales. Now her mind is whirring in turmoil and confusion, desperate to communicate with her child, hoping that one of the monks or nuns will know their language. She sees how wealthy these people are, and feels embarrassed at how poor she is. How their ten years with Chun have centered them in happiness, their wide round eyes filled with confidence and hope, while her ten years have leached out her heart. She sighs.

Now, even though they will think her even more strange, she must make her bows to the Buddha in the temple. As she passes the Elephant Bathing Pool she wishes she could tell Chun the story of how Pu Gong climbed the mountain and had a vision of a man riding a six-tusked white elephant, and above his head was a halo of colored light. Wishes she could sit beside Chun and tell how Pu Gong traveled to India and visited a Buddhist monk, who told him that the man on the white elephant was the bodhisattva Samantabhadra, protector of Hundred Mile Mountain, and told him to go back and build a temple there. The Elephant Bathing Pool is the exact spot where the bodhisattva landed and gave his elephant a bath, before settling in to forgo his own enlightenment to help others along the Eightfold Path, and to be the protector of the mountain. Chun would like this story. It hurts her not to be able to tell it—not only to her but also to Xia. With sadness she realizes that all she can do now is point to the pool, and then point to the open temple where they can see the statue of Pu Gong's white elephant, and wave her hand for them to follow her.

Again the man gestures that they need to find someone who can translate.

She cups her hand to her ear and indicates that they should listen, and they will hear the monks and nuns at prayer, the sound carrying from the Pure-Sound Pavilion, which is in the next courtyard, through the gate at the top of the winding steps. She points to his watch and tries to tell them that the monks and nuns are all at their dusk prayers now, and they will see them in about half an hour, for the evening meal. They listen, and nod—she thinks they have understood. Whether or not they have, she has no choice but to do her own devotions to the Buddha before she can do anything else on this sacred ground. She goes into the temple.

The Macys follow her. She points to the elephant, and then goes to the prayer cushions placed in front of it, and kneels down on one of them. She starts to pray, murmuring and bowing her head repeatedly to the divinity.

Clio is touched by her devotion. Xiao Lu puts it ahead of anything, even this. But why isn't she chanting with the others, with the *sangha* of monks and nuns? Why is she worshipping apart, alone? Is she part of the monastery, or not? Her sister said she was not at home with people—that she was "selfish." Living in the woods, alone.

But now, in the first lull from the shock of their meeting, Clio becomes aware of the temple. The flattened dome roof and four stupas at the corners give it a Tibetan feel, but the central arch and arched windows look almost Moorish, as does the inlaid tile work bordering each arch and facade. The chanting, guttural and harsh, sounds like the tapes of Tibetan prayer chants that Tulku, the Spook Rock janitor, played. She, Pep, and Katie walk into the temple. The elephant is life-size, cast in bronze and copper and enameled a gleaming white, with dark eyes, delicate lashes, six tusks, and a short trunk. It stands on four lotus pads, each the size of a child's plastic wading pool. The setting sun slips in and strikes a golden Buddha sitting in a silver lotus as large as a car on the pachyderm's back. Clio is awed by the sight. The angled rays burnish the Buddha a liquid, living amber, caressing each fold of his robe, each finger stopped still for two millennia in a classic *mudra*—one hand palm down on one of his crossed knees, the other raised with an index finger pointing up, in what Clio knows is benediction, but what Pep takes as a warning, and what Katie sees as a light bulb going off inside him, like he has a bright idea.

They walk around the railing that protects the statue. Looking at the elephant's backside, Clio notices that the hocks in back of the knees are worn smooth—clearly by human hands touching them, for luck. The centuries of touch have worn away the white enamel, and shining silver metal is revealed, as if of exposed bone.

"Can I rub it, Mom, for luck?"

"Good idea." Clio catches a glimpse of Xiao Lu, still murmuring and touching her forehead over and over to the ground. She feels a kinship with her, a point of contact, and thinks to join her. But something stops her. She feels that she herself has not been serious enough in her own spiritual practice, not devoted enough. A Yankee, with those stiff Hale genes. Dabbling in spirituality, never in real spirit. A suburban seeker, a dilettante. All of this overwhelms her, keeps her from joining Xiao Lu. All of this, but more. *But what?*

She feels a chill. A damp shadow is crawling down from the peaks, falling over the temple steps, and coating the stone, the rocks, the plants, and the sacred carvings with a dewy sheen that makes Clio apprehensive. She senses the mountain looming over them all, an immense, rough shape that seems ready to come to life in the near dark. She checks on Pep and Katie. He's sitting on a stone bench beside the little pool, and Katie is bent down, a stick in her hand, playing with a school of red and white carp. To Clio they both look vulnerable, and in some danger. Wherever her eye turns, there, above the interlocking temples of the monastery, is the mountain.

She shivers, and goes to Katie.

She seems fine, a twig in her hand, playing with the fish. When she's in touch with an animal, she's always fine. Clio sits beside Pep. He puts his big arm around her, holding her tight to him. She snuggles in. They sit in silence but for the monks' chanting, billowing up to fill the sails of the fleeing daylight, and the murmuring of Xiao Lu. The place, to her, seems to be caught in a time warp, ancient, the sound of a handul of voices in ragged unison chanting the prayers that have been chanted for two millennia in this decaying place, sending out songs of the spirit to float in the thick, damp air. Xiao Lu is a link to so much!

"Bare ruined choirs," Pep says, as if reading her mind. She smiles at him, and he holds her more tightly.

Xiao Lu finishes, and walks over to Katie, smiling. She kneels beside her at the pool and takes away the stick she has been using to chase the fish. Katie is surprised and doesn't understand. Xiao Lu tries to say that it is a sacred pool, and that you cannot play with the fish. Her child nods, gets up, and goes to sit next to the woman. To Xiao Lu she doesn't look happy, and she feels sorry for that. But it is a rule. Xiao Lu follows her and stands before the three of them. To disguise her turmoil, she smiles.

"I feel bad I did the wrong thing, with the fish," Katie says. "Sorry, Mom."

"I'm sure it's okay, dear, you didn't know."

"I have like a hundred questions, and I can't ask any."

"I know. It's really frustrating."

"I guess she feels that way too."

"I'll try again," Pep says, and through gesture asks about a translator.

Xiao Lu points toward the sound of chanting, which is growing even louder, echoing off the faces of the cliffs. Again she points to his watch and makes eating motions, pointing to the roof of a monastery building they can see above a wall, a moon gate of which opens to a garden. In fifteen minutes or so the prayers will end and everyone will go to dinner; the Macys can eat with them. Pep asks where they can sleep. She nods and points in the same direction as the dining hall.

During this, it's clear to Clio and Pep that Xiao Lu only has eyes for Katie. She rarely even looks at Pep and Clio, as if they are not there. Fascinated with her, she keeps touching her hand, her arm, her cheek, as if sounding a depth, to make sure that this child is real, and really here. She is acting giddy, even girlish, getting Katie to stand back-to-back with her to see who is taller—they are almost exactly the same height—comparing their hair, laughing when she sees, in the low rays of light, the blush of red in Katie's, and then pointing to the back of Katie's head, the same double whorl, which she indicates to Katie symbolizes her "big brain"—meaning wisdom. Then she takes her hand and runs with her to one of the two bronze incense holders standing as high as the two of them, and helps her light a stick of incense as large as a whisk broom and place it there. They race each other back to Clio and Pep. Both are laughing.

Katie asks Xiao Lu where she sleeps. She points back down to the series of courtyards and the gate and the forest, and then makes walking motions.

Suddenly Clio has an idea to help make contact. She takes out Ming Tao's directions—in Chinese, translated by Rhett—and spreads the piece of paper out on the bench.

Xiao Lu is startled—it's the sheet she gave to Ming Tao! She told Ming Tao that if, on one of her trips to Changsha, she found them, she was to give it to them and tell them that she wanted to see them. Somehow Second Sister *did* find her! Xiao Lu gestures to Clio for a pen. Clio hands her a Magic Marker she carries for Katie to draw with. Xiao Lu looks it over. Tilting the wedge tip she swiftly draws a map from the monastery to the Dusk-Enjoying Pavilion, and up along a stream and across a series of log bridges to a little house.

"I think she's saying, dear," Clio says, "that she lives in a house in the woods—just like Ming Tao told us."

"Mom, can you ask where the monkeys are? Tao said she loves animals."

"How can I do that, dear?"

"I'll do it," Pep says. "Xiao Lu?" He points to the map, wiggles his fingers along the path to the Dusk-Enjoying Pavilion, and then suddenly jumps, looks up, points high into a nearby tree, puts his hands down on the ground knuckles first and lumbers about and scratches under his arm and jumps and howls.

"Dad, stop!"

It is obvious to Xiao Lu that he is pretending that he has suddenly gone crazy. She laughs and makes eating gestures, thinking it's because he is hungry. He tries harder. She laughs harder, pointing to the chanting monks and making eating motions.

"I guess she doesn't know a joking monkey when she sees one," Pep says.

"Here, gimmee." Katie takes the map, turns it over, and carefully draws a picture of a monkey with a long tail, eating a banana. She can feel Xiao Lu sitting close to her. Their legs are touching, their heads close together. Her scent is like fresh earth and the eucalyptus soap her mom loves. Xiao Lu taps her shoulder, her neck, with a single finger. Katie wants to touch her hand to reassure her but can't bring herself to do it. She finishes the drawing and hands it to her.

Now Xiao Lu understands—the man was trying to imitate a monkey. She nods, holds the pen upright between thumb, index, and middle fingers, and with a series of rapid brushstrokes draws not one but three monkeys.

The Macys are astonished. With a few strokes she has captured not only the idea of a monkey, but a particular species—short arms and long legs and stumps of tails, their round, furry heads and faces giving them the look of curious kids, or wise old men. And each of the three monkeys is different, an individual with its own face and expression—one happy, one puzzled, one surprised. All done in an instant, without hesitation or correction, with an elegance of line and a deep sense of the animals.

Katie's mouth is open in surprise. In her wide grin, her braces catch the last light. Xiao Lu reads her appreciation, and smiles broadly. Then she looks at Katie's mouth, and tries to tap the metal of the braces with a finger. Katie pulls away and with a gesture asks, "Do you *know* these monkeys?" Xiao Lu nods. Katie asks, "Where are they?"

Xiao Lu tilts the Magic Marker on edge and draws a mountain peak and lacy trees, up a trail from the Dusk-Enjoying Pavilion, away from her house. She puts miniscule but clear suggestions of the three individual monkeys in the trees, and hands it back.

Katie makes hand motions for "Can we go there?"

Xiao Lu smiles broadly, delighted. She knows the monkeys well—has visited them often, wishing that she could bring her daughters there, to watch them play.

"*Ching*?" Katie says, placing her hands together. "*Ching-ching*?"

"What's that mean, honey?" Clio says, surprised that she's using a Chinese word.

"It means 'please.'" Xiao Lu is startled, and again smiles, and nods. "Great!" says Katie, and asks her, "Can we go tomorrow?"

Xiao Lu is puzzled. Katie makes a quick drawing of the sun going down, and then coming up again on the other side of the earth. Xiao Lu nods again.

Clio is surprised that Katie is so easily familiar with Xiao Lu—it's so unlike her. She glances at Pep. He is smiling, nodding. They have rarely seen Katie act this way with adults, except them. With kids she often shows an assertiveness, taking charge on playdates or on the play structure at school. But with adults she's always been shy. She'll hardly ever answer their questions, never initiate contact or conversation. Now she is, as if she's known Xiao Lu for years.

A lone gong sounds. Once, twice, and then a third time, each catching the echo off the mountains of the first, and then the second, and then the third, so that it devolves into a modulated chord that seems to arise in the high live stone itself.

A stream of brown-clad monks and then a few nuns flows out through the gateway above, ripples rapidly down the winding steps, and then switchbacks left through the gateway leading to dinner. Xiao Lu smiles and indicates to them to follow.

26

Picnic-type benches and tables are set end-to-end down the center of a cold, damp, high-ceilinged dining hall, able to seat a hundred or more. Perhaps a dozen or so monks and the few nuns are seated on the benches at the last two tables, waiting for the Macys and Xiao Lu to sit down so that everyone can eat.

Pep has read that the Buddhist monasteries were one of the "Four Olds" that Mao ordered to be destroyed. After the Cultural Revolution, on the Four Sacred Mountains—Emei Shan being one of them—many temples were rebuilt for the tourist industry, populated with token monks and nuns. They are free to practice Buddhism as long as there aren't too many of them and they don't try to proselytize. This monastery is not yet on the tourist map, and is still in decline. Following Xiao Lu to their places at a bench, Pep assesses the skeletal crew of monks and nuns that remains. All are elderly, and seem worn, much like their faded robes, which hang loosely on their spare, wrinkled frames. The robes are threadbare at the elbows, and patched. Their teeth are bad, their skin sallow. They seem barely capable of keeping the enterprise going—as if the nursing home residents are running the facility. Everything is dirty and forlorn and echoing with decay. The place is too big for the people in it. A ghost temple. And always in back of it, out there growing like the night over the temples, the black mountain.

"Kind of sad, isn't it?" Pep asks Clio.

"Yes, yes, it is. But I'm in awe of it. They've been doing this here, continuously through hell and high water, since the fourth century—almost two thousand years! Hats off to them. I only wish there were some young ones, who would carry it on."

As they walk in, the Macys see some of the monks and nuns pointing at Xiao Lu and Katie, gossiping among themselves. It is clear that everyone now knows this secret of Xiao Lu's life. The last ones to sit down, Xiao Lu and the Macys have to squeeze into the space between two of the nuns at one of the long picnic benches. Clio, Katie, and Xiao Lu slip in easily. Pep, last, has trouble fitting his big frame into the last single-person slot. He can get his first leg in okay, but when it comes to his second, it takes all his contorting to do so without hitting the neighboring monk in the back of the head with his foot. This is made more difficult by all eyes being fixed on this struggle, as if he's a living sutra—say, the Sutra of Human Clumsiness. He doesn't care all that much, for he's frantically trying to control his dirt phobia, all this encrusted gunk and current dust.

The nuns lean in toward Xiao Lu and whisper insistently to her. She seems to shrivel up, wrapping herself tightly in her vest, staring down at the empty bowl before her. Pep, Clio, and Katie are intensely aware of the change in her mood. Clearly she is embarrassed and on guard, and has no wish to relate to the nuns. She is stony in her silence, her withdrawal. The noise itself seems to bother her—she covers her ears and bows her head, as if she is trying to protect herself until she can escape.

Finally the hall falls silent. A small bell sings out.

Each monk and nun does a private meditation on his or her empty food bowl, moving lips in silent prayer. Finally the food is ladled out in wooden spoons from two king-sized steel pots.

Through gesture and his passport, Pep asks if anyone speaks English. Except for a few words—"yes," "no," "hello," "goodbye," "New York," "Nixon," "Wisconsin"—they do not. French or German? No. The Macys and Xiao Lu shake their heads—it is a tremendous disappointment, and dooms them to this sign-and-picture-drawing language. Pep then asks, through gesture, about a telephone. None. The bare bulbs dangling from cords from the ceiling mean electricity, and there's running water—but that's about it. Green tea is offered. They ask for bottled water. None. Coca-Cola or Sprite or any other bottled drink? Nothing.

"Well, Kate-zer, this is a first. If a place doesn't have Coke, it's officially designated as 'In the Middle of Nowhere.' In the old days, when they came to the end of the world as they knew it, they wrote, 'Here Bee Dragons,' and drew pictures of dragons. That's where we are. Dragon Country."

"So, dear, we have to be really careful about the water. You can either drink tea or water that's boiled and that we let cool."

"I know, Mom. It's okay."

The Macys are ravenous and try the food. It is a greasy stew with evidence of vegetables, but also of other things they cannot identify. The oil smells rancid.

"Incredibly salty!" Clio says.

"Whoa! Solid salt!" Pep says, mouth puckering. "Like eating a salt lick, yeah."

"I like it," Katie says, smiling broadly. "And look, they've got rice."

"I know," Clio says. "You want soy sauce, but there's no way to ask—"

"Jung yoo," Katie says. "Remember at Shalom Hunan they said it's called jung yoo?" She looks at Xiao Lu and mimes shaking a bottle and asks, "Jung yoo?"

"Jung yoo!" Xiao Lu says suddenly and loudly, laughing, covering her mouth with her hand as many of the Chinese women they've seen do. The monks and nuns look at Katie and point their chopsticks and laugh and say, "Jung yoo jung—"

Crack!—a sharp sound, from the end of the table. They jump. Silence.

The head monk, of great age and steely thinness. His long, lined face is crowned by shorn cotton-white hair like a dusting of snow, his chin adorned with a long, snowy goatee. He has slammed a wooden umbrella down on the wooden table. He shouts toward the kitchen. A tiny man in a spattered apron, beneath which are bare ankles and duck feet, runs in and puts a bottle of soy sauce in front of Katie.

"Shay shay," Katie says. She puts it on her rice.

Xiao Lu puts it on her rice, and even puts some in her stew. Katie follows suit.

Clio and Pep look at each other. From the very first, Katie has loved anything salty, and nothing sweet. While her friends snack on cookies and candies and sweet sugary sodas and birthday cakes with ice cream, Katie has always preferred potato chips and pretzels. So she has the taste buds of her Chinese mother.

Clio and Pep watch Xiao Lu eat. Like all Chinese, her head is down, the bowl is at her lips, and she shovels the mix of rice and stew into her mouth. She rarely looks up, and eats fast. The silence echoes with the slurps of the monks and nuns.

Pep tries not to look at the others eating, but from time to time in the cooling quiet he hears a sharp *crunch!* as a molar dispatches what at best is vegetable, at worst a lower life-form. He feels ill, and wolfs down his rice, as does Clio. Most of the monks and nuns eat slowly, chewing each bite carefully, clearly meditating on the food. Slowest of them all is the head monk. The others wait for him finish.

Suddenly he is done, and bows his head to his empty bowl. Through the windows high up under the curved eaves, rays of sunlight ride in, illuminating an army of hungry dust motes dancing their way down. In a movie,

Pep thinks, the sunbeams would fall upon this last table of the dying Buddhists, but no. They miss badly—one falls upon a neglected white porcelain appliance near the kitchen with a mangle on top, another on the filthy, pitted stone floor.

A small bell rings again. The senior monk swivels around on the bench, hawks, and spits on the floor. A few other monks partake of the ritual spit.

Pep is appalled, thinking, *TB*. They all have TB in these places and there's no shot for it—Orville Rose told him that. The new strains are untreatable, lethal.

The head monk, using his umbrella as a cane, walks toward the door. He places each foot, in once-white tennis shoes, on the stone as if the earth below, all the way through to America, feels the weight of his soles. His umbrella taps stone in time. The other monks fall in behind. Pep is still worrying about the risk of TB.

"Hop betwixt the gobs!" he says to Katie and Clio. "Attend to the phlegm!"

On tiptoe Pep leads them out. The monks' feet crunch gravel as they follow the sinuous garden path, and they walk on through the falling night toward a small temple, and disappear within. Soon there is the sound of another frail bell, and chanting.

They stand there in the misty dusk. Pep shivers. The place seems even more ominous, lonely, and cold. The sun is gone. As if a warm coverlet has been pulled off, the bone chill of the mountain surrounds them, and seeps in. Pep opens his arms to Katie and Clio, who cuddle in and under for warmth.

"Let's organize where we sleep," Clio says.

"I'll ask her," Katie says. "Xiao Lu?" She nods. Katie puts her hands under her head in the universal sign of sleeping, and asks, "Where can we sleep?"

Xiao Lu gestures for them to follow, and brings them to an aged nun who sits in the doorway of a room on the ground floor of the dormitory building. "Venerable Mother," she says, "this is my daughter Chun, whom I gave up ten years ago—"

"I know," she says, in an irritated tone, "everyone knows already."

"They need a place to sleep."

"Think I don't know that? I'll do it, don't worry."

Xiao Lu indicates that the nun will help, and that she will now say goodbye until morning. Pep indicates that they will escort her to the gate, and takes out his blue-laser flashlight and walks along with her, Clio and Katie following. He towers over her. *She's like a child—young enough to be our child. Katie our grandchild.*

The monks are still chanting, more softly than before, and more discordantly. The glow of a humming spotlight drapes the white elephant. The blue-white beam of Pep's flashlight swings here and there, bringing stones and walls into eerie relief.

They come to the massive pink moon gate in the front wall. A gatekeeper opens it. Pep hesitates, wondering whether to give Xiao Lu the flashlight. It is an ink-black night, the clouds obscuring any wedge of moon. He offers it to her. She shakes her head no and points to a wooden pole as tall as her, leaning against the door. It has a black blob on top.

Pep thinks she wants him to get it for her, and goes and tries to pick it up. He doesn't realize how heavy it is, and it tilts over and falls to the ground. Laughing, Xiao Lu bends and easily picks it up in one hand.

All the Macys are surprised—this is one strong woman.

Xiao Lu takes a matchbook from the pocket of her orange vest, lights a match, puts it to the top of the pole—it's a pine-pitch torch, alight.

Suddenly to Pep the flame and the pine-and-mist scent in the thick night air are a comfort, reminding him of Macy family summers in the Adirondacks, all canoes on silky, cold lakes and campfires and toasted marshmallows. The pine torch in one hand, Xiao Lu waves goodbye and walks lightly off down the steps, and then turns sharply into the woods.

They watch for a long while. At first the pine torch bobs along smoothly on what looks like a wide path, but then it disappears up onto the black haunch of the mountain. As they watch, it starts to flicker as the trees block the flame. And then it seems to lose weight, or energy, and weakens. Pep sees it as an uncertainty, a wavering marker of one lone human soul going home in the dark of a fierce wilderness, filled with snakes. *An uncertainty of whether one heartbeat will follow, in a civilized way, the last.*

○ ○ ○

In dim light filtering through a creaky wooden stairwell, the Macys—carrying quilts and cylindrical pillows filled with what Clio, from using similar *zafus*, is pretty sure are buckwheat shells—follow the nun slowly up three flights to a long, low room under the beams of the roof. Many narrow, wooden-framed beds are set out haphazardly. Dust is thick on the floor. Pep first, then Katie, starts sneezing. The nun turns on a bare bulb struggling at the end of a long wire. A dismal place, all cobwebs and mildew. At either end are two clouded windows.

"Yuck! Gross!" Katie says. "I can't sleep here."

"It's here or outside, hon," Clio says, swallowing her own revulsion at the filth. "We'll make the best of it and find a better place tomorrow. Come on—let's all pitch in and help—it'll be fun. Move the beds together."

For Pep, even to *touch* the beds is a challenge. He watches them try to move the bulky, rough beds, and finally helps. The nun smiles at their difficulty. Finally the beds are side by side in the middle of the room, quilts and pillows on each. They have been given three threadbare orange towels, which they place on the pillows.

With a gesture that is universal, Clio asks where the toilet is. They follow her outside to a place behind the dormitory, a long latrine on the edge of a ravine.

"I'm never going there," Katie proclaims. "I'll go in the woods!"

"Shay shay," Clio says, feigning delight and bowing.

The nun smiles, says something, and walks away. They force themselves to manage. Pep gives thanks that he doesn't have to squat.

The beds are bad, hard and irrevocable. The quilts feel damp and moldy. The buckwheat shells are the only comfort, molding themselves to the three heads staring up in the dark. They cannot bring the beds close enough together to touch each other, and Katie suggests putting the mattresses on the floor. The sound of scurrying things stops them. Katie, clutching Shirty, climbs in with Clio, and barely fits.

Silence. Clio and Pep wait for the Nightly Comment From Katie.

"I told you, Mom, didn't I?"

"What's that, dear?"

"That she'd recognize me."

"You were right."

"Now she's not a figment anymore."

"What's that?"

"Of my imagination. She's real."

"Very, Kate-zer, very," Pep says, and then, "Love you."

Katie yawns, and settles. "Love you two too."

"Call me if I need you," Clio whispers.

In the silence, the sounds from the mountain, looming unseen, close by on the other side of the wall and leaning in, intensify.

Pep hears a hoot, optimally a low-risk owl. And then a snuffling thing, at worst a bear, at best a panda. Rustling noises, and claws skittering over the black-tile roof—a squirrel, a rat? Rummaging through all the risks, he gives in to the fact that he'll never get to sleep in this distressing place, and falls asleep.

Clio lies awake, thinking of Xiao Lu. *What is she feeling right now, finding her daughter again? Is it what I myself felt when I was handed the same daughter three months after she abandoned her? No. I was handed a baby to keep; she is seeing her baby as someone else's child, to be abandoned by her all over again.* All at once Clio feels what it must be like, that ache in that heart. Her own heart speeds up. She tries to breathe herself down.

Why haven't I tried harder to engage her fully? Is it that she seems annoyed that I exist? How could she not? She wants to be alone with Katie. Still, why haven't I gone wholeheartedly into trying to make contact with her—why didn't I join her, bowing to the Buddha? It's hard not to see her as a stranger, foreign, other, but there was something else too. What was it?

The answer comes, and she shivers.

She does want her back.

◯ ◯ ◯

Her feet hardly need the torch to find the path home. For the first time she walks her path in something like happiness. Her lost daughter has come back. More beautiful than she ever could have imagined, almost like Second Sister. *Thank you for finding them, giving them my message.* Chun has grown tall; her face is the same face, her hair has the same tint of russet, the same double crown that means wisdom, the same eyes and lips. Very beautiful. Healthy and strong, more so for being given to them. *My flesh and blood.* Their *child?*

Now she is pacing around the Dusk-Enjoying Pavilion, built facing west on a level clearing at a site called Ox Heart Rock—named for the shape of a boulder perched on the edge of a waterfall, splitting the stream to fall in two cascades into a pool. Here the water sprays up into a mist. In her darkest times, the endless power of this torrent crashing against the endless strength of this rock—and the rainbows that sometimes gather in the rising mist—has given her hope. This place was here long before she was born, and will be here long after she dies. This, her life, is a single flicker of the spray, only endless in a single moment, as now, here, facing this stream. *The one pure and clean thing.*

Even when she was in the depth of despair at abandoning both her children, this place offered hope—that someday she would find the one she abandoned into the wide world, and bring her back to the one still there, Chun's own First Sister, little Xia.

Strange to see her as American. More strange to see that they are so old.

I wish that I could sleep with her on my breast tonight, and every night. I wish she could be mine again.

She feels such yearning that she stops pacing, leans on one of the decaying walls of the small Dusk-Enjoying Pavilion. The happiness of a moment ago has vanished and she is dizzy above the split waterfall. For the first time since she thought of killing herself on the mountain, she thinks of it again.

Usually, the deeper into the mountain she climbs, the farther from people and the nearer to her little hut and cave and animals, the lighter her heart feels. This night, the deeper she goes, the heavier her heart. It is as if she is leaving her baby all over again, hearing again the terrible cries—"Whose baby whose baby?"—and once again not being able to shout out, *"Mine!"*

27

Xiao Lu comes at six, just as the first light of dawn unrolls itself up over the edge of the mountain and spreads out like a comforter over the stones of the courtyard. Soon, fed by the summer sun, the light feels warm. Clio and Pep are perched, thawing out and yawning, on the edge of the carp pond, watching Katie and a nun perform incense rituals at one of the three-legged cast-iron vessels. It has been a rough night. None of them can remember ever being as cold. In the morning they ran bent double to and from the latrine, trying to clench up against the shivering to get warm— which only made the shivering worse, and made their legs shake and their teeth chatter. Late June, and they could see their breath in the air.

"I'm never sleeping there again!" Katie cried. "It's scary and gross and cold and there are smells that even Cinnamon would be a'scared of. I want a hotel!"

"There are no hotels on the mountain, dear."

"*What*? None?"

Luckily breakfast, a gruelish rice soup called *congee*, was—unlike the stringy pickles in clotted-blood-colored sauce and what might have been pork or that squirrel on the roof but had to be vegetables—*hot*.

Xiao Lu is dressed as before but without her orange vest, and carries a shoulder sack and a black umbrella. With a quick nod and smile to Pep and Clio, she goes straight to Katie and is soon grasping her own joss stick in two hands and waving it around, laughing like a girl.

"I keep feeling," Clio says to Pep, "that as of this morning our lives have changed, but nothing about it is clear."

"Agreed," Pep says. "Adding another mother ain't easy." She smiles, appreciating his lightness. "But look at her—she's so playful, seems so young—it's more like we're adding another kid."

"I *want* to embrace her, but . . ." Clio trails off. In her mind are all of the things Tao told them about Xiao Lu, things that cloud a fresh view of who she actually is now.

"Understood," Pep says. "Me too. Let's just try to stay open."

"Openhearted?"

"That too."

They set out, Xiao Lu leading, to the Joking Monkeys. She sets a fast pace, pointing out plants and birds to Katie, who is soon following close behind. Clio and Pep bring up the rear.

At first the path is gradual, stone steps carved into rock. As the forest thickens, stone gives way to mossy earth, winding ways among high pines, cedars, and old rhododendrons, their waxy, thick leaves looking to Clio like Elizabethan collars around pink blossoms as big as a baby's head. Camellias abound. The air is cool and thick with rising dew, carrying the heady scent of pine, earth, high-mountain air, and flutters of jasmine. Birds sing—even, once, the harsh calls of a nightingale. There is a sense of solidity—Clio thinks of a mantra of the Vietnamese monk Thich Nhat Hahn: *I am solid, like a mountain; I am fresh, I am free*—a sense that underneath them is a big core rock, and nothing bad can happen as long as they put the soles of their feet firmly upon it, one after the other. Yet as she watches Xiao Lu and Katie playing as much as walking on the path ahead, so lithe and spry compared to her and Pep, part of her feels the opposite—apprehensive, worn, and slight, and on the shadow side of middle-aged. Thank God for Pep. *Big and solid. Towering over all of us, especially Xiao Lu. Immoveable. The family mountain.*

The path borders a stream that thunders down around rocks and fallen tree trunks. A footstep often sinks into moss, sounding something damp and satisfying. Mists are everywhere, floating the morning, rising to eye level so the trail can be seen below but nothing above, until, in the next instant, the mist clears and they are in a tall grove of ancient sequoia. Up through the straight trunks Clio can see a congealing of mist to clouds, all puffy and moving fast toward the east, riding the big expectant sky.

Pep, out in the open air and away from the low-ceilinged rooms and vans, feels good, free. He starts to sing, "She'll be coming round the mountain when she—"

"Daddy, don't!" Katie cries out. "I told you not to. Not in front of *her!*"

Xiao Lu laughs and wags her finger at Katie—a "No, don't be disrespectful" wag. Katie laughs at this. Xiao Lu wags once more, and points her umbrella up, signaling "Move it out!" Clio and Pep look at each other.

"Super blunt," Pep says, "even if culturally determined."

Soon Xiao Lu stops. Smiling broadly, she points to a pile of poop that, in mime, she avers is that of a bear. Katie shows her delight. Xiao Lu bends close to the poop and picks through it assiduously with a stick to show what the bear ate. Seeds, small bones, and a few shreds of aluminum foil. Katie is loving this.

"Like in biology at school, Katie, isn't it?" Clio says. "Picking through the owl's nest?" Katie is too absorbed to answer. Clio shakes her head in frustration. She takes Pep aside, and whispers, "Honey, I . . . I have to tell you something?" He nods. "Last night I had a crazy thought—really scary. Out of all proportion?" He nods. "I thought, 'She *does* want her back'?"

He smiles, nods. "Not crazy at all, Clee, just not possible. Given everything, *of course* she'd want her back. How could she not? For her, we hardly exist—she wishes we didn't. What else *would* she wish? But that's all it is, and can be. End of story."

"Right. Of course. I'm overreacting. I just feel we have to be alert. Careful."

"Absolutely, and very." He smiles at her, takes her hands in his. "But put yourself in her shoes. To her this is a gift from the gods!"

They come to two logs set side by side across a hard-rushing stream. The logs are dry and level, the stream just below their feet. Xiao Lu skips across, Katie imitates her skipping, and Clio and Pep walk across. The path turns sharply up. The stream cleaves the rock more deeply. The next log bridge is higher up over a more threatening gorge. Despite the height, Xiao Lu skips easily across each time. Katie and Clio, enjoying the game now, follow her lead. Pep starts to feel uneasy.

Coming out at the third bridge, watching Xiao Lu playfully hop on one leg across, watching Katie mimic her and seeing Clio look down once and then not hop but place each foot carefully, Pep feels shaky inside. Easing up to the edge, he looks down. Big mistake. The stream is now a torrent, rushing over rocks fifty feet down—to Pep it seems suddenly a hundred. Spray blasts up from the collision of the water and the rock. The rough spray has wet the logs spanning the chasm. The three others are waiting for him on the other side. He freezes. He reasons with himself: *The logs are wide, wide as a sidewalk, and steady. They all did it, you can do it.* He steps out, and finds himself paralyzed with fear. For a second he can't make himself go on. He tries to make his foot move and can't. *Shit. A new phobia? Terrific.*

They are shouting to him from the other side. Xiao Lu skips back to him on light feet, her umbrella tapping playfully along. Laughing, she holds out her hand. He takes it—it feels like iron. This helps. Iron is what he needs. But it is awkward, she holding his hand and walking backward—it makes him even more frantic. He yells over the roar of the water for her to stop and gestures for her to give him both her hands. She tucks her umbrella under an arm and does so. He has to bend down to her level, which decreases the height over the logs, and makes him feel a little better. He can sense, through her hands, the strength of her arms, her legs, her whole wiry body, the *sureness* of it all, and tries to visualize her hands as two iron railings on either side.

Step by step, he makes it. Katie looks at him strangely, as if thinking, *What a wimp!* Clio cheers. Xiao Lu bends double with laughter, unsympathetic to his plight. It irritates him. Through gesture he asks, how many more of these before the monkeys? She raises a single finger—just one more.

The last bridge is even higher, and to him the logs seem like saplings. They slope up at a hefty angle. He thinks of the Nike slogan, "Just Do It," and starts walking across. But his body decides "Just Don't!" and balks, like a deer caught in headlights. Even taking Xiao Lu's hands seems dangerous. He feels too high up to balance, and drops to his hands and knees. He sees the embarrassment on Katie's face, but has no choice. The pounding of the stream on the boulders seems to engulf him, drowning out everything else. The logs are slippery from the spray, mirroring a slippage in his confidence. Finally, with Xiao Lu walking slowly in front and Clio walking slowly behind and Katie counting his crawling steps, he's across. He sits there, drenched in sweat, trembling. *Where the hell did this fear come from?*

"Why are you so scared of heights now, Dad?"

"Honey, I wish I knew. I never was before—well, except looking down from super tall buildings. But I think she said that's the last of 'em."

"Till we have to go back over them when we go—"

"Don't *say* that!"

"Sor-ree!"

The path turns away from the stream and walks easily, moss-soft and gradual. They go in silence through high cypress and eucalyptus. The trail, cradled in the fragrant trees and the fresh, ever-thickening mist, revives his spirits. The air is cool, with a slight breeze flowing like a stream through the rocks of the trees. They are balanced at the right temperature, the right exertion, the right levels of hunger and thirst. No one talks. As happens at such times, all, in their separate ways and to different extents, have not so much forgotten their fears and desires as come alive to how even their worst fears and desires are a small, accepted, and acceptable part of their awe. They sense the deep green of the ancient trees. Stillness, but for a splash of birdsong—sparrow and jay, the odd dove. Silence, seamless with sound. The lively quiet captivates.

They turn sharply up onto rocky ledge. The climb is steep. Xiao Lu glides up easily. Katie bounces up in a series of hopscotch jumps, but Clio and Pep have to hoist themselves up, taking the high steps one by one and creakily, palms on bent knees, grabbing the trunks of saplings. They come out upon an escarpment, a flat black shelf of rock that extends out ten yards or so to the edge of an open vista to the west. The drop down is significant. Pep feels a hit of terror, and grabs Clio's arm. Her hand is on Katie's shoulder to hold her safely back.

The only sound is of water falling hard against rock. Xiao Lu takes out the crude map she sketched the day before and points to the Dusk-Enjoying Pavilion. Then she turns and shows it to them—a small, open-sided, tile-roofed temple a few yards away, sitting on the edge of the cataract, with a clear view west. Katie pays it little attention, occupied with dragon-tail butterflies in a patch of lavender. Pep stares at one corner of the little temple, where a red-lacquered post has collapsed, bringing a section of the roof to an ominous sag. Rather than risk sitting under it, he lowers himself onto a rock ledge on the edge of the trail and closes his eyes.

Clio welcomes the distraction from the turmoil in her mind. She finds herself in an architectural/botanical heaven, finding this ancient temple in the woods. The pavilion is probably hundreds of years old, of perfect shape and design, and more authentic for its decay. Vines and bushes nibble at it, but it endures. The pavilion is placed perfectly to—yes—Enjoy the Dusk. In form it is like the Elephant Temple, but much smaller and more worn—too isolated to be destroyed by Mao's thugs, or now to be repaired. The red-lacquered posts and black-tile roof shaped in an exact hexagram, the central Tibetan stupa on top—Tang Dynasty. Around it the ancient, renewing bamboo soar to an astounding height—that of the matching white spruce—and there, lining the path, a cluster of ancient gingkoes, gnarled and weathered, immediate and prevailing for up to a thousand years.

She stands there. Despite the busy roar of the cataract, she feels caught in a stillness, like a bird caught in an empty pocket of the wind. She recalls a beloved poem Tulku gave her, by a nameless Chinese monk in the year 58, on his first journey to the sacred Emei, 'The Inner Mountain.' "I feel the mountain pushing up from below, I feel the spirit of the mountain flowing down from above. In the suffering and impermanence of life, the mountain is permanent and liberating. A mountain is unchanging. No one can take it away. A flood cannot take it, a fire cannot destroy it. The inner mountain is our spirit. Rather than build a spirit mountain, we build up envy and delusion—and mountains of anger. Our minds move too fast. "

When she comes out of her reverie, Katie is no longer at her side, and not in sight—*where is she?* She finally sees her among the trees, with Xiao Lu on the edge of the cliff. "Katie! Careful! Not so close! Come back." Clio rushes toward her.

"I'm not close to—"

"I said come back!"

Katie stands there, her hands down beside her body, palms out toward Clio, her head hanging, her eyes glaring. "What, Mom, *what*?"

Clio is reaching out to pull her back, but then notices what she couldn't see from where she was—they are not at all near the edge. Another ledge of black rock, a step down from the first, reaches out some ten yards farther.

Xiao Lu stands there staring at her, a puzzled, even contemptuous look on her face.

"All right," Clio says, putting an arm around Katie. She breathes deeply to calm herself. Rather than leading her away, she stands beside her, looking out. They are so high up that the ground below is obscured by fog or clouds. The sky is now all silvery fish scales, darkening over the mountains afloat in the west. She feels foolish at being distrustful—and yet . . .

They go back into the half-collapsed pavilion and sit on benches on its good side. Clio can see how cleverly the pavilion has been sited—for both the dusk panorama and the boulder splitting the cascade. Behind her she senses the sheer bulk of the morning mountain. The mist rises from the falls and joins with a gathering of low-lying clouds all around, obscuring the foothills and plain far below. She glances at Pep. He is holding on to an ancient, mossy wooden pillar. She takes his hand. Xiao Lu starts out onto the ledge over the falls. Katie gets up and heads after her.

"Wait!" Clio cries out. "Katie, please don't."

"Mom, come *on*. *She's* doing it."

"Kate-zer, it's a *no*!" Pep says. "It's a *risk*!"

"Please?"

"Exactly what part of 'no' don't you understand? Come back here."

"*Arrrrrrr!*" Katie twists herself around in frustration. As if each step is a humiliating defeat she has to resist and dramatize, she stomps back and sits down.

Xiao Lu is watching all this from the ledge. Why are they so afraid for her? They are very fearful. Very strange. They act like children toward her. Chun is always making a loud argument, always standing up in her selfishness. Xiao Lu was never so disrespectful of her elders, even if they accused her of being so—except her mother-in-law. But Chun is rich now, she has everything—just look at her shoes, her clothes, the watch she wears—she should know better. *I could teach her, if I had her alone and if we could share a language. I could teach her the language—it must be in her.* When she told Chun, with a laugh to show how serious she was, to show her parents more respect, she laughed in return, but didn't seem to understand.

After they have rested, Xiao Lu takes out the map and points again to the monkeys. Katie nods vigorously. Xiao Lu motions that she will now take them there. She turns abruptly and leads them away from the stream, and up. The path is steep, the footing more slippery in the floating mist, which, as they climb higher, gathers from time to time around them as fog. The man starts to breathe more heavily, and attempts to disguise it. She knows that he is terrified of the next bridge, and of going back over them all again. His chi is stuck, dammed up. He is so tall, the chi has trouble rising up to his brain.

It starts to drizzle. At first, in the humid and hot mid-morning, it is a relief. They all welcome the wash of clean, fresh water, cool on their heads, their faces.

The drizzle starts to thicken to rain. The sound of the large drops hitting the limbs and the leaves is a comfort.

The man steps into a clearing and removes his hat. He lets the rain hit his face and catches some for drinking. Xiao Lu notices a big bandage on the top of his head, black with dried blood. She smiles, asks him about it. He mimes bashing his head on a low beam. In sympathy, she laughs. The man, looking surprised at her laughter, does not laugh back, but scowls at her as if she has insulted him! Strange! He is crude, blunt, like a block of concrete. He doesn't see the subtlety of the different laughters.

The drops turn into steady light rain, and then into a downpour. The path becomes a streambed, the fat leaves of the rhodos and maples and spruce drenched, funneling the water down on them as they huddle underneath. In gusts of wind, the thick trunks of bamboo clatter—*Thwack! Thwack!*

Xiao Lu's umbrella is small, and only little Chun can get in under with her. She waits with them under the trees for the rain to stop. It does not. What a pleasure for her to stand so close to her girl! Her heart flutters like a bird in the cage of her chest, yearning to fly free. Their sides touch. Xiao Lu yearns to put her arm around her, but dares not. To draw her close, to hug her, would be heaven! She stands stiffly, on fire in the cool rain.

Soon they are soaked through, and chilled. The sky shows no sign that the rain will stop soon. The visitors talk among themselves. The woman is very quiet. She speaks in a way that seems calculated to soothe the man, but he growls at her. She snaps back at him. Chun says something to them, glancing at her, embarrassed at their arguing. The man smiles at Xiao Lu as if they've just had a family joke. He then speaks as the woman did at the beginning, in a tranquil manner. Xiao Lu wonders again at how fearful they all seem, the childish parents and the willful protected child. If they don't let Chun do anything by herself, she will never learn. The parents are not used to the hard work in life. Their hands are soft. They are not used to being out in the woods. They seem ignorant of trees, and wind and air, and water. Ignorant and fearful. How do they live? Into her mind come lines of a poem by Po Chu-I, "Passing by Tien-men Street":

> *A thousand carriages,*
> *ten thousand horsemen*
> *pass through the Nine Crossroads.*
>
> *and not one person*
> *turns his head*
> *to see the mountains.*

Now they seem to be consulting little Chun about what they should do. Is it possible? They will do whatever the child says?

Through yet another iteration of charades, Clio and Pep tell Xiao Lu that they want to turn back. They ask if there's a place to get dry and warm. She takes out the map. They huddle under the umbrella. It's gotten so dark that the man takes his blue-beam flashlight from his big-flower shirt. Xiao Lu traces a path from where they are—maybe halfway to the Joking-Monkey Zone—back to the Dusk-Enjoying Pavilion, and then not much farther down another path to her little hut. They smile and gesture for her to lead the way.

By now the trail is all water and mud. It seems a lot steeper than what they have climbed, and they step hard down on slippery rocks and roots, trying to find the next handhold on saplings and bushes, bamboo and vines. Their feet are soon soaked, and they feel like they're standing in little pools called shoes. Pep and Clio slip and fall several times, and are drenched and filthy.

Suddenly Katie calls out, "A snake!" Clio snatches her by the collar and catches her foot on a root and tumbles down upon her, both of them rolling off the trail into the tangled underbrush, shrieking and terrified that it's a deadly brown viper. Pep rushes to them, huddling in the bushes, staring.

Xiao Lu is standing on the path, leaning on her closed, upside-down umbrella jauntily. The rain pours down on her, a wet, Asian Charlie Chaplain. She is laughing.

Katie makes a motion of a sidewinding snake. Xiao Lu nods, smiles, and gestures to her feet. Pinned at the head by the crook of the umbrella handle is a three-foot-long black-and-yellow snake. Laughing, Xiao Lu bends down, finds a loose rock, and, with a single blow to the metal tip of the spine of the umbrella, cracks the snake's back. The body writhes in the moss, stops. Xiao Lu picks it up and offers it.

But Katie is distracted. "Hey, I cut my knee! Look! Blood!"

After a careful search, they find the tiniest scrape in the history of scraped knees.

"It's okay, darling. There—I've washed it off with rainwater."

"I need a Band-Aid!"

"It's nothing, Kate-zer, there's a tiny—"

"I want a *Band-Aid*!" She starts to cry.

"Okay, okay." Pep takes out a Band-Aid and tries to get it to stick to the wet knee. No luck. "Okay, honey bunny, the nice beautiful scrape will have to wait till you get dry." She starts to wail like a toddler, a real meltdown they haven't seen in years.

"I want to go home," she screams. "I want to go *ho-ohmmm*!"

"Now you're talking, kid," Pep bursts out. "Now you are *talkin'*!"

She catches herself. "I didn't mean *that*! Not home, a *hotel*. I want to go to a hotel!"

Pep shakes his head in frustration. "Fine. Whatever."

28

Back at the Dusk-Enjoying Pavilion the west wind has picked up and the temperature has dropped. The rain is turning to sleet and coming in almost horizontally. They all cover their exposed faces with their hands, and peer out at the trail. Xiao Lu takes a turn down into what looks like a stand of solid bamboo but conceals a neglected path they move through single file, and sometimes sideways. The leaves are rough and scratchy, the daylight subdued. From time to time, coming out into clearings, they can see that they are circling a western prospect of the mute, unyielding mountain, and once again they are exposed to sleet and hail. It stings their faces, their arms, their thighs. No one talks. Each feels defeated and glum. The recalcitrant mountain seems to exhale freezing vapors, filled with a metallic indifference. Soon, their wet clothes stiffening with ice, they are shivering.

Pep knows that there is a *real* risk now—of exposure. He's paid out many claims over the years on dumb Columbians done in by the cold—falling through ice, deer hunting drunk, hiking half-naked in the Berkshires. "Hurry, guys—we gotta get dry and warm fast. C'mon, family, move!"

Finally they come to a crumbling low moon gate, built centuries ago when people were much shorter. Even Katie and Clio have to duck under it. Pep, seeing it as a moon gate for a midget, bends almost double to do so. They find themselves in a mossy clearing, on one side of which, up against a dark cliff face soaring up into mist, is a small, wooden-beamed stone hut with a black-tile roof. It is so old, set so tightly against the mountain, that it seems part of it. The beams of the roof overhang the walls and glisten a deep greenish-black, as if they have lived a great part of their long lives under water. Much of the clearing is covered with moss, and the mossy walls and beams with patches of yellow lichen add to the watery feel.

As they hurry across the clearing, the sleet and hail suddenly lessen, though they still hear the wind and the pops of raindrops and hail hitting the crests of the pines. Clio immediately catches how the hut is placed so that the cliff gives shelter from the prevailing wind, rain, and snow. *Habitations tell everything about their inhabitants. Look carefully. Seek her there. You will find her.* A hermit's hut, taken over after abandonment, a pragmatic structure placed romantically. A retreat.

Xiao Lu opens the door and gestures them inside.

The single room is dim, light coming through two small windows. The Macys stand clustered, in out of the rain, listening to Xiao Lu bustling around. A match is struck, a wick catches, a kerosene lamp glows. Another match, another glow. The room is small—maybe fifteen feet square—the smoke-blackened wooden beams rising steeply to meet the ridge line in a small square, from which hangs the anchoring base of the red stupa Clio glimpsed from outside.

Xiao Lu is bending to a barrel-sized iron stove that sits against a windowless back wall, the tilted exhaust pipe exiting up into the chimney of what looks like an old fireplace. She opens the door of the stove and uses a match to light shavings and kindling, then gestures to them to get out of their wet clothes, handing them towels and bringing over small quilts and a few of her own clothes and jackets for them. Pep holds up a pair of pants that only reaches his knees, and everyone laughs. Xiao Lu makes a gesture of closing her eyes to their undressing, and turns her back to them, tending the fire. The kindling is soon ablaze, and the pops and snaps of the sap smack against the walls.

To Clio the smell is intense—heavily pine and woodsmoke and kerosene and, more faintly, herbs, old incense, and sickly sweet overripe fruit. A rough table is placed against a wall near the stove, a kitchen table cluttered to its edges with mismatched plates and cups, and different kinds of tools, and a single piece of animal fur. Sagging shelves carry a few pots, a wok, some cans of food, and old dried flowers; dried mushrooms and garlic and ginger hang down from a beam. There is no obvious order—which at first disturbs Clio. On a hand-hewn bamboo bed are the rumpled waves of a wine-dark quilt. A single chair—the arms and feet made of polished branches and the back of pieces of carved, polished wood: one piece the golden sheen of maple, another the reddish glow of pine—reminds Clio of the modern chairs made by artisans in the Adirondacks. A missing slat gives the chair a face with a missing tooth. The floor is of old, pitted stones, each the size of a large wok, laid in packed dirt. Elemental and old—maybe three hundred years or more. The orange Day-Glo vest hangs on a hook beside the door, a call from the universal plastic.

The low-beamed solidness of the dwelling, the heft of the construction, the collection of used pots and pans and simple clothes hanging from lines, the recycling of anything and everything, the resurrection of found objects—all of this speaks to Clio of a skillful but crude dedication to getting by, day to day. She admires this young woman, not only for having made it alone here, but for the simplicity she has created. No car pool, no checkbook, no planning drop-offs and pickups and vacations, not even any *shopping*—lucky her! A worker's simple life. And then she notices, papering all the walls, long scrolls filled with elegant, sweeping calligraphy.

Katie looks around. The thick smells of pine needles and earth—*like when you turn it up in spring*—and smoke left over from a wood fire are familiar. She's puzzled—but then she gets it. *It smells like Mary's Farm!* Suddenly she is back there, staring up into Velcro's eyes and hearing *cheep! cheep!* and seeing, stuck to the beam overhead, the nest and the clamshell mouths of the baby barn swallows. No nest here, but things hang from the beams, *everything's disorganized like Mary but you* know *she knows where everything is, and nobody's gonna say, "Don't touch!" or "Be careful!" or "Don't get dirty!"* She touches a rounded old wooden beam in the wall. Under her fingers is the same smooth, friendly curve as the old barn wood of the stables. *She's staring back at me like she wants to read my mind for what I think. Try mental telepathy. I'm thinking of Mary who's really cool in a live-off-the-land way and maybe you're that way too?* Katie waits, but Xiao Lu shows no response. It's hard for Katie to read her—she either smiles and laughs or looks stern. Katie still feels embarrassed by her own "meltdown" on the trail, and looks away, staring at the big rough tiles on the floor.

As Clio helps Katie slip out of her drenched clothes and dries her with a surprisingly fresh, pine-scented towel, she looks more carefully at the dozens of scrolls, some six feet long, the black-inked Chinese characters stepping down from top to bottom. Some scrolls are yellowed with age, others bright, the paper reflecting the firelight. Before a window is a long table polished to a deep mahogany, the only bare surface in the room but for, at one end, a neat arrangement of brushes and inks. *This, now, is a glimpse into an artful order, a soul. How to reach her? It?*

Soon warmth is radiating from the stove. Xiao Lu has poured water from a big plastic pail into a kettle, which she's placed on the stove. Despite Clio's—and Pep's—distaste for clutter and dirt, they are starting to feel the wonder of going from wet and cold to warm and dry, a shared sense of gratitude not in the head or heart but in the fingers and toes. Xiao Lu pours the boiling water into four unmatched cups. As she passes by, there is the strong scent of her sweat. In the cups, steam spirals up. She sprinkles dark tea leaves into the first two cups. When Katie motions "no," she stops, thinks, and adds something different to the hot water. Katie waits for it to cool, then tastes it carefully. To her surprise, it's good.

"Tastes a little like Sprite!"

"Great," Pep says, "just great." He's feeling uncomfortable, embarrassed at his panicking on the logs—and half-panicked again about how the hell he'll make it back—and the low beams and dirt and clutter are revving up all of his other pet worries. He's always been sensitive, prone to harmless phobias, and to discover another one, a harmful one, now, is infuriating. He tries the breathing exercises Clio has taught him, and starts to calm down.

"Oh God, a *spider*! A huge spider lookit the size of it!"

Spiders are the one kind of animal Katie can't abide, and Pep rushes to control the situation. "Ignore it, Kate-zer. They can't hurt you."

"*Some* can! Some can kill you!" Katie cringes. Xiao Lu bends and shoos it away, carefully.

Clio nods to her—sensing the Buddhist respect for all living things.

Xiao Lu doesn't see it; she's still focused on Katie.

Clio says to Pep, "A reincarnated soul."

"Yeah, well, if she thought it was a reincarnation of that mother-in-law of hers, she might have treated it differently."

Clio smiles at him, and then calls out, "Xiao Lu?" Xiao Lu turns, and Clio points to the tea and smiles. Pep smiles too, and gives her two thumbs up. This embarrasses Katie, who tugs his thumbs and hands back down.

Again they sit sipping in silence but for the rain on the roof. They are now inextricably linked, with so much to say—but there seems to be no way to say anything, no way to ask about her life, her parents, her husband and sister, why she left, came here—and no way for her to ask them either. Clio and Pep try through sign language to find out something more about her, try to exchange words to name things with her, but she doesn't seem all that interested in responding to them. She is only interested in Katie, and shows her how some of the utensils work, and how to stoke the fire. Katie walks around the hut with her but soon they reach the end of these utensils, these stokings, and Katie comes back to Pep and Clio, who are sipping from fresh cups of tea. The Macys have a sense of failure, and wonder if Xiao Lu feels it too. She sits sipping tea, staring at her child.

Katie feels itchy, bored stiff. Her birth mom is always looking at her, as if she expects something of her. Katie hates it when her mother does that, when anyone does that, makes her the center of attention. She swings her legs and counts and gets to eighty-seven and stops. She stares at the little black Sprite thingees floating in her teacup, tries to count them.

"Mom?" It sounds really loud when she says it. "Momma?"

"Yes, dear?" Clio is aware now of the power of that "Mom" and glances at Xiao Lu, wondering if she understands. What is the Chinese word for "Mom" anyway? Xiao Lu is looking at Katie intently—and then she glances at Clio. *Yes, she understood.*

"Mom, I really, really wish we could ask her all kinds of questions, especially about my sister, you know like about her past and her life, but I don't know how."

"I know, hon, we're all stuck, but it's important to just be here with her, spend time with her, and get to know her as best we can."

"Yeah, it's getting me depressed. She lives really basic. She doesn't even have electricity here. And what does she use for like water?"

"You may have noticed, Kate-zer, that there's a lot of water outside?"

"She drinks the water?" Pep nods. "I wonder what it tastes like?"

"Don't," Pep says. "She can. You can't."

"Even when it's from the like Hima*lay*as?" Pep shakes his head. "Okay. But she's still really, *really* poor."

"In some ways she's poor, Katie," Pep says, "but not in others."

"What do you mean?"

"Well, even though she doesn't have a lot of the things we do, she seems happy, and we know a lot of rich kids and grown-ups—like in your class at Spook—who have just about everything, every material thing they want, and they aren't happy, right?" Katie nods. "So let's just see if we can find a way to be with her, just for a little while longer today, and then we'll head back, okay?"

"Do we have to?"

"We do. We have to get back to the monastery in daylight," Pep says. "We can't risk the dark. So we've got maybe another hour. Clee?"

Clio is confused. She feels strange here, as if she senses danger—but she can't grasp what it is. Xiao Lu has wanted this for ten years, set it in motion, and now it's here but clearly it's not going well for her. In that glance was raw pain. *Once we leave, what's she left with? But better not leave abruptly, it could provoke her—she's small, but strong as hell. It's clear that she doesn't want us to be here or even exist, wants desperately to be alone with her daughter. Okay, try to engage her.*

Clio looks around again. The only uncluttered space is the table with the brushes. Brushes all neatly laid out. Ink. *Her passion is calligraphy.*

Xiao Lu still feels shaken. A minute ago, carefully watching Chun question the woman, she heard a word similar to the Chinese "Mama," saw the woman's quick response and her glance at her—a deep cut of pain. All these years, and Chun is still so far away. *I'm disgusting!—a poor, strange woman living alone in the woods. Foolish woman! What made you think this would lead to anything?*

Clio stands up. "Xiao Lu?" She points to a scroll, then to the table where the brushes are, indicating that she is interested in her calligraphy.

Xiao Lu nods, and gestures for the woman to come along. Then suddenly, as if of its own accord, her hand reaches out to Chun and she puts her arm around her shoulder, to lead her to the table. *This, my flesh and blood, this smooth-skinned beautiful girl—these two whorls from which her hair sprouted when I carried her inside. Two crowns like mine.* She stops and gestures to the man and woman, from the double crowns to the head itself, to streams of wisdom sprouting out in all directions—from her eyes, her lips—but they look puzzled, their big mouths a little open. She gives up. *These people have no art. They are simple folk.* She nods to Katie to come with her to the table.

Xiao Lu's hand feels weird on her shoulder, awkward and rough. Not moving, Katie glances at Clio.

Clio understands. It's her worst fear, this hand proclaiming, *She is mine. You may have her, have her for a long time, even all of this life, but you know that she is mine. It doesn't matter that I gave her away—now she is back.* Clio has an impulse to push the hand away—but catches herself. *Hey, don't go there. She will have her daughter for a few hours, and then we'll be gone.* She nods to Katie that it's okay to go with her.

Katie feels Xiao Lu's hand guide her to a stool in front of the table. She sits.

Though the table is in front of two windows, they are small, and the light through the rain is dim. Xiao Lu lights a kerosene lamp. The scent is acrid. Katie sneezes.

As Xiao Lu does whenever she approaches her art, she glances at the proverb she painted on the beam above: "For a woman to be without talents is synonymous with virtue." This always stirs her outrage, which focuses her attention on her art. Frees it up to flow into her spirit and through her heart and arm and hand and fingers and brush, out onto the blank sheet of rice paper, bringing the character to life. Now she hesitates, not because the outrage is not there, but because she has a different goal. She wants to talk with her daughter.

29

But how? What will interest her?

For a long moment she stares at the white scroll, and nothing comes. And then she sees in her mind's eye another piece of paper, the map they have been following, with the drawings of the monkeys, and remembers, and knows.

Animals. A monkey, but the character doesn't look like a monkey really. Start with a horse—all little girls love horses.

She picks up her brush and, looking at Katie, says in Chinese, "I will draw a picture of a horse, and then I will draw the character for 'horse.'"

Katie, embarrassed at not being able to understand, watches closely.

She twirls the brush between her thumb and finger to make a nice tip, and straightens it. She fills the inkstone, closes her eyes to settle, and in a few strokes makes a line drawing of a horse:

She shows Katie, mimicking holding reins for a gallop, and says the Chinese word. Katie nods, interested. She repeats the word, prompting Katie to say it. Shyly, quietly, she does so. Xiao Lu smiles and nods her approval, and rolls the tip again against the smooth surface of the inkstone to regain its form. In the time it takes to do this she brings the character to mind and then, as it leaves her mind and without her willing it, out flows the character for "horse":

Katie stares intently at this, and then all of a sudden sees it, sees in the character the drawing, in the drawing the animal. She looks up past Xiao Lu to Clio and says excitedly, "Mom, this is really neat, do you see it?"

"No, but tell me what you see."

"Like, in the drawing of the horse, these three strokes are the mane flowing in the wind, like they are right here in the what-do-you-call-it?"

"The Chinese character."

"Yeah, and here's the tail, and the tail of the character, and under the body these four dots in the character mean the racing hooves, and it's neat because in the character it's like the horse is galloping along so fast that the hooves hardly even touch the ground and the mane is flowing back and the wind even pushes the face flat!" Katie glances up to Xiao Lu and copies her motion of riding a galloping horse.

Xiao Lu, delighted, nods and says, "I can make it even more simple for you." Now she is into her art, the calligraphy that takes the character and simplifies it but leaves the essence. She draws this:

马

Katie nods and smiles at Xiao Lu.

It is the first time. She smiles back.

"See, Mom," Katie says, looking past her to Clio, "the horse is still there!"

"Yes," Clio says, hardly seeing the horse, because she is troubled by the smile. "I see."

Xiao Lu is already on to another animal, a deer. First, the line sketch of the animal:

Katie immediately sees what it is, saying, "A deer!"

Xiao Lu nods and then, breathing out, makes the character:

"It doesn't really look much like a deer," Katie says, shaking her head.

Xiao Lu understands, and draws just the head of the deer, with the antlers:

Katie pokes her fingers up to mimic antlers, and nods.

Xiao Lu draws the character:

Katie nods, and points to the whole deer, and indicates, "But they're different."

Xiao Lu nods and, by pointing to her own head, and then Katie's, then Pep's and Clio's, shows that this is the character for "head."

"Hey, that's neat!" Katie says. "The deer head is the character for our heads too!" She smiles at Xiao Lu.

It irks Clio—and then it irks her even more that it does.

"And," Katie says, pointing to the whole deer character and, trying to gesture with her hands, "do you have deer around here?"

Xiao Lu gestures that she doesn't understand.

"Dad, can you help?"

Pep picks up on Clio's hurt. She's making *way* too much of all this—but then maybe he would too, if it were young William here instead. He thinks he needs to lighten things up a bit. "Right," he says, thinking, *Charades.* He extends his arm and taps three fingers on it. "Three syllables." He tugs his ear. "Sounds like?"

Xiao Lu wonders why he is itching his arm and tugging his ear and smiling, and offers him more tea. He shakes his head no. She watches as he clumsily gestures, and then tries again, and finally she gets it—he wants to know if there are deer nearby. She nods her head yes, and makes the gesture of feeding them from her hand.

"Wow! They're just like her sister Tao said, they're tame and she feeds them." Katie points to her watch, and asks, "When?"

Xiao Lu says, "At dusk and dawn." Katie doesn't understand. Xiao Lu gestures, and draws a sun:

And then she gestures that the deer can be fed when the sun goes down, and when the sun comes up again over the horizon.

"Can we stay till sundown, Mom? Please, Mom, can we?"

"You heard Dad—there's no way we can walk back when it's dark, especially not with the logs." She sees Pep wince, and feels bad she mentioned it. "But maybe tomorrow morning?"

"Deer are *nocturnal*! We can't walk *to* here when it's dark either. We have to stay!"

"We can't, dear, there's no room."

"Why not? We can just sleep on the floor? It'll be a lot warmer than that dump we stayed in last night."

"I don't think so, dear."

"Please, Mom?"

"Sorry, but no. We'll ask for a warmer, cleaner place—"

"But this *already* is a lot better than—"

"No means *no*!"

Katie is startled—she almost never has heard this harsh voice from her mother. Her face falls. She glances at Clio, hoping that she'll say she's sorry for this tone of voice, but no. She's just standing there with her arms crossed over her chest.

Katie turns back to Xiao Lu, and motions for her to draw more animals.

Xiao Lu feels the tension between the two of them, like a bolt of thunder that sometimes shakes the little hut. She draws a monkey, as she did on the map. Chun smiles. She mimes a monkey, excited and frantic and looking here and there and snatching Chun's hat—all great fun, she and Chun laughing together. She gives the hat back and then draws the monkey character:

Chun stares at it and then calls out to the woman and man happily, and points at it. She understands the "joking" part, the way the monkey moves here and there, jumping and swinging. The woman nods and smiles, but it's not a happy smile, no.

And then, after pausing to roll the brush tip on the inkstone, Xiao Lu again simplifies the complex character to a calligraphic emblem:

She goes on with other animals, each time starting with the line drawing of the animal, having Chun repeat the Chinese name, and then translating the drawing, not literally but through the spirit of the animal and the meaning of the animal to humans, into the character, and then finally making it simple, a few elegant free strokes that turn the character into an art that lifts it and the viewer somewhere else. With each new character she sees that her little Chun is getting more involved—not shy at all!—repeating the Chinese words beautifully! Xiao Lu claps her hands together in delight.

As Clio watches, she can see how skillful Xiao Lu is at this. It is amazing how this woman has found a way to connect with Katie through Katie's two passions—drawing and animals. And she's moving on now to other images—a boat, bamboo—but Xiao Lu has picked up, in Katie's response to the drawing of the monkeys, that this is *it*, for her. Neither Clio nor Pep can draw worth a damn. Or pronounce Chinese words.

"Mom, will you ask her if *I* can try one?" Clio knew this was coming. "Mom, you're not listening. Can I try?"

"Yes, dear, but be careful with that ink—don't get dirty."

Katie bristles at the words; it's just what her mother always tells her when she drops her off at Mary's Farm. "It doesn't bother *her*—look at *her* fingers, okay?"

Xiao Lu takes all this in, and when Chun motions to ask if Xiao Lu can guide her in doing it, it is the moment she has yearned for. All this time, she has imagined this moment, taking her daughter's hand, transmitting her understanding of the flow of the brush, the ink, to that little hand. She takes to the moment with delight.

Chun has the brush in her hand, Xiao Lu's hand around hers. They start with a simple horizontal line, which Xiao Lu, by holding up a finger, indicates is the character for "one." Xiao Lu directs the movement of her hand, and out comes the line. Chun indicates that she wants to try it for herself. Xiao Lu shakes her head and says, "No, you're not ready to do it alone yet." Chun insists. She lets her try.

The brush splays out, the point dissolves, the line isn't a line but a blob and then a raggedy mess. Chun is dismayed and looks up at Xiao Lu, who laughs to reassure her. Xiao Lu takes the brush and puts Chun's hand around hers—her child has such long fingers, her own aren't much longer. With Chun feeling the movement, Xiao Lu shows her: she lowers the brush straight onto the paper, waits a moment, and then with a steady hand takes the brush to the right toward the end of the stroke, waits again for a moment, and then lifts the brush slant-wise backward and upward. They look together at the stroke. It starts and ends with a taut, straight, somewhat slanting line.

With Xiao Lu's hand around hers, Chun tries it. The brush holds together, and the line is at least a line:

Chun turns to the woman and man and gestures to the line excitedly. They smile and nod. The woman's smile is pained.

Xiao Lu indicates that there's another way to do the brushstroke. Again putting Chun's hand on hers, at the left end she guides her to make a little circle that binds the brush point to the paper, then lowers the brush even farther onto the paper, waits for a moment, and carries it on to the right end of the stroke. She pauses before taking the brush a tiny bit downward and returning back in the stroke she's just completed, at the same time carefully lifting the brush off the paper. The stroke is different from the other at the ends: there is a softly rounded beginning and ending.

Chun cries out her pleasure and wonder, says a word that sounds to Xiao Lu like "Coo!"

Clio watches Katie getting more and more engrossed. Xiao Lu's hand leads hers over the white paper. Katie is totally into it. The two black-haired heads are close together under the lamplight. Close and still.

After a while, Clio goes over to Pep, now lying down on the bed. She settles into the Adirondack chair. The room is too small for them to talk honestly about what is going on, and the pelting rain prevents them from going outside. Clio scans Pep's face for any trace of concern about all this, and finds none. She sits on the bed, close to him.

"Pep," she whispers, "are you worried about this?"

He sits up. "Nope, why?"

"Because maybe, just maybe, she'll, I don't know, really *like* her and want to stay here with her longer?"

"No way. She said she wanted to go home."

"That was before the calligraphy."

"Nah. This isn't her thing, this 'roughing it.' Let her play. Then we go."

"Please, honey, I'm starting to have a bad feeling about all this."

"I thought you said this was healthy for her."

"Yes, but I, well . . . I mean, suppose Katie wants to . . ." She tries to catch herself. "I know it's crazy, never mind."

"Go ahead."

"I'm embarrassed."

"Wouldn't be the first time with me, right? Fire away."

"Look . . . I mean maybe all these old, maybe even bio forces could get stirred up, and she starts to really, I don't know, *care*, or *attach* . . . ?"

"Wait. Hold it. Crazy thought. And even if she did, she's ours and—"

"Even if she *did*? You think it's possible?"

"No, I don't—"

"Well, then why'd you *say* it?"

"I didn't say it, I said—"

"What are you two arguing about?" Katie turns back to them, her fingers all black, a fresh smudge on her sleeve.

"Nothing, darling," Clio says, surprised to find herself staring more at the indelible ink on the sleeve and fingers than into her eyes. "It's getting late. Just finish up and we'll go."

She turns back to her work, her head close to her birth mom's.

"Nothing to worry about, hon," Pep says. "We're stressed out, all of us—no sleep, bad food, hypothermia—and now all *this*?! It's damn well exhausting. We let 'em finish up her drawing lesson, and that's it. End of story. Take a little rest." He yawns and lies back down on the bed, and is soon asleep.

The rain, to Clio, is no longer comforting, but seems to reflect her inner turmoil—periods of drops beating regularly as a metronome on the roof tiles, and tremendous gusts of Beethoven, and then almost stopping, but not quite. She wonders how long they'll be required to stay here, and how to—without letting on to Katie about her own concern—leave. There's something about not having words that gives Xiao Lu an advantage. And she shows absolutely no sign of doubt, or anxiety, or any other all-American neurotic splinters there. *A simple, pragmatic intelligence, sparked by art.* Clio feels strangely diminished in this wordless contest. She closes her eyes and tries to meditate, following the breath.

"Mom—look! I made this one all by myself. Guess what it is?"

Clio goes over. Katie shows her the character she's just drawn:

"It looks like someone walking, like a person?"

"Almost. Keep guessing!"

Clio stares at it, unable to go farther.

"*Scraggghhhumph!*"

They all turn to Pep, snoring—and burst out laughing. For a moment, three generations of women share a laugh at a universal and problematic quality of men.

"A man?" Clio asks.

"Yes! See, it's like a man walking."

"That's great, darling."

Xiao Lu nods proudly.

"Xiao Lu helped me on the others but this I did all by myself, do you see?"

"Yes, darling. Can you do a woman?"

"Nope. I'll ask Xiao Lu."

Even Katie's use of the name is a little jab in her gut. "Do that, yes."

Xiao Lu points to herself, Clio, and Katie, and draws the character:

"I see," says Katie, "it's a woman! It's like . . . a more solid thingee, a bigger body than a man and maybe even with breasts too? It's *more* than the man figure, y'see?"

"Yes, dear, she has a lot more to her."

Then Xiao Lu draws another character:

She points to Katie, and then to Pep—indicating a Katie-sized version of him. They get it—the character for "child," or maybe "boy." She then puts the two characters together:

"Woman and child?" Katie asks. "Is that what she means?"

"I believe so."

But Xiao Lu is miming something that makes them think of "happy" or maybe "good." Maybe, maybe not. She draws another character:

And points to herself.

"What is it?" Katie asks.

"Don't know. Perhaps it's her name. Is that your name? Is that 'Xiao Lu'?"

"Bu," Xiao Lu says. They nod. They know that this word means "no."

"Wait, I know," Clio says. "It's just her and me. Not you, Katie. Maybe it means grown-up woman?" Clio points to herself, and then to Xiao Lu, indicating that this word means the two of them are similar in some way.

Xiao Lu points to Clio and shakes her head and finger vigorously for "No!" and says sharply, "*Bu!*" Then she points back to herself alone, and says, with even more emphasis, "*Xiao Lu!*"

They still don't get it.

She points to herself, points to her belly, then to Katie, and makes the motion of Katie coming out of her belly. Smiling proudly, she points to the character, "*Mama!*"

Clio freezes, startled by the blunt force of this woman's stating, in front of her daughter, *I, not you, am her mother.* It echoes with all the times when she first was out with her baby and people said things to her like "Who's her mother?" and "Where's her mother?" and "Where'd you get her?" and "How much did she cost?" And the worst, on vacation in St.

Martin, talking with a woman at an outdoor barbecue who asked, "Who's her mother?" and when Clio said, "I am," shook her head and said, "*You can't be her mother, no.*"

Now the pain of all that comes roaring back. Clio stares at the drawings—stares at the "mother," who carries within her the seed of her child, and at the "woman," who is empty, moving frantically to some place of no consequence. Xiao Lu is smiling broadly, as if she has only a child's awareness of what she has just done. Clio looks to Katie.

Katie is looking up at her, a rare puzzlement in her eyes.

"I think, Katie, it's time to go. Pep? Wake up." He stirs, but doesn't awaken.

Katie senses that something bad has happened between the two women, some crash, like a wave into a cliff. She realizes she'd better obey. "I'll get him up, Mom."

Katie shakes Pep really hard. He rouses himself, grumbling. Katie talks to him.

Clio hears their conversation dimly. Her mind is spinning—and then stops still, narrowed to a tight focus of rage. She can't even bring herself to *look* at Xiao Lu. Survival kicks in. *Get Pep and Katie out of here—fast!*

Xiao Lu is startled. The woman roughly pulls their dry clothes down from the string stretched above the stove. They turn their backs and dress. *So soon? No!*

Pep senses Clio's rage and the breakage between the two women. "Okay, Clee, Katie, let's get a move on." Trying to control the situation, calm it down, he takes out his camera. *Nothing like the distance a camera offers. Objectify this. Souvenir it. Even art it up. But control it, yes.* "I'll just get a few shots to capture this—"

"We're leaving *now*." Clio says.

"It'll just take a sec." He's already taking quick shots around the hut. He focuses on Xiao Lu, who tries to hide her face, but the flash catches her.

She points at Katie, then at the camera. "Please take a picture for me of Chwin?"

"Chwin" hangs in the air, the only recognizable word in the sentence. Katie and Pep look at Clio.

"Her name is *Katie*," she says firmly, and settles her safari hat on her head.

"Yeah, Mom, but my whole name is Katie Chun—maybe she doesn't understand. "I'll tell her." Katie points to herself and says slowly, "Katie Chwin."

"Katie Chwin," Xiao Lu says, smiling, thinking, *It is the same as in Chinese—her last name is Katie and her first name is Chun.* Through gesture, she tells them that she wants them to stay here tonight, and tomorrow when the weather is better they can go on their trip to find the monkeys. She tries to make clear that there is room for them all—she will give up her bed and sleep in the cave, next to the house.

Katie understands that they can sleep in the bed here while Xiao Lu stays somewhere outside, and explains it to them.

"I think not, darling," Clio says tightly, hoping to forestall another fight. She takes a deep breath in, holds it, lets it out slowly. "*So!*" she announces cheerily, in control again. "Everybody ready?"

Clio leads. They walk out. The fresh air feels like a godsend.

30

The hard rain is spent, fizzled to drizzle. They stand for a moment under the overhanging roof beams, staring at the mossy courtyard and the flat stones curling from the door to the beginning of the path. Xiao Lu comes out carrying her black snake-killer umbrella in one hand, the unlit pine torch in the other. There is the sound of a stream nearby, and a bird. After the rain, the fragrances seem to hang in the air like fruit—earth and pine and jasmine and something else familiar to them all—a whole grove of ming aurelia growing near the edge of the cliff.

Clio has a single ming in a large Chinese pot in the living room, a gift from one of the Columbian New Yorkers. The tree is of the bamboo family, but with cloud-like leaves that individually look like the fluffy trees in Chinese mountain paintings—the ones where the towering mountains dwarf the tiny people. The scent of damp ming is unlike any other: fresh, tangy, almost musky, somewhat like eucalyptus, somewhat like spruce. Now, out in the open, the fragrance brings to Clio's mind the *manageable* China, the one in a pot in their living room, or in Chinese Restaurant in Columbia.

Gaining control again, Clio feels her rage unclench. It leaves her shaky and ashamed. *How could I have done that? At that crucial moment?* Shame washes over her, and clings. Scared, humiliated, she seeks her usual refuge—distance. As Pep takes photos, she senses herself withdrawing into that familiar family paralysis of no feeling, of surface perception and response—what she and her sister Thalia, as teenagers, labeled with scorn—but without awareness, then, of its truth and liability—"The WASP Freeze." And now the signature word they'd been taught to use to nail that Freeze in place comes to mind: "*Quite.*" The word brings a glimpse of order, of control, of one step following another surely on a raked gravel path of denial.

We have done it now, here with her. It's over. We have found her. Visited her. Like the obligatory Christmastime visit to one of our infuriating Hale aunts. No, not like that. For better or worse, this has been authentic. A world on fire.

"A few more shots," Pep says, pleased that his photo-therapy is working, that everybody's outside in the fresh air, calming down, everybody being friendly again.

"Do we have to, Dad?"

"C'mon, c'mon. You and Xiao Lu and Clio—and I want big happy smiles." He lines them up in front of the dark-beamed hut, Katie in the middle, Xiao Lu and Clio on either side. He mimes big happy smiles, takes a few photos, and then as they move away he notices what looks like an ancient inscription carved into the front wall, several neat rows of characters, and captures them too, figuring he'll get someone to translate it whenever. Xiao Lu gestures that he should be in a picture. Clio takes the camera and they get another few shots of Xiao Lu, Katie, and Pep—he towering over them with arms around all, a giant Hawaiian flowering plant.

Xiao Lu smiles at them in a way that to Clio seems strained, and then walks briskly up the stone path across the compound, toward the woods, Katie following.

At the entrance to the trail, Clio touches Katie's shoulder and calls to Pep.

"Just look," Clio says, relieved now that they're on their way out, "Just for one last moment. And if you *really* look, Katie, and snap your eyes closed like you're taking a picture, you'll remember it forever."

"But aren't we coming back tomorrow?"

"Xiao Lu will probably be coming to the monastery tomorrow anyway, so we can all visit there. It's safer."

"Safer from what?"

Damn, that was a dumb thing to say. "Safer from the rain and cold and exposure out here, and also it'll be easier with other people around."

"How?"

"I'm not sure, I just feel it will be."

They stand there. Xiao Lu comes back to them. The Macys take in the ancient old hut up against the black mountain, the old grove of mings and a gnarled gingko and, all around, resilient towering bamboo nestling into high pine. They say nothing, forced by the momentum of the natural world to merely take in as much as they can.

For a long moment they don't move. The only sounds are of rushing water and a lone bird singing without tune or cadence.

Then Xiao Lu turns and walks briskly into the bamboo.

As Katie hustles along behind her, Pep feels a sudden fear. He takes Clio's arm. "Stay right behind them, Clio. If she disappears off this mountain with her into China, it's over." They hurry to catch up.

○ ○ ○

The narrow path back through the bamboo is uphill, and slippery. They walk in silence, single file, Xiao Lu leading, followed by Katie, then Clio, then Pep. They gently hand off bamboo branches from one to another walking behind so no one gets smacked in the face. The late afternoon light filters dimly through the thick growth.

Pep senses a seeping terror at the idea of recrossing the four log bridges spanning the gorge, the worst one first. In the gathering dark? With the bridges slick as fish after the rain? Like the imagined rumbling in the cataract ahead, he senses a distant rumbling in his bowels, which he fears might again turn explosive. He walks on, barely noticing the beauty all around him, barely taking in the fresh fragrance of the trees and the earth and the flowers and, yes, even the rocks—that sharp metal scent of certain rocks like the scent of iron in spilled blood.

Xiao Lu sets a quick pace. Katie keeps up with her, right behind—it's like a game they're playing, a wilderness follow-the-leader—with Xiao Lu doing an occasional quick zigzag or detour into the pines, Katie following. Laughing.

A space keeps opening up between Katie and Clio. At first it is a small space, so that Katie doesn't have to hold the bamboo to keep it from whipping Clio, but then it's larger, so that Katie is occasionally out of sight around a bend in the trail. Clio calls out to her to stay back, and she does, she and Xiao Lu waiting for Clio and Pep to catch up once again. The path has been cut and used by a short, slender woman, not a tall, broad man. Pep feels gargantuan, bending under boughs, blasting through narrow passages of bamboo, banging into bushes, and getting whacked around the shoulders and face by branches and twigs.

Slowed by Pep, Clio tells Katie to take it slower, not to go on ahead with Xiao Lu.

Katie says she understands, though clearly she's not happy to be held back.

Again they move on, up. Again Clio calls out to Katie to wait, and she does.

Xiao Lu stands there holding her umbrella and torch, staring down over Katie's head at Clio and Pep. Her face shows no expression. She moves on.

It seems to take an age to get back to the Dusk-Enjoying Pavilion.

Pep and Clio rest on the benches, feeling discouraged at how much farther they have to go, worried about how much longer the light will last, and whether they will have to make the trip in the dusk or, God forbid, by torchlight. Clio can't believe that Xiao Lu does it by torchlight all the time—she seems amazingly agile and strong, hardly even breathing hard at the really tough, tortuous uphill stretches. Like a lithe animal, she's totally at home in the forest, in the twilight. Katie and she are on the ledge over the falls, laughing and playing, throwing stones down into the water. Pep calls out for them to get going. He is terrified of the first bridge down below—feels like he's walking to a trial that cannot help but conclude in his summary execution. His heart thumps wildly. He sweats hard.

The path from the Dusk-Enjoying Pavilion to the first bridge is steeply down, which seems a blessing to Clio and Pep until they realize that Katie and Xiao Lu are using the slick downhill as a kind of slalom course, running, laughing, and shrieking, so that it is increasingly hard to keep up.

"Katie, wait!" Clio shouts.

"Meetchu at the first bridge!"

"Wait!" But Katie doesn't wait; she runs on ahead with Xiao Lu.

"Clio," Pep shouts, "let's *go!*"

"Right!" Clio runs off after them through a thick clutch of woods, but they are never in sight. Behind her she hears Pep trip and curse and then fall, and stops to see if he's okay.

"Yes, yes, I'm okay, you go on! Hurry!"

Clio runs on as fast as she can, shouting for Katie over and over.

No answer.

Fear rises, invades. Breathless, she stops by the side of a deep gorge—holds her breath to listen for them. Looks around, tries to find tracks on the stony trail, to see if they've stayed on it this far—but can't see anything. The noise of the rapids below, funneled up by the walls of the gorge, is deafening—she shouts her child's name as loud as she can, over and over. Rage spews out—screaming, she picks up rocks and dead branches and dirt and throws them into the chasm. Stops. Nothing.

She goes down the twisting, narrow trail, unable to see very far ahead.

Finally there is daylight, and below her, Katie and Xiao Lu are standing together at the first log bridge. Both are smiling. Katie waves to her. She runs down to them and grabs Katie hard by the shoulders, glaring at Xiao Lu, shouting, "What the hell are you doing?!"

Xiao Lu stares back, a smile still on her face, as if this is all a game. Then she lowers herself slowly down to a squat to rest, balancing on her heels.

Clio turns to Katie. "What happened?"

"What?"

"Why did you run away?"

"I told you I'd meet you at the bridge." Katie tries to understand why her mother is so upset. Is she scared of Xiao Lu doing something to her? There was one second, maybe, when she and Xiao Lu were out of breath and hiding behind a tree when Xiao Lu moved closer and put her arms around her from behind and all at once pulled her tight against her body. When Katie turned around, her eyes were wet and there was something else there that Katie had never seen before, but when Katie pulled away she laughed, and let go. "We were just playing a game," Katie says. "She didn't force me or anything. It was fun."

"She *made* it fun!"

"But Mom, *why* would—?"

"You stay with me and Daddy now. From now on I don't want you out of our sight. *Never*, understand? If you can't see us, you are too far away! Let's go back and find Daddy. He fell down. You go first."

"What about Xiao Lu?"

"Xiao Lu will be *fine*." Clio looks back at Xiao Lu, still squatting, and now smiling. "This is *not* funny, understand? This is not funny or fun!" Clio realizes how much she relies on Pep's bulk and power. She gives Katie a push in the back to get her going back up the trail. *Quite.*

Xiao Lu watches them go. She feels humiliated and enraged—it is the worst thing that can happen, to lose face in front of her daughter. She gets up and follows, but at a distance. *This woman's fear will bring about what she fears.*

○ ○ ○

In a few moments they meet up with Pep. He is sitting down, rubbing his ankle. His pants and palms are muddy.

Clio rushes to him, takes his hands. "Are you okay?"

"Yeah. I tripped and fell, turned my ankle, that's all. I can walk on it. What happened with Katie?"

Katie stands there, head down, fiddling with a loose rock with her foot.

Clio's voice is cool, and tight. "Katie Chun?"

"Un hunh."

"Darling, please look at me?"

Reluctantly, she tilts her head up, her eyes not quite visible under the chicken beak of her China Culture Camp 2001 cap.

"Don't you *ever* do that again," Clio says. "Understand?" Katie nods, puts her head back down. "Look me in the eye." She does so. "Never go off like that. *Never*. Got it?"

"Yes!" Katie cries out, ashamed and impatient. "Sor-*ree*! O*kay*?"

"Okay. Now let's get out of here."

They go down the trail to the bridge. Seeing them, Xiao Lu rises from her squat. Pep indicates that they are to go on. Xiao Lu leads. Clio makes a point of going next, followed by Katie, so that Katie will be sandwiched between her and Pep. Xiao Lu, Clio, and Katie cross the log bridge and stop on the other side of the gorge, waiting for Pep.

224 of Samuel Shem

He stands at the end of the logs. He knows not to look down but straight ahead. They seem far away, and thin. He breaks out in a sweat, starts to feel his heart speed up, his chest tighten, trapping his breath inside an iron box. He tells himself to focus. *Stay with the reality. Wide, safe logs, wide as a sidewalk, safe as steel. Been there for hundreds of years, no problem with them. You'll be okay if you don't look down.* He continues to focus only on the logs, but suddenly notices that they are wet with the rain, a little mossy, and, worst of all, they slope downward. No question about it, they tilt at a formidable and slippery angle down to the other bank. Even on the way over, with the logs sloping upward and dry—before the rain—he barely made it over them, only on his knees and with Xiao Lu's help. He closes his eyes, tries to breathe. The others are calling encouragement to him.

He opens his eyes, looks at the wide logs, thinks good thoughts, and steps out. Not too bad. Breathe, bend lower. *One step at a time, you can do it.* Is *he* saying that or are they? He's so tight he can't tell. He places his other foot carefully—but it's the one he twisted, and it *hurts*. He tries to favor it and takes another step, but this brings him out over the chasm and he hears the roar of the water crashing on the rocks far below and there's a ringing in his ears and he feels the mist coming up like a powerful sprinkler and he knows that the last thing he should do is to look down. But as if Poe's "imp of the perverse" is perched on his shoulder, enticing him—"Look down! Look down! Jump in!"—he looks down. The height is dizzying, the water crashing crazily. He panics.

Now he's in survival mode. He goes down on all fours, clutching for something, digging his fingernails into the wet logs like a squirrel. He knows he cannot get across the logs to the other side and suddenly he's worried about getting back to the bank that is only a few steps away. He can't turn around, and he can't go on. He's terrified that his fingernails will give out and he'll start to skid down the sloping logs and lose his balance and fall and die. He hears them calling to him to crawl, one knee at a time, but he can't. He's frozen. His heart is beating crazily, randomly, like a madman is trapped in his chest. Sweat seems to pour out of his skin like blood through a sieve, dripping down. Terror. Absolute terror. A sense of impending doom.

Xiao Lu is coming back up the logs to help him, as she did before. Smiling, she bends down and reaches out her hands, but there's no way he will unfreeze again.

"Daddy, you can do it, I know you can!"

"Pep, you *have* to! Come *on!*"

He's too scared even to call back. Shaking his head no to Xiao Lu—which makes her laugh!—he slowly edges backward up the logs a few yards that seem to be an eternity, and then, feeling solid earth again, digs his feet into it and scrambles off the bridge and flips himself over on his back, panting, humiliated, heart blasting, but safe.

The three of them cross back and stand over him. He sits up, his hands clasping his knees, shakes his head, says over and over again how sorry he is but there's no way, right now—especially with his turned ankle—that he's going to be able to get over those logs.

"Are you sure, honey?" Clio asks. His answer is in his terrified, exhausted eyes.

"I feel like the biggest jerk in the world," he says. "I'm sorry, Kate-zer, it's a panic attack. I tried, but—"

"I know, Dad—you tried your best. You'll do it tomorrow, in like daylight?"

"Do you have any Valiums?" Clio asks. "Maybe, if you calmed down . . ." He shakes his head no. She tries to think. "What if we get someone to carry you?"

"Who?"

"One of those porters, the ones who offered to carry us up the mountain. We could send Xiao Lu back to the monastery, and bring two of them back. Maybe with a stretcher?"

"Good idea," he says. "That's the best bet. Let's see if we can make her understand that. Katie, we need a drawing."

They manage to show Xiao Lu what they are thinking. She nods, but indicates that it will take time to go there and come back, and that as it is getting dark all of them will have to spend the night in the hut. Clio shakes her head no, it's urgent, and the three of them will go back to the hut, but she will go on, right away. Xiao Lu nods but says she will lead them there, get them settled, and then go off to the monastery, and come back later tonight with help. They can go back tomorrow morning.

"What about you and Katie going back to the monastery with her?" Pep asks.

"Leave you alone out here? And us off in the dark with her? Forget it."

Xiao Lu indicates that they should start back to the hut.

"I'm sorry, guys," Pep says.

"It's okay, Daddy. My daddy'll be okay. I mean like you're *the man!*" She takes his hand and they walk on together, Katie matching her stride carefully to his limp.

For the first time since her blowup with Xiao Lu, Clio looks her directly in the eye. *She looks pleased. Of course she's pleased, she's gotten what she wants—another chance.* Clio feels her spine stiffen, and indicates that Xiao Lu should follow Pep; she'll bring up the rear. Slowly they go back along the overgrown path through the bamboo and pines, toward the hut.

31

By the time they reach the hut night has come. Clio tries to communicate with Xiao Lu that she should leave right away for the temple to bring back the porters, but Xiao Lu is getting things organized for their stay. She lights the kerosene lanterns and stokes the stove, and shows them where everything they will need is kept. She takes them outside again and points out the firewood, the latrine, and where her drinking water comes from—a pool formed by a little waterfall spilling over a ledge in the rock face above. Pep limps along after them. His ankle is swollen badly and hurts like hell. When she leaves, he'll ice it in the pool. Filling a plastic bucket with water, Xiao Lu carries it back into the house. She puts on water for tea, and for rice for dinner—with *jung yoo*—and shows them oil and dried vegetables and fresh fruits, and what might be pieces of dried meat hanging from the rafters. Xiao Lu arranges where they will sleep—the bed, and what looks like a small straw-filled mattress and a bulky quilt on the floor.

To Clio's surprise and Katie's delight, there are a large number of bags of a Chinese rip-off of Pepperidge Farm Cheddar Goldfish—Katie's favorite.

Xiao Lu points to the calligraphy of the deer and the dawn. Katie gets it at once.

"Mom, can we get up early tomorrow and feed Goldfish to the deer?"

"Of course, sweetie." Clio is impatient with Xiao Lu, and wonders if she's gotten the message that they want her to leave at once. She urges her to *hurry*. Xiao Lu laughs and nods, but dallies. To Clio, she seems to be stalling, as if prolonging the time with her daughter. Finally Pep and Clio lead her to the door, and she leaves. The Macys follow her outside and stand close together in the cloudy, misty night, watching the torch flicker between the pines until it might still be there, and might not. Then, feeling a sudden chill, they go back inside.

They busy themselves with making dinner—rice and soy sauce, nuts and fruit and Goldfish. Clio and Pep fight their aversion to the dirt—the dirty plates, cups, food, chopsticks—and use their sterile Handi Wipes to keep whatever their mouths touch clean. But they are ravenous, and hardly speak as they eat. With joint sighs, they finish, and sit by the fire, warm and full and safe.

"Dad, I feel kinda bad."

"Why's that, sweetie?"

"It's like *I* did this, like I made it happen? I ran and made you run and trip and made it hard for you to cross the bridge. It's my fault, and I'm really sorry."

"You didn't do it, Kate-zer. It just happened."

"I know it feels that way, dear," Clio says, "but it's not your fault."

"*Kinda* it is." She pauses. "Mom, there's one thing I don't get? When you said we have to get back to someplace safe, like the monastery, why isn't it safe here?"

"I just don't feel safe with her—or that *you* are safe with her."

"You mean she'll want me back?" Clio is startled. "I heard you guys talking in the van."

"You *heard* that?!"

"I couldn't help it, honest." Clio and Pep nod. "So I thought about it and I mean *sure* she wants me back. It'd be worse if she *didn't*, right? I really wanted to meet her and I'm super glad, I mean, it's really something to meet your *birth mom*. But it's weird because I know I should have like really deep feelings for her?"

"We all know—"

"But maybe it's because she's so different and I'm so different from her—she's so Chinese, she makes me feel I'm like less Chinese and more American. Really, you don't have to like worry, okay?"

Clio smiles and hugs her. "Thanks, but sometimes kids don't see the whole picture. Daddy and I have a lot more years than you, and, as you said after being lost, our job is to make sure you and the family are safe. So you've got to trust us on that."

"But on *what*? I mean like on our . . . our like *plight*?"

Clio and Pep smile at the word. "About making sure, honey, that if we need help from other people, we can get it."

Katie yawns. "Can I go to sleep now?"

They get her ready for bed—she'll sleep on the mattress on the floor. She lies down and snuggles into the heavy quilt and sighs contentedly. Looking at Pep, she says, "Hey, Daddy, *coazy-coazy*! This is fun! Like the time we all camped out in our tent in the backyard and . . ." She's out.

Clio and Pep clear away the dishes and clean up as best they can. Gingerly, Handi-Wiping here and there, Clio beds down with Katie on the floor. Pep scrunches himself into the small, rough bed. The kerosene lantern is turned down low. The night is so quiet it seems perversely loud. Even though his heartbeat still feels fast and weird, without Xiao Lu there they both feel a touch of calm.

"Clee?"

"Hmm?"

"Think, for a sec, what *is* the actual risk here? What's the real danger? Katie's finally got the message: be careful, and stick together. We're together; we've got food, clothing, shelter—this place has been safe for human habitation for hundreds of years."

"Call it intuition. I just don't like it."

"What's not to like?"

"Oh, nothing," she says, matching his flip tone, "I mean, just some minor thing like—as you yourself said—she'll grab Katie and instead of waiting for us at the next bridge she'll keep on going and disappear with her into China! Jesus!"

"But she's had chances already, and—"

"She has not. I've kept an eagle eye on them."

He pauses. "Don't take this the wrong way, okay?"

"How can I know, until you tell me."

"Well, right . . ." He takes a deep breath. *A risk, to say this. Definitely foreign territory.* "Y'know, my problem isn't the bridge—the bridge is the bridge. My problem is I can't get over it—" He blinks, smiles. "That's a dumb way to put it. But what I mean is, is that it's not out there, it's in here, in my head. And *that's* what's got to change, in me. So, well, maybe that's true of you too?"

"And why am I so afraid? I'm not usually."

"'Course not, usually. But, well . . . with Katie, sometimes. Even, sometimes, a bit overprotective and—"

"Don't go there, Pep. Do *not* go there."

"Sorry. Just *consider* it, okay? I mean we're both really on edge about it—it's a big-time fear, no question. But what *is* the fear, really? And is the fear commensurate with the risk? Is it poisoning the little time we all have with her? When we get home, will we look back and say, 'What the *hell* were we so afraid of? Look what we missed out on!'"

Clio says nothing, fighting to control her anger—and fighting the paralysis of the control, The WASP Freeze. She tries to follow the breath, to breathe herself down. *Okay, try to open up to the possibility that you've taken this—what Katie calls "a figment"—way too far, that she's no real danger to your child, that you're making something worse of her, for some reason that has to do with . . . with what? Closeness? Trying to keep Katie from spiraling out, away? Fear of Katie going out into this tough world with such an innocence, such trust?* Possibilities crowd in. She feels the fist of fear unclench, a little, and the merely human ease in. And then she feels an appreciation for her husband. He's hanging in there. Blunt as a pile of rocks, but as solid, too. Maybe there's something new here. Maybe, because he himself feels humiliated, he's more open?

"Pep, you awake?"

No answer. Rocklike. Good for him.

The acrid kerosene lamp is killing her throat, her eyes. She puts it out. Pitch black but for the glow of embers in the stove. She sits back down in the chair that's squeezed between the bed and the stove and the calligraphy table.

She thinks of when she was a girl, every ritual summer like clockwork at the Hale Family Compound in the Poconos, the gangs of kids running around, the olders taking care of the youngers, one game running into another and campfires with s'mores and creaky old cabins with kerosene lanterns, wood fires and smooth wooden chairs and banisters that once were birch saplings and it was good fun, free and unbridled until the hormones hit and the boys became boys and the girls, girls, and everyone grew and fell in love and got married and had kids and was happy for a while and then was miserable and stifled and she didn't marry when it was normal and had to run away to the sexy tropics—and couldn't get back.

She stares at her sleeping daughter, who even after today seems to have no sense of the hole in the core of her soul. *Stop it! How do you know what's there? Didn't she, in a moment after our visit to the orphanage, with tears in her eyes say, "I wish I knew my birth mom"? Well, now she does. And is that better?*

All at once she finds herself weeping, forcing her hands over her mouth so as not to wake her husband or child. Weeping harder for her pitiful Hale Family Practice of Forcing Yourself Not to Weep At All.

32

Pep awakens to a touch on his arm. He has no idea where he is. He stares up at a golden glowing light. *I've died and gone to heaven.* But then a face darkens the glow and a cold drop of water falls on his forehead, and he is hit by the strong scents of damp wool, kerosene, and wood fire, and he sees that the face is ancient, Chinese, the ashen-tan color of a persimmon, and wrinkled like a prune—an old Buddhist monk's face. *If this is heaven, it's the wrong heaven, and I'm toast.*

"It's okay, darling," Clio says, touching his arm, "Xiao Lu's brought him from the monastery. I think he's a doctor."

"A doctor? She was supposed to bring a *porter*—two porters—to carry me out. This guy looks like he needs to be carried out himself. What's up?"

"I tried to ask her, but all she does is shake her head no. Maybe there weren't any at the monastery, or she couldn't persuade anyone else to come."

The monk grabs him by the ears, as if they are two jug handles, and forces him to stare into his eyes, which, in contrast to his ashen old face, seem to be live coals in a dying fire. "Ow! Hey, pal," Pep says, squirming away, "take it easy!"

The monk grabs his ears harder and forces him to submit to another set of hot stares. Finally he stops, lets go, knits his brow, strokes his chin.

Pep groans. *She dragged this guy out in the middle of the night across those logs to treat me?* He looks around. Katie is asleep on the floor, huddled under the quilt.

The monk takes Pep's wrist, feels for a pulse, and his head snaps back. He drops the wrist as if it's a live wire, and his mouth, which has been a thin, wrinkled slit, pops open in surprise. He barks something grim at Xiao Lu. Both of them stare down at Pep, who thinks, *This is not a good sign.* He starts to say something but the monk tries to silence him. Pep slips his head free.

"Clee, tell him the problem's in my ankle."

Clio tries to explain this. The monk nods in a dismissive way and traces a path on Pep's body from his wrist pulse to his heart and then up to his head, mimics a man looking down at a chasm, terrified, and then traces a line back down through his heart to his ankle, which is swollen to the size of an eggplant and bruised the same color.

Pep focuses on his heart—it's racing even more crazily. At that moment the monk puts his fingers on his pulse again, more lightly this time, and suddenly, as if receiving another shock, jerks his hand back. With a smile he shakes his fingers in the air as if to cool them off. Pep tries to explain that the monk's exam is causing the symptoms he's noticing, but he gets nowhere. Finally, after cooling his fingers in the pail of drinking water, the monk touches Pep even more lightly so that it might not even be a touch at all, keeps his fingers there, and closes his eyes.

From time to time he sighs, spreading the odor of garlic and ginger through the tiny room. He lifts his fingers, places them on the other side of the wrist. For another long space of time he communes with the pulse, his face twisted in worry. Pep is getting scared, feels his heart speed up—*the damn thing seems to be beating at random!*

Clio is fuming at this useless delay. Xiao Lu has failed to bring back anyone who could carry Pep out. After what seems like half an hour Pep and Clio are not even sure that the monk is awake. His breathing is deep and regular, and he isn't moving.

Finally the monk stirs, groans, and digs in his bag.

"What are you going to do for him?" Clio asks, indicating this in gesture.

The monk stares at her with a haughty air—reminding her of the infertility doctor telling her that everything had failed. Again, but this time with insistence—as if explaining the basics of life to a child—he points to Pep's heart, then traces his finger from heart to neck to head, into the brain, and then back down to the swollen foot. And then he smiles, revealing a silver mine of repaired teeth, front and back. He removes his worn quilted coat and points to his black bag. With a snort and a fist placed over his own heart, he indicates that he is the doctor and Pep is the patient and Clio counts for nothing and should just stay out of his way.

"Honey," Pep says, "I'm a goner."

The monk takes out a box of acupuncture needles.

"It's okay," she says. "He may be brusque, but acupuncture may be just the thing."

"The *porters* are just the thing—why the hell didn't she—?" The monk barks at him to be quiet. Pep lays his head back down and pictures himself dying of hepatitis or AIDS. He sighs. At least they say these acupuncture needles are painless.

Which is why, when the intense pain hits his inner thigh, he screams. The monk curses and tells him to be quiet. Katie wakes up, mumbles, and goes back to sleep.

The needles are a torment. So much for being painless, Pep thinks, these ones must be too thick or too dull—they feel like a nail twisted in through his skin. He bites his lip until it bleeds. The placements and twirlings are bad, but worse is when the monk takes a piece of kindling and sets the end aflame, then places it on a needle the length of a ruler stuck into the soft white middle of Pep's belly. At this Pep groans, whimpers—which makes the monk's wrinkled face re-wrinkle even more tightly in hearty laughter, joined by Xiao Lu. He tries to push away the big needle in his gut—the monk's hand bats his away as if it were a Ping-Pong ball in a tight game, and cautions him with a single raised index finger not to try that trick again. Pep clenches the wooden sides of the bed, clenches his teeth, clenches his mind down on his body, fighting the burning needles.

On it goes, the monk really getting into the fire cure and Pep in hot pain and Clio in frank doubt, until suddenly, and for no obvious reason, the monk stops still, alert, as if he hears something scary outside. He puts down the wooden mallet he has been using on a picket fence of needles between Pep's toes and, barking a command at Xiao Lu and motioning to Pep not to move, hustles to find his coat and umbrella and a rolled-up bamboo mat. Then, as if late for his next patient, he hurries out the door.

"Get him back in here!" Pep cries. "He needs to take out the goddamn needles!"

Clio gets up. From outside there's the sound of a tiny bell being struck— first a dull *clink*, then a hard strike and long ring. As it ends, another dull *clink* and a long ring. A third time, then silence. Clio looks at her watch. Four a.m. exactly. She takes the flashlight and goes outside.

It is dark—a thick, heavy dark just this side of fog. She sweeps the beam of the blue-laser flashlight around the clearing. The light hits the cliff face and brings to life reflections in the skin of the rock, mica and quartz—the mineral soul of the mountain. She senses an aura of gold and silver ore all around her.

On the far side of the clearing, where the stream runs, the monk sits on his bamboo mat in a full lotus. The bell perches in his hand like a songbird, the echo of its song fading, fading, to nothing. With a serene diligence he lowers it to the ground, and places the small piece of padded wood with which he struck the bell beside it. He then gathers his heavy coat around him and chants the sutras, bowing to the Buddha.

Clio watches, startled and touched. Startled at the transformation from an irritated, haughty, even mocking doctor to a devoted old man who has given up everything and endured God knows what during Mao's China for this classic Buddhist practice—to affirm that suffering is human, that there is a cause of suffering, that the cause is holding tight, that the relief of suffering is possible by merely this, merely letting go and bowing to the Three Jewels: the Buddha, the Dharma, and the Sangha. She watches with envy and dismay.

This *matters*. This practice, somehow, will help get them back to safety. Even having the monk here makes her feel safer; they're no longer alone with her. Somehow this monk's spirit will ease her husband's fear. *This is, because that is. That is, because this is. In the compost is the flower. In the flower is the compost.* Does she believe it, this co-arising of all life? At her best, maybe. Now?

Not really, no. She wants to go over to the monk and point to her watch and say, "Excuse me, sir, how much longer do you think you'll be? Back at the temple, the bowing and chanting lasts an hour. Is there any chance that, since this is a kind of satellite service, and my husband is paralyzed with fear and we can't get out of here, you could cut it short?"

She watches for a while, feels the night chill start to seep into her bones, and goes back inside.

33

Katie, curled up asleep in the chair, doesn't get to see the acupuncture needles porcupining out from her father's body. She's set her Baby-G to go off in time for her to feed the deer at dawn. By the time she awakens, the monk has ended his meditations, come back in, unceremoniously plucked out his needles, and demanded food.

Sleepily, Katie checks in with Clio, nods to Xiao Lu, is introduced to the monk, and asks Pep how he's doing.

"Okay," he says, cheerily. "Did you have a beautiful sleep?"

"Un hunh. How's your ankle and your like panic attacks?"

"Ankle's swollen, panic's gone—as long as I'm on solid ground. This monk is a doctor—he's already started working on it." He doesn't mention his pounding heart.

"He's started with acupuncture," Clio says.

"*Needles*!? Don't let me see 'em, okay?" Clio nods. "Hey, wait—I thought she was supposed to come back with some guys to carry Daddy across?"

"So did we," Clio says, tersely.

Katie picks up on Clio's irritation. "So maybe there weren't any guys and she left a message for them to come later."

"Maybe." Clio goes to Pep.

Xiao Lu settles the monk at the table and serves him a steaming hot bowl of congee. He slurps it up quickly, and asks for another. Though his name is True Emptiness, she has heard the joke around the monastery that this thin old man has such an enormous appetite they nicknamed him True Fullness. She laughs to herself, and wishes she could tell Chun this joke.

"Mom, can I ask Xiao Lu about feeding the deer?"

"You can ask, as long as you wait for me to come with you."

Through gesture with the Cheddar Goldfish, she makes it known that she wants Xiao Lu to produce the deer. Xiao Lu gets a few packages of Goldfish and heads outside, Katie following.

"Katie?"

Katie stops on the threshold, turns. Clio, hand raised to pour water into Pep's cup, is looking at her.

"Please don't go out there without me."

"But I'll miss the—"

"I'll be right there."

Katie glances at Xiao Lu, who laughs. When Pep is settled, they go out.

The sun is barely up, more a glow than a disk. The morning, after the rain, seems to Clio all mist—scrubbed fresh, the dew hanging on the grass and big drops shining on the wide leaves of skunk cabbage and on the thinner leaves of what Katie has said is the only thing giant pandas eat, cold arrow bamboo. A dark cypress grows next to the cliff, and a weeping willow rises over a streambed. Flowering azaleas, their purple or white blossoms downed by the rainy wind, are scattered around as if a wedding party has passed by in the night. Bordering the ravine to the left are catalpas, and dragon spruce that climb straight up for a hundred feet. Clinging to the walls of the ravine are what might be thousand-year-old gingko trees, gnarled and angry looking in the easy dawn. And ferns, ferns everywhere, as big as Clio has seen in the jungles of the islands, and Panama and Costa Rica, and moss upon moss upon mulchy rotting logs. And earth. All in all, a perfect place for deer.

Katie and Xiao Lu are walking softly across the clearing to where the cliff edge cuts back into the mountain and the forest takes over. Xiao

Lu puts some Goldfish in Katie's hand, takes some herself, and faces the forest.

"*Ping,*" she calls out quietly, musically. "*Ping. Ping.*"

They only have to wait a few moments. Suddenly the mountain deer are there. Katie is amazed at how silently they come to them through the woods, how still they stand there—two, three, four—and one of them is a *fawn*! They're much smaller than any deer she's ever seen. Their long delicate faces and big dark eyes are beautiful. She wants to turn around to tell Clio but knows she mustn't move or she'll scare them away. They're wild, but they act tame. Wild mountain deer her birth mom has tamed! She stares at Xiao Lu, who nods and slowly holds out her hand, palm up, motioning to Katie to do the same. They hold out their hands and wait.

The deer, eye level with them in the safety of the rhododendrons, hesitate.

Katie watches their eyes flick from Xiao Lu to her, and then down to the Goldfish, and back up. The biggest one, with a set of small horns, takes one step toward Xiao Lu, and another, then bends his head to the Goldfish and nibbles them up.

Katie is left with her hand out. The doe looks at her, looks back to Xiao Lu, approaches, steps back, approaches again, steps back again. Katie's hand is getting tired, but she holds it as steady as she can—bringing her other hand up to support it from the bottom like she's offering a gift to a god—and sure enough, the doe comes back, nibbles the fish quickly from her palm. Her lips feel rough and strong, as if eating harsh leaves and twigs and bark has made them tough. But it tickles, too—it's all she can do to keep from laughing. The doe bounces off—like a reebok or a bongo on Animal Planet—but then stands a few feet away, staring.

Xiao Lu pours more Goldfish into Katie's hand and into her own, and the deer come back. This goes on for several turns, until finally all the deer, even the fawn, have come up to eat. Xiao Lu shows them her empty hands, and the deer, Katie thinks, almost nod. Then they walk away, *gentle-gentle,* into the woods.

Katie watches them go. Amazing how fast they disappear in real life, with hardly a sound! It's different from TV. She turns around to where Clio stands. "Mom, did you see it? They ate from my hand—there was a whole little family, a momma, a daddy, and a *bay-bee!*"

"Wonderful, dear," Clio says, smiling. Katie starts to walk back toward her.

Xiao Lu follows her with her eyes. Again the word "Mom" hits her like a branch whipping back in her face. She was totally in the moment with her daughter just now, her mind emptied of all else—this new moment is filled with the torment that often comes when she tries to be with other people, especially now with this woman. Again she feels a crush of despair, the despair that made her think of killing herself by drinking fertilizer when she still lived with her husband and his family. Even after she fled to this mountain, this despair that made her wander aimlessly, all the way to the top of Sacrifice Rock. The only thing that stopped her from throwing herself off the edge was the dream of finding her baby again. *But if I'd known it would come to this?* She stares at Chun walking excitedly away from her toward the other woman—and meets the other woman's eyes. *This angry woman* cannot *be Chun's mother. Will not be.*

Clio sees, in Xiao Lu's eyes, something she has never seen before—not just her hunger but also her desperation. She realizes that Xiao Lu sees her seeing it. For a second it scares her. But then, trying not to blink, she stiffens her jaw and clenches her teeth, sending her a message: *Don't.*

"Did you see 'em, Mom, they're really, really tame, and they come in the morning and at night, and there was this fawn!"

"I did." She smiles at Xiao Lu. "Did you thank Xiao Lu for showing them to you?"

"Nope, I forgot."

"Go back to her and tell her. Try out a few shay shays."

As Katie turns toward her, Xiao Lu glances again at Clio and nods, as if she understands what Clio is doing. They walk around the clearing, looking for more wildlife, bending and gesturing. Xiao Lu tells her the Chinese word for each thing they see and, when Katie repeats it, tries to correct her intonation. It's a game of sounds, she saying it, Katie trying to mimic it, until she gets it right and Xiao Lu laughs and claps her hands and Katie teaches her how to do a high five.

After a while they come back and stand together before Clio, like two kids without a game to play.

"What are we gonna do *now*, Mom? What happens today anyway?"

To Clio it is a familiar question. In Columbia, like many other well-off kids living in their private, protected houses, Katie is used to having her time scheduled. She often seems not so much into the current activity as checking it off from a list before the next one, and not into the next because of the looming next, until at bedtime, she'll ask about the next day's schedule. And despite the frantic scheduling, any lull is met with a petulant "I'm *bored!*" Clio has worried about her daughter living too much in the future, but she and Pep and their friends live there too. Now, with Katie looking to her for ideas, Clio looks around at the cliff and woods and hut and moon gate leading out to the high west prospect, and realizes that here, stranded on a mountain halfway to the Himalayas in primitive China, the day looms endlessly ahead. No schedule, none.

"First thing," she says, "we help to get Daddy better."

"Okay, but that's the monk's job, right? What else?"

Xiao Lu has picked up the water bucket and motions to Katie to follow.

"There's the answer. We'll just follow along to help Xiao Lu. Let's go."

○ ○ ○

When the women return with firewood and fresh spring water, True Emptiness has Pep on his stomach in bed. Clio starts to talk to Pep, but the monk silences her. Soon Pep feels a warmth on his back, between his shoulder blades.

He sighs and starts to turn over, but hands like steel bands and a sharp command stop him. Exotic fumes fill the tiny room with a complex scent suggestive of something that died painfully a long time ago. The warmth turns to heat, the heat suddenly a fire in the center of his back. *The guy's set me on fire!* He tries to struggle free but the monk has him pinned down. The pain suddenly increases, as if an insect with a big hot mouth is trying to suck his skin up in a ball and swallow it—is he doing *leeches*? Clio and Katie gasp. His cry of pain is muffled by his being facedown in the quilt. The insect releases with a *pop!* He burns. He yelps.

"Relax, darling," Clio says, trying to hide her disgust at the smell and the round red welt where a cup has been removed, "it's just moxibustion."

"It's what?"

"Moxibustion. An ancient remedy. Tulku gave us a lecture on it, on traditional healing. I think the smell is mugwort. He's combining it with cupping. Trust him."

"*Why?*"

The monk has let go, and Pep manages to turn his head to see what's happening. True Emptiness is staring at the small glass cup he's removed and cursing under his breath, as if it were defective. He throws it against the wall and it shatters, sending flying shards of glass onto the stove. Xiao Lu berates him. He growls back at her, and indicates that all of them should leave him alone with his patient.

Clio protests, in vain. "Just relax, Peppie," she says. "We'll be right outside."

"Fine. Do me one favor—when he's done cooking me, don't let him *eat* me, okay? And no fancy funeral. Just family, dog, and bird."

As they leave, the monk indicates that Pep should lie back down.

Biting down on the edge of the quilt, Pep feels a series of hot mouths starting to suck at his body, from the nape of his neck to the crack of his butt. Each sizzles for a while, sucks at the skin, and then—*pop!*—is torn off. But after a while the mugwort fumes seem to be working on his brain, as if loosening screws and leaving him in a high that reminds him of his peace movement years. *Fun years, the only time I was loose, except meeting Clio. Love does that. Loosey-goosey love.*

The monk is chanting quietly to himself, a two-tone chant: a high short note—*hm*—then a low long note like a hum—*hmmm*. Pep tunes in to the silky rhythm. *Hm, hmmm. Hm, hmmm.* Soothing. Words come to mind, latching on to the enticing sounds, in the same tone and duration: *Tight, loooose. Tight, loooose. Hm, hmmm. Hm, hmmm.* Pep finds his grip on the pain loosening, his mind filling with all the ways he lives tight—family, job, even golf, even *love*, hell, even *sex*! All these phobias—trying to tighten, to close down and live without feeling. If you *do* feel something, *kill it*. And—here's the *real* killer—if you *have* opened up once to someone so that the other person really sees you, shame comes down on you like a baseball bat! You feel *so* ashamed of *having been seen* that you *kill it off*, once and for all, so the next time you see that person you pretend that what happened didn't happen, you just go right on with the pretend-shit, so that even if you're dying of cancer you repudiate the offer of a last true touch of your child's love.

Like my own father, on his deathbed, when I went to embrace him, even kiss him, said, "Now, now, Pep, none of that puff stuff now."

Pep feels a need to tell someone. "Hey," he says to the monk, "this is working."

"*Hm, hmmm.*"

"No question I'm tight," he goes on, relieved the monk can't understand. "Getting older, I'm getting tighter. When you're old, it's not about what you *think* anymore, it's about what you *feel*, right?"

"*Hm, hmmm.*"

"So it all boils down to this. Loosen up. Either you do it or you miss it. Right?"

A pause. And then: "*Hm, hmmm.*"

34

The morning passes. Katie, Xiao Lu, and Clio do the chores: gathering and chopping wood, hauling water, washing, fixing, cooking, cleaning, starting a new quilt. The monk continues to work on Pep. He moves on from moxibustion to a brisk massage, pounding Pep's back with a wooden mallet rife with knobs, which seems to make his internal organs wobble. Next, oral treatments, concoctions of herbs, mushrooms, a slimy green and foul-smelling potion Clio thinks is the notorious bear's bile she's seen on TV, gathered from bears chained in cages with infected catheters in their bile ducts. Gamely, Pep swallows it. After each treatment, the monk stares at him suspiciously as if he hasn't really drunk or endured it, then, gingerly placing a finger on Pep's wrist, mutters a curse and withdraws to the chair to drink some more green tea and brood. The only noticeable effect of all this on Pep is in his bowels. He spends much of his time limping back and forth to the latrine.

On one trip, taking his own pulse—fast and random like two steel bands dueling—Pep suddenly thinks of his poker buddy, Marty Van Buren. Dr. Orville Rose diagnosed Marty with a heart arrhythmia, "atrial fib." When meds couldn't control it, Orville told Marty he *had* to go on blood thinners, *right away*—otherwise a clot could form inside his heart and blast up into his brain and stroke him out. Marty refused. Two days later, he stroked out. Never walked or talked again—never even played poker. Died years later a vegetable. Pep breaks out in a cold sweat. *Shit. If this is what Marty had, and doesn't stop in a day or two—I'm dead!* He shivers. *But what can I do? Take a ton of aspirin. And don't tell Clio.*

As Xiao Lu works with Katie, she points out all kinds of animals, birds, and plants, and mixes play with the tasks. Clio does her best to join in. Each chore is turned into a game, a chance for her to teach Katie the Chinese words for things. Katie repeats each one, and then Xiao Lu goes to work on the tones until Katie gets it right. Clio can hardly hear a difference in the tones, and for the life of her can't remember the words for any length of time. Katie can, and does. As if, as Katie said before they left for China, the language is *in* her, ready to come out.

Clio is amazed at how Katie, who steadfastly neglects to do her only two chores—to feed and water Dave and Cinny, and carry her dishes to the sink—is pitching in with everything, even hard things, like getting down on her knees beside Xiao Lu to clean the old stones of the floor, one by one. Side by side they work with picks and brushes, stone by stone. With each chunk of muck dug out there's a triumphant laugh—two happy prospectors chipping out gold.

Katie likes working with Xiao Lu. *She makes it a game, like a friend, and she's happy when I do good, and laughs—she's a good laugher!—and helps me on the hard stones—like cleaning out Velcro's hoofs with Mary. It's so fun to learn things—how to tip the pail to get the water from the stream without getting mud in it and how heavy water is! Xiao Lu's way strong, and even though I'm huffing and puffing—Dad said we're at like eight thousand feet—she doesn't even breathe hard. She let me chop wood, showed me how to use the hatchet so I don't hatchet my legs or fingers. The way if you put the edge of the hatchet just right and hit the back with that big wooden hammer she has it goes shhhwittt! and like magic there are two pieces of wood the inside all tan and smelling sawdusty and the grains running up and down like veins. At home Mom and Dad don't do stuff like this with me, not even fixing a flat tire or washing the windows or mowing the lawn. They pay somebody else to do it. They pay people like Xiao Lu to do their things. I wish they'd teach me themselves like she does.*

Xiao Lu indicates it's time to stop cleaning the floor and start preparing lunch. Katie stands up in front of Clio proudly, pointing to the dozen or so stones they've finished.

"Great! But you're filthy—please go wash your hands?"

"*She* isn't washing her hands."

"That doesn't mean *we* don't. I'll go with you to the spring. And remember—don't get any water in your mouth, not a drop."

Katie glances at Xiao Lu and sees that she's picked up this tension. *Like Mom thinks it's a kinda contest—but all it is really is a pain.*

When they come back from washing their hands Xiao Lu teaches Chun how to cut up the vegetables—bok choy, onion, bamboo shoots. Soon Chun is following her, matching her precise shapes. It is a slow process, a challenge to Chun. She concentrates hard and seems to admire how fast Xiao Lu does it, how fine she chops, how alike the pieces are. But Chun does it too fast. Xiao Lu grasps her racing hand, pats it, and smiles, meaning "Careful!" She and Chun stir-fry the vegetables with wood ears in the beat-up wok. Garlic and soy are added. Rice follows. It is a simple, healthy meal that Chun and the others seem to like very much.

Afterward Xiao Lu takes Chun outside again to collect small branches and logs for the evening's fire. Again Xiao Lu watches as the woman trails along behind, helping a little. She is on alert, never letting them be alone, watching like a hawk, and always glancing back to make sure the man is all right. She seems very worried and very tense. Each moment with Chun is precious!

○ ○ ○

Toward the end of the afternoon Chun asks if she can do more calligraphy.

Xiao Lu sits close to her at the table. Today she will teach her the eight basic brushstrokes that every Chinese child her age will already have learned.

Katie tries hard to follow her lead, surprised at how difficult the brush is to control, and amazed at Xiao Lu's skill. She's a good teacher, Katie thinks. She makes it fun and doesn't get impatient like her mom does, and she isn't in a hurry and doesn't seem to have something else on her mind.

After a while the strokes are good enough, so Xiao Lu teaches her the classic stroke order for each character. As she describes the stroke, she motions to make Katie see what the word is. First horizontal, then vertical, like the character for "ten":

一 十

First above, then below—like the character for "three":

First to the left, then to the right—like the character for "man, person":

First in the middle, then on the sides—like the character for "small":

First outer, then inner—like the character for "moon":

But if the outer stroke, like in the character for "sun," forms a closed square, the lower stroke is written last. "First go in, then shut the door":

Chun seems to really enjoy this, Xiao Lu thinks. Her head is bent low to the paper, the brush held upright, just as she has shown her. As she makes the characters, Xiao Lu giggles and applauds. Chun smiles at her. Xiao Lu feels a warm glow. *It's like when I was a child being taught by my own mother, and then by my dear teacher. By the time Xia was old enough to hold a brush, she had turned against me. I never taught her. Now I am teaching my own child.*

Suddenly Xiao Lu realizes she has not yet shown her the most important character, the one for her name, Chun, "Spring." She points to her, and says, "Chwin."

"Chwin," says Chun, pointing to herself.

Xiao Lu smiles and nods—the accent is almost perfect. The woman is standing beside Chun now, looking over her shoulder. Xiao Lu catches the woman's eye, seeing that she is not happy at this. Why? It is her girl's name. She wonders how to show that Chun means "Spring." She sits, puzzled. Then she realizes she can tell Chun the same story her first teacher told her—she remembers the day like yesterday! She holds up three fingers to Chun and says in Chinese, "Three," and draws the character for "three":

Then she points to the character they just drew for "man, person," and says it in Chinese and superimposes it on top of the "three":

Finally she points to the character they've drawn for "sun," and puts it below:

Over and over in gestures she paints a picture in the air above the character, pointing to each character as she makes it and saying to Chun: "Three. People. Sit. In. Sun." She pauses. "Chwin. 'Spring.'" She has Chun repeat each word, and corrects her intonation until she gets every syllable right. "Three people sit in sun—'Chwin, Spring.'" Finally Chun understands and says the whole sequence perfectly. It is her first sentence in Chinese and Xiao Lu claps her hands. Chun claps too, and turns and talks to the woman. The woman pretends to be excited. It is all Xiao Lu can do to keep from laughing at her clumsy effort.

Xiao Lu laughs and claps, says, "Chwin-Chwin," and invites her to draw it. Carefully—too carefully, so that it is chunky and out of proportion, she does. Xiao Lu takes her hand and guides her, over and over for ten "Chuns," twenty, until she is starting to relax, and then another ten or twenty until, through her relaxation, it starts to be drawn, the character starts to come alive. She smiles and laughs and pats her on the head, and then she takes her by the hand and leads her over to a wall where some of her calligraphy scrolls hang. She points to the top character of one of them—it is a "Chun" much like the character she drew. Then she points out the top character of another "Chun," but drawn with more freedom. She points out others, some so stylized that they barely resemble the first character she drew.

"Look, Mom," Katie says. "Almost every one starts with a 'Chun'!"

"Yes. She really loves that character, doesn't she?" *Obsessed. For ten years it has been her lifeline to you.*

"That 'Chun' up there," Katie is saying, "looks like a plant coming out of the earth, y'see?" Clio nods. "I'll try to copy it." She leads Xiao Lu back to the table, and takes up the brush. Twirling the tip and then inking it, she points to the calligraphy with the plant-coming-out-of-the-earth "Chun," and copies it, pretty well:

Xiao Lu nods, appreciating how well Chun has copied the character she herself copied from the photos her teacher showed her of the "Spring" character carved into ancient tortoiseshells and ox shoulder bones.

Katie says to Clio, "But she doesn't have the one from the 'New Beginnings' card you got when you were waiting for me, the 'amazing.' I'll see if I can draw it for her."

Clio feels a shiver go down her spine. *To share* that? *Our story?* But Katie can't actually tell her the story. *Relax, damnit. Let it go.*

"Here it is!" Katie is saying, proudly, tilting the paper up so Xiao Lu and Clio can see. She points to the character, and then to herself. "*My* Chun."

Xiao Lu is stunned by this, and studies it carefully. She has done many "Chuns," but she has never before seen a character like this. It is an elegant, vibrant, alive creature that forms a bridge from the ancient "Chun" to the modern—the missing link in the chain of "Chuns." It is new to her. She is thrilled, and feels a warm rush fill her body. She smiles her pleasure, and reaches out to touch her daughter's face with her fingertips, caress it.

Katie smiles, happy at the big smile from Xiao Lu, thinking, *Wow, she really likes this one. Let me do it again better.* She bends her face down close to the paper and concentrates on making this one perfect. When it smudges, she gets impatient and tries another. Finally, on the fourth try, she is satisfied and says to Xiao Lu: "Momma, this is my best one, see?"

She looks up at Xiao Lu, who is smiling broadly—and then Katie realizes what she has done.

She turns to look at Clio, hoping she hasn't heard. But she has.

35

Katie has been looking forward to feeding the deer again at sundown. As the light begins to fade, she stands between Xiao Lu and Clio, facing the woods, her open palms filled with Goldfish. Pep, leaning on the monk's staff, watches. The deer appear, and the little buck comes forward to nibble at Xiao Lu's palm. The doe and fawn and a few others hold back for a moment, then bounce toward them.

Boom! Boom! Boom! A pause. *Boom! Boom! Boom!*

The deer vanish. The monk is walking around the clearing to the beat of a small drum clenched under his arm and struck with vicious abandon by the same mallet he used for vibrating the acupuncture needles in Pep's toes. *Boom! Boom! Boom!* Pause. *Boom! Boom! Boom!* Xiao Lu screams at him to stop, but he does not. She tries to grab his arm, but in his floppy robe he is like a wave that no human hand can grasp—he keeps chanting and circling. *Boom! Boom! Boom!* It is as if he has been doing the same thing for so long, at dawn and at dusk, that it is wired into him.

Finally he stops, spreads his bamboo mat, lights a joss stick, assumes the full lotus, and begins bowing and chanting again.

Katie gestures to Xiao Lu and asks, "You think they'll come back?"

Xiao Lu shakes her head—"No, not tonight"—and gestures to come help make dinner.

After the monk finishes, and as he is rolling up his mat, Xiao Lu says to him, "Go home! Go back to the monastery! You are ruining my time with my daughter!"

"I don't leave till I fix the man."

"He's no better."

"He's no worse. I will study my textbooks. Tomorrow I work on him some more. He is a great challenge. His heart is beating bad. Great danger. But I will cure him."

"You cause trouble for me. If you don't go tonight, you don't get the quilt."

"If you don't give me the quilt, you lose your job. Where do I sleep?"

"Leave!"

"Stupid woman! Where do I sleep?"

His eyes are two rocks. "Okay. I give you one more day. You sleep in the cave."

"What cave?"

She leads him around the back of the house. The Macys follow. At the mouth of the cave, True Emptiness balks, curses, and says that not even in his days as an itinerant young monk with a begging bowl, not even during the Mao era when he hid out in the foothills of Tibet disguised as a butcher's apprentice, did he stay in a such a cave, and he isn't about to start now.

"You either sleep in the cave or you sleep outside," she says. "There's no room in the hut. I'm going to have to sleep in the cave too."

"It stinks."

"It is a sacred cave."

"Bullshit."

"There are markings on the wall. There is an altar. There are legends. A holy man lived here for many years and when he died his body stayed here untouched by animals until his bones became a pile of white dust." She points. "That pile of white dust you see in the corner there."

"What's for dinner?" She doesn't answer. He goes outside.

Katie and Clio and Pep are amazed at the sight of the cave. The dusk light eases in through a wide crack in the rock, and water drips steadily through the crack and down twenty feet into what looks like a foot-deep, carved-out basin, then through a narrow channel cut into the rock and out through the entrance. On the smooth walls Clio can make out pictographs of animals and humans, and long columns of Chinese characters. It reminds her of the caves of the Dordogne that she visited with her mother and sisters so long ago, although these drawings are stick legged and simplistic, almost like the Chinese characters they became, not the full-bodied, fluid mammoths and deer, in red and black, of Font-de-Gaume.

"Awesome!" Katie shouts up into the dome.

"Awesome! Awesomeawesome . . ." the dome echoes back.

"Lotta headroom," Pep says, staring up into the expanse, "more than any other place we've seen in all of China. Nice."

Xiao Lu brings in a load of firewood and lights a large iron stove whose scarred, rusted flue pipe zigzags unsteadily up through the crevice in the roof. Then she goes out and returns with an armload of small, sweet-scented cedar boughs. Katie asks in gesture what she's doing, and she indicates two rough-hewn beds, one large, one small, and two quilts. She starts stuffing the cedar boughs into one of the quilts, asking Katie if she'd like to help.

"Look—she's making mattresses! Are they for us?" Katie asks Xiao Lu in gesture. No, they're for her and the monk tonight. "Hey, guys, maybe we can switch? It would be so fun, like sleeping in a pine tree—it smells all tree-ey and fresh. Please?"

Pep has gotten out his blue-laser flashlight and is sweeping the recesses and the roof of the cave. Suddenly there's a fluttering high up in a far corner, and something glides easily down around them like a paper airplane. It seems to be about to hit a wall when it banks away smoothly and sails on an imaginary gray wind in spirals, graceful floating loops, and quick flips, and floats off on another tack.

"A bat!" Katie cries. "Wow!"

"Careful!" Clio cries, taking Katie's hand. "Let's get out of here!"

"Wait, Mom! They're just doing big swoops—they'll never bump into you! They're blind and fly by echoes!"

"Bats carry diseases," Clio says. "Like rabies. Let's go."

"Not really. I *studied* bats in Lucille Stotts' class! I love bats! Bats don't hurt anybody."

"Sick ones do," Clio says.

"Sure, ones cooped up by humans in zoos, but not wild ones, free ones."

Xiao Lu sees Chun's fascination and the woman's fear. She holds up her hand. A bat comes straight for it, then banks away, and comes back and banks around it again, and sails off on another unseen breeze.

"Cool!" Katie says. *Xiao Lu's really good with animals. Wild animals are like her pets. A pet bat is awesome. She loves animals and they love her. She's in symbiosis!* "That's not a sick bat, Mom, no way! And they eat mosquitoes. So they protect us from malaria, right? They're like good for us, right?"

Clio says nothing.

"Right, Dad? Low-risk, right? It would be *so* cool to sleep in here! Can we?"

Pep feels caught between Clio and Katie. Lately when Katie gets a "No" from one of them, she tries to play them off each other. She's right, he thinks, it's not much of a risk, no. Pep glances at Clio, and sees in her eyes her fear and her resoluteness—she does not want them to stay here. He knows that she feels safer in smaller, enclosed spaces, with doors that you can close and lock, like the hut. Big, high spaces—which he prefers—make her nervous. In her glance is a firm "No." But he feels he has to moderate it—Katie and she are getting into a fight about everything and anything to do with Xiao Lu, and all it does is push Katie away, toward her.

"Mom 'n I will talk about it and let you know. Besides, Xiao Lu hasn't said she'd switch and let us stay here."

"I'll ask her." Katie gestures. Xiao Lu smiles and nods. "It's okay with her." Katie glances at Clio, who looks even less open to the idea, and then focuses her hope on Pep. "Please, Daddy?"

Pep realizes he has to be firm. "Sorry, honey, we can't do it, not tonight."

Immediately Katie turns to Clio. "Mom, say yes."

"No, not tonight."

"You never let me do anything *fun*! And for your information, this would *definitely* be fun. Low-risk and fun! Like she's fun and you're not!" Katie flumphs out of the cave. Xiao Lu follows.

"Katie, come here!"

"No!" She turns and stares at her. "I'm not hanging out with you anymore, I'm hanging with *her*." She stomps away, Xiao Lu walking quickly after her.

Clio goes to the cave entrance and stares. Xiao Lu walks into the house, and comes out carrying a large wooden cutting board heaped with vegetables—spring onions, bok choy, yams, garlic cloves, ginger root. A small knife and a curved chopper lie beside them on the board. She squats on the ground beside Katie, balancing perfectly on her heels. Katie looks down at her, they exchange words, and then Katie squats down alongside her in the same way, balancing easily.

Clio has never seen Katie squat like this before, perfectly balanced, just like her. With no effort, as if her body was designed for this.

Xiao Lu and she seem, just then, like sisters sitting in the courtyard outside their family house—First Sister, Second Sister—two sisters squatting together in the dirt facing the woods, sharing an old wooden cutting board, starting to chop up the garlic and ginger and vegetables for the family's evening meal, going over the day's events as sisters do, happy just being together. Safe, at day's end, with family, protected from the world. *Located.*

○ ○ ○

"Pep? Pep, wake up, but shhh, quiet—don't wake Katie." He carefully gets up and limps on the uneven stones to the fire, where Clio is sitting on the chair. He takes the lone bench.

They are alone. Xiao Lu and the monk are sleeping in the cave. It's only ten o'clock—Clio waited until she was sure that Katie was sound asleep.

They sit face-to-face, reading each other in the warm, close glow. Pep sees the worry in Clio's face, and something else he can't identify. He's surprised at the acuity of his eyesight—no, not just that, his inner sight as well—he feels he's never really *looked* into her eyes this unflinchingly, searchingly, before. He sees her concern, her terrible fear that things are going very wrong here—and shivers. Suddenly he wants to tell her all the things he's come to understand during the monk's treatment, and share his terror that his screwed-up heart could throw a clot into his brain that would paralyze or kill him—wants to tell her *every true thing!*—but can't.

Tell her! Can't.

And in that "can't" something wells up that he's felt once or twice in his life—as a boy at that moment when he sensed the dry depth of his father's disinterest in him, and as a man when he stared with his wife into a childless future. He wants to tell her but he sees in her eyes her fright and sadness and all at once he's weeping.

"Oh shit, I'm sorry—" He tries to stop but can't.

"What's wrong?"

Again he takes a deep breath and tries to say something but keeps on sobbing, his body shaking. And then he feels her arms go around him and he understands that his tears are for her, for their baby, for all of them. He holds on to her, hard.

Holding him, feeling his shudders, her heart opens and breaks a little. She hasn't seen him like this in years. Not since they said yes to China and were handed Katie and their hearts flew up like birds and they were in love with her and each other and life itself and began living human-sized lives. As she cradles him, this poor man whose tightness restrains his anger like her tightness restrains her sorrow, she feels his terror, senses how much they have lost, how lonely and walled-off each of them has become, how the connection they made with each other and their baby has become a connection only *through* her, so that for years when they have "taken time for themselves"—a weekly movie date or dinner up in Albany or a trip to New York—all they talked about was their child. Katie has been their connection—which makes Katie's distance, now, terrifying.

Seeing him so vulnerable, for a moment she feels confused. Her instinct is to say to him, "Pull yourself together, be strong like always," but then she hears her mother's voice when her father didn't get tenure in locust entomology and crashed into depression—"Pull yourself together, Forbes!"—and she damn well will not follow that shit now. *Move! Accept him. Be with him where he is, right here, right now.* She squeezes him as tightly as she can, feeling their embrace as a life preserver in this harsh, isolating world.

They hug each other for dear life and for a long time. The strength that has seemed lost in either of them alone now seems to come back to both, in the shared flow of care, raveling them up, together. This little catch of fire, in their despair, warms them. Again they look into each other's eyes for a long moment before pulling away.

"Pep . . . I . . . thank you so much . . ."

"And you." He wipes his eyes, sighs.

"Yes." She collects herself. "But listen—we've got to get out of here. I've got a really bad sense about Xiao Lu, and it's getting worse. Why didn't she bring anyone to carry you out? We could be back in Changsha by now. Katie's moving toward her, starting to love being here, love being with her. She's hardly *talking* to me anymore—and Xiao Lu knows it. Katie's learning words, sentences. A couple of times I even saw her cover her mouth with her hand when she laughed, just like her. We're losing her—*emotionally.* Whatever I try just makes it worse! I have this feeling there's a real possibility that Xiao Lu is going to try to take her."

"Clee, *please*—"

"We *have* to take it seriously. The only thing that's kept her going all these years is the hope of seeing her daughter again. Look at the walls— over and over she writes her *name*?"

"What more can we do?"

"One of us has to be with them at all times. At night, one of us will stay awake—I'll put the chair against the door, to sleep. When the monk goes back to the monastery, if you still can't get across, we'll make *sure* he sends back the porters. And one other thing: Pep, we've *got* to stick together in this. In the cave thing, she tried to play you off of me, and she saw you waver—"

"I didn't—"

"Listen—if she sees the slightest crack between us, she'll use it. Right now, with Katie, you're the good guy. She'll still listen to you. So you've got to be really *there* with her, okay?"

"Sure. But she still looks to you first and foremost."

"When the *hell*, Pep, are you going to see how important you are to her, how powerful? *When?*"

He's startled at her vehemence. "Yeah, when indeed." He sighs. "Sorry for my outburst. Guess I'm getting emotional too."

"Sorry? Pep, it's a *treasure.*"

Choked up again, he takes her hands. "Thanks."

○ ○ ○

Sitting there in the chair in the centuries-old stone hermitage, the embers casting a smoky glow and all kinds of clutter hanging from beams or tacked to walls or lying on sagging shelves, Clio feels her own heart racing. Despite feeling Pep so much with her, she feels like she's lost her bearings on place and time, as if she's in a fairy tale with a wicked witch, or in Hogwarts, or with Odysseus in the cave of the Cyclops—how Katie loved that story—Odysseus trying to figure out how to get his men out safely, all the while wondering which of them would be eaten next. *In a way it's so simple, with the Greeks.*

The chair blocks the door, and soon she feels safe enough to sleep. But in that phantasmal hypnogogic moment just as she's falling asleep she's jolted awake by a voice—*She loves her more truly than she loves you.* She stares around. Nothing.

She takes a sip of black tea, intent on staying awake. Vigilant.

○ ○ ○

At four the next morning the monk rings his bell and starts his chanting and wakes up everybody but Katie. Xiao Lu comes in and smiles and starts to boil water and cook congee. First Pep, then Clio, goes to the latrine, the other guarding the sleeping Katie.

The monk finishes his devotions and walks into the hut and puts a finger boldly on Pep's neck pulse. He nods rhythmically, as if in time with it— which Pep and Clio take for a change for the better. But then, cursing softly through clenched teeth, he shows his frustration. His examination of the ankle is more satisfying. Given the soaking in cold water and the poultice of an ointment made from mixing some black mud downstream from the latrine with the same bear-bile stuff that Pep has been drinking, the purple color has changed to blotched lavender, and the swelling is gone. He asks Pep to walk on it. Pep nods and smiles—it's much less painful.

After an enormous breakfast prepared by Xiao Lu and Katie, the monk disappears into the cave, indicating that they all should follow. He takes a large, leather-bound volume out of his bag, opens it, and invites them to look. Clearly it is a textbook of Chinese medicine, with page after page of finely wrought drawings of human bodies crisscrossed with lines of meridians and latitudes and longitudes that make them seem more like maps than people. There are also drawings of moxibustion cups and internal organs and whole chapters on acupuncture needles and their placements. It's impressive, and they nod in appreciation of the monk's obvious expertise. He indicates that they should leave him to study. At the cave mouth they look back. He is bent low to the text, a finger tracing the pathways, with the intensity of a man wrestling his gods, or his demons.

Outside, Pep says, "Katie, I want to talk with you a sec, alone?" Clio goes off. When Katie and he are settled on a bench, he tells her how it's not good that she and Clio are getting into fights all the time, and that it's got to stop.

"Yeah, but she's like so nervous! Anything I do she doesn't like!"

"I know, I know, but put yourself in her shoes. She—and I—have a job to do, which is to keep you safe, and get you back home safely."

"But like I told you before—nothing's *not* safe here! I'm just starting to have fun and she goes wild!" She pauses. "Not like you."

"Mom and me are totally together on this, understand?"

"Not really."

"Not really understand?"

"No, *you're* not really."

"Trust me—we *are*, okay?"

Katie looks down at her running shoes and doesn't say okay.

"There's one big thing you can't do while we're here: you can't go outside the boundaries of this yard, from the moon gate to the cliff edge, from the cave to the woods over there, *unless one of us is with you*. Period. It's a rule. *Agreed*?"

Katie rolls her eyes. "What choice do I have?"

"On that, zero."

"Okay, okay!"

"Say it."

As if to say the word would destroy her very being, she grimaces and it slips out through her clenched teeth. "Agreed." She gets up. "Now can I go? I've got a lot of work to do today."

"Have fun."

"I will!"

36

Xiao Lu and Katie again spend the day in ordinary ways but for Clio's—and now Pep's—heightened vigilance. They do the usual housekeeping tasks, and also go into the woods to gather mushrooms and herbs, Xiao Lu leading them to a damp, sunlit patch of obvious fertility—there are vegetables of all sorts, carrots and Chinese radishes, garlic and onions, bok choy and sweet potato. Katie and Xiao Lu prepare another dynamite lunch—which the monk eats by himself in the cave.

Clio is exhausted from being up all night. Pep tries to persuade her to take a nap and hand over the care of Katie to him, but she can't. To stay alert, she keeps up her intake of strong tea until her fingers tremble and her lips twitch. Despite several overtures, Katie doesn't respond. Clearly she is still angry. Clio can hardly stand it.

After lunch Katie sticks close to Xiao Lu, with Clio always nearby. Katie helps Xiao Lu cut up rags for the monk's quilt, sew them together, haul water and chop wood, cook and clean. Katie makes a point of getting down in the dirt. She digs with her bare hands for mushrooms or roots or vegetables, lying on her stomach to reach into rotting holes in fallen logs or stumps and coming up smeared with mud, black half-moons of dirt under her nails, and her T-shirt and shorts the wet-brown color of the forest floor. Filthy, she smiles at Clio as if to spite her.

In late afternoon, Pep and Clio sit on the bench at the corner of the house to get away from the intense tropical sun. Katie and Xiao Lu are on the edge of the clearing in the shade of a tall old pine, playing some kind of Chinese game that involves sticks and smooth river stones and a meticulous drawing of things in the dirt, upon which Katie is sprawled on her stomach, her face sideways on one hand, carefully tracing a figure on the ground. Xiao Lu is also on her stomach, drawing—or, it seems, extending Katie's part of the drawing—with Katie's head close beside hers.

Pep asks Clio to check his pulse. She puts her finger on his wrist and looks at her watch. The sunlight makes it hard to see the second hand, and they turn and face away toward the cave, creating more shadow. She has to concentrate to find the pulse, and then try to count it. She can't—it's still too high and irregular. To Pep it feels horrific, like it's tumbling over a waterfall and crashing on the rocks below. He shakes his head in dismay. Clio turns back to Katie and Xiao Lu. They're not there.

"Oh shit! Pep?"

She starts running this way and that all over the yard, calling, "Katie! Katie!" Racing around the clearing and a ways up each of the faint paths leading into the bamboo and the woods. "Katie? Katie!" Except for the echo, dead quiet.

Back in the yard, Pep joins her. They stand, catching their breath, staring around the grove in the stony mountain pass. Clio feels exhaustion come down on her, wanting nothing more than to go to sleep and for all this to be a bad dream, yet she feels adrenaline pumping and caffeine jittering—she's on a razor's edge. She tries to think, cradling her chin in her hands, fingers to her temples, pressing hard.

"Hey, up here!"

They look up. There, up in the big pine under which they've been playing, are Katie and Xiao Lu, smiling down at them.

"We're up in the tree house!"

She and Pep stare up at the two girlish faces peering over the edge of a platform in the big old tree. "Get down!" Clio shouts. "Now!"

"Come up and see—it's really neat! The steps are on the other side."

"I said come down!"

"'Kay. You walked right under us, it was so funny! You didn't once look *up*!"

"Katie!" Pep yells up at her. "I told you—don't disappear!"

"You said don't go out of the clearing and I didn't! Jeez Louise!"

They come down on a series of wooden slats nailed to the unseen side of the tree. Clio takes Katie's hand roughly and faces Xiao Lu. "It won't work! I've *had* it!"

"Stop it, Mom, please—" Clio starts leading Katie away.

"Why are you scared of me?" Xiao Lu shouts, knowing she won't understand the words. "She is my baby, I will never harm her! You take care of her but she is *mine*!"

Clio shouts, "We're leaving. Very soon. One way or the other, we will leave!"

"Why do this to me? Is it my crime to love her?"

Katie has never seen Clio like this. Her hand on her shoulder is shaking—her whole body is shaking. Clio walks Katie toward the hut, but then instead goes up to the mouth of the cave and looks back. Pep is hobbling along as fast as he can, trying to catch up. Katie looks back at Xiao Lu standing there alone, her hands down at her sides. *She looks really sad.*

Suddenly Clio starts to feel like she's evaporating. The caffeine has burned off. The strength goes out of her, the weight of fatigue rolls in, pulling her down. "I am very tired. If you promise, Katie, to stay close, I think I'll lie down here in the sun and take a little rest? Daddy's on duty."

"I promise."

Katie watches Clio stretch out on the sunny rock, adjust her body to its shape, and soon fall asleep. Pep sits there with his back against the warm cliff, watching. Katie nestles between his bare bony knees. It feels good.

Xiao Lu is still standing there in the clearing, her hands stiffly down at her sides.

Glancing at Clio, whose eyes are closed, Katie raises her hand and waves at her.

Xiao Lu sees her wave and waves back. She is appalled at the way that the woman yells at Chun. The way they both are with Chun is so strange. It is almost as if they don't like her. They will go soon now. *How will I bear it?* She sighs and looks out at the July sun, which has made its way far down into the ocean of sky, and is now only two fingers above a far peak, the one that, whenever she sees it in shadow, makes her think of her mother-in-law's ugly chin.

Time to prepare the evening meal. She starts to go into the house, and stops, turning to see her child deeply, maybe for one of the last times before they take her away. Chun sees her seeing, and nods. She nods back. *I will not let that happen.*

○ ○ ○

Not long before dusk the monk comes out of the cave, banging his drum in a new, upbeat rhythm. He calls out to everyone in a reed-thin, piping voice to come to the center of the clearing. When they are gathered he puts down his drum, then turns and disappears into the cave. They wait in silence. He comes back with his black doctor's satchel over his shoulder and a rolled-up bamboo mat under his arm. Carefully inspecting the lay of the land in the clearing, he picks a spot for the mat. He unrolls it gently, as if it is alive and now fragile in its flatness, and makes meticulous, almost surgical adjustments of edges and alignments to sky and earth.

Then, walking in a circle around the mat, he stops at each of the four points of the compass and shouts up into the heavens, generating enormous high-pitched sound that drills the air. He cuts each shout off sharply, as if with a scalpel, so that he can luxuriate in the response from the suddenly talkative mountain. With a grand gesture to Pep and a broad smile on his face, he ushers him to the mat and urges him to sit in a full lotus position. Unable to achieve even a half lotus, Pep negotiates a Boy-Scout-at-a-campfire cross-legged sitting posture and waits. Clearly this effort, the result of the monk's daylong retreat to study his texts and spiritual sources, is the do-or-die moment.

The monk pounds his chest with his fist and points a finger like a sword at Pep's head, maybe even his brain, making slicing motions up and down.

"No way! Clio, don't let him!"

"Don't worry, we're right here."

The monk opens his satchel, takes out his tools, and gets to work. He places a few acupuncture needles over Pep's heart and twirls them, first one, then another, then another, then back to the second, like one of those acts in the Beijing Circus where a guy keeps twenty plates spinning on wobbly sticks.

The monk then lights one glass cup and places it on Pep's knee, then another on the other knee. Clio holds Pep's hand. The monk produces from his satchel a small, black-enameled box sparkling with inlaid precious stones in arcane, asymmetric patterns. He slips the bone-peg latches and opens it. Obviously the guy is pulling out all the stops, building to some kind of grand finale. Inside the box, catching the low sun, are long metal instruments thick as a pinkie, sharp at one end with a knob at the other. Before Pep can protest the monk has selected one and shoved the knobby end into Pep's left ear. As it hits the eardrum Pep screams bloody murder, and keeps screaming, for the pain is intense. Clio moves to grab the monk's hand, but he pushes her away and takes up his trusty all-purpose wooden mallet and grasps the metal stalk of the rod firmly in his left hand and raises his mallet in his right. Clio fears he's going to shove the metal rod through Pep's eardrum, maybe his brain, and again rushes at the monk, but again is pushed away roughly. As Katie screams, Pep tries to turn his head, but the monk has straddled it and is holding it firm between his knees.

"Dad, what's going on?" Katie cries.

"No, don't!" Clio shouts, and again moves toward the monk.

The monk lowers the little mallet—not to drive the rod into Pep's brain but to gently strum the sharp end so that it vibrates back and forth. Strums it with a cellist's touch, again and again.

Pep yells and yells. Clio tries to shield Katie from the sight.

Xiao Lu is laughing, not just at the antics of the angry monk but also at the Americans' fear. Haven't they ever seen someone's ears tuned and cleaned before?

With a final sharp tap of the vibrating rod, the monk yelps and pops it out of Pep's head, releases him from between his knees, and steps back to observe.

Pep is stunned. He feels like he's been plunged down way too far underwater and his eardrum is screaming, "Let me up!" He puts a hand to his ear and, feeling a wetness, sees that his hand is covered in bright-red blood. He starts to panic, but then suddenly feels that something else has happened. What is it? And then he knows.

"My heart!"

For the first time in many days he has a sense that he is back to slow and steady, his heart back to strong, full strokes—a crew rowing boldly on a river. He puts his bloody finger on his wrist pulse and sure enough, it is slow and regular. He screams. "Yesss!"

The monk comes over, feels his pulse, and screams, "Ya! Yaaaa! Ya! Yaaaa!"

Clio and Katie cheer.

The monk plucks out the last needle, pops off the moxibustion glasses, stows them away in his black bag, and bows in triumph.

He turns to Xiao Lu. "I want my dinner, and my quilt. And then I will leave."

Xiao Lu indicates that dinner is ready inside. She senses his cure as her curse.

○ ○ ○

Soon after the dramatic cure and dinner, the monk packs up to leave. Pep asks him through gesture if he's sure that this means that he won't have any trouble crossing the log bridges. The monk grabs Pep by the ears again and pierces him with his stare and makes it clear that he is absolutely sure that he will have no further problems. With one hand he makes a sweeping gesture like the sun traversing the sky—which Pep takes to mean that it could either last for one day or for the rest of his life. He re-grabs the ear, and seems to hold him there forever. Then, smiling, he chants another "*Hm, hmmm. Hm, hmmm,*" winks at Pep, and releases him. With an impresario's flourish, he hoists his black bag to his shoulder and turns to go.

Pep, still not satisfied, asks him again if he will have any trouble crossing the logs.

The monk give the universal sign of "No problem."

Clio tries to ask, "But what if it doesn't? Can he ask the porters to come?"

True Emptiness seems to understand and, full of himself now, gestures grandly—"You *doubt*?! You doubt *me*?!" Then he shuffles off into the morning forest, his big black bag sagging like a dead animal over his back. The Macys follow him a little way along the path, waving and calling goodbye.

"Tomorrow we go back," Pep says.

"Do we have to?" Katie asks. Both assure her that they have to, and she knows that there's no argument. "Okay. But can we stop and see the monkeys on the way back? They're *right on the way*, remember?"

"We'll see."

They walk back into the clearing. Xiao Lu has disappeared. They look around, and call out, and sit outside together, wondering where she went.

The sound of chopping wood echoes among the silent peaks.

○ ○ ○

At sundown, after feeding the deer, Xiao Lu motions to Chun to sit with her on the ground in a full lotus. Little Chun sits beside her and, with a quick twist of her feet and legs, does it easily. Xiao Lu nods and smiles and motions for her to close her eyes and meditate with her as the sun sets.

Pep and Clio watch from the doorway. In profile in the dusk, the two Chinese silhouettes seem much alike, sitting naturally in postures that, at their age, Pep and Clio could never attain. *I invited her to meditate with me, many times, and she never would. A full lotus is beyond me now. We are old. We started too late. It's too late to try. We can never catch up.*

Shivering, she feels the wings of death spread themselves inside her, a betrayal.

○ ○ ○

Midnight. Xiao Lu is alone in the cave. She stares at the dust of the hermit's bones. *Like him, I will die here. It is a cell where I will spend the rest of my life, alone.* She goes back out into the clearing and paces around. The loss she feels now echoes with all the other losses.

She returns to the cave and takes out her mother's little box of gods. Arranging them on the altar, she lights a stick of incense and prays to Kwan Yin, the thousand-handed goddess of compassion. At first she prays that she herself will be able to do something to stop her baby from leaving, praying until she feels the clutch of her desire loosen, a little. And then she prays that something will happen that will result in her baby staying, praying until she feels, again, the clutch of that desire loosen. Finally, ardently, she prays to the goddess—to *all* the little gods and goddesses that her mother prayed to, most fervently when First Sister never came back, never ever, day after day and night after night and month after month and year after year, never came back—she prays to them to help her let go of the pathetic clutch of desire completely.

37

"What's wrong, Katie?" Clio asks. It is the next morning. They are already at the Dusk-Enjoying Pavilion, taking a first break. She and Pep sit in the sun. Xiao Lu squats by the mouth of the path leading down to the monastery. Katie is wandering around poking in the bushes, as if searching for something. Suddenly she stops.

"Look!" she cries out. "I found it."

"Found what?"

"The path up to the monkeys. Look." She lifts the branches of bamboo and shows them the narrow path that they took before. "I brought lots of packs of Goldfish."

"I'm not sure we have the time, hon," says Pep. "To be on the safe side we'd just better go."

"They're really close! I bet it won't take ten minutes even."

"It took longer when we tried last time, and we didn't even get there."

"I'll ask Xiao Lu how long." Katie takes out the little map and, through gesture and drawing and a few words, asks Xiao Lu how long it will take them to reach the monkeys.

Xiao Lu draws a watch on the map. The monkeys are about thirty minutes away.

"See? Only thirty *minutes*! Please, Mom? Dad? I won't ask for anything else this whole trip, I promise. I want to see them so much! They're so cute! And they eat right out of your hand!"

Their daughter stands there in the fork of the path, so eager, so hopeful, that she is almost dancing. Clio just wants to get back to the monastery safe and sound. But she realizes how much Katie wants to be given this little bit of freedom. She herself was never allowed it. Her own mother was afraid that she would go too far out, and never get back—and because of that fear, Clio did just that, and that led to this.

Thinking, *It's a way of making contact with her again now. Of starting to repair the damage.*

"Pep? Shall we?"

He senses Clio has shifted, and is doing something new. "Why not? Let's go!"

"*Yes!*" Katie cries. "Thanks, Mom, thanks, Daddy. C'mon!"

They start up the path toward the monkeys.

○ ○ ○

Soon they are farther up the mountain than on their first try. Declivities. Crevasses, sheer ups and downs. Long stretches through jungle, longer stretches up flights of ancient stone steps carved into the mountain like characters into oracle bone, steps so small that only Katie and Xiao Lu can put their feet straight out on them while Pep and Clio either have to go up on tiptoe or place their feet sideways like, Pep thinks, a couple doing 'The Stroll' at a sock hop at Mount Carmel Church when as a teenager he first fell in love with being in love.

It is not a well-travelled way. Yet there are signs that at one time, when there were hundreds of temples on the mountain, it was. Every so often the path opens up to an astonishing sight. Once, a waterfall above a thundering stream, spanned by the remains of an arched stone bridge to a toy pagoda perched on an escarpment of granite. The jungle shrouds it all around. Xiao Lu leads. This stretch of path is badly neglected. She carries a large leather bag and takes out of it a long, wide knife, like a machete, and starts hacking through the bush.

The path shadows the stream, steeply up. The mountain, like a live beast, rises. The stream, fighting the rise and riding it too, carves more deeply into gray granite veined with lava-black basalt, and woven with stretches of light-colored and water-worn coral rock they've seen in temples and museums from Beijing to Chengdu. It looks friable, but is not. Soon they are so high up that they can see, on a nearby peak overlooking a sheer drop down thousands of feet, a crest of unrelenting snow.

Sometimes they cross the stream on log bridges. Clio looks at Pep anxiously, but he assures her that he is fine. His heart is beating with the slow, steady pulse of a pachyderm, his balance is exquisite, his fear is gone. He crosses effortlessly.

They stop to drink from the stream. Willow and bamboo grow where the rock gives way to soil. Filtered noon light sprays over the splashes of water, creating doomed tiny rainbows. The moisture and heat send up the scent of rich earth, mixing with that from succulent boughs of eucalyptus. No one talks. Clio finds herself staring at the machete Xiao Lu has placed on a flat rock as she washes her face and armpits. She'd like to wish it away. They move on.

After walking for a few more minutes Xiao Lu stops and signs to them to listen. At first they hear nothing. Then, faintly, screeches, like the distant sounds of big birds. Xiao Lu gestures to them to hurry. Katie jumps up and down and grabs Pep and gives out a screech of her own. She follows close behind Xiao Lu through a stretch of eucalyptus and fern, and then into a narrowing corridor between two high cliffs.

The screeching in the trees gets louder. Xiao Lu gestures to them to hurry on ahead.

Katie follows right after her, digging into her little backpack for the crackly bags of Goldfish, hurrying to get them into her hands so the monkeys will be attracted. She walks in the direction of the sounds, Goldfish in open palms like an offering.

High on a limb a monkey appears, screeching loudly, waving his arms wildly, as if calling his friends to meet these new travelers in bright-colored shirts and hats. Before anyone can say a word, another appears, and another, and soon there are ten, twenty, thirty, more, jumping around the intertwined tree limbs like frantic kids at a playground. They are small, about the size of the Macys' little cockerpoo, their fur in shadow a cinnamony color, but in sunlight a bright, fluffy blond. They have only stubs for tails, and little half-moon rims for ears poking barely out of their furry heads. Their faces, set in bowls of blond fur, have pug noses and thin, expressive lips. Eyes, large as sand dollars and set close together, give them the look of clowns, puzzled by the colorful little circus troupe of humans who are standing there staring up at them with such happy looks on their own pasty faces.

"They're so cute!" Katie shrieks, walking toward the first cluster.

The lead monkey, a big, tough, scarred male, looks down on them curiously, and with a cry launches himself out of the tree and onto the back of the lead human.

Pep feels the weight of the animal and at first is scared but then laughs. And then he hunches over—wiry fingers are searching here and there all over his body. He puts both his hands up to hold on to his hat, which the monkey is trying to get in under. But while his hands are occupied with his hat the monkey switches to the pocket of his Hawaiian shirt. Before he can slap it away the monkey rips the whole front flap of the pocket off the shirt and tries to dig for whatever is inside—his stash of aspirin and Ambien— and then he throws them away and lunges for the fanny pack.

Scared and furious, Pep smashes the monkey in the face. It flies onto the ground and leaps back up into a tree. "Watch out! They're vicious!"

Now another monkey is at his fanny pack. Pep swings at it with all his might but it's quick, and he misses, spinning around and barely staying on his feet.

The monkeys are at the others. One lands on Clio's backpack and tries to claw its way into the contents. Clio screams and spins in circles to try to throw it off.

Katie is screaming horribly—"Help, help, help!"—curled up in a ball, her hands over her head, trying to hold on to her bright-yellow beaked cap. The monkeys are like vultures over a corpse, ripping into her backpack for the glittery packets of Goldfish, trying to rip the whole pack off her back.

Pep and Clio rush to her. Pep bashes at the monkeys in rage, Katie screaming and Pep trying to cover her up with his big body and feeling Clio standing astride them both, screaming. He looks around and sees her, hat gone and backpack hanging, smashing at the monkeys with a big branch, but for every one that falls back, another comes forward, clutching, shrieking, trying to bite, clawing to get.

Total chaos. Pep gets up to help Clio, but a monkey slips in onto Katie, who screams louder. Pep dives on her again to protect her, shouting to try to scare them away, trying to beat them off with fists, going on instinct to save his little girl.

All at once Xiao Lu is there, swinging her machete, hacking at the monkeys.

Blood spurts out of one. Shrieking, one arm hanging, it scurries off to the base of a tree and cries out horribly.

The others seem even more enraged by the blood—screeching so loudly that the sound is overwhelming, echoing around the narrow rock corridor the monkeys have chosen—and attack even more viciously.

Xiao Lu is shouting, swinging her machete, ripping at monkeys in a wild fury.

Clio is terrified that the blade will hit her. She tries to protect herself from her, scurrying away like a desperate crab, leading her away from Katie.

But Xiao Lu is swinging with skill and power. She slashes another monkey, and another. Clio manages to beat back a third one with her stick. It flees, and she's able to stand and, for a second, assess.

Another monkey, the large, scarred male, has leaped down onto Xiao Lu's back and bitten her. Xiao Lu gives a bloodcurdling scream and drops the machete. It clatters on a rock. She twirls around so that the monkey is thrown off. It jumps around on the ground and then races again toward Xiao Lu. On her knees, she shields her face, her chest.

Clio grabs the machete and as the monkey leaps up toward Xiao Lu swings the blade with pure fury and catches the monkey with a slashing blow to his leg. He cries out and falls, blood running out, dark blood.

There is a moment of quiet. The pack of monkeys retreats back up into the trees. They watch as the big male staggers toward Xiao Lu, who is huddled against a boulder. He gets closer and closer. Clio sees the fear in Xiao Lu's eyes and, as she looks directly at Clio, the plea. Clio slashes at the monkey, who slips away but falls.

Clio corners him and, staring down into the beast's clown face, starts screaming and hacking at him, cursing and crying at the top of her lungs. The monkey is on his back, staring up at her. There is still a light in its eyes, but with a final vicious blow Clio splits its skull. The pink brains splatter on the gray rock of the mountain. There is blood everywhere—on the machete, on her hands and shirt and shorts and arms and legs. Shocked, overwhelmed by the killing, she stares at the bloodied machete in her hands.

She lifts her head. The other monkeys are bouncing around up in the trees like big swarming bees, screeching and gesticulating. One of them shakes Xiao Lu's umbrella like a spear. From their perches they start to throw things down at the humans—branches, bunches of leaves, their own feces.

Pep and Katie surround Clio. Except for scratches and ripped clothes, they're unhurt, amazed, relieved.

"Jeez, those are bad monkeys! And look—one of 'em has my *hat!*"

High in the dark green, in the midst of the brown-golden patch of monkeys, is a flash of bright yellow, Katie's beaked cap with the chicken logo. A monkey is waving it back and forth, as if threatening them with it.

"Oh my," Clio says, "look."

Xiao Lu is propped up against the cliff. Her bag is in tatters, spilling ripped rolls of calligraphy and broken brushes. One arm hangs limply at her side. Her shirt is torn, bloodstained. She stares up at Pep, her last thought: *black fire cursed mountain . . .*

○ ○ ○

Pep has inspected Xiao Lu's bloodied arm and back. There are bite marks and a long wound—starting in her back, going around her shoulder and down to her elbow. By applying his clean spare socks, iced with stream water, as pressure dressings, he has managed to stop the bleeding. He has cleansed the wound with alcohol, applied a whole tube of Neosporin antibiotic ointment, and is now finishing up with a startlingly white sterile gauze dressing, thinking, *God knows what those monkeys have been chewing and doing.* Finally the super first aid kit that Orville Rose put together for him has come through. Xiao Lu seems a little confused, maybe in shock.

The dead monkey looks enough like a person that they keep Katie away from seeing it, the split skull, the hacked-off arm, the gashed belly—on top of the attack itself, the sight would be too traumatic for her. The other monkeys have vanished, their high-pitched cries rising and falling in waves, crashing against the big silence of the mountain. Pep has rearranged the monkey into a rough peaceful order in the bottom of a shallow grave they dug with the machete.

"Can I see him now, Dad?"

"Not a good idea, Kate-zer. The way you love animals, it'll upset you a lot."

"No, it won't. Mary always says it's the law of nature when animals kill each other. I've seen 'em there, on the farm. I'll be okay."

They let her take a look. Standing between the two of them, Katie is somber, and silent, but dry eyed. Finally she sighs. "One thing," she says, staring down at the grave. "Those monkeys are no joke!"

Clio and Pep smile. Pep covers the corpse with dirt, starting with the face.

Katie stares at Clio, whose hair and clothes are covered with monkey blood and dirt, her freshly washed face and arms, in contrast, a strange lily white.

Clio smiles and takes Katie's hand, and Pep's, and they go to Xiao Lu, who is still propped up against a rock. "Shay shay," Clio says, "thank you." Through gestures she goes on, "You saved her life, and our lives too."

Xiao Lu nods, bows her head, understanding, saying, "Shay shay." She goes on speaking frantically, gesturing with one arm, hoping they understand: "I'm so sorry! I've been here so many times and they never attacked me! I don't know why, this time—maybe because you're so strange to them, the bright colors, the white skin. I'm so, so sorry!" She puts a hand over her face, clearly ashamed and shocked.

Clio gestures to Pep and Katie to kneel down and reach out their hands and take Xiao Lu's good hand and shoulder to make a circle. For a moment they are silent.

Then they drop hands and Xiao Lu tries to get up to lead them out but with a cry of pain she slumps back down. She seems confused, and gestures that she can't walk.

"We'll have to carry her," Pep says. "The fireman's carry—from Boy Scouts."

He shows Clio how to hold her hands so that each hand grabs one of his wrists, and his hands grab hers, making a kind of seat between them. They indicate to Xiao Lu that she has to sit on the hands, and with Katie's help she does. They start back down the mountain, the new mountain down, the dark mountain of danger defied, a mountain of late afternoon, of dying summer sun.

The Fireman's Carry doesn't work—the path is cut for single file. Pep indicates that he'll carry Xiao Lu on his back. Clio asks if he's well enough for that. He says he feels fine. They help her up. She slumps down on his back, one arm around his neck, the other in a sling made from a shred of his shirt. She feels surprisingly light.

The rains catch them. They are limping along down the mountain when the day's monsoon comes up suddenly. At first the cool drops feel good on their bruised and cut skin, and on their sweat-soaked clothing, and they keep walking. But the sun is blocked by the storm clouds, and the wind seems to come from Mongolia. The cool rain starts to feel cold.

They are soon chilled, shivering, and, because they can't see clearly and the stone steps are narrow and mud slicked, it is too dangerous to walk. They have to find shelter, but see nothing except a stand of pine and thick-leaved gingko growing out of a ravine whose face looks southeasterly. The four of them sit there under the ancient trees, huddled close together for warmth.

As wet as they have ever been. Like being thrown into a cold lake with all their clothes on. The only sounds are of the sempiternal torrent of water cutting down the mountain, and the raindrops, carried on cannons of wind, hitting the gingko bush and the fat leaves of the rhododendrons and even shaking the massive lower boughs of the pines. The horizontal rain seems to come in rollers, one long wave in that breaks and breaks and never seems to be about to subside, and then subsides, and then a lull as if the wind god is taking a deep breath, and then another big one rolls in over them, so loud and fierce that any attempt to talk is blown away, off the shoulders of the mountain, back down toward Tienja, or maybe even Changsha or Hong Kong.

It seems to go on for hours, and then it stops. They get up, weighed down by water, and take a few steps. Their clothes are cold wet rags plastered to their skin, their shoes cold lead. The sun is low and the air is chilly—in the mist they can see their breath. They need to hurry, but for a second they don't move. It is so still that even the stream seems to be listening.

After the rain
each hears
a bird.

38

By the time they get back to Xiao Lu's hermitage it is almost dark. Xiao Lu is hanging on even more limply across Pep's back, from time to time murmuring softly.

They need to stay together tonight. The hut is too small. They take Xiao Lu to the cave. While Clio and Katie prop her up, Pep moves the small bamboo bed over near the iron stove, and helps her gently down onto the mattress of pine boughs. She lies there with her eyes closed as if asleep, looking thin and frail.

Pep goes around the cave lighting the kerosene lanterns. Katie stokes the stove with kindling and split logs. Clio, holding the flashlight in one hand and the bucket in the other, fetches fresh water from the spring. By the time she gets back, Pep and Katie have fanned the fire to life. Clio puts a teakettle and soup pot on the stove to make sure they have boiling water. The iron stove soon radiates a reassuring warmth, and the water starts to boil. When Clio goes out into the chill mountain night to the hut to find dry towels and clothes for all of them, Katie follows.

When they come back they turn their full attention to Xiao Lu. They make tea and Katie's sweet drink and packaged noodles with vegetables. Pep props up Xiao Lu. They spoon it into her. Her eyes are not focusing all that well, but she drinks the soup down. Katie and Clio will undress her and wash her while Pep assesses what he has in his fanny pack for her lacerations and shock. He lays out the contents, all in a line on the crude wooden table, trying to recall what he learned from Orville, trying to make a diagnosis and a plan. As they bring the boiled water and clean clothes to Xiao Lu, Pep realizes how filthy they all are, covered with mud and blood.

"Hey, wash your hands—and then use the sterile Handi Wipes!" They look down at their hands, fingernails rimmed with black, arms scratched and bloodstained. They wash their hands, sterilize, and go to work.

Xiao Lu struggles feebly as they undress her, pointing toward Pep, embarrassed at his seeing her naked. They rig a sheet across the cave. Her clothes are worn, threadbare, filthy and stiff with caked blood and dirt. The green shoes are hardened muck, the soles like cardboard. Her dark pants are thin, torn, and stained; her boxer underpants gray. They cut off her blouse to get it over her wrapped arm, and then her gray T-shirt. For a moment before they cover her up with a quilt, Clio stares at her body, the exposed and now dirt-blackened ankles, neck, face, and arms that make the untanned skin seem stark white, the modest swirl of pubic hair and tight belly and small breasts with almost black nipples—a body worn down by years of work and abstinence, the muscles defined sharply beneath the skin. Xiao Lu groans as they move her. They try to do it even more delicately as they see, in the bright light of the lanterns, the extent of her scratches and cuts—and the wrapped wound.

First they wash her upper body and lay her back down and wash from her belly to her toes, using sea sponges they found in the kitchen to massage the warm, soapy water all over. Then they put on fresh underwear and pants and two layers of socks—she wants her shoes on but they are too filthy to use and Clio indicates that they will clean them and give them back. Then they wash her chest and back and face and hair—everything but where the bandage covers the wound on her back, shoulder, and arm. She is so dirty that they have to change the soapy water several times, going to the mouth of the cave to spill it out, watching it run down onto the moss covering the stone bones of the mountain.

As she and Katie wash Xiao Lu's limp body, Clio remembers washing her own mother during her long dying from cancer. Once, on what would turn out to be the family's final "locust" trip together, as she and her mother stood outside the Grand Souk in Marrakesh, her mother got strangely frank: "Hold the awe, Clio dear, *always*. Hold the awe." Clio didn't understand, and asked her what she meant. She didn't elaborate. A month later she was dead. Clio was seventeen.

Like washing my mother, those last endless days.

To her now, Xiao Lu's skin feels the same, toneless on the bone, her eyes have that same mix of pain and fear, the way she can't move and Clio has to move her. The way Clio can't quite get the dirt out of her hair or her ears or the creases of her body is the same. *Washing my mother, washing my child.* That first night with Katie in the Jiang Jiang Hotel, their new baby never yet having uttered a sound so they feared there was something wrong, they put her in the hot, soapy water in the sink—she pinkening—and she gave a wail and their hearts lifted! *Washing my daughter, washing my mother. My mother washing me.*

My mother washing me, Xiao Lu thinks, hazily, sort of knowing that it is no longer her mother washing her when she was a sick child in the little house by the slow river, and sort of knowing that her mother was not the one washing her mostly because she was the baby of the family and everyone was starving and then there floats into her memory who it is she feels is washing her. *First Sister, who was my mother until she disappeared, and never came back. Never came back—ever!*

"Mom, look," Katie whispers, "she's crying."

"I see, yes."

"You think we're hurting her?"

"No, dear, I think she's afraid. We'll go gentle-gentle, and she'll know we're here and helping her to get better. You stay here and dry her while I get fresh hot water so we can clean her arm and back, okay?"

"Okay." Katie takes the pine-scented fresh towel and starts to pat Xiao Lu dry, her neck and hair and then her face, looking into her dark eyes, sparkling wet from her tears. Katie is amazed at how deep her eyes seem, as if, if she could turn herself into a tiny person, she could just walk into them and go deep down like in the deep part of Kinderhook Creek under where the bridge used to be. She finds it impossible to keep looking at her but impossible to look away for long. So she just caresses her cheek, back and forth a time or two gentle-gentle, and the dark eyes get wetter and the lips turn down at the edges and she feels herself cry inside with her. *My birth mom and mom too. My body's not like my mom's, it's like hers. When Mom and I were naked trying on bathing suits I saw in the mirror her body didn't look like my body, it was strange. Now I know my body looks like hers.*

Clio is back with fresh soapy water. Pep comes over with a kerosene lamp and his Ziploc plastic bags of pill bottles, needles and syringes, wraps and tubes.

The lamp casts an acrid warm light.

"I'm not sure you should see this, Katie," he says. "It's a bad cut."

"It's okay. I want to."

"Sure?" She nods. "Okay." Pep washes his hands in fresh soapy water and sterilizer and dries them on a fresh towel. They roll Xiao Lu over on her good side and start to unwrap the bandage they put on her back and arm. He tries to be as gentle as possible, but the gauze sticks to the bloody wound and she screams in pain. Katie winces, Clio grits her teeth.

Pep takes a deep breath to steel himself. Worse than he thought. The wound is ugly, a bite on the back and a rip from shoulder down to elbow, in one place a deep slash down to what might be bone. He has come prepared. Before they left he badgered Orville Rose to give him a complete ultra-medical kit suited to high-risk people who trek alone across Africa or through the gut of Asia to Kuala Lumpur. He also took an EMT training course, and invited Orvy to dinner twice to discuss the practice of the medical arts in disastrous environments—something the good doctor knew a lot about, from his "salad days" wandering the genocidal zones in Médicins Sans Frontières, before he'd come back under duress to his broken-down hometown, Columbia.

Now all of Pep's training kicks in. He cleans and tends the wound, thinks to suture it up—but then remembers that it's hazardous to sew up bites. The bacteria in mouths are anaerobic; without oxygen they'll form abscesses and spread. He knows from the good Dr. Rose that the worst bites for infection are from humans, not animals. They didn't talk monkeys. He slathers more Betadine disinfectant over the skin, wraps the whole wound with clean gauze, and splints it with a fresh clean stick from the inside of a split log. Finally, he uses the big capsules of his stash of Levaquin, the latest broad-spectrum-Western-antibiotic-that-kills-every-thing. He and Clio prop Xiao Lu up and pop the big pill in. Katie helps her to drink it down. He thinks of giving her a shot of Demerol, but she seems calm and not in great pain—as they lower her to her pillow she looks from one to the other and smiles.

"Go to sleep," Clio says, smiling, patting her hand.

"*Wa-an*, Xiao Lu," Katie says. Clio looks at her. "It means 'go to sleep'?"

Clio smiles at her, takes her hand. They walk away.

"Mom, can I have Shirty?" Clio, as daytime Shirty-keeper, unzips her money belt, takes out the worn, soft little shirt, and hands it to Katie. Katie goes back to Xiao Lu, whose eyes are closed. "Xiao Lu?" Her eyes open. "Here, you need Shirty tonight." She gives the little guy to Xiao Lu, who moves her good hand slowly up to take it. "You use Shirty like this." Katie takes her hand with Shirty in it and moves it up to her cheek, showing her how she can hold the softness against her cheek gentle-gentle. Again tears come to Xiao Lu's eyes. She smiles. Katie goes to Clio and Pep.

"That's a wonderful thing to do, dear," Clio says. "You never gave Shirty to anyone for the night before, did you?"

"Nope. But she really needs him tonight, more than me."

The three of them get into the big bed and pull the quilt up to their chins. The scent of cedar calms.

"She risked her life to save us," Clio says.

"She was brave," Pep says.

"No foolin," Katie says, and then, in awe, "Super brave."

"Let's take a minute of silence to pray for her."

To the soft flurry of bats rushing in and out of the mouth of the cave, they fall asleep.

○ ○ ○

Clio, Pep, and Katie are so sore the next morning they can barely move. Every muscle seems made of dry leather, every scratch a flicker of fire. Groaning, they hoist themselves up and go to Xiao Lu. She lies on her side, quiet and still, as if she hasn't moved all night. Her eyes are open, and her breathing is regular, but her forehead is damp with sweat. With difficulty Pep shows her how to keep the little plastic battery-powered thermometer under her tongue, and it beeps at 101.6. He's worried. Clio sees his concern, and asks if there's any way that they can get some help. But there's no way to carry her back to the monastery, and for one of them to try to get there alone is too dangerous. They're stuck. He gives her another Levaquin.

They set about organizing the tasks of the day. Pep is in charge of medical care, fire, heavy lifting, and controlling bugs, snakes, and any other pests. Clio and Katie are in charge of tending to Xiao Lu, cooking, and cleaning. Together they will hunt and gather food and water.

It is more difficult than they could have imagined. Clio and Pep have little idea how to take care of the basics of life in the wild. Katie, having tagged along with Xiao Lu, is the expert. She shows them how to carry water—not just one bucket, leaning to one side as you walk, but using a bamboo carrying pole to bring two, making it easier to balance on the path and up the slope. She shows Pep how to use the wedge and hammer to split wood, and shows Clio where the right vegetables grow, and which mushrooms to pick (Clio and Pep don't know which are the safe and which are the poisonous ones)—even, sometimes, saying the Chinese words for them. It is amazing how Katie's mind has absorbed all of this, even the smallest detail of daily life here. Katie is in heaven directing them.

Clio and Pep are better at taking care of Xiao Lu. The Great American Antibiotic may or may not be working, but it has certainly worked on Xiao Lu's bowels. With a shameful look in her eye she lets them know that she has not been able to control herself. Clio and Katie roll her over and confront the mess. At first they feel disgusted, but Clio remembers how, with Katie as a baby, there was no disgust. It helps. They clean and dust her with baby powder Clio carries, and reassure her that she just has to let them know when she has to go, and they will bring a flat bowl to use as a bedpan. Xiao Lu smiles wanly and soon goes back to sleep.

Like being in a strange new house, they—even Katie—are awkward in their chores. Nothing they need seems close by or right; things they do find seem useless. They can't figure out what to do when. They float through the day clumsily; the meals they make are pallid. After lunch the monsoon comes again—they finally realize that in the summer on the mountain it comes every day, it's just a question of how fiercely—trapping them indoors for the afternoon. Katie goes to the hut to do calligraphy, Clio going with her. Pep stays with Xiao Lu in the cave.

The rain beats down on the stones of the path through the mossy clearing, on the roof of the hermitage, and the wind whips it against the cliff face. It's strange for Pep to sit there alone with the sleeping young Chinese woman. Occasionally she awakens, and seems disoriented and cries out. He goes to her, sits, holds her hand until she sees where she is and with whom, and calms down. He feeds her, washes her hot forehead, and smiles, and she smiles back, and soon goes back to sleep.

It reminds him of caring for Katie when she had pneumonia last year. She got more and more listless and said at first that she felt like she was going to die and then said she *wanted* to die—which sent a bolt of panic through him and they called Orville at two a.m. and she spent the night getting intravenous antibiotics in Kinderhook Memorial. He wonders, now, if Xiao Lu could die. Infections from bites, Orville said, always nasty, can be lethal. But she's strong, and tough. The next day or two will tell.

In the little hut, Katie is teaching Clio calligraphy. Trying to follow her lead, Clio feels an admiration for her, for the way that she's made a jump from doing it the Western way to the Eastern. It's hard to define the difference. It's something about not trying to make it happen, but being relaxed enough so that it happens. Katie has got it now and Clio has not. Together they laugh at Clio's clumsiness.

The rain stops in time for the evening feeding of the deer. Katie organizes this too, knowing where the deer appear, showing Clio and Pep how to creep up silently to the edge of the forest near the low moon gate, and signaling for them to be silent while she imitates exactly Xiao Lu's call to them. "*Ping? Ping?*"

The deer don't come. "Maybe they'll come if I'm alone?" Katie says.

Clio and Pep walk away, sit at the entrance to the cave, and watch.

"*Ping? Ping?*" Katie stands absolutely still, holding out her open palms with the orange Goldfish. "*Ping? Ping?*"

"She looks so young," Clio whispers.

"Young and old both."

"And almost like she's *right*, here?"

"Yes."

The deer are coming. Like parts of the leaves they part to appear, all at once they are there. They are so small that Katie seems even bigger. The buck comes first, and then beside him the doe, and the fawn. They stop and stare at the girl. Then they come up to her, first the buck, finishing a handful, and then the doe for the second handful, and the fawn for a few nibbles of the third—which the buck finishes up. The deer ease back into the wood. Katie turns to look at Clio and Pep and gives a thumbs-up and shouts, "Yes!" Clio and Pep echo back, "Yes!" The last shafts of sunlight play off the flinty face of the mountain and dance across the clearing.

Smiling, Katie walks with unusual slowness through the bars of light toward them, not in a straight line but veering off here and there as a sound from the woods or the glimpse of a bird attracts her, as if she has become *like* all this, a current of mere nature, like the mountain deer Xiao Lu has tamed.

○ ○ ○

The next day is a horror. They awaken to demonic rain, carried on scary gusts that seem driven in directly from the Himalayas. It rains all day and into the night.

Xiao Lu is worse, her fever is 102, and she is delirious and disoriented, as if a part of her has gone away, disappeared. When she's awake, she fights their efforts to help. It is all they can do to get the antibiotic and fluids into her and change the dressing. And change her clothes and sheets—she can't let them know when she's got to go. To keep the rain out, they've strung a heavy blanket across, which keeps them more or less dry, but which entraps the smell of kerosene, sweat, urine, and feces. Inside, the air is soon fetid, but it's impossible to go outside at all. Even a run for the hut or the latrine soon soaks them through.

To keep the fire going with wet wood is difficult, and to keep bringing what they need from the hut to the cave is a pain. They take turns doing this, trying to dry out in between. The mossy clearing has turned muddy. The stones are slippery—unable to see where they're going, soon all three of them have fallen several times.

In late afternoon, as Xiao Lu goes through a bad run of delirium filled with shouts and curses and sobs, Katie turns to Pep. "Dad, is Xiao Lu gonna die?"

"No, no, Kate-zer. The medicine should work soon. By tomorrow."

"What about giving her some of that monk stuff? It worked on you, Dad."

They try to get the bear bile down, but she struggles against it.

Clio and Pep start to really worry. Pep realizes that Xiao Lu could actually die—the next day or so will tell whether Levaquin works for monkey bites. Despite the gentle deer and the beautiful scenery, the attack of the monkeys has made him afraid of what else is out there. With the constant pounding of the rain, he is filled with dread of the power of all the old rock of this mountain that has been here long before they were and will be here long after they are gone. The sheer *bigness* of what they are perched upon scares him, mocks him and his pitiful little pills. Time seems trivial, and immense. Death could come at any moment to Xiao Lu—and to him, Clio, Katie—death could come anytime, from anything out there. No one knows where they are. Their bodies would be eaten, their bones scattered, never to be found.

39

As they get ready for bed, Clio feels, for the first time in China, a sudden turmoil in her bowels. Grabbing the umbrella and the flashlight, she tells them she is going to the latrine. The wind and rain are fierce. She can barely see the path down to the ditch. One shoe comes off on the way, and she holds it in her hand. At the latrine she yanks down her pants with one hand and squats and . . . and nothing. Her belly aches, she feels an urgency to go, but nothing comes. She tries, waits. Still nothing, not even gas. It's difficult to balance there on her heels, holding the umbrella and shoe in one hand, the flashlight in the other. The smell is intense. She breathes through her mouth. Finally it starts to happen, semi-solid and smelling revolting, even breathing through her mouth. And then, in the middle of it, she feels something crawling across her bare foot. The cold sweat of terror comes over her. *Brown snake I'm dead they say not to move and it won't bite you.*

She freezes, and then, feeling the thing crawl off her foot, she thanks God, but then the thing turns around and crawls *back* onto her foot and starts up her ankle. Still squatting she squirms around and puts the flashlight on it, and sees what looks like a foot-long giant red millipede crawling up her leg. She screams at the top of her lungs and kicks out with her leg to shake it off, which makes her lose her balance and start to fall, backward into the pit. Desperately she throws all her weight forward, like a rower with an umbrella and shoe for oars, and she avoids falling back into the pit but is so full of terrified strength that she reflexively springs straight ahead and finds herself sprawling in the mud of the path, both arms down hard into something soft, which she hopes is moss, a rivulet of water running over her outstretched arms. She feels the crawling thing—or now things!—creeping with sharp little tarsi up her other leg and lets out another howl and, trying to pull up her pants, gets up and then trips on the band of pants between her legs and goes down again, this time right on her face. Pebbles scratch her. Her face feels coated in a mudpack. She wails and cries and digs her fingernails into the dirt as if into a cliff to try to get up, pulling her pants up and then running as fast as she can back up the path, bamboo whipping against her.

She staggers into the cave. There's a strange howling coming from Xiao Lu. Pep and Katie are walking toward her bed. They turn when Clio comes in, and their look turns into surprise, then fear. Her face is filthy, mud on her nose and cheeks and hair, her clothes are soaking wet and dark with grime, she carries one soaked shoe and the umbrella, which is twisted inside out.

"What happened?" Pep says, over the howling.

"You okay, Mom?"

"No, I am not! I fell, I saw a . . . a . . ."

"Snake?"

"No, a bug as big as a snake—a huge creepy-crawly thing—and I, and it was revolting!" She stands there, wanting them to help her. Xiao Lu is crying. "What?"

"She had a poop, Mom, and she was lying in it asleep and she just woke up and started crying bad, so we were just starting to get her cleaned up. Can you help?"

Clio joins them. Xiao Lu looks at her and falls silent, a look of fright on her face, as if she's staring at some demon. But then, recognizing her,

Xiao Lu laughs feebly, raising her good arm a little to point. Pep and Katie stare at Clio again, and start to giggle, and then as Xiao Lu laughs harder, they laugh with her. Clio, looking down at her messy shirt and shorts and legs, takes the mirror that Pep hands her, sees the total mud bath that is her face, her muddied hair standing straight up on top of her head like a rooster, and laughs with them. Soon all of them are laughing hysterically, deliriously. They stop, start again, and finally stop enough to help move Xiao Lu, strip and change her, and lay her down, clean.

"Now," Pep says to Clio, "you."

"Y'know what?" Clio says. "I'll just go out in the rain."

"But it's cold out there!" Pep says, worried for her.

"Mom, are you crazy?"

"Yes!" She runs back out into the pouring rain and, laughing inside, twirls around in it, figuring she can't get any wetter. Waves of big, cold drops wash over her, but—like the frigid Atlantic at Annisquam when she was ten—it doesn't *feel* all *that* cold now, and to her surprise she realizes she's not *figuring* anything anymore.

She takes off her shirt and her bra and her pants and her panties, and uses the rain on her hands and fingers to wash her whole body, from her matted, muddied hair to the dirt beneath her breasts and her armpits and belly button—a big nugget there!—and in her vagina and the cleft of her butt and right down to the goop in the gaps between her toes. Feeling cleaner, she wanders here and there on the moss. The rain feels almost warm now, as if the wind has shifted to bring truly tropical clouds up from the South Seas and screw you too, Himalayas! And if at first she just walks around delicately, suddenly she lets go and starts twirling around like a dancer, like she used to dance in the steamy rain in Jamaica, just letting go and dancing. She feels dizzy but keeps on dancing, for the first time in weeks if not years not *worrying* that she feels dizzy and is dancing in the rain on a speck not on any map, dwarfed by a big, fucking-tough mountain.

As she twirls around she keeps touching, with her eyes, one stable point—not her husband and child silhouetted in the mouth of the cave, but the keystone of the arch in the moon gate, and her mind turns to a quote from Luke that Bob Marley put in a song—"The stone that the builder refused will be the main cornerstone." The two times and places come together, linked across time and space by the freedom she felt as a girl, and this sudden freedom as a woman.

And then something else happens. She realizes that she has been drowning in what she fears. Dragged down and under, scared to death of the dirt and shit and blood and strangeness of . . . of *China*! From the start she denied it, imagined she was going on this trip to China for the sake of her child. But in fact it was for the sake of her denial, to close the door on her child's past and even on her child's dream of finding her Chinese mother, to solidify that denial for all time, to nail down a "No, there's nothing we can know about where you came from." And now she's found the "Yes." Now finally, yes, the death of her denial. Her real fear all along—maybe for her whole life!—has been of opening up to the not knowing, to the dirt of bringing in someone unknown to love, to bring the unknown and different *other* into her heart as her beloved.

To bring to your bosom your hidden and mysterious beloved.

Clio dances on, drowning in the dirt of not knowing what's next and what's really there, undeniably there in who she is and who she will be.

You've had to lie about it to yourself—think you could keep it all nice and neat, clean and unknown—to really get it. The lying has led you here, to China.

She finds herself stopped still, staring at the silhouettes of her daughter and her husband in the mouth of the cave. They stand as still as she, as silenced by the rain.

China is the other that you come to love and that loves you. China is our daughter. To lose this opening would be to lose her. And you can't just do it once, opening up to that love, no. You have to do it over and over again until you die.

Naked, as she walks closer toward them, she sees the amazement in their eyes.

○ ○ ○

That night, Katie asleep, and Xiao Lu feverish and restless across the cave, they lie in each other's arms. Pep's arm is around her, his fingers intertwining with hers in their special way. Seeing her naked, and daring, has turned him on. He caresses her breast, her belly. Her summer scent of tube-fresh Coppertone mixes with the scents of the cave and the meal, the scents of hollows in rocks, of earth floors, of being inside this mountain. As he caresses her, she sighs happily. Has he ever felt so close to her? Their first summer, making love in the afternoons—but even more afterward, lying together like this but in daylight in his inherited house filled with the stiffness of two hundred years of whalers and commerce and insurance that had become a burden, a slow death. Lying there together, she with him and he with her, a "click" with each other that had something to do with their breaking free of their families and of their separate pasts. He loved her spirit. The way her senses mixed—she would hear "a velvety sound," or see "the daylight music," or talk about "the color-tumbled gardens of the Islands." She woke him up. He opened up to love, and love opened them both up to the shared vision of having a child. He suffered with her through their sterility—a shared suffering, which, to his amazement (for he had been taught the opposite), opened them up even more and drew them even closer together. And then when he—ass that he was!—at first said "No" to adoption, she kept holding the "Yes" until China opened up and led them to this.

He strokes the small of her back. She sighs, and snuggles in closer, all along him.

What I loved then and love now is the . . . yes, the vital sense that with her I could make the journey all the way to the end of life, and that to lose her would be the old beginning of death. Amen.

40

They look around. They call out. There is no answer.

A late runner of sunlight strikes the bright white of the golf umbrella that reads "GE Brings Good Things to Life—The Masters 2000," skids off over the glittering cliff face, and hurries back to the hut and the two people standing outside it. Rhett is in black—black loafers, pants, collared shirt unbuttoned two or three buttons down, black leather jacket, and a black, brimmed hat like actors wear in gangster movies. His white golf umbrella is an aberration. The woman, taller than him, is dressed for an upscale safari—khaki pants with many pockets and khaki vest with many more, and a stylish robin's-egg-blue safari hat with a many-colored feather in the band. All the logos on her clothes match: "ORVIS." Her blond hair scoots out in a ponytail. On her feet are Reeboks, pink trimmed and mud spattered. She and Rhett both wear aviator sunglasses. Both are damp from the monsoon, and out of place in this unadorned clearing in fashionless nature, the dead end of a rough path carved onto the mountain.

"Depressing!" the woman says, staring at the hut, at the ill-set stones and tilting moon gate. "You really think this is it?"

"Un hunh." He walks to the hut, shakes the rain off the umbrella, and closes it. The tip hits the roof tiles. A shower of dirty water and leaves comes down on his leather loafers and black linen trousers. Brushing them off he notices the hems of the trousers are filthy, the sides of the loafers too. Cursing, he leads her inside.

Lived in. Recently lived in. Ashes cold in the wood stove. Bed, with quilt pulled up over the pillow. Calligraphy everywhere. Smell of old incense and garlic and cooking oil and kerosene. And worse. A peasant's dwelling, one of thousands he's been in, run from, and tried for many years never to be seen in again.

"She's been here, Thalia," Rhett says, reflexively sniffing at his wrist where his cologne, Hermès Homme, affirms his talents and aspirations. "But no sign of them."

Thalia wrinkles up her nose, then sneezes. "Hard to believe people live like this. I hate this smell."

"Here." He takes out two cigarettes, lights them, hands one to her.

"I told you I'm trying to quit. It's deadly."

"Nah. It's good for you. Clears the chest." He takes a deep drag, holding the cigarette up between index and middle finger, *a la* the French sophisticate. "Let's get some fresh air."

"You call that a thorough search?" she says, following him out.

"No, I call it a downer. We'll check outside." He tiptoes through the puddles, trying to keep on the old stone path that leads toward the stream and the cliff. The sight of the lowering sun is of scant interest to him. He isn't really worried about not finding them. The monk saw them several days ago and said they were fine. They're sure to be back by nightfall. The real worry is where the hell he and Thalia are going to sleep. It took them a lot longer to get here than the monk said it would. He can't see going back in the dark. Thalia is standing beside him, looking at the sun, which doesn't seem to him to have all that far to go before it's gone. He turns to look back at the little settlement and notices the inscription chiseled into the wall of the hut, the script looking ancient and set out in short lines like a poem. The two of them draw on their cigarettes, standing awkwardly in the clearing, with no place to sit down.

"What do we do now?" she asks.

"We widen the circle, shift the paradigm. Investigate."

Metal sheets of sunlight suddenly rattle through the clouds and illuminate the clearing like, he imagines, on a film set. He lowers his aviator sunglasses from their perch on his pomaded black hair, and moves around with surprising lightness, keeping up a patter, "See, look at me, I'm investigating, investigating. Sure to be some DNA shit around here somewhere." She laughs. He leads her around, finding the latrine, the vegetable garden, the huge, wet ming aurelia, which, with the soaked eucalyptus and pine, gives a fresh scent to the oncoming dusk.

He stops, and listens. "Hey, hey, hey. Listen up."

Sounds coming from the woods, sounds of people moving toward them.

Three people come out of the forest. First is a woman in peasant shirt and torn khaki shorts and a conical straw hat, bent low under a large bundle of tied-up wood that lies over her shoulders. Next is a tall man in a torn Hawaiian shirt and a hat that looks like a cloth bowl, he too bent over, from the weight of a bamboo pole with a bucket at either end. Last a girl in shorts and a faded yellow T-shirt sporting a chicken. She carries a woven reed basket full of greens.

Breathing heavily, Clio, Pep, and Katie make it into the clearing and put down their burdens. They blink in the sudden bright sunlight, shading their eyes to see.

"Holy shit," Rhett says, staring at them.

"I don't believe it," says Thalia.

Clio, Pep, and Katie stare back. In each mind is the same word: *Tourists?*

"Pep?" Rhett calls out. Pep nods. "Wha's happenin', baby?"

"Just gathering wood," he says quietly, "fetching water and food."

The Macys stay where they are, as if suspicious of the well-dressed intruders.

"Clio? Can it be you? And dear little Kate?" She walks toward them.

"Thalia? What are *you* doing here?"

"You didn't show up at the family Fourth—it was *quite* unlike you . . ." She stares at her sister: two black eyes, scratches all over her face and legs, and filthy hands. Dirt makes dark rims of her nails and outlines the creases of her skin. Pep too is filthy; Katie's hair is unruly and her knees are caked with mud, as if she's been crawling around in dirt. "Are you guys *okay?*"

"Fine." Clio looks Rhett and Thalia up and down. She sees them as dressed ridiculously for where they are, without climbing shoes, and with no protection from the elements except those stupid hats, and that garish umbrella too wide to get through the narrow mountain paths. Their jewelry—gold necklaces and fat watches and rings and bracelets—and that potent cologne seem pathetic here.

"Don't I get a hello from my niece?"

Thalia's one of those adults who doesn't know how to talk to kids. Katie stares down and says, "Hi."

"Thank you, Kate," Thalia says. "Now. Clio, what happened to your *face*?"

"I fell down in the dark. It looks bad, but it doesn't hurt."

"Far out," Rhett says. "But what's with all the scratches and cuts?"

"From the monkeys," Katie says. "Just the monkeys."

"The monkeys?" Thalia asks.

"No joke," Katie says. Pep bursts out laughing. Clio and Katie join in.

"Where's Xiao Lu?" Rhett asks.

"In the cave."

"Cave? What cave?"

"Where we live," Katie says. "I'll show you."

Pep stares at the way that Rhett and Thalia are standing together. *My God, he's noodling her!* "Hey, Rhett," he says, "my shoulders are sore. Can you give a hand?" He motions to the carrying pole. "Just up to the cave?"

"Sure, big fella." With clear distaste for this menial task, Rhett tries to hoist the pole with the buckets onto his shoulders, spilling some water, finding it hard to balance. Pep grabs it and gets under it by himself again and slowly follows the others up to the cliff face and the hidden mouth of the cave. Rhett chatters away, something about a "business plan" he's brought along.

To Pep the words sound too loud, too vulgar. This mindless banter in the service of ambition is annoying. Thinking, *"The expense of spirit in a waste of shame."*

Pep and Clio and Katie walk into the cave, which is dark but for the glow from the fire. Rhett and Thalia hesitate at the entrance, suddenly blinded, their eyes needing to accommodate. The glow from the stove shines on a small bamboo bed, and a larger one. A sharp-edged shaft of light shoots down from far back in the cave, illuminating a large pile of milky-white dust on what looks like a primitive altar. The metallic sound of dripping water. Pep lights the kerosene lanterns.

As if the floor were paved with scorpions and snakes, Rhett and Thalia make their way gingerly to the crude chairs and the table, on which sit backpacks and, arrayed as if for an operation, scissors and knives and bandages and medicines. The smell is revolting to the visitors, for in addition to all the smells of the small hut, there is the scent of sweat and excrement and dirt, and antiseptic, which seems to congeal the other smells in a disgusting way, as vomit might. Rhett sniffs his wrist. Thalia takes out her own perfume and dabs. They watch the Macys go to the small bed and unpeel the covers, revealing a pale, thin, frightened, scratched-up face.

"This her?" Rhett asks.

"Yes. Katie's birth mom, Xiao Lu."

"Wonderful," Thalia says, without missing a beat. Standing over her, she says loudly, "Nee how nee how!" Xiao Lu stares at her and says nothing. "I . . . am . . . Clio's . . . sister," Thalia says, slowly and more loudly, as if that will make the woman understand. "Your . . . daughter's . . . aunt."

Xiao Lu closes her eyes, these loud words making her head pound. Rhett translates. She nods. Katie takes her hand. She opens her eyes and smiles.

Katie makes antler-shaking motions to Xiao Lu and points to the mouth of the cave. Xiao Lu nods and smiles, and tries to get up. She falls back down on the bed, exhausted. Pep and Clio help her up. Supported by them, she walks stiffly with Katie out of the cave to the edge of the woods, where she sits on a stone bench.

"Interesting sign language," Thalia says. "And the meaning . . . ?"

Clio finds the sound of her sister's voice irritating. There is something in it she can't identify at first. She wants to ignore it, but feels an obligation to respond. Even so, she can barely squeeze her own words through her set teeth. "Feeding Goldfish to the deer."

"Good Lord! Well, it *is* China, after all."

Clio's irritation starts to rise—but then all the air goes out of it. It reminds her of what she herself might have said. *There but for the grace of God go I.*

"Yes, Thally," she says, "it is."

41

The deer are fed, the dinner done, and the iron door to the old stove in the hut is open. The pops and crackles and slow hum of the burning wood take the bite out of the damp rising like cold breath from the exhaling mountain.

Xiao Lu, still feverish and weak, has insisted on being with them in the hut. She sits in the chair. Pep and Clio squat against the wall. Katie is at the calligraphy table, working on a new scroll. Her head is down close to the brush tip in concentration. Rhett and Thalia sit on the bench smoking, each with one leg crossed over the other as if at a business meeting.

For a while no one has said anything. The loud, fast chatter of the visitors has made Pep and Clio—and even Katie—realize how precious the silence has been.

The only sounds are the wood in the stove and, in the fluid stillness of the night as it gathers its dark satin, the calls of birds—magpies, cuckoos, silk-voiced doves, and a lone mockingbird riffing on their songs.

"Well, Pep," Rhett says, "you owe me." Pep says nothing to this. "After I got arrested, it was not fun. Five hours of interrogation by the thugs in Tienja. Why was I illegally bringing Americans nosing around *a restricted zone*? A night and a day in jail to teach me a lesson. I give them all the cash you gave me. They put me on a train back to Changsha. My boss fires me.

All the while I'm wondering what happened to Katie. I was really down, really bummed. But then I lucked out."

"How?"

"This beautiful lady shows up in Changsha." He smiles at Thalia, puts his arm around her. "She asks me to find you. An urgent matter—especially as your visas have run out, and you're illegal in China. Illegal *big-time*."

"Big deal," Pep says happily. "Big damn deal."

"Could be, fella, could be a *real* big deal when you try to get home. Anyway, I call the Dripping Cave and find out that Katie came back, and that you went off to find Xiao Lu. But I can't go back *through* Tienja to get here, I gotta go *around*. The *long* way around. A pain in the ass. Days, nights. Bad conditions. But me and this foxy lady do it. The rest is history." He puffs, pleased with himself.

"Yes," Thalia says, "there was quite a kerfuffle when you weren't at Annisquam. Not like you, you've never missed, and with no explanation? And then, when we found out you weren't on your scheduled flight? Frightening. I volunteered to go find you. Once I found Rhett, it was easy. It was good fun."

"My luck is turning, Pep. You owe me, *big-time*."

Pep says nothing to this.

"I'm talking insurance—life, property, the whole enchilada. Like we discussed before." Rhett takes out a navy-blue folder embossed with "Deloitte and Touche," and reads the Chinese title: "'The Platinum Rice Bowl: Private Insurance in the New China.' Y'see, Pep, when Mao guaranteed everyone a level of security—starting with having enough food—he called it the 'Iron Rice Bowl.' Now, the safety net is gone. 'Platinum' is good, don't you think?" He waits for Pep to answer. When Pep doesn't, he goes on with his pitch. "The market? At *least* nine hundred million people. Market cap? Billions. What better collaboration than you and me, Pep? Chinese-American. Cutting-edge. The New Millennium. Look! Spreadsheets, Pep, spreadsheets! Like I said, 'With your good looks and my brains . . .'" He laughs. "What do you think?"

Pep wishes he'd stop talking and go away, and remains silent.

Thalia seizes the opportunity. "Good," she says. "Right. Now. Let's organize our trip back. Tomorrow, first thing, back to the monastery—it's so quaint, isn't it?—almost Disney—and then Changsha tomorrow night at that great hotel—I hear Kate *loves* the pool, don't you, dear?"

Katie's head lowers a millimeter farther toward the tip of her calligraphy brush.

"So then," Thalia says cheerfully, "the five-star hotel, and then home?"

The question floats around the tiny room like a moth with bad timing.

Clio feels her body stiffen. "No, we're not ready to leave yet."

"Why, why not? You've been here for days and days, and . . . and to be honest, sis, you're a *mess!*" Clio's vehemence seems to startle her. She tries to stop, but like a car engine that keeps popping after its power has been cut, she blurts out, "You're *all* a mess!" Clio looks at Pep, and Katie looks up too—and they all laugh. "Go ahead, but you can't think only of yourselves. What about your family, your friends—your *dog*, for Christ's sake? Your friends are frantic, and the kennel fellow is at his wit's end!"

"We've got to make sure that Xiao Lu is all right. She was bitten by a monkey."

"All the more reason to get her good medical care."

"As soon as she's up and about, strong enough to walk," Pep says, "we will."

"Kate, dear, aren't *you* ready to go home? It's only early July—the summer awaits!"

"No way, *Thal.*" She looks up, says, "Trust me," and lowers her head again.

Thalia blinks, as if slapped. Her jaw drops. New dental work, mostly gold.

Clio sees that her sister finally has understood something of what has gone on here. She watches as the worry lines that grew and deepened all through Thalia's catastrophic marriage to—and endless trench-war divorce from—her Beverly Hills *uber*-Freudian analyst, Shapiro, now spread across her face like a fractal pattern in a cracked windshield. She looks so *old.* Feeling sad for her, Clio takes a gentler tone. "You see, Thalia, we've been with Xiao Lu for several days without a translator. This, now, is a very special time. Rhett, we need your help."

"Fine." He looks at Pep. "Deal?"

"No," Clio says. "No deal."

Her directness surprises him. "Why not?"

"If you're going to translate for us, it's important you be here in the right spirit."

His face curls in distaste, as if he's bitten into a bad scallion pancake.

"You're too much! Hitting me now, after all we've been through, with this touchy-feely shit?"

"Welcome to the insurance industry," Pep says. He spreads a banner in the sky and quotes his slogan: "Insure With the *People* People—Whale City Insurance."

Rhett stares at him, at Thalia, who shrugs and rolls her eyes. He gets it, and groans. "Let me get ready." He closes his eyes, and takes three deep breaths. Three more, less deep. He opens his eyes. "Ready."

Xiao Lu listens, through Rhett, as they tell her about their lives in a village called Columbia New York America. Chun tells her about her dog and bird and school. To Xiao Lu it seems very strange. She asks how can Chun have a dog made of spice and a bird with a face of a peach, and a school make of spooks?—of evil spirits? When Chun and the others hear this, they laugh. At first she hears their laughter as anger, and is embarrassed. But then Wong translates it better, and she laughs too. Then it's their turn to ask questions.

She tells them about her own mother and father, about growing up on a farm near the river, about being born in the last Year of Starvation when the fish and frogs and even snails were gone and they combed the hillsides for *anything* to eat, and about the disappearance of First Sister. The Macys tell her about seeing Tao at the police station, Rhett finding her, about her taking them to visit her husband's family, and about the vicious reception they got from her mother-in-law.

"Did you see Xia?" Xiao Lu cries out. "Did you see daughter Xia?"

"No," Clio says. "We tried, we asked people and looked around as much as we could—for her and your husband—but we had to get back, for the train."

"No, we didn't." This is from Katie, without looking up from her work.

"We had planned to," Clio says. "But that's another story."

"What is that story?" Xiao Lu asks. Katie tells her how she ran away to keep them from leaving. "I thank the gods, Chwin-Chwin, that you ran away. Maybe some day you will meet your big sister, Xia. She is twelve now."

"Yes!" Katie says, giving a thumbs-up. "My big sister! Like lately I've really missed not having a big sister or brother, and now it's coming true? Mom? Dad? Can we?" As soon as she says it, she senses like a bad jangly sound in the air their discomfort at how she's put them on the spot in front of everybody, especially Thalia, and feels bad. "Sorry," she says quickly. "Like sorry *really*. Okay?"

Clio is startled at Katie's sensitivity to her and Pep. Has she ever done that before, tuned in so acutely to the feeling in a room? It's a giant step for her, coming out of all this pain. Clio glances at Pep, sees him seeing it too, and she smiles at Katie and nods. Pep puts his hand on Clio's shoulder.

Katie, having made herself the center of attention, shies away again, head down. She feels sheepish for blurting it out, but also feels a glow, a tingly warmth all over from the top of her head to the tips of her toes. *Mom understood, and Dad too.*

Clio asks Xiao Lu, "What happened to First Sister?"

Xiao Lu visibly stiffens, and bites her lip. She asks to look at the little jade on the red thread around Clio's neck. Clio shows her. She inspects it carefully.

"It's a Kwan Yin," Clio says. "I got it in Changsha."

Xiao Lu nods. "After I had Xia, they wanted me to have a boy. I went to a temple and prayed to Kwan Yin for a boy. But it was a beautiful girl. It was you, Chun."

"And then what happened?" Clio asks.

Xiao Lu lowers her eyes, and doesn't speak.

Thalia comes over to Clio and whispers, "Do you think it's right for Katie to be hearing all this? I mean, she's only ten, and it could get, you know, worse?"

Clio looks up into those familiar eyes of shallow blue, and all at once sees the shallowness as a sign of the depth of the suffering beneath, sees the damage to her sister's soul, leached out not by what Thalia feels, but by the soul-death of not being *shown* how to feel. *These are the tarnished emblems of my own past.* She puts her hand on her sister's arm. Thalia seems to stiffen. "Katie's ready," she says, as kindly as she can. "Trust me." She turns to Xiao Lu. "You kept her for one month?"

"Yes." Again she falls silent. *Shame! Shame! You set this horror in motion and now you're paying for it. Tomorrow they are gone and you will die.* She takes a deep breath. "I wear this." She shows Clio her own jade. Clio and Pep lean closer, trying to make out the image. "My mother prayed to many gods—to our ancestors, to the Tao, to the sun god and moon god and the day-after-tomorrow god and to the Buddha. She gave me this Buddha when I left home. It is very old, and rubbed so much over many centuries that it is almost gone, but I know, and anyone who wears it knows, that it is a Buddha." She gets up, falls back into the chair, and then, with Pep's help, goes to where Chun is sitting and shows her the worn jade Buddha. "When my mother—your grandmother—died, the only thing I took with me was her little box of gods. Here, look." She limps over to a hollowed-out shelf in the rock wall, takes a little faded red box, brings it back over to the calligraphy table. She takes out, one after the other, carved and chipped wooden and jade figurines of animals and suns and moons and stars and a Buddha or two. Katie finds a statue of a tiny ox, says the Chinese word for it, and matches it up with an ox calligraphy they have done.

"Pep," Clio says, "your fanny pack?" She unzips it, looks in the packet of the tickets and passports, and finds the carefully folded piece of paper. She hands the fanny pack back to Pep. "Xiao Lu?" She turns. Clio gestures to her to sit down beside her again. Without a word, Clio unfolds the piece of paper.

Xiao Lu feels as if she has been hit by a hammer. It is the note that she wrote and put in her baby's swaddling clothes before leaving her in the celery, ten years ago. Seeing the note, seeing her own desperate characters, seeing the traces, in the slight tremble of the hairs of the brush, of her grief and rage, she feels the phrases like daggers: "*I myself don't have the strength to do anything against it, let alone overthrow it. But I believe on this big world there must be some kind, good-hearted uncles or aunties who can rescue my little daughter Chun, born July 25. I would be happy to be a cow or a horse in my next life to repay your boundless favor and infinite kindness.*" It all comes back, her sitting up against their once-beloved guava tree, alone and unloved at dusk, writing. She tries to control her feelings but they break out in a flood. She bends her head into her lap, ashamed to show this to *her*, this weakness, bends down over the paper in her lap and sobs—it is there all over again, *there*, her doing that terrible thing to this tiny, delicate baby. Head down, she sobs. The spasms rip at her fresh wound, making her cry out in pain and sob even more savagely.

And then she feels, as she hasn't felt for many years, a woman's hand on her shoulder, a woman's arm around her neck, drawing her to her, and she lets herself be drawn to her, and buries her head in her breast and lets herself cry and cry, murmuring, "Mama, Mama . . . Mama," over and over again, hoping it will not be heard but ferociously wanting it to be heard, not only now but in the past. Wanting *her* to understand she always loved her more than life and letting her go was her death sentence. She weeps, and when she feels the woman holding her weep with her, weeps on, as if she will never stop.

Finally, she pulls away and looks, just once, into the other woman's eyes. There she sees the same thing as in her own, sees the human grief at the twisting of their lives, and the twisting together of their lives, and at last—at last!—feels seen.

Clio, looking into her eyes, all at once sees her less as a woman or mother than as a child, the age her own child could have been—should have been, if only, if only. A poor, desperate child, coming back. Her mother, her daughter, her granddaughter. The red thread of shared sorrow unraveling back, and raveling back up, as care.

Xiao Lu feels all their eyes upon her, the pressure coming down on her ears and eyes like when, as a girl in the river, she dived too deep. She struggles back up, goes on. "After I left you, Chwin, I wanted to kill myself. I wondered every day if you were all right, wondered where you were. I wondered about you *every single day*. For ten years I missed everything! The day you first crawled, your first word, your first step. I tried to imagine where you were, who you were with. I stayed alive at first for little Xia. But I refused to try again for a son, I *refused*, do you understand? I will *not* give up a baby again!"

Her rage fills the small room. She feels it tight inside her, a fist.

"They turned Xia against me. I left, came here. I wandered around in the woods, every day deciding this would be the day that I killed myself, that I would jump off a cliff. There are a lot of cliffs here, aren't there, Chwin-Chwin?"

Katie, staring at her now, nods.

"I had no hope of seeing you again, dear little one, and for that I almost did kill myself. But I also have . . . one other person. First Sister. She is my beloved sister, who raised me, with my mother. When she was fourteen, First Sister went to Tienja, to a meeting of the Red Guards in a schoolhouse there. No one ever saw her again. We tried to find her." She looks at Katie. "I tried . . ."

"Do you think she is still alive?" Clio asks.

"She *is* alive," she says, her eyes glittering like black mica.

The vision of this young woman, this First Sister, coalesces in the small room, as present as if she just walked in, much like when, at a certain hour of the evening in such rooms all over the world, all those present fall silent, and in the shared stillness it is commonly believed that there are angels passing overhead.

"And *I* am alive too," Xiao Lu goes on, fiercely. "Not like others who give up their babies and years later realize what they have done, what it *means* to give up your baby—and kill themselves!" Her heart feels like it's on fire, smoldering. "I will *not* become another of the missing girls." With her good arm, slowly and deliberately, she wipes away her tears. "I began to search for you. I went back to the market. I went back to the orphanage . . . I could not do anything—I'm poor, and ignorant, and timid, but . . . then Second Sister, Tao, found you."

"Like a miracle!" Pep says.

"I'm so sorry for what I did! I think of her every day. Now I can't bear to . . ."

Lose her again, Clio hears, in the silence. She senses the moment as a delicate fabric that might just, with the right words and despite its delicacy, hold.

"You don't have to," Clio says, her voice softened by her tears. "Now that we know. It's a gift, what you've told us."

"Yes, thank you," Pep says, wiping away his own tears, "for her."

Silence—but for the crackle and hum of the burning wood.

Clio stares into the flames. *Reaching on and on, but never reaching. Combustible, eternally. In the wood, the fire; in the fire, the wood.*

"Xiao Lu?"

They turn. It's Katie, looking at Xiao Lu from the calligraphy table.

"Yes?"

"Why did you give me up?"

Even before Rhett finishes translating Xiao Lu looks stunned. In the ten years of every single day in which she has thought of this child, she has imagined answering this question. Now, the usual answers echo in her mind: *I had to. I was forced by my family. We didn't have enough food. They said we had to have a boy. People said it was a better life for you. If I did not give you up, you might have died, or been killed.* But now with her child looking at her, waiting for her to say something, she realizes that none of these answers are reasons, they're just stories she made up. Before she says anything Chun asks her another question.

"I mean, is it something I *did*?" Rhett, translating, hits the word hard.

"No! You were a wonderful baby, a beautiful, curious baby—your eyes then were like your eyes now, they seemed to reach out and hold the world in their grip!"

"Well, um . . . was it something wrong with me? Like how I looked, or—"

"No, no, Chun, you were perfect! There was something wrong with *me*!"

"Like the one-child-per-family thing?"

"I had one child already, but they said it would only be worth it if you were a boy."

"Why?"

"Because they are stupid and care more about money than girls!" She lowers her eyes, ashamed of this childish outburst, and goes on, with her head down, "I . . . I could not stand up for you, with them. Not that they were at fault, your father and grandparents. No, it was me, my fault. They were doing what they had been told to do—and I knew I shouldn't do it. I could not stand up to do what I knew I should do, as your mother who carried you inside her. I could not do it and I am sorry!"

She thinks she will cry again, but she is all out of tears. These are the accusations sent from her ancestors—no, not them, they would approve of her giving her girl baby away—but sent from the gods, from those little statues and icons lying in her mother's box. She is out of tears, out of anger, out of words. She has nothing left but her shame. She can no longer look at Chun or the others—these three dear, kind souls!—and gets up suddenly and somehow finds herself out in the clearing on the stones, and then on the cliff edge beside the willow, staring down into the stream and the rocks far below, feeling desperately alone. The waterfall roars up at her.

Arms tighten around her arms, Clio and Pep are on either side of her, holding her back, talking to her. *They are scared I will kill myself.*

They talk to her, through Rhett, the words at first seeming to come from far away. They are worried about her, they don't want her to hurt herself. Everything's okay. They forgive her.

Clio takes her by the shoulders and turns her so they are face-to-face. "Tell her, Rhett," Clio says, "that she *saved* . . . Chun's life, and that we will always be grateful to her, *always*."

"Saved our lives too," Pep adds, "risked hers for us all."

As Clio holds her, faces her, Rhett repeats this.

Xiao Lu looks up into Clio's eyes, sees the truth of this, and nods. Embarrassed, she turns away, looking out into the great expanse that stretches from this mountain to the next. The fishhook of the new moon is resting on its curve. The bright jewel of the Evening Star shines just above the upper horn as if it's about to fall into the curve and rock back and forth like in a cradle—it reminds her of sitting out under the stars of a summer night, her mother telling her stories about all the gods in the sky.

42

Rhett and Thalia are in the hut. In the cave, Pep and Clio and Katie are awake in the large bed, Xiao Lu still awake in the other. When any of them moves, the light from the wood stove makes their shadows jump like liquid ghosts against the calcified wet of the rock walls. The bats are out for the night. Clio is using Pep's flashlight to read to Katie, yet again, *The Little House on the Prairie*. Xiao Lu lies quietly, her arm freshly bandaged. The wound is healing. Her energy is coming back. Rhett and Thalia are anxious to get back to civilization and are pushing to leave tomorrow.

After a while Katie yawns loudly and says, "I want to go to sleep." Clio closes the book and puts her arm around Katie, who snuggles in. "Goodnight, Mom, Dad."

"Goodnight, dear."

"'Night Kate-zer. Have a beautiful sleep."

"Okay," Clio says, "now everybody says goodnight to Xiao Lu. In Chinese."

"*Wan-an*," Katie says, echoed by Clio and Pep.

Xiao Lu lies there, knowing that it is the last night she will see her baby. She wants something more, but does not know what. She lies there rigidly, a thousand images racing through her mind.

"Mom? Dad? This is our last night here, right?"

"Probably," Clio says.

"And we can't stay here any longer?"

"No."

"Can I sleep with Xiao Lu tonight?"

For an instant they each pause, and then, almost in unison, each says, "Yes."

"But you'll be right here too, right?"

"Of course," Pep says, "for sure."

Xiao Lu hears them talking. She hears the pine boughs creak and footsteps on the stone and sees her little girl gesturing to her to move over and give her some room. She feels the pine boughs respond as Chun gets into bed with her. She is afraid to move.

They lie there for long moments, side by side. She is afraid even to breathe.

Then the girl yawns loudly, says something, and lifts her head. She puts her good arm around her and feels her head settle onto it and in the settling start to relax—once, twice relaxing—and she breathes, and soon her baby is asleep in her arms. She looks at her face, and she sees in it the face of her lost one, and then the faces of all her lost ones, alive now in the breathing of her child. She vows to stay awake the whole night this way, for it is not only her baby in her arms again but it is she herself in her mother's arms and her dear lost sister back and all the floating dead come back to life, and for the longest time she is aware of feeling every touch of her daughter's skin against her own, a lost world found, until an edgeless sleep, of love redeemed, prevails.

43

Maybe Chang-O the moon goddess,
Will pity this single swallow
And join us together with the cord of light
That reaches beneath the painted eaves of your home.

Rhett translates this, the calligraphy on the wall of the little hut, as they sit in the clearing finishing their lunch. "The name of the poem is 'To a Traveler,'" he says, "the signature is Su Tung P'o."

"Did Xiao Lu do the calligraphy?" Pep asks.

He asks her. "No, it was here before she came. She thinks it is ancient."

"Worth a fortune," Thalia says, "if you could crack it off the wall in one piece." She smiles. "Well, then, are we almost ready to go?"

Clio, irritated, snaps, "No, we are not."

Thalia lets out a sigh of disgust and boredom.

Katie, Clio, and Pep have spent the morning doing the usual chores and delights—the deer, the fire, the cooking, the cleaning, the calligraphy. Xiao Lu is much better, stable on her feet again, and even though her arm is in a sling she says she is ready to walk back to the monastery with them.

They carry the plates back inside and make fresh tea. Then they sit, using Rhett to ask all the questions that they could not before. Pep is interested in finding out about the family history of illnesses, to pin down Katie's risk factors. Clio asks about Xiao Lu's marriage, about Xia, Katie's sister, and about the circumstances of her giving up Katie. Katie sits at the calligraphy table, listening. Thalia announces she does not want to hear "all the gory details," and goes outside to read her latest *New Yorker*.

Xiao Lu tells them about her decision to give Chun up and about the trip to Changsha. She takes out her one souvenir from the trip, the pair of pink plastic sandals she has never again worn. Then she asks Clio, "Why don't you have your own baby?"

The bluntness startles Clio—she looks to Katie, to see how she takes this.

"She doesn't mean anything, Mom," Katie says, reassuringly, "she just doesn't know how we put it."

Clio smiles and nods. "We tried," she says, "tried incredibly hard." She glances at Katie again and decides for the first time to tell her. "Every month I had to take my temperature, first thing in the morning, and when I was 'right', I had to call Pep to come home, to make love. And then every month, when my period came, month after month, it was like something had died—and some part of us had died." She sees Pep nodding in sympathy. "Once, I did get pregnant. We were so happy! Finally! We celebrated—yes, Katie, celebrated, told people. I felt such a *glow*! And then, after about two months, in the middle of the night I . . . lost the baby." She can't keep talking, looks down, and then up at Pep. He has tears in his eyes, and tears roll down her own cheeks, turning to salt on her lips. She looks at Katie, and sees in her fallen face a sadness, and a puzzlement too. "I lost her."

"You know . . . I mean . . . it was a her?" Katie asks, her voice trembling.

"Yes."

"I would've had a big sister?"

"That's right, honey."

"But you do," says Xiao Lu.

"Yeah. But if you had her, Mom, maybe you'd never 'a had me. It's all kinda *weird*. Did you ever get pregnant again?"

"No," Pep says. "We tried, tried hard, went to doctors, everything. Never. Maybe it was just that by the time we tried to have children, we were older."

"Why were you so old?" Xiao Lu asks.

Clio smiles. "We didn't meet until we were older—I was in my thirties, Pep even older. I left my family, wanted to have adventures, see the world."

"And I never fell in love before," Pep said. "It was love at first sight. We fell deeply in love—crazy about each other. But even as much as we loved each other, the pain of losing our baby was so depressing, we couldn't even *think* of adoption for a long time. When we finally did, we found out that it was almost impossible for us to do. The rules were against us, because we were older, and we hadn't been married long enough. We started to argue with each other, we fought—a lot. For a while it seemed like we would split up. The marriage almost died. Just because of the rules."

"The rules were against me too!" Xiao Lu says, passionately. "The rules, and my in-laws. The rules almost killed us both, Chwin-Chwin."

"But we couldn't give up," Pep says. "Life without a child, for us, wasn't really life. We felt so depressed, walked around in a daze—like facing death every day."

"Until we heard that we could adopt from China," Clio says. "The moment we heard, we knew it was right."

"Why was it right?" Xiao Lu asks.

"I was always drawn to China. My best friend, Katie's godmother, Carter, spent years in Asia, some in China. As soon as I heard 'China,' I said, 'Yes!'"

"And my family," Pep says, "is from an island called Nantucket, and they were whalers, and sailed to China to trade in silk and tea and rice and opium, hundreds of years ago. For me, too, it was *so* right—a big 'Yes!'"

"Can I tell Xiao Lu about the 'Chun'?" Katie asks, excitedly. They nod. "Well, I wasn't there when it happened but—" She stops. "I mean I *was* there, but not *there* there, I mean I was born already *here* and in the orphanage, but I wasn't there with them when it happened like I'm going to say?"

Rhett, with a contorted brow, tries to communicate this, and fails.

Breathlessly Katie goes on, "So then like they were supposed to go to China to get me, but they didn't get their documents like their police record ready in time, so their friends went to China to get *their* baby first. And it was Christmas and they wanted to give their friends a Christmas card to welcome them home, and they found one. It had a Chinese character on the front and on the back it said that the character meant 'New Beginnings,' it was like from the third chapter of a real old Chinese book called the *I Ching* and—" Rhett slows her down, to catch up.

"What is *I Ching* book?" Xiao Lu asks Rhett.

He stops and thinks. "Not sure." He turns to Pep. "What is the *I Ching*? We never heard of it."

Clio and Pep are amazed. Sure that they aren't pronouncing it correctly, they try to explain what it is—*The Book of Changes*, thousands of years old, one of the oldest books in the world, a classic in Chinese, a book of prophecies, of fortune telling?

No, neither of them knows it.

"Astonishing," Clio says to Pep.

"Thank you, Chairman Mao," he says. "I guess that by their generation, it had been totally wiped out."

"*Whatever*," Katie says with irritation, wanting the stage back. "So then this character for 'New Beginnings' is all about a plant born in the dark from a little seed and *chaos looms*!" She smiles. "But then it rises up from the earth into the nice beautiful light. And the card seemed so cool to them they didn't give it to their friends but *they kept it for themselves*! They even like made a *banner* of it, and *hung it up in their bedroom*! Because they were going to have a 'New Beginning' in their life. And then, and then . . ." She looks at Clio and Pep and rubs her hands together with excitement, letting out little giggling squeaks. "And then *two weeks later* they got a call from the adoption lady, with news from the orphanage in China. And the lady said there were only *two things* they knew about their baby: her *birthday*, and her *name*. And her name was . . . *the same name as the character on the card; it was Chun*!"

Xiao Lu's eyes get big. She flushes and takes Clio's hand.

"My dad started crying and my mom fell down on the floor!" Katie screeches with delight, goes to the table, and gets her calligraphy to show them. "And of all the like *millions* of Chinese characters, it was *mine, me*! And this is the 'Chun.' See?"

毛

It is the character Katie drew a few days ago. Xiao Lu understood, then, that it was a bridge between the ancient pictograph and the modern character, a bridge unknown to her. To have it come to her this way, this lost character from her lost daughter, with the *karma* of connection between her life and the lives of these kind people, is astonishing. She sits there speechless, nodding. Then she gets up and shows them, in two "Chun scrolls," the other two characters, and explains how this is a bridge. And how it all means "New Beginning," or "Spring."

They ask the meaning of the scrolls. Rhett translates. "Spring returns flowers no fade," he says—the literal translation. He tries again, "When Spring comes, the hidden flowers come up and blossom." He reads others. "'When Spring winds stop, moon shines clear'; 'A Spring child, when a woman is twenty-eight, is good fortune.'"

○ ○ ○

After lunch, it is time to leave. Pep produces his business card, Clio writes down all their numbers and e-mails—"in case," Katie says, "she gets a computer." They talk about bringing her to Columbia on a visa.

Rhett takes photos of them standing in front of the house, at the cliff edge, with the fragrant ming aurelia, in the house, and in the mouth of the cave. At the flash the bats squeak and scatter, gliding here and there, and finally seek deeper dark.

To Xiao Lu the walk back to the temple is funereal, reminding her of the journey with her mother's body in the wheelbarrow, her half-crazed father trailing along behind, up the mountain from the river to the run-down little temple where the monks would do the cremation. Was Tao there, then? She can't recall. This walk seems even worse. *She is in good hands, yes, but how will I bear it again without her?*

Clio is worried. First that something will happen to keep them from getting there—but also that nothing will happen and that the wheel of loss will merely turn. She walks along, listening to Thalia's inane chatter. Finally she says, "Would you mind not talking? This path is an old pilgrimage path between the monastery and the Dusk-Enjoying Pavilion. Would you mind walking in silence?"

"But why? We've got to amuse ourselves somehow."

"Well, then walk ahead or behind—I don't care, just don't spoil it!"

"Now you just wait a second, missy! I came all this way—"

"*Shut up!*"

Thalia looks mortified. Settling her Great White Hunter hat with a *harumph* that Clio can barely keep from laughing at because it reminds her of the precious English literary novels they were forced to read in Mr. Parkman Howe's Academy for Girls, Thalia stomps off to where Rhett is lighting another cigarette, using the smoke to try to discourage the pestilential insects. Clio feels great—lighter, freer. Her sister is stirring up her old rebelliousness, her wish to break free and do outrageous things in wild places. She wonders, *Why, then, did I ever go "home"? Why the hell did I ever go back?* She finds herself wishing now that the way back were forgotten, hidden away, and she an empty boat, floating adrift.

○ ○ ○

When True Emptiness spots Pep, he breaks into a big smile and bows a formal Buddhist greeting. For the first time in his life Pep Macy bows to someone too. The monk motions him into his office. Pep insists Xiao Lu go first. Appalled at the severity of her monkey bite, the monk sets off a string of red firecrackers, and then, gathering the spent gunpowder and paper and mixing it with what could be rancid Tibetan yak butter, makes a poultice and wraps it from shoulder to elbow in a snow-white Red Cross bandage. He gives her a packet of medicine.

He then ushers Pep and Rhett into his consultation room, a former classroom of the monastery, long abandoned. All along one wall are hundreds of two-foot-tall carved and painted wooden Buddhas, primitively done, as if by novices. The colors are faded, the paint chipped, but the hundreds of eyes are somehow insistent, although insistent about what, Pep can't tell.

Katie, Xiao Lu, and Clio are immersed in the carp in the reflecting pool outside.

Thalia is buying souvenirs in the Elephant Temple Gift Shop.

True Emptiness puts his fingers on Pep's pulse and nods proudly. He does a more careful communion with the pulse, checks out the ankle—and for some reason does an extensive sounding of Pep's armpits. He says that *almost* all problems are cured, but that more medicines are needed. He goes to an old floor-to-ceiling cabinet, rummages around, and returns with a fistful of matter that he parcels out into paper packets. He writes down the doses, timetables, and route of administration, one of which, to his own great hilarity, is up the butt. Pep asks if these will assure his continued health. The monk holds his thumb and forefinger together in front of Pep's eyes, and lets them go in the universal sign of "Poof!"—fairy dust being released, vanishing up into nowhere, not even air.

"Take this correctly," he says, "and you'll be forever smiling and talking. Smiling like an idiot and clucking like a chicken!" They all laugh.

"How long do I take the medicine?"

"Not long," he says. "Only for *this* lifetime." He laughs again, bows, and starts to leave. But then he stops and asks Pep to remove his hat. He peers at the scars of Pep's chronic scraping of skin off his scalp from bashing into the low beams of China, and is not pleased. He sets off a string of *green* firecrackers, and applies the same gunpowder, yak butter, and white bandage. He bows goodbye.

Rhett and Pep go out and tell Clio, Katie, and Xiao Lu the good medical news to much delight. No one knows what to do next. The moment hangs, neglected.

Xiao Lu gets up, thinking, *I can't stand this.* She says, "It is time to say goodbye."

"Don't you want to stay for dinner," Clio asks, "and for the dusk meditation?"

"No. My food is better, and I do not often meditate with them."

"But I thought you were a Buddhist?"

"No. I do not believe in religion. My mother did, with her little box of gods. I do not. I heard once that God has no religion. I believe that."

"*Your* food," Pep says, "*is* better. It is delicious! So fresh and healthy!"

"Yes," Xiao Lu says, "the food here stinks. It was one reason I had to find another place to live, away from them and their religion and their food."

"Rhett," Clio asks, "did she really say 'stinks'?"

"'Stinks' is a refined translation. In Chinese it's a lot more literal."

Xiao Lu is speaking again. "I will go now."

"But you'll be back again tomorrow?" Clio asks.

"No. It is too hard."

"Well, um," Pep says, "let us walk you back to the main gate?"

"No. I go alone."

"Wait," Clio says. All at once, as if it is her own, she feels the depth of this young woman's pain, losing her child again. She has a sense that she has become *like* her, wanting nothing but her child. "Listen," Clio says, hearing her voice as insistent, frantic, as if trying to catch a dream, "we'll be back, you'll come to America—"

Xiao Lu takes this in, and wants to be polite and say yes, yes, of course. But she has never been the polite one that says yes, yes, of course. "No, that will not happen."

"But it will, it can, and I—"

Xiao Lu stops her with her hand on her arm. "No."

Clio hears this "No" as the dead weight of ten centuries of things in this empire not working out for its Xiao Lus. *As opposed to our flicker of two centuries that still, despite the duplicity and violence toward less lucky ones at home and brown-skinned others abroad, still holds out the illusion that we are an exceptionally good if not the best country in the world with our democracy and money that foreigners crave—and, hey, that things can work out if you just do what we want and buy our films and TV that will make you happy and that show you that things really can. Yes!*

She feels Xiao Lu release her arm. Their eyes meet. Hold for a moment. *No.*

Xiao Lu looks from Clio to Pep, and then to Chun. "All of you give me strength. Soon I will go back and visit my other daughter, Xia. *Your* First Sister, Chwin-Chwin."

Xiao Lu bends slightly so that she is face-to-face with her child. She takes off the jade Buddha and places it around her neck. "From my mother, through me, to my daughter." She looks at her then as if for the first time, looks at her in the care of this other woman, this other country, and feels it as unbearable and bearable. She takes her in, all of her, in the way that she took her in before she let her go the first time, thinking it was the last time she would ever see her, as this time might be too.

Katie looks into her eyes. "Can I ask you one more thing?" Xiao Lu nods. "What time was I born?"

Xiao Lu smiles. "You were born as the sun came up, about five in the morning. We call it the 'springtime of the day.'"

"Shay shay," Katie says. "I'm glad I know."

"Goodbye, Katie Chun," she says, but she does not move, cannot move yet.

Katie looks down at her shoes. Then she looks back up. Xiao Lu has tears in her eyes. Katie says, "Goodbye, Mom."

Katie watches as Xiao Lu seems to tremble from inside, as if she'll fall, and so she reaches out and puts her arms around her and hugs her and feels the thin body shake horribly as if collapsing—like *she's* the little girl!— and then she feels arms around her too, not Xiao Lu's arms but her mom's and dad's arms shaking and shaking because they're crying really hard! All of them standing there together and she feels something break free inside her and she's crying her eyes out too, just crying her heart out with everybody. They stand there together for a time, and the world around them disappears for a moment too. *I'm with everybody in the world I love and who loves me too.* They ease apart.

Without another sound Xiao Lu turns and walks quickly across the long, sunbaked courtyard. The thin, childlike figure, one arm wrapped in a white bandage with a red cross, the other carrying the unlit torch, walks out through the somber and capricious moon gate toward the green wall of mountain forest, and vanishes.

44

After the parting, a silence comes over all the Macys. They find themselves wandering aimlessly around the courtyards and gardens and temples. There is a strange feel to what remains of the day, as if it, too, is wandering aimlessly around, a confused child waiting for the rest of the hours to fill up again. They are depressed and distracted. Worse, each feels a distance from the others—just when they sense they should feel close. They are aware that it is the distance of loss, of the empty space where the young woman has been. No, not so much her, but more the web of feeling strung between them all, woven out in the woods and on the paths through the woods, woven around all the gnarled tree roots seeking life among the rock, woven in the way the sky as the rain came seemed to fall into the earth, woven in the hut and the cave. The distance straining between the ones who stayed and the one who is gone. The one who stayed, and the ones who are gone.

In the afternoon the three of them sit on a bench in the shade. After a while Thalia appears.

"And what are your plans for the summer, Clio?" Thalia asks.

"Nothing, really."

"No camps for Kate?"

"Sure there are camps, but nothing we have to be back for."

"Which ones?"

"The usual—tennis, horseback, swimming—"

"I hate those camps," Katie says sullenly, "except horseback. And the ocean's always too cold to swim."

"And you?" Clio asks.

"*Well!*" Thalia says, in the definitive voice that reminds Clio of their much-feared Aunt Urania. "I've got a new Navigator. Good fun."

"Navigator?"

"The new Lincoln Navigator—the biggest SUV there is—you know the Lincoln Continental?" Reluctantly Clio indicates that she does. "Got it from the settlement with my Freudian. I'm going to *Navigate*! The kids are gone, Dr. Ed the Sadist is paying through the nose—enormous!—I mean both his nose and his payments—and I'm taking my first road trip *ever*, to see all my old friends."

"Nice," Clio says. "Pep, Katie? Let's put our things in the attic where we'll sleep? And see if we can get them to cook you noodles for dinner?"

The smells in the kitchen, and the cobwebs and dank in the attic, drive them back outside. They wander around peering into barred, locked temples and empty classrooms, the musky shadows a relief from the final, pounding heat and glare of the sun.

For suddenly the sun is brutal. They realize that for the past several days they have been living in a high rainforest, with an umbrella of trees over their heads and a crisp breeze blowing not only from the fertile western valleys but from the foothills of the Himalayas. Now, in the monastery, they feel exposed. The sky is clear and still. The sun crashes down incessantly on the stone courtyard, as if stacking itself up in flat slabs for the long, freezing night on this scary mass of rock.

The monastery is by now familiar, so old and solid it seems safe. Compared to the woods out there, it seems civilized. But something is missing.

Pep and Clio sit on a stone bench at the top of the two hundred steps up from the path. They can see for miles out into the western prospect, watching the lowering sun, and can keep an eye on Katie, sitting in the Elephant Temple with a notebook and a pen trying to draw the white elephant, the lotus, and the Buddha.

As they sit there, a long line of porters climbs up, approaches them, and passes by. As far as they can see down the stone steps there are porters, all bent under loads of sacks lashed onto bamboo frames. Each load dwarfs its man, piled from where the pack rests on the man's lower back to high up over his head. From the careful way the men place their feet and stagger, the loads must weigh over a hundred pounds each, maybe two. The men are young, the men are in midlife, the men are old. They wear only rope sandals with a loop around the big toe, and are dressed in raggedy shirts, some with Chinese characters, others proclaiming "Nike," "IBM," "Abercrombie and Fitch." They each have a half-gallon plastic milk-bottle dangling from a ratty cord attached to the top end of the bamboo spine, a water bottle within easy reach. Most of the plastic bottles swaying back and forth have been emptied along the way, fuel to keep these bodies climbing thousands of feet and many hard hours from below. Hanging from a piece of cord from the other spine of bamboo is a faded rag, with which they wipe away sweat. They use a thick wooden stick with a metal tip to climb with. At each step up, a hard, crisp *tap* echoes, loudest as they pass, fainter above and below: *tap . . . TAP . . .*

tap. From time to time one of them will stop to rest. It is an elaborate ritual, for they never put down their loads. The "tap stick" is T shaped, and when a man wants a rest, he smoothly slips the stick into the bottom of the bamboo frame, the T fitting into a T-shaped crossbar. Then the man leans back on the stick, resting his legs from the load, but unable to move. When they rest, most take out a cigarette and smoke. Then they go on. With barely a glance, they pass by. An endless stream of burdened men, climbing thousands of feet up. Then down. Then up.

One older man stops in front of them, gasping like a stranded fish, and lights a cigarette. Other men move slowly past him. Pep stares into his eyes. The eyes seem both sunken and bulging. Pep is struck by what is in them. Sunken into a world that only he knows and that Pep can only dimly glimpse, and bulging at what?—at chancing upon this Westerner, at suddenly meeting the stare of this rich, foreign, tall, well-fed Round Eyes sitting there without a two-hundred-pound load on his back.

Pep is mesmerized. He holds, and tries to read, this man's gaze. There's no resentment in these eyes, merely an acknowledgment that *this is who you are and this is who I am*. But there's something more: a desperate *curiosity*. These eyes seem to be asking, "*This* isn't a life, is *yours*?"

The question rocks Pep back on his heels.

The man hoists his load, removes the stick that has been holding him and it up, and starts to climb the next set of steep steps, *TAP . . . Tap . . . tap . . .* taking his place in the line. Already the next man is climbing into view, *tap . . . Tap . . . TAP . . .*

"Whoa!" Pep says to Clio. "Did you see his eyes?"

"I did. Like an accusation."

"More a challenge—like he's saying, 'What's the load *you* carry? Big house, big cars, stuck-up expensive school? Yeah, you're rich compared to me—so what? Why?'" Despite the sun, Pep shivers. "*Insurance*? You know, Clee, there never even *was* insurance, till the Medici thought it up. People used to take care of each other. When someone got sick or died we used to take care of them and theirs. Now? Forget it. And this is what we're passing along to Katie?"

"I know. It's depressing."

"Lonely too."

"Deadly," she says. "Like watching a sunset alone. How can we take care of each other, locked up all day in our Navigators, buzzing around?"

Pep nods, with a grim smile. He sits there in the hot sun, quietly. "I feel so down, Clee—like there's something desperately wrong with the way we're living."

"And the way we're showing *her* how to live." She feels a wave of sorrow, and then the air goes out of even that, so she's left with an airless dismay, a paralysis that she senses will just get worse when, at home, she buries it under her errands.

"Really depressing," he says. "To see it all so clearly right now, here."

"But what the hell are we going to *do* about it, Pep? To sit here and get a glimpse, to understand this—to really feel it—and then just go right on with life as usual? That's worse than never understanding it at all. 'Blessed be the Thalias!'"

"Honey, we gotta start living it, or it'll destroy us."

Clio looks at him, surprised at this moment of clarity together. "Yes, we do. Live or die, but don't just wander through."

They sit, face-to-face, eye-to-eye, holding the awe.

Like making sure, Clio thinks, *when you are saying goodbye to someone— even for a day, or for a night when you're tucking them in to bed—that you look into their eyes and hold that look, because every time might just be the last time you see them alive.*

"Pep, when you said goodbye to Xiao Lu, did you really look into her eyes?"

He understands. Thinks about it. "No. You?"

"No."

"Mom? Dad?"

Clio and Pep turn and see Katie coming out of the Elephant Temple, her notebook under her arm. As she gets closer, they see that she is not happy.

"Look—I tried to draw the elephant, but it didn't come out too good."

"It's not that bad, honey—"

"Mom, stop it! It's *bad*, okay?"

"Okay. It is pretty bad."

"Not even *pretty* bad. *Bad.* It is *ugly!*"

"Okay. Bad."

"Agreed," Pep says. "*Ugly!*"

"So then I thought, okay, I'll do like what Xiao Lu does, I'll draw the *character* for elephant she taught me, okay?"

"Great."

"But it's not great, 'cause it's hard with a lot of lines and I can't remember it too good. I drew this." Katie shows them a character that looks a lot like an elephant.

"It looks a lot like an elephant, honey."

"Sure does," Pep adds.

"Guys, that's the *problem*! It looks *too much* like! It's supposed to be a . . . what?"

"An abstraction of—"

"Yeah, a metaphor like in Greek?" Clio nods. "But it isn't! It's just it *itself*!"

"Calm down, calm—"

"*I'm not calming down, Mom*! This is *important*. Listen to me, will you?"

"You're right," Clio says. "Don't calm down. I'm listening."

Katie waits to see if she is really listening. Finally she sees that she is.

"So then I decide to go back to basics, and draw what I know, you know?"

"Like?"

"Like a horse. The first thing Xiao Lu taught me. First the stick figure of a horse, then the old character, then the modern, and it was great, and I knew if I did it I would feel good about it, right?" Clio and Pep nod. "So I did it, and look!"

They do. It isn't very good. The stick figure looks like a horse, but the character doesn't, it doesn't have much *lift* up off the pictograph into the art. The modern figure has even less.

"Yeah, I see what you mean," Pep says, "they're not too good."

"Not that good at all," Clio says.

Katie is startled—*they told the truth?* "No, they're not," she says, "and you know why?"

"Why?" they both ask, at the same time.

"'Cause I don't have my real brush, the one she gave me! And I don't have my real inkstone! All I've got is this dumb ballpoint pen from the Drippy Hotel!" As soon as she says that, she finds herself thinking, *And I don't have her!*

"Well, where's your brush and inkstone?" Clio asks.

"I forgot 'em! I left them at her house! Can we go back and get 'em?"

Pep and Clio glance at each other.

"Sorry, hon," Clio says, "we can't."

"There's no time now, and we leave tomorrow morning."

"Shit!" Katie says. Clio stares at her. "I know, it's a swear and I'm sorry."

"It's okay," Clio says. "You're old enough now for a swear once in a while."

Katie is staring at her, and then at Pep, silently making a plea: *Please, Mom, please, Dad, don't make it nice anymore, just show me you get it and then tell me. Tell me.*

"And," Clio goes on, "you don't have *her* with you either now, to help?"

Katie stares at her, and in her mind is a memory of sitting at the table in the hut, the scents of woodsmoke, garlic, and ink all around, her head bent close to the character that is really an animal, almost alive, and the scent of her birth mom—pine, rain, turned-up earth.

"Yeah," Katie says, "I miss her already, really *bad*." She snuggles into Clio's arms.

○ ○ ○

All of them are bedding down for the night. Outside the tremulous arc of their candle it is deeply dark, cold, and scary as only a big mountain in a foreign wilderness can be. In the attic the damp cold is almost cutting. Pep, Katie, and Clio are on one side of the room, Thalia and Rhett on the other. The meal has been foul, the bedding is stale. It makes all the Macys miss the fresh vegetables and sweet cedar mattresses of the little hut and cave on the shy side of the mountain.

Rhett has located two bottles of beer, which he and Thalia are sipping.

"Okay, gang," Pep sings out. "Bedtime. I'm taking orders for sleeping pills." He holds out his palm. "Ambien reds, five millipedes, Ambien whites, ten millipedes—"

"Stop that, you cad!" says Thalia, laughing. "I'll take a white."

"For me, of course," Rhett says with delight, "the red."

Hungrily, Rhett and Thalia reach for the Ambiens, pick a couple of pills each out of Pep's extended hand, and drink them down with their beers.

All say goodnight.

Rhett and Thalia are soon afloat in that rich, syrupy sleep of the drugged. They stir as the gongs chime at four in the morning but, groggy, go back to sleep until the sun clears the silent heart of the peaks and the monks start calling to the soul-mountain for their feeding at six. They look around. Katie and Clio and Pep, and all their things, are gone.

PART FOUR

The days grow long, the mountains beautiful.
The south wind blows over blossoming meadows.
Newly arrived swallows dart over steaming marshes.
Ducks in pairs drowse on the warm sand.
—Tu Fu (713–770), "South Wind"

45

Pedaling hard uphill on the rackety bicycle, the girl thinks, *I won't give up until I reach the fork in the path.*

The branches of the persimmon trees scratch her, but she puts her head down and pedals on. She remembers how the red-dirt path, all rutted and twisty, keeps going up until where the tree is, that one lonely fig tree at the fork. *This time we'll go the new way, to the right. When we got to the village down below it was easy to find out where they live. It's not far now.* "See, I *told you, didn't I?" I said to them. "I said trust me—we'll find 'em."*

From the day they showed up again at her little hut in the woods, Xiao Lu was determined. As soon as she was healthy, she would go back. And they would go back with her, no question. This morning down in the village, Xiao Lu wouldn't take no for an answer—she was tough. *I've been right almost every time in China except when I ran away—and if that hadn't happened then, this wouldn't be happening now. But is this gonna be right too?*

Katie clenches her teeth, pushes hard, harder, and when the bike slows after a hard push she takes a quick glance back and doesn't see anybody. It's a steamy morning in late July. She wants to wipe the sweat off her face because it's mixing with the sunscreen to make some weird goo that's stinging her eyes but she knows that if she takes her hand off the handlebars to wipe it she won't be able to make the next turn of the wheel and keep moving up. It's like if she can make just one more turn of the pedal this whole adventure will turn out well, but if she gives up it will tilt like a bicycle defeated and wobble and throw her off, down into the red dirt. Eyes stinging, she does one more hard push. The bike moves at first barely but then when the pedal goes all the way down it moves faster and everything else but pedaling gets blotted out, and she puts her head down and does one more and when she looks up she sees it just up ahead, the fig tree at the fork in the path. *I'll stop up there and wait for them to catch up. I'll go, "La-dee-da what took you so long?"*

Catching her breath, she looks around. To the left, the path goes up to the house of the scary grandparents. To the right the path dips into a valley of rice fields. A lot of paddies climb the hills like steps on either side. Some fields are green, others are flooded with no sign of planting and reflect the sun in wedges. Far down in the valley she sees somebody working in the field, a white shirt with a golden straw hat, bobbing up and down like a bird. *I think they told Xiao Lu to go down there, way down there, maybe three farms or five, and that's where they'll be.*

"Katie? Wait!"

Katie watches them walk their bikes up toward her. First Clio, in her straw hat, then Xiao Lu, hatless, smiling up at her—she's always smiling at her now—and then Pep, huffing and puffing and bent down almost double over the small bike like a clown in a circus act. Katie laughs at the sight of him, his big knobb-ley knees going here and there, his face sunburnt red, his nose like a half tomato, skin peeling.

They come up to her and stop to rest.

"Thank God we don't have to go up there again," Clio says, nodding to the left fork.

"Up to the beautiful nice grandparents?" Pep says. "Hey—how 'bout we drop in for a cup of tea and a torrent of abuse? Shall we take a vote?"

"I vote no!" Katie says.

"No," Clio says.

"Xiao Lu?" Katie communicates, in gesture and a few Chinese words, what the choice is. Xiao Lu's eyes get big, her mouth falls open, and she shakes her head no.

"Good," Pep says, "I vote no too."

Xiao Lu gestures to the other fork of the path, the one leading down alongside the rice field with the bobbing figure.

Her eyes are different, Katie thinks, *as if she could start crying really easy. It's a big thing for her to bring us to them, for her to see them again after so many years. She's scared of what she might find there—real scared. I'm scared too. They might be mean like the others!*

Clio nods to Xiao Lu. Xiao Lu gets up on her bike and sets off, Clio following.

"Excited, Kate-zer?" Pep asks as he walks his bike alongside Katie.

"Yeah."

"Gonna be great to meet your beautiful nice sister, eh?"

"Yeah, Dad, like as great as your meeting my beautiful nice birth dad too!" He looks like he's swallowed a toad, the slimy thing caught halfway down his throat. She laughs and gets up on her bike.

"You little foozle! Ha! Haha!" He grabs the seat of her bike and pushes her a few steps along. She screeches—"Heeeee!"—and with a hard push he lets go and she keeps on going, fast and faster down the slope.

Feeling his push, the bike floating along, she remembers the moment when she learned to ride. He had been teaching her, running alongside and holding the bike while she pedaled, catching her when she was about to fall. It seemed she would never get it. But then one warm evening as he ran along beside her and she wobbled and wobbled as if once again she would fall, he ran faster and she pedaled faster and suddenly he seemed a little behind her and he had already let go of her and it worked!—as if he was still there pushing her but he wasn't, he'd let her go on alone and she was floating, flying, screeching with delight, and he was still with her and not.

She glances back. He's pedaling hard to catch up. She hurries after the two women, thinking, *My mom and birth mom side by side, how cool is that?*

But he's given her too hard a push for the sudden downhill. She flies way too fast down the long slope and is suddenly scared that she's just gonna crash into them on the narrow path or have to steer off into a paddy and she cries out, "Hey, watch out, *here I come!*" and they turn and seem to be laughing because as if by magic the red-dirt path swells out like a big belly into a road wide enough for everybody and they make a place for her to slip on in between them and grab her and slow her down and hold her, Clio by her shirt and Xiao Lu by her handlebars until she moves with them and they move with her along into their pace, all of them suddenly a living character of three people riding in the sun.

"Look! No hands!" They look back. Pep is barreling down toward them, hands high in the air. He brakes hard and swerves dramatically, tires spitting red dirt, and, laughing, joins them. He rides on the outside of Xiao Lu.

The three women and the man ride along together seeking a girl named

Xia, whose name means "Summer." And if you could ask each of them what they are feeling at just that moment, each might say in their own way that they are feeling part of something else, part of something at the heart of the universe, a universal law of love.

Notes

With appreciation of the marvelous volume *China: Empire of Living Symbols by Cecelia Lindqvist,* translated from the Swedish by Joann Tate. Addison-Wesley Publishing Company, Reading MA 1989.

With appreciation for constant scholarly and cultural advice on China from professor and friend Tianja Dong, Westfield State University, Massachusetts

Note on the two different translations of the "Birth Mother's Letter": on Page 64, the Americans are reading the English translation; on page 290, the letter is being read by Xiao Lu, who of course makes and the correct Chinese translation.

Note on the Chinese character "Chun": As to the word 屯. It is supposed to be the very original character 春 in its most ancient form. Originally "Spring" was symbolized by the growth of a bud, like a sprouted broad bean, which is the synergy of energy of growth—the "Qi." The original form of the character 屯 is this bud. These two words were supposed to be interchangeable by people three or four thousand years ago. And later 春 incorporated 日.

About the Author

Bestselling novelist SAMUEL SHEM is known as the author of the three million copy–selling modern classic, *The House of God*, which with dazzling humor describes the horrors and banalities of working in hospitals—and is required reading for medical students and doctors. A Rhodes Scholar and Harvard Medical School faculty member for over three decades, Shem is currently Professor of Medicine in Medical Humanities at NYU Medical School. He has given over sixty medical school commencement addresses on "Staying Human in Medicine." His other books include *The Spirit of the Place*, named *USA Book News* Best Novel of the Year and Independent Publishers Best Novel of the Year in 2009. His award-winning play *Bill W. and Dr. Bob*, co-written with his wife, Janet Surrey, about the founders of Alcoholics Anonymous, ran for ten months Off-Broadway in 2013. Surrey and Shem are co-authors of the 2015 book, *The Buddhas's Wife: The Path of Awakening Together*. He was a visiting artist/scholar at the American Academy in Rome in 2012. He lives in Boston and Costa Rica, together with Janet and their daughter. www.samuelshem.com

About Seven Stories Press

SEVEN STORIES PRESS is an independent book publisher based in New York City. We publish works of the imagination by such writers as Nelson Algren, Russell Banks, Octavia E. Butler, Ani DiFranco, Assia Djebar, Ariel Dorfman, Coco Fusco, Barry Gifford, Martha Long, Luis Negrón, Hwang Sok-yong, Lee Stringer, and Kurt Vonnegut, to name a few, together with political titles by voices of conscience, including Subhankar Banerjee, the Boston Women's Health Collective, Noam Chomsky, Angela Y. Davis, Human Rights Watch, Derrick Jensen, Ralph Nader, Loretta Napoleoni, Gary Null, Greg Palast, Project Censored, Barbara Seaman, Alice Walker, Gary Webb, and Howard Zinn, among many others. Seven Stories Press believes publishers have a special responsibility to defend free speech and human rights, and to celebrate the gifts of the human imagination, wherever we can. In 2012 we launched Triangle Square books for young readers with strong social justice and narrative components, telling personal stories of courage and commitment. For additional information, visit www.sevenstories.com.